DUE DILIGENCE

DUE DILIGENCE

Jonathan Rush

Thomas Dunne Books
St. Martin's Press ⧢ New York

THOMAS DUNNE BOOKS.
An imprint of St. Martin's Press.

DUE DILIGENCE. Copyright © 2011 by Jonathan Rush. All rights reserved. Printed in the United States of America. For information, address St. Martin's Press, 175 Fifth Avenue, New York, N.Y. 10010.

www.thomasdunnebooks.com
www.stmartins.com

ISBN 978-0-312-55977-9

First Edition: May 2011

10   9   8   7   6   5   4   3   2   1

DUE DILIGENCE

1

It was raining in Memphis, where the Delta flight out of LaGuardia connected for the leg to Baton Rouge. Pete Stanzy sat in the executive lounge and made some calls. The layover was meant to be an hour, but a delay on the Baton Rouge flight had stretched it to an hour thirty. Then it stretched to an hour forty-five.

Stanzy was a tall man with dark curly hair running to gray, dressed in a charcoal gray suit. His copy of *The Wall Street Journal* was on top of his briefcase on the seat beside him. He couldn't help glancing at it. In the cab to LaGuardia at six in the morning he had gotten a text message from John Deeming. "Seen page 12 of the Journal yet?" Great start to the day. Pete had just about been able to hear the cackle of John's laughter coming off the screen of the cell phone.

Pete Stanzy and John Deeming were managing directors at Dyson Whitney, a New York investment bank. Dyson Whitney didn't have much in the way of its own capital to gamble and had therefore avoided the trading losses and toxic loans that had brought down the big Wall Street names during the credit crunch. It lived off the fees it earned for advising on corporate deals and selling the bonds for the company debt that financed them. But deals had been hard to come by and the competition was fierce. Dyson Whitney had survived the chaos of the financial crisis, but it had come through it like a hungry dog on the prowl—lean, anxious, sniffing for scraps in a world that had turned meager and bleak.

Within that world, Pete Stanzy and John Deeming covered similar sectors, energy, electricity, utilities. They were both about the same age, early forties, with the same career options, looking for the same promotion. There wasn't much love lost between them.

Stanzy finished his calls and picked up the paper. The article on page twelve was a short piece, like fifty other articles in the *Journal* every week. Pete looked at it for probably the hundredth time that morning. The headline said it all: HALE ENERGY TO PAY $800 MILLION FOR FLORIDA GAS & LIGHT.

It was an open secret that Florida Gas & Light had been on the block for months. Pete himself had been pitching it to just about anyone who'd stand still long enough to hear his spiel. And now it looked as if someone had actually gone and bought it. Pete did the math. Eight hundred million. Assuming the usual cut of around thirty basis points for a deal of this size, three-tenths of a percent of the price, that would yield a fee of around $2.4 million. According to the article, Citibank was handling the deal. Two-point-four million was chicken feed to a bank like Citibank, even with deals hard to come by. And the guys at Citibank who had put the transaction together—and Pete had a pretty good idea who they might be—couldn't possibly need a deal as badly as he did.

Pete reread the article. He was sick of looking at it. He got up and threw the paper away.

The executive lounge was about a quarter full. People waiting on flights in Memphis on a Thursday morning. Laptops were out. In one corner, three men and a woman were sitting around a low table covered with papers and Coke cans. Other people were watching CNN on a flat screen. Over by the buffet, there was a big guy with long ashy-blond curls wearing a red suit. Pete watched him, wondering what the suit was about, until the man happened to look around and catch his eye. He looked away. Outside, a plane took off and disappeared into the gray sky. Rain fell on the tarmac. Pete tried to put Florida Gas & Light out of his mind. He tried to focus on the reason for his trip to Baton Rouge.

He was going down there to meet with a CEO called Mike Wilson. In ten years Wilson had taken a sleepy little electricity company down in the bayous called Lousiana Light and grown it into an outfit with operations in seven states and an international portfolio of plants that took in a clutch of countries in Eastern Europe and Latin America. Not the biggest utility company in the country, but one of the most exciting. Wilson's strategy was to pick up old, undervalued electricity plants with scope for large efficiency improvements, bidding aggressively and borrowing to finance the acquisitions. Wall Street loved the Louisiana Light story and the stock price reflected it. Mike Wilson had a golden touch, always in the right place at the right time. After Katrina sunk half of New Orleans, Louisiana Light picked up a half-billion-dollar federal grant to fix a network that would have needed upgrading anyway. Not even the financial crisis burst the bubble. Lousiana Light kept on acquiring. Even in the worst days of the crunch there had been credit available for companies Wall Street believed in.

A few months back, Stanzy had been talking to Wilson regularly, pitching a whole bunch of deals. Even thought he might hook him. Wilson showed interest for a while, asked him to keep showing him stuff. Then it all dried up. The Louisiana Light CEO hadn't even returned his calls.

Then yesterday afternoon, out of nowhere, Stanzy got a call from Wilson asking if he could come down to talk. Wouldn't tell him what it was about, just asked if he could get himself down to Baton Rouge. Told him he wouldn't be wasting his time.

Stanzy went through his files and reviewed the deals he had pitched to Wilson, made a few calls to check the state of play. A couple of the targets were out of reach now. Some of the deals might still be on the table. But he doubted Wilson wanted to hear about them. Stanzy figured Mike Wilson was like just about every other CEO he'd ever met. They'd tell you they weren't going to waste your time and then they'd go right ahead and do just that. Call you up every six months or so and ask you to come see them about some kind of fictitious deal they had no intention of doing, just to hear what people were saying about their own company and get a little free advice on the state of the industry. Maybe the morning's news about Florida Gas & Light was coloring Stanzy's thoughts a little, but this was going to be one of those trips, Pete could feel it.

Sullenly, Stanzy watched the rain fall outside. The longer he sat in that lounge, the less he felt like getting on the plane to Baton Rouge. Bottom line, he needed a deal—he needed one now—and unless Wilson was going to give him one, every minute he spent with him was a minute wasted. He had been to Baton Rouge too many times and wasted way too much time with Mike Wilson already. Stanzy was half-tempted to turn right around and go back to New York. Maybe the delay was some kind of sign. Pete glanced at his watch. If they pushed back the flight any longer, he decided, that's what he'd do. He'd get on the first flight back to LaGuardia and give Mike Wilson a call and say they'd canceled the flight.

A minute later, they called it.

The guy in the red suit got up and walked out. No briefcase, no hand luggage, nothing. Stanzy picked up his briefcase and followed him.

Ninety minutes later, Pete Stanzy was in Baton Rouge. Wilson's secretary had sent a driver. They headed downtown.

He tried to think positive, get himself in the right frame of mind for the meeting. Maybe Wilson was going to throw him a bone, give Dyson Whitney a junior share in selling the bonds to finance some kind of transaction, raise a couple of hundred million in debt. Pete did the math. Say a hundred million. That would be a fee of a half million for raising the finance. Realistically, say a quarter million. A quarter million . . . it was hard to stay positive over that. Wilson could have told him about it on the phone. For a quarter million, he thought in disgust, he didn't have to spend a day coming down here.

Away on his right, the tower of the state capitol came into view, the insane skyscraper built by Huey Long. If there was anything Katrina should have blown down in the entire state of Louisiana, thought Stanzy irritably, that was it. From the previous times he had come to see Mike Wilson, Pete knew you couldn't make a trip down here without someone reminding you at least once. Tallest state capitol in the United States.

"See that over there?" said the driver, right on cue. "That's the tallest state capitol in the United States."

"Really?" said Pete drily.

"Yes, sir. Thirty-four stories. Huey Long, he was assassinated there. Yes, sir," said the driver, nodding to himself. "Nineteen thirty-five. Shot to death right there."

Served him right, thought Pete, for building the thing.

"You can see the bullet holes in the walls," said the driver, still nodding.

Stanzy watched it go past. His thoughts drifted back to the *Journal,* to page twelve. He wondered if there was some way to cut into the Florida G&L deal. The article said it was an agreed bid, but if he could find another bidder, someone who'd offer more, he might be able to put Florida G&L back in play. It would mean fighting dirty, but Pete Stanzy was desperate enough for a deal to fight any way he had to. It was a long shot, but not impossible. The world of mergers and acquisitions was full of the ghosts of apparently rock-solid bids that had dissolved like a spring snowflake on Wall Street the minute a higher bid appeared.

He'd need someone tough, someone credible, someone with a reputation in the industry as an aggressive acquirer who was prepared to bid fast, and bid high.

Mike Wilson? Stanzy frowned. That was an interesting idea.

The driver turned off the highway they had followed in from the airport. Then they swung left at a corner in front of some kind of church with a tall, thin spire. Two minutes later the car pulled up.

Pete Stanzy was deep in thought.

The driver glanced back at him. "Here we are, sir."

2

Mike Wilson's hand was already swinging for Stanzy's as he came out of his sixth-floor office. He was a big man with a look of rude health. Full head of silver hair, broad in the shoulders, fleshy face, tanned skin. He took Stanzy into a large office with plate-glass windows overlooking the river.

"Sit down, Pete," he said. He gestured to a suite of armchairs at one end of the room. "Coffee?"

"Sure," said Stanzy.

Wilson put his head out the door. "Stella!" he called. "Can we have some coffee?"

Wilson came in and sat down opposite Stanzy. There was a wait for Stella to come back with the beverages.

"You been busy?" said Wilson to kill the time.

"Pretty busy."

"You see Hale Energy's buying Florida G and L?"

Stanzy nodded.

"Didn't you pitch Florida G and L to me one time?"

"See what you missed out on?" replied Stanzy.

Wilson laughed. "Hell, Pete, that's a chickenshit operation."

Stanzy sat forward. The opening was there and he decided to take it. "I'll tell you something, Mike. You could have it for nine hundred million."

"Really?"

Stanzy nodded. "Florida's just using Hale to flush out the bidders."

"Hell they are!"

"You want me to talk to them?"

"Always trying, aren't you, Pete?"

"I'm telling you, Mike, there's an opportunity here. I can't divulge everything I know," said Stanzy, his voice dropping slightly as if he were about to tell Wilson something especially confidential, "but let's just say I've had some discussions, and I can tell you for sure that nine hundred will get you in the game. Now, I know in the past I said you could get it for seven, but the market's moved on. The point is, we have to act fast. Go in over the top with an aggressive bid, blow everyone else out of the water. Trust me, that's the strategy for this one. That's how to take it. Nine hundred, Mike. Let's put it on the table and it's yours."

Wilson gazed at him for a moment, as if considering it. Then Stanzy saw that the other man was toying with him. Wilson laughed again. "You talk to them if you want, but not about me. I'm not interested. I got other fish to fry."

Stanzy sat back. Didn't look like he had a hope in hell of getting Wilson to bid for Florida Gas & Light. It was going to be one of these free advice sessions. Another one. Stella brought the coffees. She was an efficient woman of about fifty with dark hair in a bun, neat figure in a cream-colored dress.

Stanzy gazed out the window as she poured the coffees. It wasn't a view of the Mississippi you'd see in any tourist brochure. Barges, factories. Industrial.

"Cream?" said Stella.

"Thank you, Stella," said Wilson. "We can manage."

Stella put the jug down and left.

Wilson waited for her to close the door, then turned back to Stanzy. He gestured at the cream jug. Stanzy shook his head. He picked up his coffee and took a sip of it, black.

Wilson was watching him.

"I appreciate you coming down," he said.

Stanzy nodded. "What can I do for you?"

Wilson's eyes narrowed. "I got a deal in mind."

Stanzy set his coffee down. "What kind of deal?"

"We're confidential, right?"

Stanzy nodded.

"You ever heard of a company called BritEnergy?"

Stanzy tried to conceal his surprise. BritEnergy was one of the larger electricity companies in Britain, worth at least as much as Louisiana Light itself.

"At current stock prices, they're valued slightly higher than us," said Wilson, as if reading Stanzy's mind.

Stanzy nodded. "I didn't pitch BritEnergy to you."

"Someone else did."

"Who?" asked Stanzy, hoping like hell it was Citibank.

"Doesn't matter."

Mike Wilson stood up. He walked across to the window and stood looking out.

"My board feels the company needs to take a new strategic initiative. We need a major acquisition. Until now, we've been opportunistic, incremental. We've created our portfolio by buying an asset here or an asset there."

"Seems to have been pretty successful."

"At this point, we've gone as far as we can go like that," continued Wilson, ignoring the interjection. "We've become a global player, after a fashion, but for a global player we're still too small. If we continue taking a piecemeal approach, our reach is always going to be limited. There are gaps we're not going to be able to fill. It's time for us to leapfrog our growth. We need to establish a platform so we can double and double again. That's my vision, Pete. The only way to do that is to acquire a sizable company that can fill the gaps we have. In particular, my board feels we need a major strategic presence in the European Union and they've tasked me with the job of making that happen."

Stanzy watched Mike Wilson's back. *My board feels* . . . Stanzy knew what that meant. Mike Wilson's board was stuffed with more friends and well-wishers than your average wedding party.

Wilson turned around. "Your thoughts?"

Stanzy shrugged. "Mike, you haven't given me anything to think about yet. If you want a strategy talkfest, go to McKinsey. When you're ready to do a deal, come to me."

Mike Wilson smiled. He came back and sat down. "BritEnergy."

"You're looking at some kind of merger?"

Wilson shook his head.

Stanzy stared at him. "You want to buy it?"

"You got it. An acquisition, but a friendly one."

"What makes you think they're interested?"

"The strategic fit is fantastic. Our portfolios are complementary, like a hand and a glove. Hell, Pete, put our two sets of assets together, you get a map of the known world."

"What makes you think they're interested?" repeated Stanzy.

"Let's just say there have been discussions."

"What kind of discussions?"

"Early discussions."

"Price?"

Mike Wilson shook his head.

Stanzy didn't reply. There was no such thing as a discussion without price. That wasn't a discussion, it was just words. He watched Wilson with irritation. This was just bullshit. Wilson had gotten him down here to run the idea past him and see how he'd react, just as he'd expected. Pete Stanzy had been to Baton Rouge way too many times to do this again.

"You seem skeptical," said Wilson.

"Not at all. I'm sure it does make a lot of sense. So does putting Chevron together with ExxonMobil. And Toyota with Ford. So do a lot of things. The only problem is, both sides have to want a deal or it doesn't matter how much sense it makes."

"Pete, there have been discussions. I can't tell you any more right now. There have been serious discussions."

"All right," said Stanzy. Mike Wilson was still a potential client, even though he had just gotten him to come all the way down to Baton Rouge for what was turning out to be a monumental waste of his time, and Stanzy was trying to be patient. But his irritation was getting the better of him. "What is this, Mike? You want advice from me on this thing? You want me to tell you what I think?"

"I don't need you to tell me what you think. I know what to think."

"Then what do you want?"

"I told you what I want, Pete. I want to buy BritEnergy."

"Then let's cut to the chase. Are you looking for a pitch here? Is this going to be a beauty parade? Who else are you talking to? Merrill? Goldman? Morgan Stan—"

"What I'm looking for," said Wilson, cutting across him, "is to do this deal very quickly and very quietly, in exactly the way I want it done."

Stanzy's eyes narrowed. It was beginning to dawn on him that this might not be a monumental waste of time at all. Suddenly, it seemed as if Mike Wilson might actually be talking about something very real, very immediate. And very big.

All at once, Stanzy was powerfully alert. He just hoped he hadn't rubbed Wilson the wrong way by being so brusque with him.

"How quickly?" he asked.

"Quickly. Can you do it? I want the best team you can field."

"You're not talking to anyone else?"

"I don't have time for a beauty parade."

No time for a beauty parade? Pete Stanzy didn't quite believe that. For a deal this size, every bank on Wall Street would scramble. Wilson could have Goldman Sachs, Merrill Lynch, Citibank, Morgan Stanley, all of them strutting their stuff inside forty-eight hours.

"Mike," said Stanzy carefully, still looking for the catch, "you've got a relationship with Merrill Lynch, right?"

"That's right," said Wilson.

"And you're telling me you're not even talking to them?"

"My relationship with Merrill Lynch didn't stop you coming down here and pitching me all kinds of chickenshit like Florida G and L."

"But I didn't pitch you this one."

"You want me to go to Merrill? Is that what you're saying, Pete? Are you telling me Dyson Whitney can't handle a deal this size?"

"No," said Stanzy hastily. "We can handle it. Absolutely."

"Then I would have thought you'd kind of want the business." Wilson raised an eyebrow meaningfully, watching him.

Stanzy frowned. "They know you're interested? BritEnergy, I mean."

"I want to have the whole thing agreed in a month," replied Wilson, which wasn't exactly an answer to the question.

Pete Stanzy looked at him skeptically. In a month?

"I told you. I wasn't joking when I said I want it done quick. And quiet. All right, Pete, let's cut to the chase, as you said. How much?"

Stanzy's mind raced, running the angles. The whole scenario was highly unusual, to say the least. By any standards, this was a big deal—by Dyson Whitney's standards, a huge one. For a deal of that size, you'd normally expect to offer a discount on the fee. Twenty basis points, 0.2 percent of the price paid for the target, was what you'd probably get as an advisory fee. Maybe only fifteen. You might start by asking for thirty basis points and let the client beat you down to twenty. Maybe he should start low right away to make sure he got it. But who was he competing with? For whatever reason, Wilson was offering him the deal on a platter. No beauty parade, no competitive pitch. He was almost begging him to take it. So maybe he should start high. Thirty-five? Maybe even forty? But Wilson might get pissed. And however much Wilson wanted Stanzy to handle this deal, he couldn't possibly want to give it to him as much as Pete Stanzy wanted to have it. He *had* to have it. So go low. But why should he? Wilson wanted him to have it.

"Pete?"

"Forty basis points," said Stanzy impulsively, almost wincing even before the words had come out.

There was silence.

Stanzy wished he could take those words back, make it thirty. Jesus, why hadn't he made it thirty? Or twenty?

"Done," said Mike Wilson.

Pete stared at him in disbelief.

"But nothing if we don't win," said Wilson. "You got that? Don't give me any of that retainer shit, Pete. I don't care how many shareholder votes we get—if we don't get to the takeover threshold, there's nothing in it for you."

Oh, we'll win, thought Stanzy. And he would be a legend. The man who got forty basis points on an eleven-billion-dollar deal. He did the math. In about a second. Forty-four million in fees.

"I'll send you a draft letter of engagement tomorrow," said Stanzy. "In the meantime, we'll get right on it. It's Thursday today . . . you'll have a first cut of the valuation on Monday. That soon enough? We'll meet."

Wilson nodded. "I'm running down to Colombia tomorrow to check out our operation down there. I try to get down there once a quarter. Probably run over into Saturday. Monday's good. Set up a time with Stella."

"Okay. Mike, what are your thoughts on how you're going to finance the deal?"

"Stock and cash," said Wilson. "Say three-fourths and one-fourth as a starting position."

"That's one-fourth cash?"

"That's right."

"You got that or are you going to have to raise it?"

Wilson didn't bother answering that question.

"So how you gonna raise that? Debt or equity?"

"Debt."

Stanzy nodded. One-fourth cash. Say 2.8 billion. He did the math. Say fifty basis points arranging fee on the debt. That was another fourteen million in fees right there.

Stanzy pulled out a notebook. "Who do we talk to?"

Mike Wilson didn't reply.

"Who's on your team? Finance guy? Head of strategy? Who do my guys talk to?"

"No one," said Wilson. "Me. You talk to me."

"But my guys are going to need someone to—"

"Your guys talk to me. If you need to talk to someone else, ask me."

"But you must have had people working on this," said Stanzy.

"I don't think you understand, Pete. I said I wanted this done quietly, exactly the way I tell you to."

"Okay. I understand, Mike."

"Do you?" Wilson watched him carefully.

Pete Stanzy put his notebook away. For forty basis points, he'd do it blindfolded and standing on his head if he had to. "We'll talk to you, Mike," he said. "No one else."

3

His cell phone was in his pocket, but Pete Stanzy resisted the temptation to take it out. He kept his face blank. Never say a word in front of a company driver, he knew. Never give a hint of what you're feeling. And never, ever, *ever* pull out your cell phone. Do that, and before you know it you're wrapped up in the conversation and you've forgotten there's anyone listening in the front seat.

Instead, he sat in silence as he was driven back to the airport, running the numbers in his mind. Savoring them. Forty bips on the advisory fee, on a price of 11 billion. That was 44 million. Another 14 million for selling the bonds that would provide the debt. Fifty-eight million. And they'd need a bridge loan while the bond sale was arranged. Dyson Whitney didn't have the capital to provide a bridge of 2.8 billion, or anything like it. They'd have to go to one of the majors for that. The usual premium on a bridge loan was 4 percent. Say Dyson Whitney got a 25 percent cut of that. Say the loan was paid out in six months. That was another 14 million. Add that to the fifty-eight, and the total fee to Dyson Whitney was 72 million. Say a round 70. Seventy million for the firm—of which around 6 million would go straight into his own bank account as bonus out of the fee.

Pete forgot the eyes of the driver watching in the rearview mirror for a moment, and smiled. Not bad for a morning's work.

These were big numbers. The kind of numbers you'd deal with at a Morgan Stanley, at a Goldman Sachs, not at a third-tier bank like Dyson Whitney. On the scale of acquisitions, it wasn't exactly an AOL and Time Warner, but it wasn't chicken feed. In any given year—in a good year—there might be a total of a couple of hundred deals of this size worldwide. Right now there were probably half that number or less, and the first-tier banks got just about all of them. Stanzy couldn't wait to see John Deeming's face when he heard about this. He forgot himself and smiled again. Good-bye, Dyson Whitney. Do a deal like this, and who knew which bank might not come looking for him?

Already, the desperation he had been feeling that morning seemed far in the past. Had that really been him, scheming to muscle in on some chickenshit Florida deal? Eight hundred million? What was $800 million to a guy who'd just pulled down an eleven-*billion*-dollar play?

He ran through the numbers again, for the sheer pleasure they gave him.

On that half-hour drive to the airport, Pete Stanzy did once or twice ponder the strangeness of the way it had happened. There were all kinds of things that might have given him pause. But it wasn't too hard to think of reasons to explain them. Mike Wilson had probably had a dispute with Merrill. That happened with clients all the time. And suddenly, just when he needed an investment bank in a hurry, he found himself without one. And if he called for a beauty parade to find a replacement, with a half-dozen banks all strutting their wares, you could just about guarantee there'd be a leak from one of them. And Wilson must have been impressed when Pete pitched to him back in the spring, so why not go straight to him? Why not? It was possible.

And the forty bips was unusual. More than unusual. But there were probably all kinds of good reasons Wilson had agreed to that as well.

Besides, Stanzy wasn't committing irrevocably to anything yet, not until the letter of engagement was signed by Mike Wilson and approved by Dyson Whitney's own mandates committee. That wouldn't happen until next week. He would have plenty of time to check out Louisiana Light when he got back to New York. Ask around, do a little digging, find out whether there were any problems with Louisiana Light that he should know about before he took Mike Wilson's forty bips.

And what? *Not* take them? Pete shook his head, amusing himself with the absurdity of the thought. Forty bips . . . he ran through the numbers, turning them around and around in his mind, like things so precious and beautiful you can hardly believe they really exist, and if they do, they might shatter before you can get ahold of them.

That was what he started to think about now, the long, twisting, obstacle-laden path that lay between him and that prize. Any deal, even the most apparently straightforward and mutually agreeable, can break down over any number of potential points of dispute. It isn't done until the ink's on the page. A deal of this size, with the added complication of the transatlantic dimension, would be as fragile as any. Stanzy began to plan. He pulled out his notebook and started to jot down some points.

At last, in the airport, he pulled out his phone and called one of the vice presidents at the bank.

"Menendez!" he said. "We need a team."

"What's going on?"

"I'll fill you in when I get back. Just get hold of a team. Two associates and an analyst."

"Associates are tight, Pete. We got rid of so many. Every time I talk to Fischer, he's fucking telling me he's got no one."

"We need a top team, Menendez. Tell Fischer. I don't care what he has to do. Tell him I need the best we've got. Tell him I want Sammy Weiss. You got that? Tell him to get us Sammy Weiss. This is big, Phil. Tell Fischer this is big."

"What's happening, Pete? You got a deal? You big swinging dick! You've got a deal, haven't you?"

Stanzy grinned. "I got something, that's for sure. Get a war room, Phil. The lot. This is ultraconfidential. I'll be back at eight. I'll fill you in then."

"What's going on, Pete? What? Tell me now."

"I'm in Baton Rouge. Figure it out. And Phil, when you talk to Fischer, see if you can get someone on the team who's a Brit."

4

Bernard Fischer had the worst job at Dyson Whitney. That was saying something, considering all the other jobs he'd had at the bank. Over eight years, he had worked up from analyst, through associate, to vice president, which was one rung on the hierarchy below managing director. The problem was that he wasn't just any VP. For the period of one year, he had been tapped to be VP in charge of staff allocation.

Being VP of staff allocation had a downside. You got lied to, threatened, yelled at, and generally abused by anyone at VP level and above. The upside? Bernard Fischer was still waiting to find one.

Allocating staff at Dyson Whitney meant distributing the analysts and associates among the various projects in the bank, trying to balance the near-hysterical demands of table-thumping MDs and VPs against the limited realities of the available pool. Analysts were the lowest grade in the bank and did the worst of the grunt work. After about three years, if they survived that long—and about half of them didn't—they were promoted to associate. Associates would serve about three years before having the chance to become a VP. When it came to analysts and associates, the only thing anyone cared about was whether they were going to deliver the work they were told to do. Every MD and VP had favorites. Everyone thought they knew who were the big producers and who were the losers. Everyone wanted experienced associates who could be told what to do and left to get on with it. Bernard Fischer found himself struggling to satisfy demands out of an unusually shallow pool of associates that had been left after a round of layoffs earlier in the year. No one seemed to ask themselves how the green first-year analysts who had just been recruited would turn into the experienced associates to replace them if no one was prepared to staff them on their teams and teach them the trade. Before he had become the staffing VP, Bernard Fischer wouldn't have asked it, either. By now he had worked out the answer. Only no one else much wanted to hear it.

And now he had Phil Menendez on the phone, shouting in his ear. Phil was the loudest, most foul-mouthed VP in the bank, which wouldn't have been so bad if only he had a vocabulary of more than about three expletives that he continually repeated.

"Phil, I cannot give you Vince Cozzi," Bernard said for the fifth time. "Why don't you understand? He's in the middle of a deal."

"I don't give a fuck!" shouted Phil.

"Obviously. But Bob Waite does. You want Vince Cozzi, Phil, you're going to have to talk to Bob."

Bob Waite was an MD. He hated Phil Menendez, who hated him back. Phil didn't have a snowball's chance in hell of getting an associate off one of his teams.

"Get Pete Stanzy to talk to him," said Bernard.

"I gotta get this team today!" yelled Phil.

Bernard sighed. "Phil, I've given you Sammy Weiss. Sammy's a great associate, a top producer. You wanted Sammy, right? You asked for him. Okay, I've pulled him off something he was doing for Dale Bronson. You understand what I already had to go through with Dale for that? You want to thank me?"

"Yeah, right."

"And I've given you Cynthia Holloway."

"She's crap! We should fire her ass."

"You *wanted* her, Phil."

"I wanted a Brit. Don't we have another Brit?"

"She's the only one."

"Jesus Christ! I told you, she's crap. I wouldn't let her give me a blow job."

Unlikely to be an issue, thought Bernard. He had a printout of the staffing sheet on the desk in front of him. He ran his eyes down the sheet, mentally evaluating the ones who were free. Phil had knocked back just about every other name he had suggested. "Jeez, Phil. Two out of three you wanted, I've got for you. The third one, I can only tell you what I've got left. I offered you Nick Bromgrove and you won't take him because he didn't perform on the Alphaguard deal—"

"He's a jerkoff! Didn't we fire him already?"

"What about Steve Pippos? What did you say? He couldn't find the severance terms on some guy down in Florida—"

"We should fire him as well! What a useless fuck!"

Bernard shook his head. There was no point going through the names again, Phil had something against them all. "Well, all I've got left for you is Rob Holding and Ben Levi."

"Who are they?"

"They're analysts, Phil."

"What kind of analysts?"

"Analysts," said Bernard cautiously. "Dyson Whitney analysts."

There was silence for a moment. Bernard winced. It would take about two seconds more for Phil to realize why Bernard hadn't mentioned them before.

"You're selling me rookies!" yelled Phil. "You're selling me fucking rookies!"

"Phil, I'm telling you what I've got—"

"Do you know what kind of a deal I've got here?" demanded Phil, who had no idea yet himself. "Do you know what this deal is gonna mean for the bank?"

"How can I know that, Phil? You won't tell me anything about it."

"I can't. Do you know how confidential I have to keep this?"

"Look, you're going to have to choose," said Bernard. "Otherwise, you're going to have to take it all the way up to the Captain. I bow out."

Phil was silent. The chief executive of Dyson Whitney, or the Captain, as he was known, hated getting involved in staffing disputes. Pete Stanzy wasn't going to thank him if he got the Captain involved.

"Choose, Phil," said Bernard.

"What were their names?" growled Menendez.

Bernard glanced at the staffing sheet on the desk in front of him. "Rob Holding and Ben Levi."

"What are they like?"

"How would I know? They're rookies, Phil. Joined a few weeks ago. We must have thought they were good enough to work here."

"Oh, that's great."

"You can have either of them. They've been given stuff to keep them busy. Nothing that anyone needs."

"Mother*fucker*."

"Well?" said Bernard.

"You're killing me here. This is the judgment of Samuel."

"Solomon," said Bernard. "And it's not."

"What? What's not? What the fuck are you talking about, Fischer?"

Bernard sighed. "Who do you want, Phil? Holding or Levi?"

"Give me the first one," said Menendez grudgingly.

"Rob Holding? He's the one you want?"

"No, he's not the one I *want*. He's the little fuck you're forcing me to take."

"Rob Holding it is," said Bernard. "He's on extension 4327. I'll pull him off what he's doing. You want to tell him or shall I?"

"You tell him," said Phil. "Tell him to be in my war room at eight o'clock."

"Tomorrow?"

"Tonight!"

"Where's your war room?" asked Bernard.

"I don't know yet. If he can't find it by eight o'clock, it'll just show what a fuck he is."

"You want me to tell him that?"

"If you like," retorted Phil Menendez, and slammed the phone down.

Bernard Fischer put down his phone. His office, like the offices of the other VPs, was separated by a glass partition from the bullpen where the analysts and associates sat at their computers. There were about forty of them out there, gazing seriously at computer screens, punching at keyboards, or talking into phones. Bernard knew that he must have met Rob Holding a few weeks back during the induction program for new analysts when he had given a talk on staffing. He looked around the bullpen. There were a number of faces he didn't recognize. He had no idea which one belonged to the rookie he had just assigned to Phil Menendez. Rob Holding was just a name on a staffing sheet.

Bernard Fischer ticked it off, writing *Phil Menendez* alongside it. "Rob Holding," he murmured as he wrote, "may God have mercy on your soul."

5

The Beneventi Cement Company was a midsize cement manufacturer headquartered in Turin, Italy. According to the annual report on the screen, it had just had a pretty poor year. A damn poor year. The Beneventi Cement Company, thought Rob with a wry smile as he copied the key figures into a spreadsheet, would be lucky to issue another annual report if it kept going like that.

Rob Holding had never heard of the Beneventi Cement Company before and he was unlikely to hear of it again. Its name just happened to be on a list of 214 cement manufacturers that someone in the bank had e-mailed to him. The same person, whom Rob had never met, had also e-mailed the spreadsheet into which Rob was supposed to enter the main data on every company on the list after downloading their financial accounts from the Net. Rob didn't know why he was doing this. Apart from the fact that he had been told to.

Rob was six-one with dark hair, a good physique, and a winning smile. He came from a middle-class family in Pittsburgh. Rob had an older sister, Sherryl, who got hitched to a real-estate guy who took her to Arizona. That was fine with Sherryl. She couldn't wait to get out of Pittsburgh. Life had gotten hard for the Holdings, as it had for a lot of families across the Rust Belt. Rob's father had been a technical draftsman at an auto-parts manufacturer. He lost his job back in the late nineties when the company closed down and hadn't held a steady job since. Rob's mother was a schoolteacher, a big believer in the role of community. Kind of a Hillary Clinton disciple. It was only with gritted teeth that she had been able to bring herself to vote for Obama after he beat Hillary to the 2008 nomination, and she still hadn't recovered from the disappointment. She had devoted her entire career to the public-school system. Year by year, she got more distressed at what she saw.

His mother had instilled something in Rob. Some part of her idealism had rubbed off. Or maybe it was seeing his father lose his job when he was barely forty-five, right in the middle of what should have been the most productive years of his life. Rob had an itch in him to do something, to make a difference. He just hadn't worked out what it was yet.

Of the two children in the family, Rob was the gifted one. He didn't have any money to back him, but he had enthusiasm and drive. He worked nights to get through Penn State, then found himself with a part scholarship to law school at Columbia, graduating fourth in his class. Out of law school he joined Roller, Waite & Livingstone, a major Wall Street law firm, and after a couple of years he was about ready to think about paying off some of his debt. But this wasn't the thing for him, he already knew that. Contracts, bid documents, offerings documents for major corporations. After the initial buzz of getting a job at a firm of that caliber, the shine wore off. He looked at the Roller Waite partners and knew he didn't want to be like them in another ten years, even the ones he liked. Whatever it was that he wanted to do, this wasn't the place to do it. In the meantime, he had worked alongside a bunch of investment bankers on deals where Roller Waite was doing the legal work. The investment bankers were sharp, energetic. The kind of people who got things done. They were the ones who called the shots. He got to know a couple of them who had started out as lawyers before making the switch. They told him to do an MBA. He began to think about it. Six months later, he was out of Roller Waite. Now, two years on, he had an MBA from Cornell, a load more debt, and had interviewed with just about every investment bank on Wall Street.

Dyson Whitney wasn't his first choice. Like everyone else, Rob had imagined himself with a job at a Goldman Sachs or a Morgan Stanley. But recruitment on the Street was low and there were plenty of guys Rob knew, good guys, who hadn't even gotten an offer. Besides, you didn't necessarily finish up where you began. Work hard, do well at Dyson Whitney, and in a couple of years, who could tell where he might end up?

It was about six weeks since he had started at the firm, along with eight other new joiners. Bernard Fischer had given them a talk during their induction week, and although Bernard may have forgotten the names of the inductees, they remembered him. They remembered the things he told them. As analysts, they would be assigned to teams working on deals and other transactions. They wouldn't have much choice over their assignments, at least not for the first year or two. Between projects, MDs and VPs would get them to help out on pitches or marketing materials they were preparing. Bernard warned them that the pressure to get this stuff done might be just as great as the pressure during a live deal. They shouldn't be under any illusions. Didn't matter what they had done before. At this point, Bernard had paused and looked long and hard around the room. "Two of you," he said, "have law degrees. I've read your profiles. We've got a particle physicist and a neuroanatomist here. You know what? Doesn't matter. Doesn't matter what you were told during recruitment. The reality is, no one cares. You're the grunts, the dogsbodies. The only criterion anyone will apply is your ability to get stuff done. Do that, and people might want to use you. Keep your utilization up, and you might just survive long enough to give this same talk to someone else one day."

If that was supposed to be intimidating, it had the opposite effect on Rob. He didn't mind hard work. Throw it at him! How else could you learn? Hard work was what he was here for.

On his first morning at his desk, a voice had called up and told him to put together a chart of Argentinian and Chilean exchange rates against the dollar, yen, and euro since 1990. After Rob sent it off, he never heard another word about it. Then there was a press search to produce profiles of the board members of a housewares chain in the Midwest. There was a search for companies that were comparable to a half-billion-dollar wine producer in New Zealand. Rob e-mailed that to an associate who sat not far away from him, and he figured it might have something to do with a real deal that someone was trying to execute. But the associate didn't tell him what it was for. That was how it worked. No one told him anything. He wasn't staffed on a deal, so it seemed that people just threw stuff at him. Half the time, someone would call up and tell him to drop what he was doing and start on something else.

The guy Rob sat next to in the bullpen, Ilan Golani, was a senior associate who didn't say much. At first Rob had asked him an occasional question. Ilan didn't show much interest in answering. Supposedly he had been a pilot in the Israeli Air Force and he acted like he was still dropping bombs. Steve Pippos, a second-year analyst who sat across from him, was friendlier. Rob had met him during the recruitment process.

The new analysts hung together, comparing notes. Only three had been staffed on genuine fee-generating transactions. The deals weren't flowing, people said. Without deals, there was no way to get your utilization up. A couple of the analysts were real doommongers, saying they'd all be fired if things didn't pick up soon. Rob didn't know how seriously to take that. Apparently, there'd been a round of firings of associates a few months earlier.

He just wanted to get himself staffed on a deal. Any deal. Didn't matter how big or how small. Didn't matter what kind of company. Heavy goods manufacturing or ladies' lingerie—he didn't care. He just wanted to get the chance to show what he could do. In the meantime, he knew, his best bet was to do the work he was given as quickly and as well as he could. Although this latest thing . . . 214 cement companies, without even knowing what it was for. That was enough to put a dent in anyone's enthusiasm.

He typed in the figures from the Beneventi report. When he was done, he typed the next company name into Bloomberg, trying not to think of all the names that remained.

"Rob?"

He looked up. It was Steve Pippos, peering down at him over the divider that separated their desks.

"You ready?"

"What for?"

"The photo. Didn't you get my e-mail?"

Rob didn't know what he was talking about. "When did you send it?"

"Ten minutes ago. Come on, they're looking for people to feature on the website. They want to put up fresh photos with biographies." Steve grinned. "They said they wanted some mean-looking mugs, so obviously I thought of you."

Rob smiled. At least it would get him away form the cement manufacturers for a few minutes.

"Come on. Let's go. They're taking the photos in facilities."

They went down a couple of floors and had the shots taken.

"You know," said Rob as they were coming back up in the elevator, "some of the new guys are saying if we don't get staffed on a deal pretty soon, we're gonna get fired."

Steve nodded. "Probably."

"Really?"

Steve grinned. "They just hired you. They're not going to fire you. They just fired a bunch of associates. They're thinking a couple of years ahead. You're the guys who are going to replace them when business is good again."

"Yeah, but how long do they wait? What if there're no deals?"

"There's always a deal eventually. How long since you started?"

"Six weeks."

"I went ten weeks before my first deal. Then I was on one after the other for eight months solid."

"But what if there isn't one?"

"You'll get staffed, don't worry. And when you do, you won't know what hit you."

"I don't care about that. I don't care how many all-nighters I pull."

"No?" Steve laughed. "Be careful what you wish for."

They got back to their desks. The list with the names of the entire world's cement companies was lying just where Rob had left it. The message light on his phone was flashing.

Rob hit the button for his voice mail. He heard Bernard Fischer's voice. A moment later, he broke into a grin.

6

The door opened and in marched a short, stubby, bristling man with a close-shaven head, like a cloud of aggression blowing into the room. He slammed the door behind him.

"I'm Phil Menendez!" he announced. "Sammy, I know. I'm guessing you're Cynthia. That makes you Rob." Phil didn't pause for confirmation. "All right, listen up, you jerkoffs. I've just spent the last hour with Pete Stanzy. Any of you know Pete? Sammy, you do, right? You two? Doesn't matter. He doesn't know you, either. Doesn't know you now and won't know you later. Show the Shark a team where the MD doesn't know the name of the analyst at the end of the deal and the Shark'll show you a team that's done its job. Okay, here's the deal." Phil grabbed a marker and turned to a whiteboard. "Louisiana Light," he said, and wrote it up. *BritEnergy,* he wrote underneath it. "Okay. *We* are buying *them.* You ever heard of them? You, Cynthia?" He stabbed at the whiteboard with his finger. "You ever heard of this operation?"

Cynthia, a thin blonde of around thirty, frowned.

"Jeez!" growled Phil. "I told Fischer. I told him you'd be fucking useless."

There was a knock on the door. Phil opened it irritably.

"I got a printer here," said an office guy, glancing around the room and taking a good long look at the whiteboard.

"Later!" said Phil, and he slammed the door again. "Okay! Secrecy! Top level." He erased the names from the whiteboard. "Nothing's said or taken out of this room. Is that clear?"

Sammy, Cynthia, and Rob nodded.

"Shredder! You got no shredder, Sammy!"

"We'll be getting one," said Sammy calmly. He was a tall red-headed guy with clear blue eyes.

"You get a fucking shredder in here!"

"We're getting one, Phil."

Menendez glared at him suspiciously. Sammy didn't bat an eye. There were four desks crammed into the war room, but that was about all. The rest of the equipment was yet to arrive.

"Okay, listen." A cunning gleam came into Phil Menendez's eye. "This is a genuine mother*fucker* of a deal. Understand? We're talking ten, eleven billion."

Menendez paused. Rob glanced at Sammy and Cynthia to see their reaction. Cynthia's jaw had dropped. Sammy frowned for an instant, then resumed his deadpan expression.

"And there's more," said Menendez.

"What?" asked Cynthia.

"Wouldn't you like to know?" Menendez turned to Sammy. "Okay, we need all the usual stuff on this one. And no screwups, Sammy. You understand me? No fuckups. The Shark'll kill you. This is too big."

Sammy nodded.

"First review's on Monday. Pete and I will be going down to Baton Rouge. We'll want the basics—valuation grid, first cut of the integrated financials, decision-maker analysis. You know the drill."

The words flew over Rob's head.

"The rookie'll do the football field. She can cut the model. Sammy, you take the decision makers and the other stuff and make sure these guys don't fuck up."

Sammy nodded.

"Okay, what'll we call them? Huh? Code names." Menendez snapped his fingers rapidly. "Come on, we need code names for these guys. Our guys start with an L. What about Leopard, huh? Big fucking leopard going hunting in the jungle." Menendez laughed. "I like it. Huh, what do you think?"

"Sure," said Sammy.

"All right. What about them? Something with a B."

"Bat," said Cynthia.

Menendez stared at her as if he'd just been hit in the head with a fence post. "What the fuck? Bat? What the fuck's a bat?"

"A bat's one of those—"

"I know what a bat is!" Menendez shook his head in amazement. "Bat! Some shitty little bat! You think a leopard's gonna eat a fucking bat? A leopard's not gonna get out of *bed* for a bat. Jesus, what the fuck do you think we are?"

"What about Buffalo?" said Rob.

Menendez looked at him. "Buffalo. Not bad. A big juicy buffalo our leopard's gonna sink his teeth in. The Shark likes it. Okay. Leopard and Buffalo. Project code? Don't worry, Pete and me've got a name already. Project Forty." Menendez grinned, just waiting for someone to ask him why.

"Why?" asked Rob.

"Don't you worry." Menendez looked at his watch, then glanced around the room, as if seeing it for the first time "What the fuck is this, Sammy? This is a war room? This is a jerkoff. You haven't even got a phone."

"The phones are coming," replied Sammy.

"When? Come on. Get to work!"

"Phil, we're not set up. We'll get the room set and we'll do some work planning, and then I think we should go home and get a good night's sleep. We're going to need it."

"Sleep?" demanded Menendez, spitting the word out. "You expect the Shark to care if you want sleep?"

Sammy didn't reply. His gaze didn't falter.

Rob watched him.

Menendez snorted in contempt. Then he turned around and walked out.

The door shut loudly, leaving a portentous silence in the room.

"He's going to murder us," said Cynthia quietly.

Sammy glanced at her. Cynthia was a third-year analyst, up for promotion to associate at her next review. Originally from London, she had an MBA from Northwestern and had been in the States for six years. The rumor in the bullpen was that Cynthia had been lucky to survive her last review a few months back and needed a great review this time around, or it would be her last.

"Who's this 'shark' he kept talking about?" asked Rob.

"That's what Phil likes to call himself," said Sammy.

Rob looked at him in disbelief.

Sammy nodded. Deadpan.

"He's going to fucking murder us," murmured Cynthia again.

Rob was inclined to agree with her.

"Don't worry about Phil," said Sammy. "All he cares about is the work gets done. Do that and you'll hardly have to talk to him. That's my job."

"This is a big deal, right?" said Rob.

"Sounds like it. That doesn't matter. What we have to do is the same whether it's eleven billion or eleven million. Just treat it like a regular deal."

"What was that stuff Phil was talking about when he said there's more?"

Sammy shrugged. "That's just Phil blowing off."

"You think there's stuff we don't know about this deal?"

"There's always stuff you don't know about a deal. Listen, Rob, this is your first project, right? This should be a big learning experience for you. It's part of my job to help you get that. As a team, our job is to do a great job for the client, but personally, your goal is to get a good review. Get a bad review, and no one will want you on their team. Your life at Dyson Whitney will be nasty, brutish, and short."

"Very short," said Cynthia.

"All anyone wants to see from a first-year analyst is that you can do the work you're given. That's it. That's how you get your utilization. Focus on that and leave the rest to me. All I ask is that you let me know early if you're getting into trouble so I can help you out and keep everything on schedule. Don't be a hero. If you're not sure, ask. Okay? Ask."

Rob nodded.

"It's going to be intense. For however long this takes, you're going to be working your butt off. That's the deal, but you know that already, right?"

"Sure." Rob smiled. "That's what I'm here for."

Sammy hoisted himself onto a desk. "Tell me a little about yourself."

Rob frowned, wondering where to start. "I just got my MBA."

"Where from?"

"Cornell."

"Before that?"

"I was at a law firm. Roller, Waite and Livingstone."

Sammy nodded. "You didn't like working there?"

Rob smiled. "I didn't like sitting across the table from you guys. I worked on a couple of deals. Smaller deals, not like this one. I thought, I want to be on the other side of the table."

"Why?"

"Looked like you were having all the fun."

Cynthia snorted.

Sammy ignored her. "What else? You married?"

"Not exactly."

"Girlfriend?" He paused for an instant. "Boyfriend?"

"Girlfriend," said Rob. "She's an editor at a publishing house. Lascelle Press. It's kind of a small imprint. You probably haven't heard of it."

"I lived on a Lascelles Avenue once," said Cynthia.

"What do they publish?" asked Sammy.

"Fiction, mostly. The Great American Novel." Rob grinned. "You got one in your drawer? They're always looking for it."

"She got a name?" asked Sammy. "Your girlfriend?"

"Emmy," said Rob.

"Is she ready for this?"

"What?"

"For what you're about to go through."

"Why not?"

"Why not?" said Cynthia. She smiled knowingly. "I just hope Emmy's got a picture to remember you by."

. . .

"The meeting with Leopard's on Monday," said Sammy to Rob when they were together again in the war room at seven o'clock the next morning. "That gives you three days to come up with a valuation. Here's how you do it. Day one, you select companies that are comparable to Buffalo. Day two, you do a first estimate of their valuations. Sunday morning, you'll refine it. By Sunday noon, you'll have a first cut of the valuation grid for Buffalo. Sunday afternoon, you refine it again. Sunday night, it's ready to go."

Rob smiled. Yeah, he thought, and I might just solve world poverty and end global warming while I'm at it.

Sammy stared right back at him. Deadpan.

"How many comparable companies?" said Rob.

"I like to have twenty," replied Sammy.

Twenty? Rob still wasn't sure if Sammy was kidding.

"But this is a little rushed. Ten should do it for the first cut." Sammy grabbed a piece of paper, flipped it horizontally, and ruled up a chart. Across the top he wrote the headings for a series of columns, saying the titles out loud as he wrote them: "Country, market share, market capitalization, earnings, employees, divisions, assets . . ." Sammy flipped it across to Rob when he was done. "Get that information, we'll rank them, pick the ten most comparable."

"So I should start with BritEnergy?"

"Buffalo," Sammy corrected him. "We use the code names. And yes, you're right, you should. Buffalo first. You need to know what you're comparing with. Then go to the major stock indexes here, in Europe and Australasia, look at the electricity sectors, pick the names, and start working through them." He pushed the ranking chart across the desk to Rob. "Remember what I said yesterday. If you've got a question, ask." He turned to his own computer and began to scan whatever it was that was on his screen. "This isn't an MBA case study. This is for real."

By the time they sent out for pizza that night, Rob had a ranking chart of sorts for a list of companies, with a bunch of gaps. By the time Sammy called a halt at midnight, some of the gaps were filled.

"You've got enough," said Sammy.

"But there's all kinds of—"

"Eighty-twenty," said Sammy. "Twenty percent of the effort gets you eighty percent of the way. You've heard of that, right?"

"Eighty-twenty," said Cynthia mechanically from her desk. She turned around, weary, hollow-eyed. "Around here, you live or die by that."

"Let's look at what you've got," said Sammy to Rob. "Print me out a copy."

Sammy took the chart off the printer and glanced at it with an expert eye. "Not bad." He picked up his pen. "We'll take this one," he said, circling the name of a German electricity supplier called ERON. "This one in Britain. This one." He circled more names. "This one. This one. This one. This one. These. This one. These two." He paused, surveying the data. "And this one here, in Australia." He pushed the chart back to Rob.

Rob counted the circles. Fourteen. That morning, Sammy had said he only wanted ten.

He looked up. Sammy was watching him. Rob didn't say anything.

After he left, he got a cab to Emmy's apartment.

He was exhausted. Dead beat. He sprawled in the back of the cab, watching the buildings going by outside. He thought about the names on the ranking chart he had produced. He had been so caught up in the work, he hadn't had time to think. But suddenly it struck him that it was an incredible amount of information, an incredible amount of stuff he'd learned. A lot of it was a blur, but through the blur were some definite shapes, definite areas of knowledge. He knew about the industry, the whole global industry. And it wasn't just the information he'd gathered, but *how* he'd done it, how he'd managed to get coverage of the industry so quickly. The sheer pace of it was the biggest learning experience of all. Only now, comparing what he knew when he walked into the war room that morning with what he knew when he walked out, did he understand how much he had actually covered in a single day. If someone had asked him before he started, he probably would have said it would take a week.

He smiled. That was really something.

The cab moved up Eighth. It stopped at a set of lights somewhere in the Fifties. On the corner across the street, a bunch of people were lining up to get into a club.

Sammy had told him to be back at seven. Seven o'clock on a Saturday morning. With fourteen selected companies to value. In one day.

A guy with a shaved head stood at the door outside the club. His scalp gleamed yellow in the lamplight. Rob saw him say something. A couple of girls at the front of the line laughed. Rob watched them. It was one o'clock on a Friday night. Those people were out having fun, and he was in a cab after eighteen hours shut up in an airless room with maybe five hours' sleep ahead of him before he had to be back there again. He should have been pissed.

But he wasn't. Rob realized that he didn't envy the people outside the club one bit. Instead, he felt a strange exhilaration. He had worked plenty of late nights at Roller Waite, but he had never felt like this, not once in his time there. This is what he'd gone to Cornell for. This is what he had studied two years and gone deeper and deeper into debt to do.

Maybe it was tiredness playing games with his mind in the back of the cab that Friday night, but when he thought about the war room, Rob couldn't wait to get back there.

7

The thunderclouds had been building up all afternoon. Storms are frequent in October on Colombia's Caribbean coast. The tropical air became denser, the sky darker. Finally, at around six o'clock, the storm broke. Thunder rolled through the air, forks of lightning jagged across the sky. The fronds of palm trees bent back until they were almost snapping. A wall of water came down, drenching the streets of the colonial town of Cartagena. The rain swept across the tarmac of the airport outside the city, pelting into the sleek white shape of the executive jet that was parked there for the second day running.

The rain went on for hours. Downtown, in the casinos of the Bocagrande district, no one noticed.

Tourists favored the Las Vegas–style places like the Casino Royale. But there were others. The Casino del Rio didn't admit yankee tourists in shorts. It had no slot machines. Its open gaming room was small, with only a dozen tables. The clients who went upstairs came with recommendation. Eduardo Velazquez, the general manager, knew their likes and dislikes, and made sure that each was catered to.

Velazquez came out of his office. He was a small, fine-boned man, dark-complexioned, with thin black hair slicked back from his forehead. He walked along the corridor on the upper floor. Each room in the casino was named for one of the rivers of South America and decorated with murals of river scenes. Velazquez stopped at the Orinoco Room and went inside. He exchanged a glance with the croupier, then with the auditor, who had discreetly called him from his office. The serving girl, Concepción, was out of the room, getting a drink for one of the clients.

Velazquez stood unobtrusively beside the auditor. With a practiced eye, he appraised the value of the chips in the middle of the table. Eighty thousand dollars. Two of the men at the table were Colombian. One was a son of one of the wealthiest ranching families in the country, claiming ancestry of pure blood back to sixteenth-century Spain. Eduardo Velazquez doubted that. No one's blood in Colombia is pure. The young man was pale, thin, with elegant hands. Usually, those hands put down more chips than they picked up. The second Colombian was shorter, darker, pockmarked. The source of his wealth was shady. Narcotrafficking was rumored. Velazquez had no idea if this was true. In Colombia, whenever the origin of a man's wealth is unknown, cocaine is mentioned. Whatever the source of his money, at least ten times a year he would come to the Del Rio to squander it. He always had a cigar in his mouth. The air of the room was heavy with its smoke.

The third man at the table was a fat Brazilian businessman. When he was finished at the table, he would expect to take to his room the girl who was serving the drinks. He liked the girls to be young, tall, and with short hair. Velazquez knew this. The Brazilian would pay five hundred dollars for the pleasure. Concepción was willing.

The fourth man was an American. A good-looking man, healthy in the way of a certain kind of American, with a full head of silver hair. He came to the Del Rio four times a year to play poker. His particular preference was that there should be no other Americans at his table. Each time, Eduardo Velazquez arranged it.

The American had taken two cards; each of the others had taken one. The Brazilian folded right away. Velazquez knew his style. A real man when he had a paid-for woman in his bed, but he didn't have the balls to carry through a bluff. Concepción came back with a drink for him. His hand wandered over her ass as she put it down.

The narcotrafficker put twenty thousand on the table. The young rancher thought better of his hand and put down his cards. That left the American. Velazquez watched from beside the auditor. An interesting matchup, these two. The narcotrafficker, Velazquez knew, was like a street dog, a real mongrel. He would bluff with such aggression and back it up with so much cash that he could sap the confidence of almost any opponent. The American was harder to read. A smarter player. But there was something about a mongrel that makes him hard to beat.

The American watched the narcotrafficker for a moment. Then he put twenty on the table, and another twenty.

"I'll raise you," he said.

The narcotrafficker exhaled a cloud of cigar smoke. He put twenty on the table. Then he gazed at the American with narrowed eyes, toying with a set of chips in one hand. He muttered something in Spanish to the son of the rancher, who smiled. The narcotrafficker raised one eyebrow at the American. The American didn't react.

He put three twenty-thousand-dollar chips on the table. "I raise *you*."

Bluff, thought Velazquez. Must be. He had nothing. *Nada*. But it would cost the American more than sixty thousand dollars to find out.

Two hundred and twenty thousand dollars on the table now.

The American put down sixty thousand. Then he put down one more chip. Ten thousand.

"I'll see you," he said.

The narcotrafficker put down his cigar. One by one, he turned over his cards. Two sixes. Two twos. And a seven.

The American nodded slightly to himself. He threw down his cards.

The narcotrafficker laughed lustily. He muttered something to the son of the rancher. The younger man grinned.

Eduardo Velazquez was surprised. He wondered whether the narcotrafficker thought he had been bluffing. Probably. Two pairs. But it was the American who had been bluffing. It was hard to beat the narcotrafficker that way. That was what the American should have learned. If he was smart, he would remember that. The narcotrafficker would do the same thing next time, and the time after. He only played one way. Bluff harder and harder still. You could lose to him to start with, but after a while, if you had the money to keep going, you could turn him to your advantage.

Still, if the cards were unkind to you, nothing would help.

The American got up. "I'm going to take a breather," he said to the croupier.

"Will you come back, *señor?*" asked the croupier.

"Sure. Just give me a few minutes."

Velazquez went to the door.

"*Caballeros?*" said the croupier to the other players.

"*Vamos,*" said the narcotrafficker impatiently, and he threw a twenty-thousand-dollar chip on the table.

Velazquez opened the door for the American and followed him out.

"You would like to speak with me?" said Velazquez when he had closed the door behind him.

The American nodded.

"This way, *señor.*"

Velazquez led him down the corridor into his public office. From there a door led to his private office, into which no one but Eduardo Velazquez himself ever entered.

Velazquez showed him to a seat, then waited.

"I'm kind of stuck here, Eduardo."

"Yes?"

"I'm pretty much at the limit, right?"

The manager nodded. He knew already that the other man was at the limit of the credit he had with the casino. That was the reason the auditor had called Velazquez to the room. The ten-thousand-dollar chip with which the American had seen the narcotrafficker's hand had been the last one he had. He was two hundred and fifty thousand down on the night.

The American shook his head. "Lady Luck's gone AWOL on me here. Not a single decent hand all night. That's gotta change."

Velazquez didn't say anything. There was nothing he hadn't heard before, about why a person wins, or doesn't win, and why only one more hand will surely see him winning again.

The American gazed at the rug, talking to himself more than to the manager who was watching him. "Thought I was gonna get it all back on that one. I only needed one for a straight. Instead I get a pair, and he's sitting there with two." He laughed disbelievingly. "Hell, he thought he was bluffing me!"

Velazquez waited. "What shall I do, Mr. Wilson?" he asked eventually. "Shall I call Mr. Prinzi?"

Mike Wilson didn't reply right away. His face had a troubled frown. Then he took a deep breath and nodded. "Yeah. Call Mr. Prinzi. Say I need another two hundred K."

"Two hundred thousand dollars?"

"Yeah. That ought to be enough. Cards can't keep going like this."

"Very good." Eduardo got up. "Excuse me for a moment."

"Say, Eduardo. Hold on a second. Make it four."

"Four hundred thousand?"

"Yeah."

The manager nodded. He went into his private office. A few minutes later he came out again, holding two piles of chips, ten tens, fifteen twenties.

Velazquez smiled, holding out the chips to Wilson. "As always, Mr. Prinzi was pleased to guarantee your credit."

8

The alarm hit him like a punch in the face. Rob bolted upright, then fell back again. He felt nauseated, clammy, disorientated. He looked around. Emmy was lying next to him.

Sunday morning. Sunday morning at six o'clock. Sunday morning at six o'clock after finishing work at two on Saturday night. And he was meant to be in the war room in half an hour.

Emmy stirred. Her long hair was draped across the pillow. She put her hand to her face for a moment, then dropped it.

She was lying on her side. The cover showed the curve of her hip. Under the cover, Rob knew, her T-shirt would have rucked itself up.

Sunday morning wasn't made for getting up at six o'clock. Sunday morning was made for having long, delicious sex with Emmy. And then going back to sleep until noon.

"Baby?" she murmured sleepily, without looking around. "You getting up?"

"Yeah," he said.

But he didn't move. He was hungry for more sleep, but knew he couldn't have it.

"Honey, you know we've got dinner with Greg and Louise tonight."

Rob frowned.

"You remember?"

"Have we?" said Rob, hoping the arrangement would somehow dissolve just because he questioned its existence.

"Rob . . ."

"Why didn't you remind me?"

"When, Rob?" Emmy rolled over. She looked at him, eyes bleared with sleep. "The last two nights, you've come in after I've gone to sleep and you're gone before I get up."

Rob nestled down. His let his hand wander down under the covers.

Emmy shook her head. "Go on, Rob. You gotta go."

Rob didn't go.

"Go on. I'm too tired. I want to sleep." She pushed him away and rolled over again.

"You just want me to get out."

"That's right," she said, talking into the pillow. "I just want you to get out so I can sleep."

Rob sat up on the side of the bed. "It's gonna be late tonight."

"How late?"

"I don't know. There's a big meeting with the client tomorrow and we've got to get a document done. I don't think I can make dinner. You go without me."

"I don't want to go without you. He's *your* friend, Rob."

"Yeah, but you like Louise."

"Yeah, right. Miss Snookums."

"What's not to like?"

Emmy didn't respond.

Rob waited a moment, wondering if she had fallen asleep again. "Will you call them?"

Emmy sighed.

"Make it another night."

"What night?"

"I don't know. Maybe it won't be so busy after tomorrow. Later in the week, huh? Tuesday, Wednesday."

Emmy nodded, eyes closed.

Rob watched her. "What are you going to do today?"

"Don't know. There's always a manuscript to read."

"I'm sorry, Em."

She shrugged. "Go on, you'd better get going."

Rob nodded. They had hardly had a chance to say a word to each other in the past couple of days. Their longest conversations had been when he called each night to say he was going to be back after she had gone to bed.

He leaned over and kissed her. Then he got up.

"What are you wearing?" Emmy said as he walked into the bathroom.

"Same as yesterday."

"You'd better get back to your apartment and pick up some clothes."

"Right," said Rob. He turned the shower faucet. "I'll add it to the list."

The valuation grid was like the outline of a football field. On the grid were positioned four black circles, each of which represented the possible value of BritEnergy according to a different valuation methodology. Simple. And behind that one simple page were the annual reports, regulatory filings, brokers' reports, and literally thousands of pages Rob had looked through on comparable companies to figure out where those four dots should sit.

The first cut of the grid was supposed to have been ready by noon Sunday. By four o'clock, when Phil Menendez arrived, Rob had just about gotten it done.

Menendez took it out of his hand, held it like it was a reeking dog turd, and started jabbing. He pointed at one of the circles. How did Rob estimate that? What were the comparables? Where were the numbers? What about that one? And that one? Pretty soon Rob was searching through the piles and piles of paper on his desk.

"He's a piece of crap," said Phil to Sammy, as if Rob weren't in the room. "Look at this stuff." He tore up the copy of the valuation grid. "And you, Sammy, you've been jerking off in here."

Then he turned away to deal with Cynthia.

Rob looked at Sammy. Sammy gave him a slight nod. They huddled.

"Go back and check over these . . . and these . . . and these . . ."

"But Sammy . . ." whispered Rob.

"He's happy," murmured Sammy. "Trust me. It's a first cut. Eighty-twenty. It's going to have errors. He knows that."

"What the fuck is this?" exploded Menendez behind them, hunched over Cynthia's computer.

Menendez came back at about nine o'clock that night. After that, he didn't leave. He worked over and over the document that was going to Baton Rouge the next morning, giving drafts back to Sammy and peering over the shoulders of Rob and Cynthia and cursing while he waited for Sammy to give a new draft back to him. Rob had no idea what was in the document. All he knew about was the four-blob grid on his screen and the endless pages of figures in the documents on his desk and in his computer. Every so often he would come up with a new valuation for a comparable and he'd move one of the blobs a quarter inch up or down, and he'd e-mail the new version to Sammy to do whatever Sammy was doing with it. Then he'd be back in the figures. A fog of tiredness descended on him and he just kept moving muzzily through the numbers.

At some point he realized that Phil Menendez had settled in for the night, and no one was going home. He wondered if he should call Emmy. He looked at his watch. A quarter to one. Too late. If he called now he'd only wake her.

He kept crunching the numbers.

At about four o'clock he became aware that Phil and Sammy were talking about his latest version of the valuation grid. He turned around.

Menendez stared at him. "What the fuck are you looking at? You got nothing else to do?"

"Listen in," said Sammy.

Menendez snorted in contempt, then ignored him. He and Sammy were talking about the value of BritEnergy, which was what the valuation grid was all about. The four blobs gave somewhat varying figures. They decided to give the value a range of 11.25 to 11.75 billion. Where the client chose to pitch the offer within that range would be a question of the negotiating strategy.

The last draft was done just before seven in the morning. Phil, who had gone upstairs, reappeared in a suit, face and head freshly shaven, and leafed through it disgustedly. He lingered over the valuation grid, the sneer on his face getting deeper and deeper.

"It'll do," he said eventually. He put three copies of the document in his bag. "It's full of mistakes. Sammy, I want them fixing this stuff. I don't want you guys bugging off." Then he left to catch a cab for LaGuardia, where he was going to meet Pete Stanzy for the flight to Baton Rouge.

Sammy got up and closed the door after him.

"Good job," he said.

"You're going to tell us he's happy, right?" said Rob.

"Very."

Cynthia stood up. "I'm getting out of here."

Sammy nodded. "Let's go get some sleep. Be back here at four. Phil's gonna call."

Cynthia grabbed her bag and walked out. Sammy turned around and started leafing through a pile of papers on his desk.

"You not going?" asked Rob.

"Soon," murmured Sammy. "Go on, get out of here. Get some sleep. Be back at four."

Rob looked through a couple of documents, remembering a detail here or there that he had wanted to check. Nothing important. Yet something kept him in the war room. Over the past seventy-two hours, he'd had maybe ten hours' sleep. Yet he wasn't ready to leave. He didn't know what had gone into the document Phil Menendez had just taken with him, other than the valuation grid he had worked on. Yet there was something immensely satisfying about having seen that document go, despite the sheer physical ordeal that it took to get it into shape, despite Phil Menendez's yelling and cursing. Or perhaps because of them. It had been a baptism of fire. He'd gone into it, and he'd come out the other side. He wanted to hold on to the moment. He knew it was unique, a first experience, something he'd never have again no matter how many times he went through the same thing. He wasn't ready to let it go.

He saw that Sammy was looking at him. Maybe guessing what he felt.

"You all right?" said Sammy.

Rob smiled. "Yeah. Thanks, Sammy. I mean . . . you know, thanks for all your help."

"We're not done yet."

"I know."

Sammy nodded. "Go on. Get out of here."

Rob sat for a moment longer, then got up. "See you at four."

"Right," said Sammy, and he had already turned back to whatever he had been doing.

Rob left. He walked to the elevator. He was exhausted, but in a good way. Like Sammy said, they weren't done yet. He guessed they'd hardly started. But that was why he was here. That was what it was all for.

As he got out of the elevator, Steve Pippos was arriving for work. "Hey, Rob," he said. "You look like crap."

Rob grinned. "Thanks. And good morning to you."

"Pulled an all-nighter?"

Rob nodded.

Steve laughed. "See, remember what I told you?"

"And remember what *I* told you?"

"You're working with Phil Menendez, right? What's the deal? Who is it?"

"Can't tell you," said Rob, feeling a tingle of pleasure as he said it.

"Secret, huh?"

Rob nodded.

"Big, huh?"

"Couldn't say."

"Well, I know one secret. I heard we're getting forty bips."

Rob looked at Steve, not quite comprehending.

"I heard we're getting forty bips," said Steve. "Our fee. Forty basis points on this deal."

"Forty?" said Rob. "That's kind of high, isn't it?"

"No," said Steve. "Mount Everest is kind of high. Forty bips is somewhat higher. Pete Stanzy's crowing."

Pete Stanzy? Rob's mind was blank.

"Your MD." Steve peered at him, then laughed.

"We're getting forty bips? Why?"

"Because the analyst is so great, apparently. I don't know, it's just a rumor. Who knows if it's true? Go on. You going to get some sleep?"

"Yeah."

Steve gave him a friendly shove. "Go on, then. You deserve it."

Steve left him behind and headed for the elevators.

Rob went out the door into the chilly air of a crisp New York

Monday. Around him, the sidewalk was full of people on their way to work.

Rob shook his head, trying to clear his mind. It wasn't a rumor, he knew. That was why they had called the deal Project 40. That's why Phil Menendez had looked so smug when he said it.

He was working on a deal where they were getting forty bips. Great! It made it an even better deal to be part of.

Suddenly the accumulated exhaustion of the past three days and nights hit him. He was too tired to think straight. The forty bips—true or not—went out of his mind.

But it was very much in mind the next evening when the mandates committee convened in the boardroom of Dyson Whitney.

9

The mandates committee met every second Tuesday at six o'clock to review the new business brought in by the MDs and to approve the terms of engagement. Clients always demanded changes to the bank's standard letter of agreement, which were negotiated individually by the MDs involved. The committee's role was largely a formality. Most Tuesdays it was done by six-thirty.

But not this Tuesday. Bob Browning, or the Captain, as he was known, stared at the letter in his hand. He was on the fourth page.

"Is this a typo?" he said.

Lou Caplan, the bank's general counsel, craned his neck to see what the Captain was looking at.

"It says here we've got an advisory fee of forty bips." He looked at Caplan. "Is that a typo?"

"No, Bob, I don't believe it is," said Caplan.

Browning raised an eyebrow. He turned the remaining pages of the letter. "This is our exact letter. No changes. Isn't this our exact letter, Lou?"

Lou nodded. "Looks like it, Bob."

"Did Pete talk to you about this?"

"No. But if there aren't any changes, he wouldn't have to."

"Can you remember a letter we never had to change? Not even our indemnity clauses?"

Lou shook his head.

The Captain glanced at the others around the table. They shook their heads as well.

There were various myths about the way the Captain had acquired his epithet. He had been an officer in Vietnam, which is where it might have started. More likely, it had something to do with his piratical dealings back in the eighties, when he was close to Mike Milken, the junk bond king. Those were the glory days of Dyson Whitney. Thanks to the Captain and a couple of other aggressive MDs, the bank got a healthy piece of the first leveraged buyouts that were to become the hallmark deals of the decade. Then the big boys muscled in, and Dyson Whitney was pushed to its usual place at the back of the line. Bob Browning left for Salomon Brothers. After the Salomon takeover by Smith Barney, he came back to the chief executive job at Dyson, and had held it ever since.

Beside him sat Frank Nardini, head of mergers and acquisitions, Pete Stanzy's direct boss. In addition to Lou Caplan, the others at the table were Tom Dixon, who was the next most senior MD in mergers and acquistions after Frank; John Golansky, head of capital markets; and Bruce Rubinstein, head of credit risk.

"What do you think, Frank?" asked the Captain, putting the letter down. "Has Pete run this past you?"

"He mentioned the deal to me, I don't know, Thursday, Friday. Told me it's an eleven-billion-dollar play. Said he was counting on getting forty bips." Frank Nardini shrugged. "I thought he was kidding."

"Looks like he's got it," said the Captain.

"Looks like he does."

"So it's kosher?"

"Bob, all I know is what I know. He told me he was going to get it and it looks like he got it."

The Captain looked at Lou. "What do you think, Lou?"

Caplan hesitated. As the in-house lawyer at an investment bank,

Lou Caplan lived his entire life under fire. Investment bankers hate lawyers, even the ones they pay themselves. Lawyers are cautious. They're paid to point out obstacles, pitfalls, and any other reason they can find to back off from an opportunity because of problems that might arise later. To investment bankers, caution is poison. It's the toxic sludge that separates them from their fees, and if they had a choice, they'd hose it away along with every lawyer on Wall Street.

"I don't know, Bob," said Lou diplomatically. "The client didn't change the letter, but on the other hand, we propose those indemnities because we think those are the ones we think we should have." Lou allowed himself a wry smile. "Maybe this particular client just saw how fair that was."

That was so ridiculous the Captain decided to ignore it.

"Frank," he said, "you know anything about this client?"

"Not really," said Nardini, whose own area of expertise was aerospace and defense. He glanced at the letter. "Some electricity company in Louisiana, I think."

"Any of you guys know anything about it?"

There was silence for a moment.

"I'm not so sure we don't have a problem," said Tom Dixon.

The Captain looked at him sharply. "What kind of problem?"

Tom shrugged.

"Do you know this client?" asked Frank.

"John Deeming does. He says there might be something going on. The client has a relationship with Merrill Lynch. It's done all its acquisitions through them. This is a substantial deal, their biggest deal ever by a mile, and they come directly to us."

The Captain shot a glance at Nardini. Nardini shrugged. They both knew about the situation between John Deeming and Pete Stanzy. If Pete was about to pull off an eleven-billion-dollar deal at forty bips, you couldn't trust anything John said. And John, as everyone knew, was one of Tom Dixon's protégés.

"Tom, I think you'd better declare an interest here," said the Captain.

Tom Dixon grinned. "All right, I declare it. But that's what John said. He does know the industry. He knows it as well as Pete."

"Yeah, but he didn't get the deal, did he?" said Nardini. "What was John's last deal? A couple of hundred mil? What was it? Milwaukee Sewage or something?"

"All right," said Dixon. "Jeez, I don't know. I'm just saying what he said, all right? By the way, he asked me not to let Pete know he'd spoken to me."

"Tom, hold on," said the Captain. "That's not good enough. Are you saying there's a problem or not? Let's get this clear. What you're saying is John says the client's got a relationship with Merrill. Is that it, Tom? Is that all you've got?"

Tom shrugged. "That's it. I just felt I had to raise it."

Nardini glanced at the Captain and rolled his eyes.

Bruce Rubinstein coughed. "I don't mean to intervene . . ."

"What is it?" asked the Captain.

"Well, normally I wouldn't comment on the matter if it was just an advisory fee on an acquisition . . ." Rubinstein paused, turning the pages of his copy of the letter. The Captain watched him impatiently. Rubinstein was the kind of guy who made a thing of the fact that he couldn't be hurried. "It does appear that we'll be raising a considerable amount of debt to get this deal off the ground."

John Golanksy grinned. "Looks like it," he said. Stanzy, knowing he needed an ally at the committee table, had given John Golansky the lowdown in some detail.

"In which case," said Rubinstein, "I agree with Tom."

Dixon's eyes narrowed. He rarely found himself in agreement with Rubinstein, and it didn't make him feel too comfortable when he did. As head of credit risk, it was Bruce Rubinstein's job to make sure that the bank's exposure to the portfolio of debt it was selling on behalf of its clients didn't pose a threat to Dyson Whitney itself, and if necessary to advise restrictions. It was also his role to cast an eye over the long-term quality of that debt. Not because it would hurt Dyson Whitney financially if the client later defaulted—the loss would hit the investors and other banks to whom they had sold the bonds—but because of the damage it would do to Dyson's reputation and ability to sell further debt in the future. This role was an essential part of the checks and balances in any bank, as were Lou

Caplan and his in-house lawyers, but it put Bruce Rubinstein and his team in conflict with just about every other executive at Dyson Whitney, whose sole aim was to get transactions completed. And there was no one with whom Bruce's role put him in greater conflict than John Golansky, the head of capital markets. Golanksy's guys were the ones out there selling bonds into the market. They got their bonuses according to how much debt they could shift, and so did Golansky. They wanted as much debt as they could get, and once it was off their hands, they couldn't care less if the client defaulted.

But that wasn't the only reason for the hostility between Rubinstein and Golansky. Until recently, Bruce Rubinstein had been head of capital markets himself. His greatest success was handling a bond placement for a pharmaceutical company called Alesco, a $3.2 billion placement that was completed under intense pressure of a deal that was in danger of collapse, and he never stopped reminding people about it. But the Alesco placement, and just about everything else that succeeded in capital markets, had in reality been managed by Rubinstein's deputy, a fast-talking Nebraskan called Joe Allen. The Captain had been planning to move Allen into Rubinstein's job when Allen suddenly announced that he was going to Morgan Stanley. The Captain would have kicked Rubinstein out and put Allen behind his desk the same day if he could have persuaded the Nebraskan to stay. Instead, Allen walked—together with half the capital markets team—and the Captain was left with Rubinstein running the operation, minus Joe Allen, just when the Alesco deal had finally gotten Dyson some credibility in the corporate debt market. As fast as he could, the Captain sidelined Rubinstein into credit risk and recruited John Golansky from Deutsche Bank, giving him double Rubinstein's salary and a huge incentive package to build the debt business.

"Are you saying you know something about this client?" said Golansky

"No," said Rubinstein. He looked Golansky in the eye. "I'm saying I'd like to."

Rubinstein and Golansky squared up to each other across the table. Golansky was a big, powerful guy who had played college football and looked like he still had the physique under his shirt to throw a tackle. Rubinstein was a small, balding, dapper man with a large pinky ring on his right hand. Golanksy looked as if he should have been running a gym; Rubinstein looked as if he should have been running an antiques shop.

Golansky turned to the Captain. "Are we seriously saying we're going to refuse this mandate? Are we saying we're even considering that?"

"Delay it," said Rubinstein, "until we can do a little research."

"Yeah, which the client's likely to accept. That's going to make him real happy." Golansky shook his head in disbelief. "Let's just stop to think what we're talking about here. This would be the biggest deal Dyson Whitney has handled since . . . I'm relatively new, so I may not know all the history, but would that be the Transcom deal back in 2003, Frank?"

"This is bigger," muttered Nardini.

"Bigger? Really?" said John, as if he hadn't realized. "And it's not as if deals are exactly falling out of the sky. And if we're talking about selling two-point-eight billion dollars of debt, well, I *have* handled bigger debt placements than that—"

"The Alesco loan was bigger," said Bruce Rubinstein sniffily. "Three-point-two billion, and we placed it in four days."

"As I was about to say," continued Golanksy pointedly, "I have handled bigger debt placements, but not since I came to Dyson Whitney."

"Precisely my point," said Rubinstein smugly.

"Like hell it is!" retorted Golansky. "Excuse me, but I seem to be hearing that we're thinking about refusing a mandate because some client signs the letter and gives us the fee and the indemnities we want. Like that's some kind of crime! So let's be clear. Is that what this comes down to? Is that the bottom line? Because if it is, I honestly don't know what we're doing here. And to be frank, Bob, I certainly don't know what *I'm* doing here."

Golansky looked directly at the Captain. Bob Browning was perfectly well aware of his meaning.

There was a troubled silence at the table.

"Lou?" said the Captain eventually. "What do you think?"

Lou Caplan frowned. "I think we ought to get Pete Stanzy up here."

Stanzy was ready. He was expecting the call. He went down to the boardroom, and when he saw they were looking at his letter of engagement, he gave them a grin. "That's some letter, huh?"

The Captain nodded. "Pete, we just want to clarify a couple of things."

"Shoot."

"There are a number of things about this letter that are unusual."

"You like the fee, Bob?"

"Yes," said the Captain, "I like the fee. How did you get it?"

"Negotiation," replied Pete smoothly.

"Tough negotiation?"

"Not unreasonably. The client's looking for us to be extremely fast and responsive on this."

"Did you ever see a client who isn't?" said Rubinstein. "Doesn't mean they pay forty bips."

"He likes what we offer and he's prepared to pay for it."

"And no quibbles over the indemnity clauses?" asked Lou Caplan.

"Not really. My client's very focused on the things that really matter."

"And these don't?"

Stanzy didn't reply. He allowed himself a tiny smile. That was for the Captain. Browning, he knew, would have allowed himself a smile at that question as well—or a belly laugh, more likely—if he hadn't been sitting there as CEO.

"Okay." The Captain frowned. "That's a little unusual, isn't it? Wouldn't you say that?"

"I'd say it's very unusual," said Pete, as if there were nothing more agreeable to him than to admit it. "Mike Wilson wants this done very quickly and very quietly."

"Show me a client who doesn't," said Nardini.

"No, this is for real, Frank. This wasn't a competitive pitch."

"I was going to ask you about that," said the Captain.

"It wasn't," said Stanzy. "That's what I mean, Bob. Wilson wants this done quick and quiet. I've told him we can do it exactly the way he wants it done and he's prepared to pay for that."

"I understand the client has a relationship with Merrill," said Bruce Rubinstein.

"Who told you that? John Deeming? Well, Bruce, they do have a relationship with Merrill. And you know what they say, places like Merrill leak like a sieve. I told you Mike Wilson wants this done with the absolute most confidentiality. That's why he's gone away from Merrill and Morgan and Goldman and anyone else you'd expect him to go to with for a deal this size. He's very strategic. He wants to blind-side the competition. He wants this coming from a direction no one's going to expect."

"Why us?" asked the Captain.

"He knows me. I pitched a few things to him at the start of the year. It's not for me to say . . . I guess maybe he was impressed."

"Did you pitch him this one?" asked Nardini. "BritEnergy?"

"Absolutely," said Stanzy without hesitation. "You should see the fit. If you know anything about the industry and if you've got a global perspective, you'd have to be blind not to see it."

"Why didn't he do it then?" asked Tom Dixon.

"When I pitched it? That, Tom, I don't know. You'd have to ask him."

"Why did he decide to do it now?"

"Ditto. Maybe he saw the light."

"Do you think it's a good deal for the client?" asked the Captain.

"That's a good question, Bob. Yes. Unreservedly. I think this is a very good deal for the client. The strategy's rock solid."

"Would you recommend this to a shareholder?"

"Yes, Bob, I would. Again, unreservedly. There's an extremely compelling rationale for this deal. Like I said to Mike Wilson when I pitched it to him, put the assets of these two companies together and you've got a map of the known world."

The room was silent. Pete Stanzy emanated certainty, confidence, control.

"I'd like to add," said Golanksy, "that I think this is a very good deal for the bank. Personally, Pete, I think you ought to be congratulated. It's not just the fees, it's what it'll do for Dyson Whitney's reputation. We can all build on this. We've needed something like this for a long time."

"Thank you, John," said Stanzy. "I think it's a good deal for Dyson, too. I have a first-class team on the engagement. I met the client yesterday with the initial outputs and he was very impressed with what we'd achieved. That's why he signed."

There was silence again.

"Do you think this deal will succeed?" asked Nardini.

"I think it has a very good chance, Frank."

"I notice we have no retainer," said Tom Dixon. "We get no fee at all if they don't complete the acquisition?"

"That's correct."

"And what's the threshold they need to achieve?"

"In the UK, it's ninety percent of the shares, I believe."

"Ninety percent? And we get nothing if they don't reach that?"

"Like I said," said Pete, "I think this deal has a very good chance. The logic is extremely strong. Most important, Mike Wilson is determined to make it happen. He's a strong leader and he's absolutely committed to it."

Pete Stanzy waited.

There was silence. Everyone at the table knew there was something questionable in the story they were hearing. The size of the fee made no sense, nor did Pete Stanzy's explanation of it. Yet they also knew how badly the bank needed a deal that was big enough to remind people that Dyson Whitney existed, to make them sit up and take notice. This was the one.

They looked at the Captain.

"How fast does he want to do this deal?" asked the Captain eventually.

"Fast," said Stanzy. "As fast as it can be done. The parties are already talking. I'll be frank with you, Bob. If we don't drive this as hard as we can, we may as well stop now. If Wilson gets the faintest sniff that we're not two hundred percent commited, he'll go somewhere else. He's not going to wait around for us. And with this deal on the table, he won't have trouble finding someone to do it for him."

"He'll have trouble fighting them off," murmured Golansky.

Frank Nardini nodded.

There was silence again.

The Captain cleared his throat. "Pete, I just want you to be able to tell me there isn't something wrong here, there isn't some kind of Enron sitting under this company. That's all I'm asking. Just tell me there isn't some kind of dirty stuff going on and they're not paying us a big forty-bip fee so we don't look too closely at anything they've been doing."

Pete Stanzy smiled. "I'm no auditor, Bob. The auditors say she's clean."

"They said that about Enron," muttered Rubinstein.

"Can you tell me that?" said the Captain. "Can you tell me there's nothing that's going to come out when this deal goes public? Pete, no matter how big this deal is, Dyson Whitney can't afford to be involved in anything like that. If we get into litigation . . . Look, we're not that strong. We're just keeping it together. You know that. If we get into litigation, the deal flow will dry up completely and it'll be the end of us. I'm not exaggerating."

"Bob," said Stanzy seriously, "this is a great, robust American company that's taken its business model and exported it to a dozen countries around the world. Let's get this straight. Louisiana Light is a success story. It's a growth story. And Mike Wilson is a great leader. A visionary leader. Now he's about to make this company even bigger and stronger by making an acquisition that creates an awesome growth platform and may well change the dynamics of the entire industry on a global level. That sounds like a pretty good story to me."

"And me," said John Golansky.

"Exactly," said Stanzy. "This is the kind of deal Dyson Whitney should want to be involved in. In fact, I'd say more than that. Given where we are today, from our own perspective, it's the kind of deal Dyson Whitney can't afford *not* to be involved in."

Stanzy stopped himself from saying anything else. First rule of making a pitch, he knew, was never to oversell. And this was as much of a naked pitch as anything he had ever said at an investor roadshow.

The Captain frowned. At heart, he was a deal maker. A play like this got him tingling down to the end of every last fiber. And there was no way the bank could turn away a fee like this. It was inconceivable.

He looked around the table, giving the others a last chance to speak up. No one did. Bruce Rubinstein hesitated for a moment, then looked away. He was on thin ice with the Captain. There were only so many times he could challenge him.

"All right," said the Captain. "Looks like we're agreed." The frown disappeared and he broke into a grin. "Well done, Pete. Go out there and make it happen."

At about the time that the mandate committee was breaking up in the Dyson Whitney boardroom, a limousine delivered a slim, dark-haired man in his late thirties to the American Airlines terminal at JFK. He had one small carry-on bag and a briefcase. He checked in at a business-class counter and went to the executive lounge to wait for his flight to be called.

From time to time, as he waited, he looked around with a slightly furtive air, as if to see whether anyone had noticed him.

At last he heard his flight number and got up to board.

Seven hours later, eight A.M. local time in London, he disembarked at Heathrow Airport. A driver was waiting with a sign saying MR TOM BROWN. The driver took him through the morning traffic to a hotel in Kensington, overlooking Hyde Park, where a room was booked for him under the same name.

His name wasn't Tom Brown. It was Lyall Gelb, chief financial officer of Louisiana Light.

10

Donato's was an old-style neighborhood Italian place with red-and-white–checkered cloths and wax-encrusted Chianti bottles on the tables. Real wax-encrusted Chianti bottles, from years of candles burning down, not the kind someone's made by purposely melting candles to give the place a homely look. Ercole, who was about sixty, took the orders, opened the wines, and generally ran the place. His wife, Teresa, did the cooking, with help from a Mexican guy called Esteban, who did the chopping, the cleaning, and the washing. Teresa wouldn't let him near the pots. They had a waiter called Ricky. He was an old guy, silver-haired, but everyone called him Ricky, as if he were a kid. And that was it. Ercole and Teresa closed in August, and everyone took a month's vacation. First of September, the doors opened again.

Rob and Greg discovered the place when they were at law school together at Columbia. They hadn't been friends at first. Greg's background was well-to-do with family money on both sides. His father was a partner with a big advertising firm, they had an apartment in Manhattan and a house on Long Island, and Greg had gone to a fancy private school and then through Princeton. Rob, on the other hand, was working nights at a deli on Ninth to supplement his scholarship. But in their second year they shared a seminar course in torts and found themselves hanging out. Two more years of shared all-nighters studying for law exams cemented the friendship. After law school, Greg had joined the DA's office. Wall Street didn't interest him. Greg would tease Rob a little, asking him how a job at Roller Waite was going to help fulfill his great urge for social justice. Rob teased him back, saying it was easy to go work at the DA's office when your salary was only the icing on the cake of your trust fund. Besides, Rob didn't know that prosecuting a succession of pimps, thieves, and drug pushers had much to do with social justice. It seemed to him it had more to do with the opposite.

Greg had been with his girlfriend, Louise, for about a year and a half. Louise was a thin woman with a large head, wide-boned face, and black hair cut straight across the forehead. She had a strange, striking beauty. Or maybe it was just unusualness. She did some kind of art thing in the Village with textiles and rubber that she never deigned to explain very clearly, obviously believing that people like Rob and Emmy would never be able to appreciate its true cosmic significance. Neither of them much liked Miss Snookums, as they called her between themselves. But Greg was besotted with her. He still was, unfortunately, because it had been clear for a while to anyone else that Louise was cooling toward him. Whatever had initially attracted her to Greg was gone. She had never exuded a lot of warmth, but her brusqueness toward him was worse each time Rob and Emmy met up with them. It was getting embarrassing to see it.

Emmy had rescheduled the dinner for Wednesday night. Rob picked her up in a cab on the way uptown to the restaurant. Work was still going on in the war room, but Rob told Sammy he needed a couple of hours and that he'd be back, then he'd stay until whatever time it took. Cynthia had done the same thing the previous evening, so Rob figured he could as well.

The cab ride was the first time they'd had together in days. Emmy told him about a manuscript she wanted to bid for. It was a story about a woman's struggle to cope with her son's mental illness, and Emmy thought it was beautifully written—honest, moving, without sentimentality—and would hit a spot with a female readership, maybe even turn out to be a bestseller. More important, she loved it. She desperately wanted to be its editor, but there was interest from other parties. The bidding had turned into an auction and she didn't know if Fay Pride, the editorial director at Lascelle Press, was going to let her put in a high enough offer.

"Doesn't she like it?" asked Rob.

"She likes it, but I don't think she sees the potential like I do. And this woman can write, Rob. She can really write. There's going to be more. Personally, I wouldn't be bidding for just the one book. I'd be offering her a two-book deal."

"And you don't think you'll get it?"

"I don't know. We could have had it all to ourselves, that's what's so frustrating. The agent came to us first, thinking we'd be the perfect home for it, which we are, but Fay took so long deciding that the agent took it out to the market and now she says she's got four publishers interested. When that happens, the price gets crazy. And you know us at Lascelle—we don't do crazy prices."

They arrived first. Ercole came out from the back, beaming. He seated them and went to get a bottle of wine. Verdicchio, the wine of his home region in Italy.

"Cheers," said Rob. "Here's to that book. Let's hope you get it."

"Cheers," said Emmy, and raised the glass to her lips.

Rob put his glass down. He glanced at Emmy.

"What?" she said.

"Nothing." He leaned over and kissed her.

Rob knew he was lucky to have Emmy. Being with her had always felt easy. But recently there was something between them. When he went to Cornell for his MBA he had already been with Emmy for a year. He had subletted his own apartment and would stay with her whenever he came to the city, even though it would probably have been natural to give up his apartment entirely. It would have been even more natural to give it up and move in with her after he finished his MBA and came back to New York to start his job at Dyson Whitney. His apartment was too small for two and Emmy had a nice place in one of the old brownstones on the Upper West Side. It belonged to her grandmother, who lived in Florida. He was pretty sure Emmy was expecting him to move in, but he never opened the question and somehow they never really had a proper discussion about it. A couple of times he mentioned something about how it would be kind of odd for him to live in a place that belonged to her grandmother, and Emmy said she didn't see why it was so odd, but she never pushed the conversation to where it could have gone, and neither did he. He wasn't sure if it was only him who was avoiding it or if it was Emmy as well. Either way, he had always been relieved whenever they got close and it didn't go the distance. Because when you talk about moving in with someone, you've got to talk about what it means. Where it's heading. The big question. And he didn't know if he was ready for that.

So when he had come back to the city a couple of months earlier, he had ended up moving back to his own place on West Thirty-ninth Street. In name, at least, because he spent about 90 percent of his time at Emmy's anyway. But that wasn't the same as having talked about it. And so now there was this thing, this unresolved question waiting to be dealt with, where it had never felt that there was anything between them before. Most of the time everything was still great, but sometimes, when Rob looked at her, he caught a certain look in Emmy's eye and he was sure she was thinking about it. He had evaded it, and she knew he had. He knew the frustration was building up in her. It was going to come out. It had to, at some point. Probably when he least wanted it to.

He just wished it weren't there. If there hadn't been this thing between them, everything with Emmy would have been perfect.

Greg and Louise arrived. Ercole fussed over them. Greg gave Emmy a kiss and Louise turned a cheek to Rob. Ercole was pouring them each a glass of wine.

"Did you come in the car?" asked Rob.

"Cab," said Louise brusquely.

Greg had just gotten a new car, a blue BMW Z4. For the past few weeks he hadn't talked about anything else. Louise refused to let him drive her, as if to take all the pleasure out of it for him.

"Parking," said Greg, shaking his head and putting on a smile. "It's a killer."

"I bet it is," said Rob.

"So you had to blow us off Sunday night." Greg lifted his glass. "Cheers to that! Looks like we've lost you to your new job."

Rob laughed. "Cheers."

"What was happening on Sunday? Better be good."

"It's just this deal I'm working on."

"*Just this deal*," said Greg. "Listen to him. How long have you been waiting to be able to say that, huh? How long?"

Rob grinned.

"You guys should feel honored," said Emmy. "This is the first night off he's had in a week."

"Sure is a privilege," muttered Louise.

"Hey, baby, come on," murmured Greg.

Louise looked away.

Ercole came back with menus. Rob always had the same thing, spaghetti with meatballs followed by the veal scaloppine. Greg always started with the marinara.

"So, what's this deal that's keeping you so busy?" asked Greg after they'd ordered.

"I can't say," said Rob.

Greg looked at him doubtfully.

Rob smiled. "I'll tell you when it's finished."

"Everyone'll *know* when it's finished," said Greg. "What's the point of being friends with a hotshot investment banker? We want to know now!"

Rob shook his head.

"He won't even tell me," said Emmy.

"Does he talk in his sleep?"

Emmy laughed.

Louise got up. "I gotta pee," she said, and headed for the bathroom.

She took her time. When she came back, Ricky came out with their first courses on a tray. He shook a little. Teresa never filled the soup bowls right to the top.

"Who's having the meatballs?" he said.

"Ricky, who always has the meatballs?" said Rob.

"I always ask," said Ricky fastidiously. "Ladies first. Who's having the minestrone?"

Emmy put up her hand.

"Okay. A minestrone for the lovely lady." He put the soup down, shaking it all the way to the table. "And asparagus . . . for the other lovely lady. And a marinara . . . and the meatballs . . . *Buon appetito!*"

"*Grazie,* Ricky," said Rob and Greg, putting on the most flamboyant Italian accents they could muster. Ricky shook his head, waving his hand dismissively, and shuffled off.

Rob and Greg grinned at each other.

Greg started twisting his fork in his marinara. "So what's it like, seriously, working on this deal?" he asked, putting a forkful in his mouth.

Rob was digging into his spaghetti. "Seriously?" he said. "Intense. It's very intense."

"Like when you were working at Roller Waite?"

Rob shook his head as he ate a mouthful of spaghetti. "No. Not like that at all. I mean, we worked pretty hard at Roller Waite, we had our moments, but not like this. This just explodes. Suddenly there's this deal and everything's time critical and you're crunching through an incredible amount of data and it's all eighty-twenty, eighty-twenty, what do I have time to cover and what do I leave? You live or die by eighty-twenty because you never have time to do everything. That's the difference. When you're working in a law firm, you have to cover everything. I mean you don't, but you do, if you know what I mean. That's where the time goes. Here, the coverage is potentially infinite, so you're constantly selecting. What do I need, what can I leave, what do I absolutely have to have before I can go on to the next thing?"

"So what do you actually do all day?" asked Greg.

Louise sighed ostentatiously and stared out the window.

"Well, mostly, I get yelled at."

"What?" said Emmy. "Someone else is yelling at you? Honey, that's my job."

"Baby, there'll always be room for you." Rob looked back at Greg. "No, really, the VP who runs the team is so abusive you could just about sue him for breathing. It's not just me he yells at, it's everyone. Every time he walks in it's like, get ready, here he comes. And every second word's a curse word."

Emmy frowned.

"And when he's not yelling at you?" said Greg.

"Mostly, I crunch a bunch of numbers. See, my job is to figure out the value of the company we're going after, so I've got these estimates and I'm working and reworking them, trying to get more and more accurate. To be honest, Greg, I'm so deep in that side of it, I don't even know what the other guys are doing. I don't even see the document my numbers go into. I just give them what they need." Rob picked up his spoon and took more of his spaghetti. "I guess that doesn't sound so great. But actually, I don't mind. The learning curve is like . . ." He pointed straight up at the ceiling. "Awesome. I don't mind being yelled at if I'm learning stuff, right? And Emmy doesn't really want to see me, do you, Em?"

"Occasionally would be nice."

Rob grinned. "All those times when I was at Roller Waite and I thought, Should I, shouldn't I? Greg, you remember? Should I go back to school and take on all that extra debt? Remember?"

Greg glanced at Emmy and rolled his eyes. "How could we forget? The great drama of the century."

"Well, I think I made the right choice."

"On the basis of . . . ?"

"Yeah, I know." Rob laughed. "One week of working on a deal."

Rob took another mouthful of spaghetti. There was silence for a moment as everyone ate.

"Well," said Greg. "That's the thing, right? To choose the right options. There's an opportunity at work which I've been thinking about and—"

"Oh, for God's sake!" Louise said suddenly. "Can't we talk about something else? Can't we talk about anything but work?"

"Sure, honey," said Greg quickly. "What would you like to talk about?"

"Your car," said Louise sarcastically. "We could talk about that for a change. Or parking. Parking's a killer."

Greg didn't say anything. He twirled his fork in his marinara, frowning.

Rob looked at her. "What would you like to talk about, Louise? Why don't we discuss something you're interested in?"

Louise gazed at him silently.

"Nothing? What about what you're doing? Why don't you tell us about that? Last time we spoke about it, I think it was rubber puppets, wasn't it?"

"Marionettes," said Louise. She almost hissed it.

"And what are you doing now?"

Louise didn't reply.

Rob watched her for a moment longer, then turned back to Greg. "I'm interested, Greg. Where *do* you park the car?"

They finished their first courses. The next course arrived. Greg came back to what he had been going to say. He wanted to hear what Rob thought about it. The DA's office was expanding the team dealing with corporate fraud. The volume of work had rocketed since the credit crunch and more cases were coming onto the roster all the time.

"They're not exactly Bernie Madoff, but there are some pretty big cases. They've asked me if I want to join the team. I guess it'll be good for my career, but I'm not sure if I'm really interested. What do I know about corporate crime?"

"You'd learn."

"These cases drag on for years."

"Well, you've got to be interested in that kind of thing," said Rob. "That's the most important thing. If you're not interested, forget it."

"Would you be?"

"That's not relevant."

"But would you?"

"What?" Rob grinned. "Instead of prosecuting the pimps and the drug pushers? That'd be a hell of a thing to give up."

"Come on, Rob. What do you think? Really?"

"I'd do it. Sure, I'd do it."

"Someone needs to," said Emmy, putting her fork into the mushroom risotto she had ordered. "Look what those crooks did to the economy."

"Most of the people who messed up the economy weren't actually crooks," said Rob.

"What were they?"

"Idiots."

"Then they were criminally idiot," said Emmy. "And criminally greedy. You can't let people have that much power to affect other people's lives and let them be guided only by their own personal greed. That's just wrong. They can hurt the lives of millions of people."

"I agree," said Rob. "We had a system of regulation and enforcement that allowed the idiots and the crooks to flourish. And why did it do that? Because it was the same idiots and crooks who created it. They ran it. Madoff was chairman of the NASDAQ, for God's sake. The biggest corporate crook in our history!" Rob laughed. "You couldn't script it."

"And it wasn't like no one knew," said Emmy. "There was that guy—what was his name? That guy who tried to blow the whistle on him."

"Harry Markopolos," said Rob. "That's true. And why did no one listen to him? Because the system didn't back him up. The system wasn't there to do it."

"Do you think you would have believed Markopolos?" said Greg.

Rob looked at him. "What do you mean?" he asked, taking a mouthful of his scaloppine.

"Would you have believed him? He's standing there saying Bernie Madoff's a crook, and everyone else is saying Madoff's a genius. Pillar of society, big donor. Who are you going to believe?"

"Sure. It's a tough one. But the regulatory system has to be objective, it has to look at stuff on its merits." Rob put his knife and fork down. He was serious now. "Bernie Madoff was a facade. Anyone who looked at the fundamentals purely on their merits would have to have said that all the signs showed there was nothing solid behind him. He was one set of lies built on another. But no one in authority did. Markopolos did, but when he brought his suspicions to the regulatory authorities, they didn't want to know. But that's what you've got to do. If that happens, if you find something like that, you've got to follow the signs. You've got to hold on to them. You've got to ignore all the bullshit and follow what's real to wherever it takes you and call it like you see it. And keep calling and calling and calling it until someone listens."

"Hard to do," said Greg. "Imagine the pressure. Your job, your income. You'd put everything at risk."

"Damn right. But if you're not prepared to do it, what are you? You might as well be one of the crooks."

"So you'd do it?"

"I hope I'd do it. I hope I'd have the strength."

Greg smiled. He glanced at Emmy. "When are we ever going to knock the idealism out of him?"

Emmy put her arm around Rob's shoulder. "Never, I hope."

Rob shrugged. "Sorry, that's just how I feel. You asked me and I told you." He took a sip of his wine and looked at Greg. At some point, Louise had gotten up to go to the bathroom again. "So are you going to join this corporate fraud team? What do you think?"

"I don't know," said Greg. "I'm still thinking about it."

In the cab downtown Emmy was silent, thinking. Eventually she turned to Rob. "You know when I heard you talking back there, about that stuff Greg was talking about, you know what I thought? It should have been you."

"What?"

"Joining that DA's team."

Rob smiled incredulously.

"Greg's a nice guy. You know I like him a lot. But he's got no fire. He's got no passion. No drive. And you have, Rob."

"I don't think that's fair on Greg."

"Sure it is. Don't you notice how he always asks you before he does anything? Every decision. He always wants to hear what you've got to say."

"I like to hear what he's got to say as well."

Emmy looked at him skeptically.

"I don't know," said Rob. "Greg's a good guy, that's all I know."

Emmy nodded. "So you're honestly going to tell me that doesn't appeal to you? What Greg was talking about? Going after corporate crooks, people who have really hurt other people with their greed and dishonesty?"

Rob shrugged.

"You wouldn't think about it?"

"Emmy, I've just started a new job."

"Which mostly consists of being shouted at by some abusive VP, apparently."

"There's more to it. I've been two months an investment banker. I'm just learning what it's about. It's a little early to start thinking about something else, isn't it? Besides, what does Greg get paid? His BMW didn't come compliments of the DA's office, in case you're wondering. It's a lot easier for him."

"You don't have to drive a BMW."

"And I don't. But I do have to pay back a shitload of debt."

"You could have paid it back by staying at Roller Waite if that's all that matters to you."

"It's not all that matters to me. You know it's not." Rob paused. "Let's leave the corporate crime to Greg, huh? If I worked for the DA's office, yeah, I'd probably join that team. Of course I would. But I don't. Em, the deal I'm on is a really big, interesting deal and I'm lucky to be on it. People would kill to be on this deal. I'm just gonna do exactly what I'm told and get through it and hopefully enjoy it and learn a hell of a lot on the way through."

"And then?"

Rob smiled. "Having been such a great success, I'm going to get myself on another great deal. And get a big bonus for my trouble. And maybe take us both to Paris. And not to a crummy hotel like the one we stayed at in London last year. How does that sound?"

"It sounds good."

Rob nodded to himself. But he could see the way Emmy was watching him. He knew that look. "What?" he said to her.

"Nothing. I'm sure you'll do great on this deal. And on the next one. You always do, Rob. I just wonder how long it's going to satisfy you."

11

The American Airlines flight left Heathrow at nine A.M. local time and by eleven-fifteen in New York it was taxiing to its stand at JFK. Then there was an hour's layover before the Delta flight, and an hour's delay during the layover in Atlanta. It was almost seven-thirty by the time Lyall Gelb walked into Mike Wilson's office in Baton Rouge.

Wilson was in a tuxedo. He was hosting a fund-raising dinner that night for the Louisiana Relief Society, one of the charities where he was a trustee. He should have been there for cocktails at seven. Dot Mendelsson, his girlfriend, had already been on the phone about a half-dozen times demanding to know where he was. These events were the kind of thing Dot lived for.

Wilson sized Lyall up as he came in. Gelb always had a furrowed, slightly worried look to his face.

"Well?" said Wilson. He threw himself down in a chair.

Gelb nodded.

Wilson grinned. "Sit down, Lyall! Come on, lighten up. Looks like you've come from a funeral. Couple of years' time, look at the company you're going to be head of."

Gelb sat.

"So what'd they say?"

"They like the fit," said Gelb. "They've had a couple of guys working on it. They agree, it's everything you could ask for. The geographic footprint is perfect. It's like we were made for each other."

"See! Did you give them that line about the hand and the glove?" Wilson slapped his thigh. "I knew they'd love that. Brits love that stuff. Gloves, scarves."

"I think we can do the heads, Mike."

"Good," said Wilson. "That's what I want to hear." The thing most likely to kill a friendly deal, Wilson knew, isn't a shareholder revolt or a counterbid, but failure to agree on who gets the top five or six posts. Executives who are happy to cut thousands of jobs as part of a deal are usually less happy to include themselves on the list.

"You were right about their finance guy," said Gelb. "Oliver Trewin. He's sixty-seven. He'll take the golden handshake."

"See, Ly? No competition. You stay CFO."

"They liked the idea of the joint counsels. As for the chief operating officers, theirs becomes operations director for UK and Europe, ours for the U.S. and Rest of World."

"Everyone's a winner!" said Wilson, smiling broadly.

"As for Bassett, Mike, that's something you'll have to deal with."

"Sure," said Wilson. Andrew Bassett was the CEO of BritEnergy. From what he knew, Mike Wilson didn't rate him. Bassett was fifty-nine and probably just wanted a knighthood to cap off his career, like every other British CEO Wilson had ever met. "I've told you how we'll do it. We tell Bassett he gets to be CEO in two years. Until then, Ed Leary stays chairman, I'm CEO, and Bassett's chief operating officer. In two years I become chairman and Bassett gets to be CEO, with a view to succeeding me as chairman in another few years. Right? That's what we tell him. But you know that won't happen, Ly."

Gelb looked at him silently.

"In two years, it's going to be my board. I give up the CEO job and become chairman. But the board doesn't appoint Bassett." Wilson shrugged. "Nothing I can do about it. You know what? They appoint you. At that point, we say good-bye to Mr. Bassett, give him a big golden handshake, and send him comfortably on his way."

Gelb didn't reply. He wasn't comfortable with such naked deception, and Wilson knew it. Lyall was a genuinely religious man. Every Sunday, he and his family took their seats in church. Wilson found a kind of pleasure in seeing the other man's discomfort. Mike Wilson didn't have a religious bone in his body. To him, it was a kind of softness.

"Will he fall for that?" asked Gelb quietly.

"Just tell me why he won't."

Lyall didn't say anything. He had seen enough of Mike Wilson to respect his judgment of character. It was something to be feared.

"You'll have to discuss that with Bassett yourself," said Lyall eventually. "That's not my place."

"Sure," said Wilson. "What else?"

"I'm concerned about what Stan's going to say."

Wilson considered that. Stan Murdoch was the chief operating officer of Louisiana Light. The plan called for him to become operations director, excluding UK and Europe, reporting to Bassett, who would be COO of the merged group. Stan wasn't going to like that. Eastern Europe was where a whole clutch of Louisiana Light's international plants were situated. Murdoch was going to have to give them up, leaving him with the South American assets of Louisiana Light and the Far Eastern and Australian plants that belonged to BritEnergy. Pound for pound, it was just about a fair trade, and the Eastern European plants were by far the least efficient and dirtiest in the portfolio. Some guys would have been glad to be rid of them, but not Stan. Getting those plants up to standard was a matter of pride for him and the job wasn't done. And Wilson had a hunch Stan wasn't going to like being told he would be reporting to someone he had never met.

That was the main reason Wilson hadn't told Murdoch about the deal yet. At this point, only four people in the company knew about it. Mike Wilson and Lyall Gelb, Doug Earl, the general counsel, and one of Gelb's analysts named Dave Sagger, who'd been doing the grunt work on the deal. They had put Sagger into a hired office off-site to quarantine him, and every couple of days Lyall went out there to look over the numbers he was producing. Sagger was something of a loner, the perfect guy for the task. Everyone else on Gelb's team had been told he'd been given compassionate leave because of a death in the family.

"Leave Stan to me," said Wilson at last. "What else?"

"Nothing," said Gelb. "Except they want to know a price."

Wilson grinned. "You don't say?"

"They knew I wasn't there for that. But this is all smoke, Mike, until we've got a price. They know that as well as we do."

Mike Wilson nodded.

"There's no point having any more discussions until we get that on the table," said Lyall. "If they like the price, they'll set up a data room and we can go ahead with due diligence as quickly as we want."

"They said that?"

"Yes. That's where we're at. We've got to put up or shut up."

Mike Wilson stood. He walked to the window. Below him, the lights of a couple of barges drifted downriver. "What will they say to eleven-point-five?"

"Eleven-point-five of what?" said Lyall. "Eleven-point-five billion in cash, they'd probably jump at it."

"Three to one, stock and cash, just like we said." Wilson watched the barges. One was moving out of sight.

"I have no idea what they'd say to that," replied Lyall. "Genuinely, I don't."

"You think we should offer twelve?"

"That's above the top of the Dyson Whitney range."

Wilson shrugged. "Three in cash, nine in stock." The barge had gone now. The other one followed. Wilson turned around. "I don't want to get into a price negotiation, Lyall. I want to bid, I want them to take it. I want it to be so sweet they don't even think about saying no. That's what we need. Maybe we go over twelve. Maybe we go higher."

"Higher?"

"I told you, I want to bid, I want them to take it."

Gelb was silent.

"Lyall, you know what their balance sheet looks like."

"Of course I know what their balance sheet looks like! Jiminy Creeper, Mike, I know it backwards."

"Then you tell me, how much debt are they carrying? Twenty, twenty-five percent?"

"Twenty-two."

"Twenty-two percent debt." Wilson laughed incredulously. "Any company with that kind of leverage deserves to get eaten. It can carry, what? Sixty? Sixty-five? There's your three billion right there." Wilson paused. "And that leaves us room for more, right?"

Gelb didn't reply. He knew all that, better than Wilson.

"Lyall, we'll get the cash. We'll have every banker on Wall Street lining up to lend against a balance sheet like that. Hell, Lyall, you couldn't ask for a sweeter deal. We borrow the money to buy them against the strength of their own balance sheet."

"You said you wanted to bid higher."

"We can get more."

"I don't know what our board's going to say."

"Our board'll do what they're told to," said Wilson brusquely. Then he laughed. "Hell, Lyall, they want us to do this deal. That's why we got new contracts, right?"

Both Wilson and Gelb had recently had their contracts renegoti-
ated, and Wilson had made sure that large incentives were included
to execute a major acquisition in Europe. The bonus Wilson stood to
earn was considerably larger than Gelb's, but Lyall's wasn't trivial.

"I've been talking to Stanzy and his debt guy," said Wilson.
"Name of John Golansky. You know him?"

Gelb shook his head.

"Time you did. Time you started speaking to both of them. I'll
bring you in on the next conversation. They're going to get us a
bridge loan to cover the deal, then they'll sell down the loan after it's
done. They're thinking of going to Citi for the bridge. They asked if
I wanted to use Merrill, throw them a bone." Wilson laughed again.

"What's their premium on the bridge?" said Gelb.

"They figure four percent. I'll leave the details to you when you
talk to them."

Gelb was silent. Wilson could see him running the numbers in his
head.

"We'll get the cash, Lyall. Remember what I told you? I could
have got Stanzy to do this for twenty bips. You would have, wouldn't
you? Well, you would have been wrong. For twenty bips, Lyall, I
would have gotten Stanzy's brain. For thirty, I might have gotten his
heart. For forty bips, I have his soul." Wilson cupped his hand, as if
holding Stanzy's soul in his palm. "Pete Stanzy would sell his own
mother to do this deal. He would put her on the block and auction
her off himself."

Lyall Gelb looked up. Sometimes Mike Wilson scared him.

Wilson closed his fist. "If we're going to get this done, that's what
we're gonna need."

"What about BritEnergy?" asked Gelb quietly.

"What about BritEnergy?"

"You don't think they're going to figure this out? You don't think
they'll realize we're going to load their balance sheet with the same
debt we raise to buy them?"

"Nothing illegal in that."

"What happens when they figure it out?"

"*When* they figure it out? Hell, Lyall, why the hell do you think I'm so confident we can get them to do this thing? A fifth-grader could figure it out."

Gelb didn't get it.

Mike Wilson smiled pointedly. "They're still talking to us, aren't they?"

Gelb watched him. He was right.

"This is a deal, Ly." Wilson leaned forward. His tone became quieter, conspiratorial, even though there was no one else who could possibly hear them. "As long as everyone's a winner—us, them, the bankers—the deal goes through."

Wilson gazed at Gelb with curiosity. How could someone who was so brilliant at weaving his way through webs of financial regulations—genuinely, frighteningly brilliant—understand so little about the realities of a negotiation? Or maybe that's what he should have expected. Cutting a deal is like bare-knuckle fighting. Structuring finances is like tuning a piano. Bare-knuckle fighters and piano tuners don't have too much in common.

"Bassett's still talking to us, right? What does that mean? All he's worried about is what he gets out of this thing, and right now, he thinks he's going to get enough. 'Sir Andrew!' He's a winner. And don't worry about where the cash is coming from. The bankers will deal with that. All you have to do is give me the stock price. Just keep it up for me, Ly."

Their eyes met. The company's next filing, for their third-quarter results, was due at the end of the following week. Since Mike Wilson aimed to use Louisiana Light stock to pay for the majority of Brit-Energy, the level of the Louisiana Light stock price was critical. If the stock price fell, he'd have to offer more. And even if he did, against the background of a falling stock price, they might well walk away.

"Let's give the market something to smile about."

"I'm squeezing all I can, Mike."

Wilson smiled. "Just as long as you're not doing anything illegal."

Lyall winced. He hated it when Wilson said things like that.

"There's nothing left after this," said Lyall quietly. "I want you to understand that, Mike. The cupboard's bare."

Wilson shrugged. There was always more from somewhere. Gelb had never let him down.

"I'm serious, Mike. After this, there's nothing else. The filing after this, I don't know what happens. There'll be nothing to show."

"Just give me this one. Keep the picture pretty."

"And then?"

"We do the deal."

"Before the next filing?" said Lyall disbelievingly. "In under three months?"

Wilson nodded. "This is the last time Louisiana Light files as a single entity. Doug says we can do it. He's looked into the UK regulations. He says we can get it all done in ten weeks if everything goes right."

"If everything goes right? Jiminy Creeper, Mike! Do you know how many things can go wrong? Have you even—"

"We'd better make sure everything goes right then, hadn't we?"

Gelb stared at him.

"Just keep the numbers up next week," said Wilson. "We'll get out of this, Lyall. Trust me. Give me this one last filing. Let's not make it ridiculous, but let's make it pretty."

Gelb didn't leave right away. After two days out of the office he had things to do. Later, one of the company drivers took him home. On the corner of North Street, St. Joseph's Catholic Cathedral with its tall spire loomed pale in the moonlight.

Lyall worshiped as an Episcopalian, but he had been brought up a Catholic. In Baltimore, his mother had been active in the church and the family was at Mass every Sunday. It was a deeply traditional congregation with an old Irish priest, Father Ahern, who raved about sin and damnation. Lyall remembered the crust of white spittle Father Ahern always had in the corners of his mouth. Lyall was sent to a Catholic school, along with his brother and three sisters, and there was Sunday school as well, with Father Ahern drumming the catechism into them. Sometime in his teens, however, Lyall started to question his faith. In college, far from his mother's gaze, it lapsed altogether. It was his wife, Margaret, who brought him back to religion. She was from a strong Episcopalian family in Memphis. When Lyall got together with her, he realized how much he missed that spiritual component in his life, how important it was to him. The spirituality, the faith, not the Catholic ritual. And definitely not old Father Ahern with his fire and brimstone. He settled comfortably into Margaret's Episcopalianism. It caused trouble with his family. Or with his mother. Still did, sometimes.

Lyall gazed at the cathedral as the driver waited for the traffic light to change. He had never been in there. Twice a day, morning and night, he passed it, yet he had never been inside in all of the six years he had worked at Louisiana Light.

The kids were in bed when he got home. Margaret greeted him with an embrace. It was good to feel her in his arms.

Margaret laughed, disengaging herself.

"Tired, honey?" she said.

Lyall nodded.

"How was London?"

"It was okay."

"Everything go well?"

"Yeah," said Lyall. "It went fine."

"What is it?" Margaret frowned. "Is something wrong?"

"No." He sat down. "Come here."

He pulled her to him. She put her arm around his shoulders.

"I'm sorry I had to be away," he said.

"That's okay, Lyall. I understand."

"No, I'm sorry, honey. I'm really sorry."

Margaret didn't say anything. She knew Lyall hated to be away from the family. She knew he kept his business trips to a minimum. She was grateful for it. He didn't need to apologize.

"How are the kids?" said Lyall.

"They wanted to see you tonight."

"I know. I'm sorry. I had stuff to do. We're filing next week, and there's . . . you know . . ."

"You still can't tell me what's going on?"

"I can't, honey. I'm sorry." He hadn't told Margaret about the deal, even though he trusted Margaret to keep confidentiality even more than he trusted himself. Confidentiality wasn't the reason. Recently, Lyall had avoided saying anything about work at home. It was like polluting the one thing in his life that was still pure.

Margaret watched him. She knew Lyall trusted her. If he couldn't tell her what was happening at work, it wasn't as if he would have told someone else. She just hoped nothing was wrong.

"Sorry," said Lyall again.

"It's okay. Becky had a bellyache today."

Lyall looked at her in alarm. "Bad?"

"She came home from school with it."

"And?"

"She didn't eat much. She went to bed early. I went up a little while ago and she was asleep."

"I'll go look at her."

They got up and headed for the stairs.

Their other two children, Deborah and Josh, were asleep in their rooms. Becky was awake. She lay on her bed, wide eyes watching from her pillow.

"How's my baby?" said Lyall, and he sat down on the edge of the bed and leaned down to hug her.

Becky winced.

Lyall stopped. "Becky?"

"It hurts," she whimpered.

Lyall looked around at Margaret. She came forward anxiously. "Becky?"

Becky grabbed Lyall's hand. She squeezed. "It hurts, Daddy."

"Where?"

"In my tummy. Bad."

Lyall and Margaret glanced at each other.

"Has she seen a doctor?" said Lyall.

Margaret shook her head, fear showing in her eyes. "It wasn't this bad."

12

Rob stared at the number. Then he started to smile.

"We've got a typo here," he said. "Pretty important one."

Behind him, Phil Menendez and Sammy looked around. Cynthia continued working at her computer.

"Where?" said Sammy.

Rob slid the document across. Sammy had asked him to proof it. It was an early draft of the discussion document that Mike Wilson was going to take with him when he flew to London to meet Andrew Bassett. The meeting was on Monday. Wilson was flying out Sunday. It was now Saturday afternoon, which gave them twenty-four hours to get it right.

"Where's this typo?" said Sammy.

Rob pointed. "Twelve-point-five billion. That should be eleven-point-five, right?"

"No," said Sammy. "Twelve-point-five billion. That's the offer."

Menendez had already turned back to whatever they had been looking at on Sammy's computer.

"But we ranged it. Eleven-point-two-five to eleven-point-seven-five."

"Yeah. Leopard's offering twelve-point-five."

"That's over the top of the range."

Menendez turned. "It's over the top of *your* range. So what? You think your range is so great? Suddenly it's the Bible?"

"We didn't just pull that out of the air," said Rob. "We did a hell of a lot of work to get to—"

"A lot of work," said Menendez derisively. "I should show you what a lot of work is."

"I think if we've got a range—"

"What? You got an issue?" Menendez stared at him. "We haven't got time for this. You got a problem?"

"I haven't got a problem."

"You got something you want to say? You haven't got enough work to do?"

Rob looked at Menendez's belligerent, pop-eyed face. "No," he said.

"Good. That's about the smartest thing you've said all day." Menendez turned back to Sammy's computer. "Look at this crap here." He pointed to something on Sammy's computer screen. "Do what the Shark says. Right? Just fucking do it, Sammy."

Sammy nodded.

"I'll be back at eight. Make sure these guys don't fuck everything up." Menendez got up. He threw a glance at Rob and left.

There was silence.

Sammy sighed. "Rob, there are some things you shouldn't question in front of Phil."

"Like anything," muttered Cynthia.

"You're saying I can't ask?" said Rob. "Sammy, if you're telling me I can't question anything, I think that's an issue."

"You can ask what you like," said Sammy. "I'm just telling you, Phil doesn't take kindly to it. He's not interested in questions from analysts. I'm not saying it's right, I'm just telling you how it is. You can accept my advice or not, it's up to you."

"Did we advise Leopard to go in at that price?"

"Twelve-point-five?" said Sammy. "I don't believe so. I believe the client favored a strategy of going in high to get immediate agreement. We suggested eleven-point-seven-five, twelve if he wanted to make the deal look really sweet."

"And he went in at twelve-point-five?"

"That was his call."

Rob took the document back and looked at the offer page again. Twelve-point-five billion—4.2 billion in cash, the rest in stock.

"I thought we were going a quarter cash. This is a third."

"Client's call," said Sammy.

Rob was silent. Stock prices could move up or down. Cash in hand was certain. More cash in a deal was like an additional bump in the price.

Sammy and Cynthia turned back to their computers.

"If we think it's worth eleven-point-seven-five billion max, our client's throwing away three-quarters of a billion of his shareholder's money."

Cynthia clicked at her keyboard.

"We're agreeing to that."

Sammy turned around. "It's a valuation, Rob. We could be wrong. It could be worth thirteen. Maybe Leopard's getting it cheap."

"What about you, Cynthia?" said Rob. "What do you think?"

Cynthia entered a couple of numbers, scrolled down the page, entered a couple more numbers. "The offer's crazy," she said, eyes still on the screen. "But they want the deal, right? So they're going high to make it irresistible."

"They want it so much they'll throw away almost a billion dollars?"

Cynthia shrugged. "It's just our valuation, Rob. Who says we're right?"

Rob shook his head. "This is crazy. This is just wrong."

"It's a negotiation tactic," said Sammy.

"You don't negotiate like this. Come on, Sammy. That's not negotiation. That's surrender."

Sammy watched him.

"Don't you think something odd's going on here? This guy goes in at a price that's a full three-quarters of a billion over the top of our range. Why? He's got so much money he can't get rid of it quick enough?"

"He wants the deal done quickly. It's a tactic. You go in high, you get the deal."

"Yeah, but why do a deal if you're going to destroy three-quarters of a billion in value?"

"I told you, Rob," said Sammy very quietly, very deliberately. "It's just an estimate. His valuation may be better than ours."

Rob stared at Sammy. Then he shook his head. "You don't believe that. You saw the work I did. Hell, Sammy, you did half of it yourself. You know what went into it." He turned to Cynthia. "You don't believe that. Do you believe that?"

Cynthia didn't reply.

"Neither of you believe it! Come on, Sammy, what are we talking about here?"

Sammy shrugged.

"Sammy?"

"We're talking about our client." Sammy's tone was still patient, but there was an edge to it now that hadn't been there before. "Our client has given us a mandate to advise him, and we're executing it. We get an advisory fee because we *advise*. If the client doesn't take our advice, that's up to him. Valuation isn't an exact science. We may be wrong. The client may be right."

Rob shook his head.

"Rob, you were a lawyer before. This isn't that different. You have a client. You serve his interests. You give him advice. You lay out the options. He listens, makes his judgment, gives you instructions. You follow them."

Rob gazed at Sammy. But there was nothing more to be read in Sammy's eyes. They were steady, cool.

He glanced at Cynthia.

"All I care about is getting a good review on this project," she said. "Just let that fat bastard Menendez give me a good review."

"Exactly," said Sammy. "We're all in this together. Every one of us wants the same thing, to get a good review. Rob, you're doing a good job. Just keep doing that. That's what Phil's really saying to you. Focus on what you've got to do and don't worry about anything else. That's how you get ahead here."

Rob watched him.

"No one gets a good review when someone on the team acts up," said Sammy. "Everyone suffers. You understand what I'm saying, Rob? *Everyone* suffers."

Cynthia was looking at him.

"I understand," said Rob.

"Good. Now, when this thing moves to the next stage, you'll go to London to do the due diligence. You done that before?"

"Only as a lawyer."

"Okay, this'll be another learning experience for you. That's what you should be getting out of your first assignment, as much learning as you can get. So, can you keep doing the proofing?"

"Sure." Rob turned to the next page of the document. It showed a history of Leopard's share price. There had been a sharp dip at the start of the year, then the price came back.

"What caused this?" he said to Sammy.

Sammy glanced at the page. "Nothing. A revenue writedown. Don't worry about it."

Emmy came out of the bedroom, bleary-eyed.

"What time is it?" she said.

Rob glanced at his watch. "A quarter past two."

Emmy yawned. "When did you get back?"

"A couple of hours ago."

She looked at him in surprise. "What are you doing? You still working?"

"There's just a few things I need to check."

"What?"

"Nothing. It's just work." Rob looked at her. Emmy's hair was mussed, and she was in a long T-shirt. "Stand there like that much longer, and you'll force me to act."

"Will I? And what *action* will you need to take?"

"You don't want to know."

Emmy rolled her eyes. "I'm going back to bed."

Rob nodded. "I won't be long."

"Don't wake me," she said over her shoulder. Then she stopped and turned back. "I meant to tell you, I bumped into Greg today. You know that bookshop on Sixty-third? The one that does the readings? I saw him as I was coming out. Rob, he didn't look too good. I think things are pretty bad with Miss Snookums. You haven't seen him since Wednesday, have you?"

"When would I have had the chance to see him, Emmy?"

"You should give him a call. Have a beer with him. You know, just you two."

"If I can make the time."

Emmy raised an eyebrow.

"I know. You're right. I'll make it."

Emmy nodded, then headed for bed.

Rob watched her go. He looked back at his computer. The screen showed a page from the Louisiana Light annual report.

He had realized something that afternoon after he had dared to question the Shark. He knew virtually nothing about Louisiana Light. He could cite chapter and verse about fourteen different electricity companies around the world, and more than chapter and verse about BritEnergy, but about Louisiana Light he could say hardly a thing. He thought it was about time to find out.

They were up to their eyeballs in debt. That was immediately obvious from the most cursory examination of the financial pages in the annual report. But that didn't prove anything. Many of the companies he had analyzed were carrying a lot of debt. The electricity business was a hugely capital-intensive industry, and if you were going to grow—as Louisiana Light had done so spectacularly—you were going to suck in capital. Debt wasn't bad as long as you had the revenue to service it.

That was the thing that had gotten him thinking. The revenue writedown in January that Sammy had mentioned.

Following the writedown, the share price had dipped by around five dollars. That was about ten percent of the stock price, or close to a billion in value. A search of the Louisiana Light filings on the company website had quickly revealed the reason. An announcement of a $208 million writedown of revenues that had been booked in their Hungarian operation. The announcement said it was a one-off due to exceptional market conditions brought on by the credit crunch. Could be. But that $208 million writedown caused a billion-dollar dip, which suggested the market wasn't so sure it wasn't the tip of a fivefold-bigger iceberg. Yet eventually the market must have bought the line. Within a couple of weeks the stock was back up to where it had been.

How did you write down revenue? Writing something down meant you were revising a figure you'd already claimed up front. But you were only supposed to book revenue as you earned it, so you wouldn't need to write it down later, because you actually had it. Or that's what

Rob thought. He was no accounting expert, but he had taken corporate finance as part of his MBA and he had the basics. But he also knew accounting rules were riddled with so many exceptions that even experts had trouble following them. And the less developed the jurisdiction, the more profuse the exceptions.

Maybe in Hungary you could book revenues ahead if you had certain kinds of contracts. Maybe that explained it. But then, if you were going to understand the numbers in the report, you'd need to know about that.

That got him thinking. If you went back to the time when they booked that revenue, would you have known they were claiming it even before they'd earned it?

He started going back through earlier annual reports. Louisiana Light had entered the Hungarian market with an acquisition in 2004. Through one report after the next, Rob tracked the revenue statements. There was nothing anywhere about booking revenues up front.

If it was only $208 million, compared with Lousiana Light's total revenues it didn't really matter. But what if there was more? How would you know? There was nothing to indicate the $208 million that had been booked. Maybe there was another $208 million, or $408 million, or a billion. If you couldn't distinguish the $208 million from the rest of the company's revenue, how could you trust a single number you saw in these reports?

Rob closed the computer and thought about it. Surely it couldn't be that obvious. He must be missing something. If he could reach that point within a couple of hours of looking through the filings, if he could conclude that you couldn't trust a single number in those reports, anyone else could. There were analysts who did nothing but spend their whole lives looking at companies in the electricity sector. Rob looked at the share price chart again. A billion in value off. Mike Wilson must have had some explaining to do to the market. Whatever he said, it must have worked. The share price came back up and stayed up. Obviously no one was worried. Why should he be?

And surely if something at Louisiana Light was really wrong, the credit crunch would have exposed it. Anyone with shaky foundations, he thought, would have been swept away by now.

But it still didn't seem right. The Leopard was up to its neck in debt and within the last year had written down revenue that had been claimed sometime in the past. And now it wanted to do this deal and was throwing three-quarters of a billion above the top of the range at the target to try to get them to agree. Not to mention paying forty bips to its investment bank along the way. That had seemed like some kind of a coup for the bank before, but now it seemed suspicious.

Red flags. That's what they were, and they were everywhere.

During induction, there had been an hour's session on ethics from one of the MDs. He talked about something called Know Your Client, which was a set of guidelines to help you understand your client's situation so you could give the best, objective advice. It was also supposed to help you figure out if your client was doing something wrong. Red flags, he called them. Things to watch for, indicators that there were problems. One of them, Rob remembered, was if your client wanted to pay you in a foreign currency. "If he wants to pay in rubles," said the MD, "you know something's wrong." Then he said, "If you're dumb enough to take your fee in rubles, you don't belong at Dyson Whitney." And everyone laughed, which is why everyone remembered it.

Another red flag they had been told about was when a client accepted your terms too quickly. Rob didn't know how quickly Leopard had accepted Dyson Whitney's terms, but how much negotiation could there be if you walked away with forty bips?

And offering above the valuation range? The MD hadn't mentioned that one, but it seemed like a red flag to Rob.

Yet Sammy and Phil Menendez claimed not to think so. It was just a range, they said. The client could do what he wanted. He could go above or below. It was just a range.

It didn't seem right. You could explain one red flag as a coincidence. Maybe two. But he had three.

If he could spot them—a rookie six weeks on the job—then so could everyone else. All Cynthia cared about was getting a good review. And he didn't expect anything from Phil Menendez, who was clearly pathological. But for some reason he expected more from Sammy. But why? What did he really know about Sammy Weiss? A week on a team working together under such intensity can make you think you know someone, but you don't really know them at all. The only thing he could really say about Sammy Weiss was that he was obviously a star producer, someone that even a psycho like Phil Menendez grudgingly respected. And what makes you a star producer in a place where an associate is supposed to focus on his work and not bother anyone with questions?

Rob knew what Sammy had been saying to him that afternoon. Focus on your work, and the collective animal that was the team would protect you. Ask the wrong questions, and you were on your own. No one would shield you.

But that didn't take the red flags away. They were still there, all around, brighter, redder the more he thought about them.

They pointed to one clear conclusion: Louisiana Light was desperate to do this deal. Why would they be desperate? Because a deal was the only way out. Of what? What could be so wrong that a deal was the only thing that could save you?

Rob thought about it. Who were these people at Louisiana Light? He opened the computer again. At the start of the report was a message from the chairman. Some guy named Edward Leary. His face was at the top of the page. An old guy with kind of a flat, almost bald head. On the next page was the message from the president, Michael T. Wilson. Rob skimmed it. All about how great they'd done in navigating through the downturn. Managing their costs, but not being blind to opportunity. Using it to position the company for the next stage of its growth by investing selectively in high-potential assets that came to the market.

Over the past week, Rob had heard Wilson's name about a thousand times. There was a picture of him at the top of the page. Healthy, fleshy face, full head of silver hair. Usual kind of corporate shot, half left profile, middle-distance gaze.

Rob turned a couple of pages. There he was again, with his executive team around him. Arms crossed, chin up.

He didn't look desperate. He looked confident and strong.

But what if, behind that facade, he *was* desperate? What would be his next move?

Louisiana Light was filing its quarterly results later in the week. Anyone doing a deal would want to put out a good set of results. But if you were desperate, thought Rob, you'd put out a set that were extraordinary.

No. That would be too obvious. It would raise suspicion on the part of Buffalo. You'd put out a set that were good, above trend. Not extraordinary. Solid. Enough to keep the stock price up, maybe bump it a little.

He looked over Louisiana Light's earnings results for the past few quarters. Growth of a very attractive six to eight percent, excluding the Hungarian writedown.

Nine percent, thought Rob. If Mike Wilson was desperate, that's what he'd want to put out.

13

Ed Leary sipped his coffee, trying to concentrate. He was sitting in the Houston boardroom of SRK Exploration, and John Sadower, CEO of SRK, was giving his management update to the board. Sadower droned on, showing charts with columns of dense little numbers that no one wanted to have to look through.

SRK was an independent petroleum exploration outfit that did most of its work on contract with the oil majors. The S in the name stood for Sadower, who was one of the founders. The other two, Bill Robertson and Hugh Koch, had cashed out of the business years earlier. John was seventy-one, but he showed no signs of leaving or even thinking about succession. For the board, that was becoming an issue.

Sadower was a small, neat man with a trim, white beard. Originally from Minnesota, he had turned himself more Texan than John Wayne, string ties and cowboy hats and big buckles on his belts. Not only was he the CEO of SRK, he was also the chairman of the board. This made getting the succession question on the agenda a doubly tricky proposition. A couple of the other directors had called Leary up before the meeting. They wanted to force the issue. Ed agreed that it needed to be raised, but he wasn't going to go out on a limb to do it. Eventually, they concluded that one of them should talk to Sadower privately after the meeting to make sure it was on the agenda next quarter. Ed didn't volunteer. In the end, Doug Anderson, another nonexecutive director, agreed to do it. Doug had arranged to stay over in Houston and have dinner with Sadower after the board.

SRK was one of five directorships that Ed Leary held. The others included Louisiana Light, where Ed was chairman. At sixty-nine, three years after retiring as CEO of Holt Engineering, Ed was content to play his part as one of the battalion of elder statesmen who criss-cross the country to sit on boards and run the governance of America's corporations. Custodians of American capitalism. That's how Ed thought of himself. He also had a three-hundred-thousand-dollar consultancy arrangement with Holt that took a day or two of his time each month. Ed had no desire to return to the trials and tribulations of day-to-day management. He marveled that John Sadower still had the stomach for it.

Sadower continued talking. Ed's mind wandered. He was flying home that night to Boston, then the next night he had to fly down to Baton Rouge to be ready for a Louisiana Light board on Wednesday morning at which they were going to review the results for the quarterly filing. Maybe he should have stayed in Houston, he thought, and gone on to Baton Rouge the next day. As it was, he wouldn't get home much before one in the morning, and he would be leaving at four the same afternoon. He grimaced. Maybe he ought to cut out these Houston meetings. He had been on the SRK board six years. Six years was enough. There was a fight coming with John Sadower. It wasn't going to be much fun. Ed had a feeling that Sadower was going to have to be pried kicking and screaming from the chairmanship of the company he had founded.

Maybe he should change his flight, he mused. Maybe stay in Houston tonight. But he didn't want to do that. His wife, Catherine, had breast cancer. The breast had been removed four years ago but the cancer had come back in all kinds of places. She was fighting it. Thin, weak. Ed didn't like to be away. He knew, when he dared to think ahead, there'd be time for that later. Too much time.

A secretary slipped into the room. Everyone glanced at her, hoping she was looking for them. Anything to have a break from listening to Sadower. She caught Ed's eye and moved quickly around the table. She slipped a note into his hand and waited as Ed read it.

"Tell him I'll call when we break for lunch," he whispered.

The secretary nodded. She slipped out of the room.

It sounded as if John Sadower was finally wrapping up his presentation. Ed glanced at the note again.

Mike Wilson needs to speak with you.

The secretary found Ed an office he could use. He called Mike Wilson's number.

"Mike?"

"Hold on, Ed," said Mike. "I don't want to talk on the cell phone. I'll call you back."

"Can't we—"

"What's your number? You still at SRK? You got a land line?"

"Yeah, I'm in some office. Hold on . . ." He read the extension number off the phone.

"Got it," said Wilson. "I'll call."

Ed put the phone down, wondering what this was all about. After about a minute the phone rang.

"Mike?"

"That's better," said Wilson. "Ed, guess where I am."

Ed shrugged. How should he know?

"London!"

"London, England?"

"The same." Wilson laughed.

"What are you doing there?"

"That's what I've called about. Ed, get ready. Are you sitting down?"

"Yes."

"Ed, I've done us a deal."

Ed frowned.

"Ed?"

"Yeah, I'm here, Mike."

"I've done a deal like you asked me to."

"When did I ask—"

Wilson laughed. "Not *you*. The board, Ed. Hell, you guys already changed my contract so I'd do a deal."

"Oh." Finally Leary realized what Mike Wilson was talking about. "The new strategy."

"That's right, Ed. I've done it!"

"That's fine, but . . ." Leary frowned. "We haven't formally talked about what kind of deal we're looking for, have we? What kind of target we want."

"Ed, you don't think I know what kind of target we want? Come on, who else is going to know?"

"How advanced is this thing?"

"I told you, Ed. It's done." Wilson laughed again. "Pending board approval, of course."

"You mean you've already . . ." Ed stopped, trying to get it straight in his mind. "Hold on, you mean you've *already* done it?"

"I've been meeting with the target CEO here in London today."

"You mean they're British?"

"You bet they are, Ed."

Leary shook his head in confusion. He didn't know whether a CEO was meant to do that, go as far as talking to the CEO of a target company without talking to his own board first, or at least to the chairman. Mike Wilson ran things at Louisiana Light pretty much the way he liked, Ed knew, which was fine by him, because the stock price showed that Mike obviously knew what he was doing. Ed Leary didn't understand too much about the electricity industry or the way Louisiana Light did business and he didn't think it was his role to get in the way, as long as everything was going smoothly. But he didn't want to be some kind of a lame duck, either. He didn't want to be taken for granted.

"Ed, listen. I've had to do this in a hurry. Literally days. Out of my control. I'll explain it all when I see you. The important thing is, they like the deal and you will, too. They're happy. The price is right. It's going to their board Thursday. And you know what? Get this! We get a break fee of a hundred and twenty-five million if they approve and then another bidder comes over the top."

Ed almost dropped the phone. "A hundred and twenty-five million? That's the break fee?"

"Yeah. Standard. One percent."

"Jesus, Joseph, and Mary, Mike! How much are we offering?"

"Twelve-point-five billion."

Ed did drop the phone. He scrambled to pick it up.

"Ed? You okay?"

"They're bigger than us!"

Wilson laughed.

"No, wait." Ed tried to get his thoughts together. "You've already met them? You've agreed?"

"It goes to their board Thursday. They'll approve. It's in the bag."

"Who's doing the work for us?"

"Dyson Whitney."

"Who?"

"Dyson Whitney."

"But we use Merrill Lynch."

"Not for this."

"Why?"

"Look, Ed. I'm moving fast. Their board's going to approve Thursday. Our board's meeting Wednesday, right? It's on our agenda."

"No, it's not."

"It is now."

"How can it be?" demanded Ed. "We haven't seen anything. We've got no papers. Something like this . . . we can't just talk about it. We've gotta . . . we need—"

"Relax, Ed. You'll get everything. Everyone will get a paper first thing when the meeting starts. You'll have time to read it, then we'll talk about it."

"And you expect us to vote?"

"We have to. Time's of the essence here. Listen, Ed, this is a fantastic deal. The strategic fit is perfect. Wait till you see it. You don't get an opportunity like this every day of the week."

"And you're sure it's okay to give us a paper and expect us to read it and then—"

"Ed, I've talked it through with Doug Earl. He says this is the way to do it. Give him a call to check it out. He's on his way back from London now. Give him a few hours and give him a call. It's all above board."

Leary was silent.

"Now, Ed," said Wilson. His tone turned admonitory. "You're going to back me on this one, aren't you?"

Ed knew that tone in Mike Wilson's voice. There were times when there was no way to say no to Mike Wilson. At least he couldn't do it.

"Ed?"

"Yeah, Mike. I guess. If this deal's really as good as you say."

"I'm going to be counting on your support, Ed."

Leary nodded. "But . . ."

"What?"

"Twelve-point-five billion, Mike. Where are we going to get that?"

"It's all taken care of. Don't worry. You'll see all the details on Wednesday. You know what, Ed?"

"What?"

"This'll make you chairman of a twenty-three-billion-dollar company!"

Ed thought about that. Holt Engineering, at its height, had been worth maybe a tenth of that. No, less.

"Now, how does that make you feel?" said Wilson.

"That . . ." Ed shook his head. The truth was, it was absurd.

"Twenty-three billion, Ed. I like the look of your stock options now."

Ed Leary felt like laughing, it was so ridiculous. He did laugh. "What about you, Mike? What did we agree in your new contract? What was the bonus for doing a deal?"

"Oh, I really couldn't remember, Ed," said Wilson, joining in the laughter.

Ed Leary laughed again. He didn't know why. Something seemed tremendously funny. He just wasn't sure what. "How much was it? Ten million in cash for you and another ten in options?"

"Something like that," said Wilson. "Not that I want it. Twelve million, I think. Ed, I wouldn't even know. Last thing on my mind."

They were still laughing. Suddenly Ed stopped. "How are the results? For the quarterly?"

"The results are good, Ed. You're gonna be very happy."

"Mike, seriously. If I'm going to support you on this thing, you've got to be straight with me. Be honest. This is a good deal, right?"

14

Night had fallen in London when Mike Wilson got off the phone with Ed Leary. He looked out the window of the hotel room. There was no moon in the sky. Below him was Hyde Park, a vast, black emptiness, like a huge lake.

He turned around and sat down. The room was overdecorated, too many patterns on carpets, curtains, furnishings. The British idea of old-fashioned luxury. Made him feel claustrophobic.

Wilson thought with satisfaction about the meeting he'd had with Andrew Bassett that afternoon. Bassett wanted the deal almost as much as he did. Wilson sensed that he had gotten the other man absolutely right. He knew exactly which buttons to press. "Sir Andrew," Bassett could already hear himself being called. He could see himself two years ahead, CEO of a big global company, and that was all he could see right now. Like anyone who wants something badly, thought Wilson, Bassett believed anything that made it seem as if he could get it. But an awful lot could happen in two years.

Doug Earl, the company's general counsel, had been with him for the meeting. Lyall Gelb was meant to have come, but it turned out that one of his kids had to have an appendectomy and Lyall didn't want to be away if he could avoid it. Besides, what with the disruption of the kid getting sick and going to the hospital and having the operation, Gelb had lost a lot of time. Normally, he would have worked the entire weekend before a quarterly filing. Wilson had managed at the meeting without him. Lyall had already met the British team anyway, and the offer was so generous that he wasn't needed to help squabble on the terms. On the contrary, Andrew Bassett could hardly believe the numbers he was looking at.

Wilson smiled to himself. Everyone's a winner, he thought, and the deal goes through. Wilson had learned that lesson from the master himself, Ken Lay. That was in the early years of Lay's career, before he took his eye off his business and started thinking he was some kind of statesman, when he was still the smartest operator around. The smartest operator Wilson ever saw, that was for sure.

Mike Wilson had started his career at an Atlanta-based utility called Georgia Electric. After a couple of years he moved to Inter-North, a gas company based in Omaha, where he first met Stan Murdoch. In 1985, both he and Stan were executives at InterNorth. That was the year a certain Kenneth Lay, head of Houston Natural Gas, came knocking. Lay's proposition resulted in an acquisition and merger of the companies. Within a year, the combined company that resulted would be renamed Enron.

Wilson wasn't there to see that happen. After the deal, like most InterNorth executives, both he and Stan Murdoch found themselves surplus to requirements. They went their separate ways, Wilson as president of Carolinas Electric, a small Charleston-based operator, and Murdoch to the electricity generator Arrenco. But Mike Wilson was there to see the takeover, and the manner of it left an indelible impression on him. InterNorth was three times the size of Houston Natural Gas, and technically InterNorth, not Houston, was the acquirer. Yet it was Ken Lay and his boys who ended up in charge. Even though he was a victim of Ken Lay's ruthlessness, Mike Wilson was awestruck by Lay's efficiency and guile. There were all kinds of rumors about the secret promises he had made to get the InterNorth board to the table. Over and over, in the years since then, Wilson had analyzed the sequence of actions. He had come to two key conclusions. The first was that Lay pulled it off by making all the main players believe they were going to be winners from the deal. The second was that you could make people believe they were going to be winners even when everything else pointed to the opposite, as long as they *wanted* to believe it. The day he was kicked out of InterNorth, Mike

Wilson vowed that if he ever did a deal himself, he would do it like Lay.

That was what he was doing now. Andrew Bassett wanted to believe he was going to be a winner. Everything Wilson had said to him at their meeting had been designed to make him believe that he was right.

Wilson got up and poured himself a scotch out of the minibar.

Doug Earl was already on a plane back to the States. Wilson had kept the company jet. He told Doug he had other business to attend to that night. He didn't. Not Louisiana Light business, anyway.

He glanced at his watch. Almost nine. Three o'clock in Baton Rouge. He thought of ringing Dot. Dot Mendelsson was a society divorcée. As head of the biggest company in Baton Rouge, Mike Wilson was a pillar of local society. Member of the board of Louisiana State, patron of the Baton Rouge Arts and Sciences Museum, trustee of half a dozen charities. Dot and he moved in the same circles. It kind of made sense. The sex wasn't frequent, and it wasn't great, but that wasn't too important. Mike Wilson had a different, more powerful compulsion. It was a relationship of convenience for both of them. Wilson had two ex-wives and five children. He wasn't looking for any more of either.

Wilson didn't call her. Maybe later.

He sat and sipped the scotch. A certain kind of pressure was building up inside him. For a while he just sat there, feeling it grow. He knew what it was. He sipped his scotch in minute portions, barely letting the fluid touch his lips. It was a kind of tantalizing, agonizing pleasure to resist the impulse, to tell himself that he might not give in. That this time, for once, he might just withstand the temptation. To let the pressure build and build, even, as he did, knowing he wouldn't resist in the end. He knew it from the moment he had sent Doug Earl off in a cab to Heathrow. He knew he would succumb. That only intensified the pleasure of resisting.

But first, there was a phone call he had to make.

Wilson put down the scotch and dialed a number in New York. He waited as it rang.

"Yeah?" The voice was high-pitched, nasal.

Mike Wilson had never met Tony Prinzi and had no desire to.

It was only through a voice on the phone that he knew him. He had been told that Prinzi was a short man, squat, almost a Danny DeVito lookalike.

"Tony?" he said. "It's Mike. Mike Wilson."

"Mike Wilson. This is a pleasure. How are you, Michael?"

"Not bad, Tony."

"How did you make out the other night?"

"Not so great."

"No luck?" There was a chuckle. "So I heard."

"Tony," said Wilson, "I just wanted to let you know, that deal we talked about, it's on track. I don't want you to have any doubts on that account."

"I appreciate you telling me, Michael. Not that I was worrying, but . . . one does wonder from time to time. The clock ticks. You understand me?"

"I thought I ought to let you know. The cut I get will cover everything. It's more than enough."

"That's very good, Michael. Thank you for calling. You've set my mind at rest. Not that I don't trust you. If I didn't trust you, both your legs already would be broken."

There was silence.

"That's just talk, Michael." There was another chuckle. "Don't worry about it. Is this why you've called, to tell me this?"

Wilson hesitated for a moment. "Actually, I was wondering, Tony . . . you might get a call."

"Where from might I get this call?"

"London."

Another chuckle. "Michael, always on the move. I never know where I'm going to hear of you next."

"I wonder if you could oblige," said Wilson.

"You tell me your deal's on track?"

"Absolutely."

"Then it would be a pleasure."

"Thank you, Tony."

"Michael, don't thank me. Thanking is for friends." There was a last chuckle, and the line went dead.

Wilson put down the phone. He tried to put the last remark out of his mind. And the one about his legs.

He refilled his glass, sat down again, sipped, tried to rediscover the mood. Soon it was back. Now that the call was out of the way, he could truly savor it. The futile resistance, the knowledge that he would succumb, the game that he played with himself in pretending that he mightn't. There it was. His skin prickled with the exquisite agony of it.

He wanted to gulp down the drink, but he forced himself to sip. Slowly.

Slowly.

At last he finished the scotch. He grabbed his jacket and headed downstairs.

The doorman flagged down a cab for him.

It was a tall, stucco-coated terrace building in Knightsbridge. Mike Wilson had been there before.

He paid the cabbie and got out. A doorman in a top hat was standing at the top of the steps. He opened the door. Inside was a hallway, black-and-white tiles on the floor, wood panels on the walls, with an open doorway on the other side.

"Good evening, sir," said a young woman in a black dress, blond hair pulled back in a ponytail. She got up from a small desk. "Are you a member?"

Wilson couldn't remember seeing her before. "Why don't you tell your manager Mr. Wilson's here," he said quietly. "Mike Wilson."

The woman glanced at a black man in a suit who was standing on the other side of the hall. "Would you wait here a moment?" she said to Wilson, and disappeared through a door in the wood paneling behind the desk.

Wilson glanced at the black guy and smiled. The black guy smiled back at him. Mike Wilson walked farther into the hall, conscious that the black guy was watching him. He stopped at the open doorway.

There were about ten tables in the room ahead of him. Roulette, blackjack, craps. Croupiers stood behind them. The room wasn't crowded. Slow night, perhaps. But it made no difference to Wilson. His pulse raced. His throat was dry.

He watched. He was in the last, most delicious stage of resistance. Somewhere in the back of his mind, he knew he could still turn around and leave. He would hold on to that thought for a little while yet, intensifying the pleasure, heightening it, like holding off an orgasm, before he abandoned himself. It was better than sex.

"Sir?"

Mike Wilson turned with a start. The young woman had come back. A man in a tuxedo was with her.

"Mr. Wilson," said the man, oozing an unctuous smile.

Wilson nodded impatiently.

"Lovely to see you back, sir. Awfully sorry about the delay. Melanie's new."

The young woman smiled apologetically.

"Well, we can't blame her for that," said Wilson.

"Very understanding, sir." The man motioned Melanie away and she went back to her desk. "Come this way, Mr. Wilson."

The man led him into the room beyond the hall. They walked briskly between the tables. On the other side of the room they went through a door and came to a staircase. The manager led the way up the stairs. At the top, there was a door on each side. The manager opened the door on the left.

"After you, Mr. Wilson. I'll just make a phone call, shall I?"

Wilson nodded. "Make it two hundred."

"Sterling?"

Wilson nodded again. He went inside. The room was large, with two tables. There was a bar, and a couple of women circulating with drinks, and a couple of men standing to the side and watching the tables. Most of the players at the tables were men. One was a woman who was wearing a white trouser suit. She glanced at him. Wilson met her eyes, then kept looking around the room.

The manager returned. "Mr. Prinzi was very happy to oblige." He placed a pile of chips in Wilson's hand. "Two hundred thousand pounds, Mr. Wilson."

Wilson nodded, eyes on the tables.

"Just ask someone to let me know if I can be of further service, sir. Any of the staff, Mr. Wilson."

The manager waited a moment, then left. Mike Wilson gazed at the tables. He felt the chips in his hands, cool, smooth. The woman in the trouser suit glanced at him again, but now he was utterly unaware of her.

The last shred of resistance tore away.

15

The sideboard was stocked with coffee, juice, pastries, and fruit. Between eight-thirty and nine on Wednesday morning, the members of the Louisiana Light board of directors arrived in the boardroom on the sixth floor of the company headquarters in Baton Rouge. Mike Wilson greeted them genially, exchanging a word with each one about family, business, golf, laughing warmly at the pleasantries. There was nothing to show that he was a man who, thirty-six hours earlier, had lost the equivalent of a hundred and eighty thousand dollars of borrowed money in a London casino.

At nine they took their seats. The board consisted of eight members. Mike Wilson, Lyall Gelb, and Stan Murdoch were the executive directors. Ed Leary, the chairman, headed the five non-execs. Dave Ablett was CEO of Ventura, a Boston-based software company. Gordon Anderton was managing partner of Anderton Doolittle, the international recruitment firm. Mal Berkowitz was CEO of Tufts Engineering, in civil engineering and construction. And Imogen DuPont was a former Louisiana Secretary of Environment, now a senior partner in Molyneux, Garth, Porter & Cabel, the biggest law firm in Baton Rouge. Everyone, with the exception of Imogen DuPont, would have described himself as a personal friend of Mike Wilson. Every one of them, including Imogen, had benefited from some kind of consultancy or business arrangement with Louisiana Light, and confidently expected to continue to do so.

Doug Earl, the company counsel, attended the meetings and took the minutes. Donald Lepore, the sales and marketing director, and Hannah Grainger, the head of personnel and corporate affairs, were other nonboard members who usually attended, but the previous day Wilson had asked Stella to let them know they wouldn't be needed at this one.

Ed Leary called the meeting to order, then handed over to Mike Wilson.

"When you look at the agenda," said Wilson, "you'll notice there's been a slight change since the board papers were sent out to you."

A couple of the directors had already opened the files in front of them. Now everyone else did.

"We have a very exciting development to discuss today. Ed has kindly allowed me to adjust the agenda to be sure we cover it, right, Ed?"

Ed Leary nodded.

"You're not trying to get out of showing us the results, are you?" said Mal Berkowitz, and he grinned. Every board has a joker. Mal Berkowitz was Louisiana Light's.

"Not at all," said Wilson, grinning right back.

"No surprises, I hope?"

"Only good ones, Mal."

Mal Berkowitz laughed. "Them's the ones I like," he said, and he moved his eyebrows up and down quickly in what he thought of as his Groucho Marx impression.

"What is this?" whispered Stan to Lyall Gelb, who was sitting beside him. He pointed at the first agenda point. "Acquisition of Brit-Energy. You know about this?"

Lyall didn't reply.

"Ed's allowed me to deal with the new point first up," said Wilson. "Now, as you can see, it's an acquisition." He paused. "Quite a sizable acquisition. As you know, we've agreed on the need for a new global strategy, and that strategy is based on the idea of acquiring a partner based in the European Union who can fill the key gaps in our portfolio. Well, you may be surprised to know how far advanced we are in the process. Pleasantly surprised," he said, with a nod to Mal Berkowitz. "There's quite a pressure of time, which is why we couldn't get a paper to you earlier. Lyall's now going to give you each a copy of the relevant document, and I'm going to ask you to leave it behind in this room when you go this afternoon. Not that there's a trust issue," added Wilson, as Mal Berkowitz started rolling his eyes and was obviously about to make a quip. "Confidentiality's paramount, that's all, and we have a fiduciary duty to take the standard precautions." He glanced at Gelb. "Lyall?"

Gelb pulled a set of documents out of his briefcase. Stan Murdoch watched him. Lyall went around the table, handing a copy to each person. He had personally photocopied them that morning, and each one was individually numbered. The document was a slightly altered version of the Dyson Whitney PowerPoint presentation that Wilson had taken to Andrew Bassett two days earlier.

The atmosphere in the room had changed utterly. There was a palpable sense of expectation.

Lyall sat down.

"What the hell is this?" whispered Stan Murdoch.

Lyall nodded toward Mike Wilson.

"I'm going to leave you while you look at the document. Please read it carefully. If you have any questions, make a note of them, and I'll take them when I come back."

"I have a question," said Imogen DuPont.

"What is it?" said Ed Leary.

"You've given us a document to look at, Mike. What exactly are you asking us to do today?"

Leary looked at Mike Wilson.

"I'm asking you to vote on it."

When Wilson came back, the atmosphere in the room was concentrated. Most people at the table were still reading through the document. Wilson had given them slightly less time than he figured they would need in order to finish it. He didn't want discussion starting without him.

He waited a few more minutes. Then he glanced at Ed Leary. Ed cleared his throat. Imogen was still reading. She was the last to look up.

"I'm gonna take questions first," said Wilson. He looked around, waiting for someone to start.

There was silence. That was either very good, Wilson knew, or very bad.

"Nothing?" He waited a moment longer. "Hell, I knew it was good, but I didn't realize it was this good. Let's take the vote right now, huh, Ed?"

Ed Leary was startled.

"Only joking," said Wilson. "All right, let me run through everything quickly and see what we have to talk about. BritEnergy, as you will have seen by now, is a first-class company with a first-class portfolio of international assets." Wilson turned the pages of his own copy of the document. The first couple dealt with BritEnergy, its history, reach, and operations. "Why don't we go straight to page five?"

Page five showed a map of the world with the Louisiana Light and BritEnergy assets represented by tiny images of their corporate logos. The arc of assets ran up from Chile, through the United States, across to Britain, through Europe, and down through Asia to end in southeastern Australia.

"This just about sums up the rationale for the deal. We're talking generating plants, wires, retail operations. I think you'll agree this creates an impressive portfolio. In fact, I think it's unmatched by any other company in the industry."

"It's the whole damn world," murmured Mal Berkowitz. Beside him, Dave Ablett nodded.

"The deal gives us an integrated company with financials that are very robust," said Wilson. "Turn to the next page."

Page six showed a proforma profit-and-loss statement for the combined Louisiana Light and BritEnergy company over the next two years.

"Now, we've used conservative assumptions," said Wilson. "We've assumed an average five percent cost savings in corporate center heads and other compressible costs. That's certainly less than we'll actually achieve. We think we'll get ten, and probably fifteen percent if we squeeze. The bankers wanted to factor that in but I said no, let's go conservative, just do the numbers with five percent. But the point is, we're talking cost savings as well as the strategic logic of putting the two portfolios together."

"So these figures show five percent?" asked Dave.

"Correct," said Wilson.

"What about the balance sheet?"

"You'll have seen that on the next page."

Mal Berkowitz nodded. "This is good."

"They're very strong on the balance sheet," said Lyall Gelb. "That'll help us with . . . you know, our issues, and it means we can finance the acquisition in the capital markets and still reduce the overall leverage of the combined company."

"I think what Lyall's saying is their balance sheet is strong enough to carry the extra debt we'll need to take on when we buy them," said Wilson. He paused. The cash they would need to finance the acquisition was the big point, he knew. "Let's go to the next page." He waited, watching them.

"I wasn't sure about this," muttered Dave Ablett. He glanced at Mal Berkowitz for a second, and then scanned the page, frowning. "Is this right, Mike? You're actually talking about—"

"Correct. Four-point-two billion," said Wilson crisply. There was no point being defensive about it. Talk it up, like it was something to be proud of.

Dave was still studying the page. Mal, studying it as well, whistled softly. Wilson glanced at Imogen DuPont. She was watching Dave and Mal. Gordon Anderton caught Wilson's eye and smiled.

"Let's be clear," said Wilson. "The offer is eight-point-three billion in stock, four-point-two billion in cash. I'm rounding a little. At current stock prices, the stock swap we agreed is around five to two. Five-point-one to two, to be exact."

"Mike," said Dave Ablett, "I wanted to ask you, where does this come from?"

"Which part exactly?" said Wilson.

"The valuation. We're valuing them at twelve-point-five billion, right?"

"That comes from Dyson Whitney."

"Dyson who?"

"Our investment bank," said Wilson. "They're advising us on this."

"I thought we use Merrill."

"Dyson Whitney has a strong electricity specialty. I've been a little disappointed with Merrill."

"So this is their valuation?"

"Correct. I'll be honest with you. We're toward the top end of their range. But this isn't a bargain hunt, Dave. This is a quality acquisition. I don't want to put this company in play, I want to buy it. And I don't want to get into a bidding war."

"But this company . . . it's kind of . . ."

"What, Dave? Big?" Wilson laughed. "Damn right, it's big."

"Maybe rather than buying it we should be looking to have some kind of a partnership."

"You mean a merger? Why merge when we can buy 'em?"

"Can we? You're sure?"

"Yes. I met with Andrew Bassett, the CEO of BritEnergy, in London on Monday. This is an agreed bid, Dave. These are the exact terms Bassett's taking to his board tomorrow."

There was silence. Only now did the board members realize how far the matter had actually advanced. It was almost a done deal.

Ed Leary watched Dave and Mal closely to see how they were going to react to that. Besides him, they were the only non-execs who gave any real input on business issues. Gordon Anderton, the headhunter guy, never had anything to say unless they got onto the soft stuff. Imogen DuPont, who had recently left the state administration, was window dressing, a potentially useful conduit to her friends in the Democratic Party. It was only her third board meeting. She knew a lot about rules and regulations and very little about business. Stan Murdoch hadn't said anything, but Stan never said much in board meetings, and Leary didn't expect him to. He assumed Stan must have already known about the deal. Ed Leary had no idea that Stan hadn't been aware of it before sitting down at the board table that morning.

Lyall Gelb could feel Stan Murdoch's eyes boring into him.

Dave and Mal glanced at each other. Like Ed Leary, they were out of their depth. These were the kind of numbers they only dreamed about. When it came to adding $4.2 billion in a single chunk of debt, they didn't know where to start. But neither of them wanted to show it.

Imogen DuPont spoke up. "Shouldn't you . . ." She looked at Ed Leary in consternation. "Shouldn't this have been cleared with the board first? I mean, before it got to this stage?"

"Well, Imogen," said Leary, "sometimes there are pressures of time . . ."

"You could have convened a telephone conference."

"We had to move very fast on this," said Wilson. "I don't think we want to get caught up in the technicalities."

"No," said Ed Leary. He laughed a statesmanlike, paternalistic laugh. "We don't want to get legalistic, Imogen."

Imogen looked at the others for support. Glances shifted uneasily.

"Why don't we move along?" said Wilson. "You'll find some of the key staffing issues on page fourteen. I'll remain the CEO, Andrew Bassett will be COO. Stan's director of operations for U.S. and International. Their current COO, Anthony Adams, gets UK and Europe." Wilson paused for an instant, glancing at Stan Murdoch. Stan was staring at the document. His jaw was set tight. "Lyall stays CFO. Their finance guy is ready for retirement and he goes."

Lyall nodded.

"We'll keep two heads of personnel for the moment. Makes sense given the differences between us and the UK. Our strategy position is vacant so we'll keep their guy. Gordon, you want to put our search on hold?"

"I've got a shortlist, Mike."

"Well, the shortlist just got shorter. Don't worry, Gordon, there's plenty of other work we'll need doing. What else? Company counsels," said Wilson, with a glance to Doug Earl. "Again, we're going to keep both, given the regulatory differences."

Doug nodded.

"Now, I know what you really want to know. As far as the board goes, initially we'll have a shared structure. Just put the whole two boards together. Ed'll be chairman. Their chairman, Sir James Duncan, will be deputy. All of you will be on it."

"Where will we meet?" asked Mal.

"London and here. We'll take turns. At some point we'll rationalize the board."

"But we're buying them, right?" asked Mal.

"Definitely. Legally and, more importantly, in the business itself. We've got the chairman, the CEO, the CFO," said Wilson, numbering the posts off on his fingers. "All three of the main jobs. Plus a majority of the board. Hell, I'd say that's an acquisition, wouldn't you?"

Mal grinned.

"But we want to do this friendly, not hostile. We've got to make it easy for them. The last page shows a proposed timetable for the acquisition. All going well, we see it being consummated in ten weeks."

Mal Berkowitz let out an appreciative whistle.

"That's right. Not bad, huh? Ten weeks, you'll all be on the board of a twenty-three-billion-dollar company." He glanced around the table. "Ladies and gentlemen, for a transatlantic deal, I believe this is as good as it gets."

Wilson stopped talking.

"Questions?" said Leary. "Dave? Mal?"

There was silence for a moment.

"I guess we have to take the valuation at face value," said Dave Ablett.

"I'd say it's a fair price," said Wilson. "I'm not saying it's a steal, Dave. I'm not trying to kid you. I could've gone in at twelve-point-two-five, say, or even twelve, but we'd be in a bidding war and who knows where the price would go. Probably way higher. This way, we get an agreed bid and a one percent break fee."

"One percent of twelve-point-five billion? We should hope it fails," quipped Mal.

"No, Mal," said Wilson seriously. "This is a good deal. At twelve-point-five, it still leaves a lot of upside."

Imogen shook her head. "Ed? I'm still uncomfortable with the length this has got to without the board knowing."

"Well . . ." Leary frowned. "What would you like to do about that, Imogen?"

"Well, I mean . . . should we get an independent opinion on the quality of this acquisition?"

"Imogen," said Mike Wilson, "we really are under extreme pressure of time here."

"Why is that, exactly?"

"Because BritEnergy is extremely anxious about being put in play. If we can do the deal in the kind of timeline I've outlined, they'll go for it. It it's going to drag on, they'll walk."

"That doesn't make sense," said Imogen.

"It makes sense," said Dave Ablett impatiently. "That's business. Take my word."

Wilson glanced pointedly at Ed Leary.

"Imogen," said Ed, "I don't believe we have the luxury of getting an independent opinion at this stage, desirable as that might be. I think Mike has put a very professional assessment to us and I think we're going to have to go with that. Does anyone else disagree?" Ed looked around. No one spoke up.

"Well, I'd like to register it," said Imogen. "I'm sorry, Mike. I think this went just a little too far without the board being informed."

"You want to register that in the minutes?" said Ed Leary.

"Yes, I do."

"Doug," said Ed. "You want to register that?"

Doug Earl made a note. Wilson had to stop himself from rolling his eyes. If that made Imogen DuPoint happy, fine. Lawyer stuff. Like registering something in the minutes was going to make a difference.

"Well, I guess there's only one question then," said Dave Ablett.

"What's the name of the new company?" suggested Wilson.

Dave laughed. "No, that's another one. Where the hell are we getting this money from, Mike?"

"Not a problem," replied Wilson. "As I said, the combined balance sheet will comfortably carry it. Turn back to that page." Wilson waited for everyone to leaf back to the balance sheet. "Lyall, does that balance sheet include the extra four-point-two billion of debt?"

"Yes, it does."

"See, Dave? That's *with* the extra debt included."

Dave studied the proforma balance sheet again. He nodded.

"Kind of preempts the agenda point on the issues with our debt covenants, doesn't it?" said Wilson.

"Sure does," said Mal Berkowitz.

"Dyson Whitney is confident on the loan. You can always get

credit for a good deal. Hell, if you remember, at the height of the credit crunch, Pfizer managed to borrow twenty billion-plus to buy Wyeth and the banks were fighting each other to give them the cash. And that was when half of them were on life support from the government. Dyson Whitney is looking for a bridge from Citibank. With this balance sheet, I'm assured it won't be an issue." Wilson paused. "If the banks like this deal enough to underwrite four-point-two billion for it, I think we ought to just stop for a second and think about what that says. You ask me, it says a whole lot about the quality of the opportunity we're looking at."

Gordon Anderton nodded loyally.

"So effectively it's down to the stock price?" said Dave Ablett.

Mike Wilson nodded. "The swap ratio we agreed is five-point-one of theirs to two of ours. I think we can be pretty pleased with that. Five-point-one to two, provided there are no major movements. Now, talking of the stock price, here's the good news. The results for the quarterly filing tomorrow are strong, even by our high standards. I think you'll be very satisfied when we move on to look at them. In fact, I think you're going to be quite pleased. Right, Lyall?"

Gelb nodded.

Wilson laughed. "Come on, Lyall. Crack a smile! We have a great quarter and already he's worried about how we're going to beat it next time. Lighten up, Lyall. Let's smell the roses occasionally."

There was laughter. Lyall Gelb forced a smile.

"Obviously, given what we've just been talking about, this is an important filing," continued Wilson. "I've got Hill Bellinger lined up to do the PR. We need to make sure these results get noticed and have the right effect on the stock price. Hill Bellinger always does a great job. Lyall and I will be on a conference call tomorrow with the analysts as soon as the results go out, and I'll be doing a bunch of interviews. We're going out strong with these results. They're really something to be proud of. Anyway, we're jumping ahead. Ed, is there anything else we need to cover here?"

Ed Leary looked around. "Are we done on this?"

Wilson waited.

"Actually, I have a question," said Leary.

"Shoot."

"What *is* the name?"

Mike Wilson laughed. "Always leave the big issue for last, huh, Ed? Look, I think we will need to think about the name, and I know the BritEnergy guys would like us to make some kind of a change so it doesn't look like they're just being swallowed. Personally, I like something simple, like LLB Energy, from Louisiana Light and Brit. What do you think?"

There were a couple of grimaces around the table.

"Yeah, right," said Wilson, smiling. "Everyone's a critic. Okay, right now, we're not doing anything. First, I'd like to get the deal done. We don't overlap in any significant markets, which is part of the beauty of the deal, so it's not an urgent question. At the start we'll stay separately branded in our own markets. A little later, we will need to think about rebranding." Wilson looked at Gordon Anderton. "Gordon, you guys do branding work, don't you?"

"Sure, Mike."

"Good, then there'll be a little work there coming your way."

Anderton smiled.

"And Imogen, we'll be using Grayson Arpel in New York on the deal—I think we need a major Wall Street firm for this one. But anything else, you know, the local stuff, you know you've got that, right?"

Imogen nodded. Slightly. Wilson wondered whether he'd gone a little too far with that. He made a mental note to be more subtle with Imogen in the future. It was impossible to embarrass a guy like Gordon Anderton, but Imogen obviously had some self-respect.

Leary nodded. "Well, okay. I think we need to vote. Do we approve this bid?" He looked around the table.

Dave Ablett nodded.

"I do," said Mal Berkowitz.

"Wait, wait, wait," said Imogen. "What exactly are we voting on?"

"Jesus Christ!" muttered Dave Ablett. Mal Berkowitz rolled his eyes.

Ed Leary stared at her in confusion. "We're voting on whether we approve this bid. You know, do we want to buy this . . . BritEnergy." He appealed to Wilson. "Is that right, Mike?"

"Pending due diligence," said Wilson. "It's all in the timetable on the last page. Today we need to approve it in principle. Obviously, the next step is to do the due diligence to check it out."

"Well, I just don't know if we can do this," said Imogen. She glanced at Wilson for a second, then looked around at the others on the board. "Even in principle. I mean, do we have enough information? One short document and this discussion? I mean . . . this is a pretty big question. We're talking about the whole company!"

"What would you like to do, Imogen?" asked Leary.

"Well, I want to know if the rules allow us to do this with such . . . limited information?"

"Doug?"

"I believe so," said Doug Earl. "Pending due diligence, like Mike said."

"And do we agree with that?" Imogen asked the others. "Maybe we should vote on whether we think we can answer that today."

"What the hell more are we gonna know tomorrow?" demanded Mal Berkowitz.

"I'm just saying . . . this is very limited. This is *very* rushed."

"This is business, honey," muttered Dave Ablett snidely.

"*What* did you say?"

"Now, now . . ." said Leary. "Let's be civil. Ummm . . . Imogen, I don't think we need to be too legalistic. Huh? That's not how we do things around here. We'll have a chance to revisit this when the due diligence is done. Is that right, Mike?"

"Sure," said Wilson.

"All right," said Ed. "Imogen, is that okay? It's pending due diligence. Now let's vote on the motion. Dave, Mal? You said yes?"

They nodded.

"Gordon?"

"Count me in."

"Imogen?"

Imogen DuPont looked around at the others one last time. But there was no support for her. Everyone else wanted to get on with it.

"I approve it on condition that we do a thorough due diligence of BritEnergy to verify the offer price and likely benefits of the deal. And I want to see the report and have enough time to read it properly before anything else happens. Can we register that?"

"Doug," said Ed, "can we register that?"

Doug nodded. Wilson smiled to himself.

"Mike, I take it you approve. Lyall, you, too?"

"Yes," said Lyall.

"Stan?"

Stan Murdoch hadn't said a single word during the discussion, just listened and watched. The boardroom of Louisiana Light, he knew, wasn't the place to challenge Mike Wilson.

"Stan?"

Mike Wilson was watching him.

"Sure," said Stan.

Ed Leary smiled. "Then I think it's unanimous."

"Conditionally," interjected Imogen DuPont. "Doug, have we got that?"

"Conditionally," said Ed Leary. He turned to Mike Wilson. "Congratulations, Mike. I think I speak for the entire board when I say we hope you get there."

"Thank you, Ed."

"What's the next step?"

"Our quarterlies are out tomorrow, as we all know. That's important because of the stock price. As far as the deal schedule goes, BritEnergy's board meets tomorrow as well. If they approve like we've just done, we start due diligence."

16

The television over the bar was tuned to some kind of news channel. Sandy Pereira gazed at it mechanically as she sipped her beer. She glanced at the guy behind the bar, who smiled at her. Sandy smiled back, but not so as to encourage him.

Sandy Pereira was twenty-six, good-looking, and unhappy. A

journalism major out of NYU, she had been with the *New York Herald* for a little over three years. The *Herald* wasn't exactly the kind of paper she had dreamed of joining when she was at school. Like just about every other journalism student—at least the ones who didn't want to work for *Vogue*—she had dreamed of investigative reporting, Watergates waiting to be exposed, Pulitzer Prizes. A job at the *Times*, at least. Certainly not a yellow paper like the *Herald*. But the world wasn't like the dreams you have in college, and it was only a lucky break through a friend of a friend that had even gotten her an interview with one of the *Herald*'s editors.

She worked the city beat, putting together human interest stories, ideally involving the little guy standing up against City Hall, the Transit Authority, the Parks Department, the NYPD, the Taxi Commission, or any other government agency. She also gathered snippets of smut for the "No, New York!" column. This was a kind of negative column that her boss, Rosie Mandelstam, had dreamed up about a year ago. When it came to gutter journalism, no one had her finger on the pulse like Rosie, a chain-smoking, hamburger-munching, gravel-voiced tabloid veteran who looked like Barbra Streisand carrying an extra forty pounds in weight. No one knew better how to tickle the masses' G-spot. The *Herald*'s readers loved "No, New York!" Anything obscene, prurient, seamy, or plain stupid went in, excluding pedophilia and sex crimes. Rosie knew where to draw the line. Apart from that, the grosser the better. People burning their genitals with fungicide or getting their lips glued together. Old ladies dying in their apartments and not getting found for months. Bullying by condo boards. People being cruel to cats. Pet abuse was a big winner. So was pet pampering. The stupid things rich people did were always good, the more extravagant and sickeningly wasteful, the better. The story about the woman with the poodle that had a different cashmere coat for every day of the week won a Groan of the Month Award from the readers.

Groan of the Month. Not exactly the Pulitzers Sandy had dreamed of at school.

A lot of the stories came from calls to the Groanline, which was another stroke of popular genius from Rosie. Give the people a voice, she said, and they'll speak. And how! The Groanline number was listed at the bottom of the "No, New York!" column. Half the calls were complete hoaxes, and part of Sandy's job was to weed out the more unbelievable of them. But not to weed too hard. Rosie taught her the necessary skills of the gutter press, the kind of things they didn't exactly teach at NYU. Like the timeless art of stealing stories out of other newspapers, especially the ethnic press, which was a rich fishing ground for tales of the bizarre and the unnatural. And the difference between a denial and a failure to confirm, which was the difference between having nothing and having a story. Never ask a question, Rosie taught her. Tell them you already know, then demand that they comment.

Fortunately, there weren't any bylines in the "No, New York!" column. Sandy found it uncomfortable to tell people exactly what she did. She said she was a journalist and tried to leave it at that. But people always wanted to know more. If pushed, she'd say she worked for the *Herald,* which was bad enough. Her mother thought she still did entertainment listings, which was what she had started with. Sometimes she pestered her to know when they were going to let her do something new. Sandy let her keep pestering.

Rosie wanted six snippets a day. "This is New York," she'd say. "There's gotta be six disgusting things happening out there!" There must have been, but finding them was the tricky part.

There hadn't been much today. Among the usual dross of unbelievable or unprintable garbage, the Groanline had thrown up some story about a kid who'd been tossed into a commercial refuse container by some other kids and had stayed there a whole night before someone pulled him out. People walked past but ignored his calls. When Sandy called back on the number they'd left, there was only some lady called Morgenstern who didn't know a kid called Kevin, the one who was supposed to have spent the night in the bin. Hoax. Sandy might still use it. She hadn't decided yet. Technically, she was supposed to verify the stories before she submitted them. Like a real journalist. But this wasn't real journalism. And what was the nonexistent kid called Kevin and his nonexistent friends who had thrown him in the nonexistent bin and the nonexistent passersby who had ignored him going to do? Sue her? No one believed anything they read in the *Herald,* anyway.

On days like this, Sandy sometimes came down to Gaston's, a bar on Baxter Street across from the DA's office. If you waited around long enough, you'd always see a couple of the DAs. It wasn't hard to strike up a conversation with them. Sandy had gotten to know a few of the DAs and occasionally they threw her something. A couple of the DA guys were cute. Sandy liked the idea of them fighting for justice. She liked to romanticize it. When she saw the cute ones, anyway. She knew one of them real well. In fact, she'd known him a couple of times.

Sandy looked around the bar. The place was pretty empty. It was still early. She thought she recognized a guy at one of the tables. No one she'd ever talked to, but maybe she'd seen him with the other DA guys before. He was with someone else. The second guy was kind of cute. Nice smile. The table beside them was free. Sandy picked up her beer and went over to it. The two men were deep in conversation. They didn't even notice her sit down.

"I don't know what it is," murmured Greg, staring into his drink. "She's changed. It's only . . . I look back, I remember what it was like, I see how different it is. But it's only recently. I mean it isn't, but it seems like that. When I look back, I realize it's been going on for a long time. It's only now I see it."

"You're the frog in boiling water," said Rob.

Greg nodded, smiling sadly. "Yeah. The frog. The water's been boiling and I haven't known it. Now I'm cooked."

The minute Rob saw him when he arrived at the bar, he thought how terrible Greg looked. Sleepless, miserable. Rob was glad he had made the time to have a beer with him. The work in the war room was grinding on, but there had been a lull that afternoon as they waited to update their work once Leopard released its latest quarterly results, and he had managed to get away. Leopard's people must have been working the numbers up to the last minute in Baton Rouge because they still hadn't sent the figures through and they were due to file that afternoon. Rob didn't want to think about the amount of work he'd have to do once the numbers arrived.

"When did you realize it?" asked Rob.

"It just hit me. On Friday, while we were having Japanese . . . don't laugh."

"I wasn't laughing. Having Japanese is as good a time as any."

"Jesus, Rob. Having fucking Japanese!"

Rob did laugh. Greg shook his head helplessly.

"I'm sitting there, and I'm looking at her, and she's got this vacant look in her eyes, like she just couldn't care, and suddenly I think, who is she? I mean, who is she? And then you know what? I tried to remember the last time we laughed or kidded around. You know what I mean. Or had sex."

"She was never much of a laugher at the best of times."

"Yeah, but we had sex. I mean, it must be three months."

"Jesus! Three months?"

At the next table, Sandy stole a glance at Greg. Three months? Maybe she could use this.

A young DA told me yesterday he hadn't had sex with his girlfriend for three months. "Things have changed, but she refuses to talk about it." How are our crimebusters supposed to do their best during the day when they can't get any at night? Come on, lady! New York can do better. Put out or get out!

Thin, thought Sandy. Very thin. No sex for three months. Half the married bedrooms in America would tell that story. But no one admitted it, that was the thing. Titillating. A young DA. Call him a "prominent" young DA. And possibly make something up about the kind of cases he specialized in. What kind of cases were sexy?

Rob sighed. "Well, I'm not surprised. Emmy and I have thought things haven't been great between you guys for a while."

"Really?" Greg looked at Rob in surprise.

Rob nodded.

"Maybe Emmy could talk to Louise," said Greg hopefully.

"I don't think so, Greg. You know, Louise . . ."

"What?"

"She's not, you know . . ."

"What?"

"Come on, Greg, you know she's not very easy to get on with. She doesn't . . . you know . . . *connect*."

Greg stared at Rob, aghast. "You mean you don't like her?"

"I'm not saying that."

"What about Emmy? Doesn't Emmy like her?"

"Greg, does that matter?"

"Emmy doesn't like her, either?" Greg was dumbfounded. "Neither of you? All this time? You never liked her? Why didn't you ever say anything?"

"You liked her. That's what mattered. We liked her for your sake."

"What's that mean? For my sake. That doesn't make any sense."

"You know what I mean."

"No, I don't."

"Look, Greg. You liked her—we liked her."

"No," said Greg. "See, that's where you're wrong. I didn't like her. I loved her. That's the difference. I *loved* her, Rob."

"I know you did, buddy. I know it, Greg."

Sandy's heart contracted. It was so sad. So romantic. And best of all, was true. She had to use it. Somehow.

"What are you going to do now?" asked Rob.

Greg shook his head.

"Have you thought about it?"

Greg sighed. He stared into his beer. "Do you think it's possible just to fall out of love with someone?" He looked up at Rob. "Just like that? Over a California roll?"

Sad Sushi, thought Sandy, instinctively grasping for a header. Tearful Teriyaki?

"I don't know," said Rob.

"I think that's what's happened."

Rob wasn't so sure. He didn't think Greg had fallen out of love with Louise. Not yet. But it looked as if he realized he needed to. That was a big step forward.

"Well, if it's happened, it's happened, Greg. You know, I think it happened to Louise a long time ago."

"I guess so," murmured Greg. He shook his head. "It wouldn't happen with you and Emmy. The perfect couple."

Rob didn't say anything to that. No couple was perfect.

"I'm not jealous," said Greg. "It's great. You two guys deserve it."

Rob shrugged. "So what are you going to do?"

"Do you think it might be a phase Louise is going through?" said Greg.

"You mean like something that's going to pass?"

"Yeah."

"I don't know."

"You don't think so, do you?"

"I don't know," said Rob. "Anything can happen, but . . . I wouldn't bet on it."

There was silence. Sandy glanced at them again. Greg was staring vacantly at the table.

"You don't know what you're going to do?" said Rob.

"What would you do?"

Rob sighed. He said it as gently as he could. "Greg, I think maybe it's time to move on."

Greg frowned. "I think . . . I think I have to think."

Rob watched him. "Maybe you should take a couple of days off work. Tell them you're sick or something."

Greg didn't reply.

"You need a place. Use mine until you find something."

Greg shook his head. "My folks have the apartment. They're only there during the week."

"You don't want to do that. Listen, I practically live at Emmy's. Seriously, you'd be doing me a favor. The mice could use some company."

"Really?"

"Sure. Absolutely. Just let me know."

Greg nodded. For longer than was strictly normal.

"Greg?"

"I really appreciate that, Rob. I might just take you up on it. You're a good friend, you know."

"Like you haven't done stuff for me."

Greg looked tearful. His eyes were moist. "I appreciate it. I just want you to know that."

"Hey, you don't need to say that."

"But I want you to know it."

"Okay. Greg, I know it."

"Sorry."

"Okay."

Sandy rolled her eyes. Guys! Why didn't they get up and hug?

"What's happened with that new job you were telling me about?" said Rob. "You decided yet?"

Greg shook his head. "I haven't been able to think about it."

"Yeah. Probably not the best time to make any decisions." Rob checked his watch. "You want another beer? I've still got a little time before I've gotta head uptown."

"You going back to the office?"

"Like every night. One more beer won't hurt. Same again?" Rob looked at the bar. "I'll just . . ." His voice trailed off. "Just give me a second . . ." he murmured. He stared at the television.

Sandy glanced at the TV to see what he was looking at. A reporter was talking. There was a company logo on the screen behind him. Sandy tuned in to the reporter's voice.

". . . stock price rose after the company reported a strong quarterly performance, beating market expectations and apparently putting to rest any lingering concerns from earlier this year that profits were under threat. Company chief executive Michael Wilson attributed the result to a strong performance across the board, and particularly in the company's East European operations, the outcome of a program of cost control and efficiency improvement. With earnings up a fraction over nine percent, Wilson said the results showed that the upward trend in growth at the company was based on sustainable fundamentals. Looking at the numbers, I don't think anyone would argue with him, Dave."

The picture cut to the studio anchor.

"So, good news for Louisiana Light shareholders," said the anchor. "In other company news, aluminum giant Alcoa today announced the suspension of its development program in . . ."

Rob shook his head. "Nine percent," he murmured.

Greg looked at him. "What is it?"

Sandy took her eyes off the television.

"Is that your client?" said Greg. "Louisiana Light? The one you wouldn't tell me about?"

"And putting their stock price just where they want it." Eastern Europe, he thought, remembering the Hungarian writedown. If you could write down, what was to stop you from writing up to get exactly the results you wanted?

"What are you saying?" said Greg. "Are you saying they're manipulating their results?"

"What?" Rob looked at him. "Jesus, Greg. No, I'm not saying that. It's confidential, right? You can't say anything."

Sandy froze. She was absolutely, utterly still. If she could have, she would have stopped her heart beating. Everything in her strained to hear.

"And you think they're overstating their earnings?"

"I don't know. I told you, I'm not saying that. Greg, this is serious. I didn't say anything, okay? I didn't tell you who they were. If their name gets out, this whole thing we're doing will be over."

"Okay. Don't worry."

"Forget I said it, huh?"

"Okay," said Greg. "It's fine. I didn't hear anything."

Sandy looked down. There was a bag on the floor with a company name. She twisted down, pretending she had dropped something, to see the name. Dyson Whitney. What was Dyson Whitney?

Rob pushed his chair back.

Sandy straightened up.

Rob went to the bar. Sandy looked away, trying to keep herself from glancing at Greg, who was still sitting at the table. Her mind was racing, trying to figure out what to do. A plan came into her head. She tried to figure out if it would work.

Suddenly she got up and left.

She walked a short way up the street in the direction of uptown, than waited. She ran over everything she had heard, on the television, at the table. The plan she had just made. She could barely contain her excitement. And trepidation.

She had to wait about fifteen minutes. Then Sandy saw the two of them come out. They separated and he walked up the street toward her, as she had hoped. She was literally shaking with nerves.

Then she went right for him.

"John Williams!" she said loudly, trying to keep the tremor out of her voice.

Rob looked at her in bemusement.

"John?"

"Sorry, I think you must be mistaken."

"Really? I'm sorry. Aren't you John Williams from Dyson Whitney?"

Rob frowned.

Sandy put out her hand, hoping like hell he didn't see it quivering. "Sandy Pereira."

Rob shook it. "Rob Holding."

"Really? From Dyson Whitney? Rob Holding?"

"Yeah."

"Oh." Sandy laughed. "I don't know why I thought you were John. I've only met him a couple of times. Hey, you guys work with Louisiana Light, don't you?"

Rob stared at her.

"They reported their results today, did you know?"

Rob was still staring.

Sandy pushed a card into Rob's hand. "I work on the finance page of the *Herald*. True, we may not be the *Journal*, but we do our bit. Louisiana Light reported earnings nine percent up today, did you know that? We've been hearing Louisiana Light has been overstating things a little. Do you want to comment on that?"

"I . . ." Rob searched for something to say.

"We understand there are serious doubts over their results. What do you say about that?"

"I don't say anything."

"So you don't deny it? Good. Can I quote you on that?"

"Quote me? No, you can't quote me! Quote me and I'll sue you. Look, Ms. Pereira, I think I should just . . ." Rob stopped talking and pushed past her.

"Rob," called Sandy as he hurried away. "Call me. You've got my card. Call me."

He dropped into the subway entrance and was gone.

Sandy stood for a moment longer. She could have yelled with excitement. *Yes!* For the first time since she left college, she felt like a real journalist.

She grabbed a cab for the office. She headed right for Marvin Koller, the guy who handled what passed for the finance page of the *Herald*. And had made a number of passes at her.

"Marvin, someone just told me Louisiana Light is pumping their stock price."

"Yeah, and the pope's a Catholic. Come over here, honey. We'll pump something else."

"Marvin!" said Sandy. "You're disgusting! Listen to me. Some guy from Dyson Whitney told me Louisiana Light's pumping their stock."

Marvin looked at her more seriously. He was a pudgy, scotch-soaked lecher in a third-grade suit, but he still had a nose for a story.

"What's Dyson Whitney?" asked Sandy.

"It's an investment bank."

"Well, Louisiana Light's one of their clients. He said they're manipulating their results."

"Why?"

"He didn't say. But it's a secret."

"A secret?"

"It's all over if it gets out. He said they're overstating their earnings."

"Hold on." Marvin switched to Bloomberg on his computer. "What did you say they were called?"

"Louisiana Light."

"Louisiana Light," murmured Marvin, typing in the name.

Sandy could see him reading the screen. She went a little closer, trying to see. Not too close.

"You're right. They reported earnings up nine percent. Their stock price went up a dollar eighty." He looked at Sandy. "What did he say exactly?"

"He said they were overstating things. They were putting their stock price just where they wanted it."

"Just where they wanted it . . ." murmured Marvin. "But he didn't say why?"

"No. Only it'll be all over if it gets out."

"What will?"

"Everything. Everything they're doing."

"What's everything? Be specific! What? What is it?"

"I don't know. But it'll be bad, Marvin. Real bad."

"Real bad?" Marvin scratched his nose. A rodentlike gleam came into his eyes. He looked at Sandy suddenly. "Did he say he had evidence?"

Sandy hesitated. "Yes," she lied.

"What?"

"He wouldn't tell me."

"Who is he?"

"Marvin, he won't talk."

"Where's the proof?" demanded Koller.

"He won't give it to me."

"Go back and fuck him."

Sandy rolled her eyes.

"You already fucked him?"

"This is all we've got, Marvin."

Marvin Koller glanced at Sandy, evaluating her. For once, not in the usual way. Why would she make this up? She wouldn't know enough to make this up. Koller thought about it. Word it carefully. Report it as a rumor. Age-old journalistic technique. Set the hare running and see what comes out of the trees to chase it.

"I want to work on this with you, Marvin," said Sandy.

Koller shrugged. How long would it take to work on a ten-line piece of innuendo?

"Marvin?"

"Okay. Jesus, relax. It's not like we've got Hitler's diaries."

"I want a byline."

"You want a byline now? On rumor, lady, we don't do bylines. Trust me, I'm protecting you."

"I want a byline!" said Sandy.

"I'll give you a credit on the page. Additional reporting."

Sandy thought about it.

"Take it or leave it, honey."

"I'll take it."

The *Herald*'s first edition hit the streets at three A.M. By seven, Reuters and Bloomberg were both reporting the story. At nine-thirty, the New York Stock Exchange opened for business.

17

TRICKY SWITCHES

Hearts were aflutter yesterday as electricity generator and distributor Louisiana Light turned in its best quarterly earnings in two years. Michael T. Wilson, CEO of the company, is the darling of the markets again. Or is he? A little birdie tells me that the folks at investment bank Dyson Whitney have their doubts about those earnings, and they should know, now that Louisiana Light is one of their clients. Tricky switches in the Baton Rouge control room? Is everything quite as picture perfect as it seems? Just where did those extra earnings come from, Mr. Wilson?

Mike Wilson froze. The fax showed part of a page from a newspaper and the article had been circled in black. It had come through from Amanda Bellinger, senior partner at the PR firm Hill Bellinger, and Stella had left it on his desk. It was the first thing he saw that morning as he opened his briefcase.

The stock price, he thought. What would this do to the stock price?

The phone rang.

"It's Ms. Bellinger," said Stella. "She wants to know if you've seen the article yet."

"Tell her I've just seen it. I'll get back to her."

Wilson slammed the phone down. He scanned the article again. Who'd written it? No byline, obviously. Not man enough to sign his name.

The phone rang again.

"What?"

"Ms. Bellinger won't take no for an answer, Mr. Wilson."

"Put her through."

Amanda Bellinger came on the line. "Mike, this is outrageous!"

"What's going on?" demanded Wilson. "I put out our best results in two years and pay you guys to get the message out and what happens? Huh? What happens? Look at this!"

"Obviously this didn't come from us."

"Who did it come from?"

"Is there any truth in it?"

"Of course not!" snapped Wilson. "It's innuendo! It's slander! We'll sue the motherfuckers."

Amanda Bellinger coughed.

"Did you hear me, Mandy? We'll sue the motherfuckers!"

"I heard you, Mike. Listen. It's the *New York Herald*."

"So?"

"No one believes anything in the *Herald*. They'll assume it's garbage."

Where there's smoke there's fire, thought Wilson. That's what everyone would assume.

"We need a strategy to deal with this," said Amanda. "'Contain, control, consign to history.' That's my motto when it comes to things like this. In a week, it'll blow over."

A week, thought Wilson. In a week, a lot of other things might have blown over as well. A lot of other things might be consigned to history.

"Mike?"

"Yeah," he said. "Work out a strategy and get back to me. I've got things to do."

"Mike, we'll handle this. I'll call you later."

"Yeah."

Wilson put down the phone. He switched on his computer and stared impatiently at the article as the machine booted up. Someone had talked to the newspaper, he thought. There was just enough truth in it. Someone must have talked.

The bankers? *"A little birdie . . . at Dyson Whitney . . ."* Maybe it was the bankers. But what did they know? How could they know anything?

He typed in his password. Finally the computer was on. He turned to the screen and checked the stock price.

"Jesus Christ!"

Wilson sat back in his chair. It was someone who knew something. Must have been. He frowned in thought. Who?

Mike Wilson picked up the phone.

"Stella?"

"Yes, Mr. Wilson."

"Get Stan Murdoch in here."

"Sit down, Stan," he said.

Stan sat in one of the armchairs on the other side of the office. Wilson got up from behind his desk and joined him. He hadn't talked to Murdoch since the board meeting two days earlier. There had been too much to do. The previous day had been taken up with calls to press and analysts, puffing the results. But it had been a mistake to neglect Stan. Mike Wilson saw now how big a mistake it had been.

"Coffee?"

"You pulled me out of the production meeting, Mike."

"Okay. I get it. I'm sorry. This is important, Stan."

Stan waited.

"Interesting times, huh?" said Wilson, looking for a way in.

Stan watched him. He was a taciturn kind of man. Never said much at the best of times.

"You know the old Chinese proverb? 'May you live in interesting times.' "

Stan's eyes narrowed slightly.

"You know, interesting times . . . trouble . . ." Wilson glanced around for a moment, trying to figure out what to say next. "I guess it was a surprise for you, the other day."

"The fact that we're buying a company that's bigger than us? Yeah, I'd say that's a bit of a surprise."

"You're not too happy about it, are you, Stan?"

Murdoch shrugged. "Don't know too much about it." He shifted in his seat. "Lyall seemed to know about it."

"He was the only one, Stan. Secrecy . . . you know."

"Doug knew about it."

"Hell, Stan! Of course Doug knew about it. He's the general counsel."

"You don't trust me, then?"

Wilson laughed. "Stan, how long have we worked together?"

"Long enough," muttered Murdoch.

Stan Murdoch was a tall, lean man with tanned, leathery skin and blue eyes. Looked as if he spent all his days physically out in his plants. He didn't, of course, not nowadays, but he looked like it. Probably would have if he had the chance. Stan was an operations guy. He was a great operations guy, as Wilson knew from their time together at InterNorth, which was why Wilson's first move when he took over at Louisiana Light had been to headhunt him and bring him over to head up operations. He was a guy who took orders and executed them. Mike Wilson had assumed that's what he'd do this time around, as he'd always done in the past.

Wilson got up. He went to his desk and came back with the *Herald* article. He gave it to Murdoch and sat back in his seat.

"You seen our stock price?" he asked as Stan read the article. "I just checked. We're six bucks down." Wilson scrutinized him closely. "You know anything about this, Stan?"

Murdoch shook his head. He put the article down. "Where's it from?"

"The *New York Herald*. Some fucking scut sheet."

"Why are you worried then?"

"Because . . ." Wilson stopped. The quickest way to kill the deal was to bring down the stock price. Even Stan must know that. "You don't want this deal, do you?" he said.

"I told you, Mike, I don't know too much about it."

"Listen, Stan, we had to give them Europe. Hell, it just . . . it makes sense, Stan. They're in Britain. They get to run Europe. You get to run everything else. What's wrong with that?"

"Nothing's wrong with that."

"Talk to me, Stan."

Murdoch shrugged. "That's what you're saying, so that's how it is."

"Let's see what we can do."

"What can we do? This is what you've agreed to, right?"

"Jesus Christ, Stan! It's not like we're talking about prize assets. They're crap. You've been busting your butt for years to get them up."

"I *have* got them up! Give me more time, and I'll get them up even better."

"Stan, come on. Get real."

"What about the numbers we posted yesterday, Mike? Weren't they real? Where did they come from?"

Wilson narrowed his eyes. Was that a threat? Or was it possible that Stan really didn't know?

Was it possible, thought Wilson, that Stan didn't know what kind of contracts Louisiana Light had signed in order to get hold of plants in places like Hungary and Poland, how little flexibility they had in setting prices, no matter what happened to the cost of oil and coal? Was it possible he didn't realize how much they had borrowed in order to pay for them, or that no matter how well Stan pushed up performance in those plants, it had been clear for a long time now that it was never going to be enough to service the debt? Much less provide the kind of earnings growth the market had come to expect from Louisiana Light and which Lyall Gelb, until now, had managed to make the market believe they were delivering.

Maybe, thought Wilson. Maybe it was possible. Stan was an operations guy. A straight-down-the-line operations guy. Focused on efficiency, effectiveness, output. He didn't know anything about finance. Maybe he really did think it was his plants, and the improvements he had managed to eke out of them, that had delivered Louisiana Light's growth trajectory.

"I'm going to ask you straight," said Wilson at last. He pointed at the article on the coffee table between them. "Did you leak that, Stan?"

Stan Murdoch stared at him. For so long that Wilson began to feel uncomfortable.

"Did you talk to that newspaper? Did you give them the information in that article?"

"Are you telling me it's true?"

"I'm not saying it's true," retorted Wilson quickly. "But I want to know whether you said it."

Stan whistled softly. "You sure do want this deal, don't you?"

"Just tell me, yes or no."

"You sure are hot for it."

"Yes or no?" demanded Wilson.

"No."

"Good." Wilson shook his head. "Why couldn't you just say that?"

"Because I don't know how you could ask me," replied Murdoch, and he gazed directly into Wilson's eyes.

Wilson looked away.

The phone rang. Wilson got up. It was Stella.

"I've got Dave Bracks on the line from Merrill Lynch," she said.

Wilson rolled his eyes. Dave Bracks must have seen the article. Now he was calling to find out what was going on with Dyson Whitney. Bankers! Like they owned you.

"Tell him I'm busy. I'll call."

"Yes, Mr. Wilson."

"And hold everything."

"Yes, Mr. Wilson."

Wilson put the phone down. He stood for a moment, thinking.

Everyone was getting what they wanted out of this deal—or thought they were getting what they wanted—except Stan. Ed Leary thought he was going to be chairman of a $23 billion company. Andrew Bassett thought he was going to be the CEO in two years, with a knighthood. So did Lyall Gelb, without the knighthood. The

BritEnergy director of operations thought he was going to get all of Europe. Only Stan Murdoch thought he was losing.

But in a deal, everyone has to be a winner. Everyone who matters. A single person who feels aggrieved, if he's senior enough, is capable of spiking the whole thing. If there was one lesson Wilson had learned at InterNorth, that was it. And right now, Stan Murdoch didn't think he was a winner.

Did Stan have the power to spike the deal? How much did he know about what Lyall Gelb had been up to?

Nothing, probably. He was an operations man, not a finance guy. He took no interest in that stuff. But as an executive director, he had seen certain documents, occasionally he had even been required to sign things. One had to assume, thought Wilson, that if he put his mind to it, he knew enough.

Wilson went back to his seat.

"Okay, Stan," he said. "Let's see what we can do here. The European assets . . . I just don't think that's negotiable. The Brits are in the EU. Hell, Hungary, Poland—half those countries are in the EU as well. Makes sense from every angle for the Brits to manage it."

Stan didn't say anything.

"Come on, Stan. I didn't mean that before. I know you wouldn't leak some ugly lie like that. I just had to ask, you know. I've got a responsibility. I'm asking everyone."

"I wouldn't leak anything," muttered Stan. "How many plants have we bought? Have I *ever* leaked anything?"

"I'm sorry, Stan. I had to ask. I've said it, I'm sorry, all right?" Wilson paused. "Come on, Stan. What can we do?"

Stan shook his head. "We could have discussed this thing."

"Is that it? I'm sorry. Maybe I should have. It's just . . . the secrecy and all. Maybe I got a little carried away. Besides, I know you, Stan. I know the kind of guy you are. You'll do whatever's best for the company. You never put yourself first." Wilson paused, trying to gauge what effect this appeal had.

"You've got me reporting to this Andrew Fassett," said Murdoch.

"Bassett. Is that a problem?"

"He's some English guy."

"English guys are good," said Wilson.

Murdoch grimaced.

"Stan, come on. That's only on paper. Hell, you'll always have an open line to me. You know that."

"Funny. When I came here, I knew exactly what the deal was. I'm your head of operations. I report direct to you. Who is this Fassett guy?"

"Do you want to meet him? Would that help?"

Murdoch smiled sardonically.

"Stan," said Wilson, "do you want to leave?"

Murdoch didn't reply. Wilson tried to read his face. Maybe that was what he wanted. Maybe that was what all this was about.

"If you can't live with this, and you want out, I respect that." Suddenly, Wilson thought he could see how to make Stan Murdoch a winner as well. "Stan, how much is your severance package?"

Murdoch shrugged.

Wilson tried to remember. Stan's salary was around four hundred thousand; bonuses and options would double that. The severance was probably . . . a million, maybe.

If he never worked again, how much would he need? How much would be a lot for a guy like Stan? Not much, probably. He wasn't extravagant. As far as Wilson knew, he and his wife lived a pretty quiet life. They had a place in Baton Rouge, a second house somewhere near Lafayette, he seemed to remember, where Stan went fishing. That was their only indulgence.

"I'll triple it," said Wilson. "I can't put it in writing right now, you understand, but you have my word. You know me. If I say it, I'll do it."

Murdoch watched him.

"Is that enough? I figure, you know, we'll need a consultant as well. Someone who knows the business." Wilson was pretty sure he was on the right track now. "Huh, Stan? Maybe a few days a month. I figure someone like that would be worth another two, three hundred a year."

Murdoch nodded. "You sure do want this deal, don't you?"

"Times are changing, Stan."

"We've done pretty good up till now."

"Times are *changing*. We'll get left behind. Come on, Stan. You were never a big-picture guy. Leave the strategy to me. You're an operator. You're a great operator. Let's be clear. I don't want to lose you."

"But you're prepared to?"

"I want you to do what's right for you and Annie. If you want to kick back, put your feet up, that's fine. Hell, how old are you Stan? Sixty-one? Sixty-two, right? You deserve it."

"You'd be happy if I did that?"

"No, but if that's what you want . . . Stan, the company's bigger than any one person. You know that. It's bigger than me, it's bigger than you, it's bigger than anyone."

"Yeah, only some guys know how to use it better than others, don't they?"

Wilson didn't say anything to that. He gazed at Stan, trying to work out what he meant. Murdoch knew him better than anyone else at Louisiana Light, better than anyone in Baton Rouge. He knew him from the InterNorth days. Back then, Mike Wilson hadn't been so circumspect in the way he handled his personal life. A lot of executives at InterNorth gambled hard, but none harder than him.

"Company jet," said Stan. "Takes you wherever you want to go. Whenever you feel the need."

There was silence.

Then Wilson laughed. "Yeah, the travel's a killer, isn't it?"

Murdoch stood up.

Wilson stood up as well. "We got a deal? If you want to leave. It's up to you, I'm not asking you to. But if you do want to leave, you happy with that? What I said to you?"

"I'd say it's very generous. I don't know that I deserve such a generous offer."

Wilson laughed. "You deserve every cent." He put out his hand. "So we've got a deal?"

"If I want to leave?"

Wilson nodded.

Stan shook his hand. "Okay, Mike," he said, and he turned to go.

"You going back to your production meeting?"

Stan looked back at him and nodded.

"How often do you have that?"

"Once a month."

"We do this deal and you want to go, that means you've only got two, three more of those to sit through."

Murdoch gazed at him for a moment. "I guess that's right."

Wilson smiled. "How does that make you feel, huh? Probably feels pretty good."

Murdoch opened his mouth to say something, then thought better of it. "I'll see you later, Mike," he said, and left the office.

Wilson watched him go. Everyone was a winner, he thought. Even Stan.

Now he was going to get this mess with the *Herald* sorted out.

18

He was in fighting mood. The initial shock had gone and left him itching to hit back. Wilson glanced at the time. Almost ten. Eleven o'clock in New York.

He picked up the phone to Lyall Gelb. Gelb had been taking calls from analysts all morning.

"What are you telling them?" asked Wilson.

"What do you think? It's baseless."

"Okay. Get in here. We need to figure out what the fuck to do about this."

As he spoke, Wilson was looking at Bloomberg on his computer screen. The stock price was 44.40, almost six dollars down from its close after the quarterly results were reported. He picked up the phone to Stella while he waited for Gelb. Calls had been coming in for him from all over. Bankers, lawyers, anyone who knew anything about the deal, and a bunch of people who didn't. He told Stella to cancel his meetings for the morning. While he was speaking to her, a call came through from Amanda Bellinger in New York. Wilson took it. Bellinger had been trying to find out more about the source for the article.

"Tell me," said Wilson

"The guy who edits the financial page at the *Herald* is called Marv Koller."

"Never heard of him."

"I should hope not," said Amanda. "Horrible man. Worst kind of lizard."

"You've had something to do with him?" asked Wilson.

"Once or twice. Anyway, I've spoken to him this morning."

"Who gave him the story?"

"He won't reveal his source, naturally. Said he'd be happy to give you right of reply. Wants to interview you."

"When?" demanded Wilson.

"Mike, don't be ridiculous! That's exactly what he wants. He's got nothing and the fact that he wants to interview you proves it. The only thing he can hope for is that you come out and say something that gives the story legs. Otherwise, it's going to wither on the vine. We just need to sit tight and let it wither."

"You don't think we should threaten to sue him?"

"Mike, for heaven's sake! Oh my God! Mike, don't even think about that."

"We should sue the motherfucking lizard!"

"You're not going to sue him," said Bellinger.

"Won't it look like we've got something to hide if we don't hit back hard?"

"No, that's exactly what'll make you look like you *have* got something to hide. No one takes the *Herald* seriously. You take them seriously only if there's something serious to be taken."

"What if we send some kind of a letter demanding a retraction? Maybe we send it to some other paper as well so they publish it."

"You won't need to send it to anyone else, Mike. Marv Koller will publish it for you."

"Good!"

"And then he won't retract. And what are you going to do then?" Wilson was silent.

"Mike, you're angry. I understand. But trust me, the way to handle this is to deal with it like it's beneath contempt. Here's the line we take. We're above this kind of garbage. We're not going to dignify it by a response. Yesterday, we put out a great set of results. Judge us by our actions, not by innuendo. Mike, how does that sound?"

Wilson thought about it. It sounded kind of meek. His instinct was to hit back, not turn the other cheek. "You really think that's the best thing?" he asked doubtfully.

"It's the only thing, Mike." Amanda said it with utter conviction. "It's the only way to handle this kind of stuff."

"I shouldn't talk to him?"

"Mike!"

"Okay. Look, talk to Jackie Rubin in our press office. My secretary says she's been bugging me for a press release."

"No! No press release."

"So talk to her, will you?"

"Of course. That's what I'm here for. Mike, leave everything to me. I'll call Jackie up right now. You don't do this through a press release, you do it quietly. I'll talk to the key people on the Street myself. But quietly, Mike, understand? Subtly. Understated. I'll tell them I've talked to Koller, he's got nothing, the best he can do is ask to interview you. They'll recognize it for what it is, a fishing expedition. No one takes the *Herald* seriously. If you overreact, that's when they'll start sniffing around."

"Okay. Let's go with that for a start. I'm gonna talk to Doug Earl down here on the legal side as well—" There was a knock on the door. "Mandy, hold on."

Stella came in. "I have Mr. Gelb outside, Mr. Wilson."

"Have him wait, Stella. I'll come out when I'm ready."

"All right, Mr. Wilson."

"Okay, Mandy," said Wilson when Stella had left. "You handle it like you said. Now, we've got something else to think about."

"Yes, I realize that," said Amanda. "The source."

"The *Herald* guy, he wouldn't have just made this up, would he?"

"No," said Amanda. "I don't think even Marv Koller would make something up entirely out of nothing. Although if it was a slow day . . ."

"Then I'm going to assume there's a source," said Wilson. "Someone's spreading lies about us, Mandy."

"Clearly. The first thing to ask is who could have something to gain from it?" Amanda paused. "And you seem awfully worked up about this, Mike, if you don't mind me saying so."

"Are you serious?" demanded Wilson. "Have you seen what it's done to the stock price?"

"With respect, Mike, if it is garbage—which I'm sure it is—then it'll blow over soon enough. If not, your next set of results will disprove it, won't they? So if there is any damage, it's short term. And so, I'm thinking, if you're so worried about a little short-term damage, there must be something happening in the short term."

Wilson didn't reply. Amanda Bellinger was smart.

"Mike? Is there something else I should know?"

"Listen, Mandy. I can't tell you yet. When it's time for you to know, you'll know."

"So there *is* something?"

"Mandy, how long have you worked with me? You'll handle the PR, I promise you, but I can't tell you what it is yet."

"Okay, Mike. That's fine. Let me ask you, how important is this thing you can't tell me about?"

"Very," said Wilson.

"And it's something that . . ." Amanda paused. "Say your stock price goes down further over the next couple of weeks, that's going to make a difference?"

"Yes," said Wilson.

"A big difference?"

"Yes."

"A make-or-break difference?"

"Mandy, don't ask me anything else. I can't answer it."

There was silence from Amanda. She'd probably already figured out there was some kind of a deal on the stove, thought Wilson.

"Okay," said Amanda. "We need to get this source. Like I said, I start with the motive. Who stands to gain from starting a rumor like this?"

"That's exactly what I've been thinking."

"And?"

Wilson thought. It wasn't Stan.

"Anyone?" said Amanda.

BritEnergy itself could benefit by starting a rumor, thought Wilson. Drop the stock price, get a better deal. But that would be a dangerous game to play. Could make Louisiana Light look so bad that BritEnergy's own board wouldn't approve the deal. Besides, everyone was a winner already. That was the whole point.

"No," said Wilson. "Right now, I can't think of anyone, Mandy. But we're going to try to figure it out."

"All right. Let me know if you do. In the meantime I'll see if I can find anything out at my end. Discreetly. I did notice one thing. There was something a little odd in the *Herald* today. I had one of my people check a few back copies. Apparently, there aren't usually any bylines on the financial page, just Koller's imprimatur. Today they had someone else credited with additional reporting."

"You think that's important?"

"Can't hurt to find out. Listen, Mike. This is important, right? If you had to, you'd spend a little money on this?"

"How much?"

"I don't know. Five figures. Maybe a hundred thousand. Would that be out of the question?"

"No, not if it could shut this down. Why do you ask?"

"It's just a thought." Amanda paused. "Let me see what happens. I'll let you know if it comes to anything."

Wilson called off. Amanda Bellinger put the phone down.

She stared out the window of her office, thinking about Mike Wilson. New York traffic moved below her. Absently, she began to finger her brooch.

He was forceful when he was angry, she thought. Impetuous. Like a bull butting at a tree, needing an outlet for his rage. Violent, virile, hotheaded.

Her mind wandered.

She raised an eyebrow, half in surprise, half in pleasure. Amanda, she thought, you're getting quite wet.

In his office, Wilson waited until Gelb sat down. "Where's the stock?" he asked.

"Steady. Forty-four-point-nine last time I looked."

"That's back up a little."

Gelb shrugged.

Wilson watched him. He didn't like the way Gelb looked. Drawn, dark bags under his eyes. As if he hadn't been sleeping much. Wilson didn't like the discouraged tone he heard in his voice.

"How do you think it happened?" said Wilson.

"I don't know."

"I talked to Stan. It wasn't him."

"Can you be sure?"

"I'm telling you it wasn't."

"Maybe it was someone else from the board."

"No." Wilson shook his head emphatically. "That wouldn't happen. Why would they? They're all going to get something out of it."

"What about Imogen DuPont?"

Wilson laughed.

"What, you don't think she'd leak just because she's a lawyer? She was a politician, Mike. Don't forget that."

"Hell, Imogen DuPont wouldn't know enough to tell whether a revenue's been booked up front, down back, or upside down. All she cares about is following the rules."

"The article was vague. Just the kind of thing you might say if you don't know anything about the details."

"Please," said Wilson. "Forget Imogen DuPont. Let's try and get to the bottom of this."

Lyall grimaced.

Wilson looked at him sharply. "What's wrong with you?"

"Last few days, I've been getting stomach pains." Gelb rubbed at his belly.

"You got an ulcer?"

"I don't know." Lyall winced again.

"You should see a doctor. By the way, how's Becky?"

Lyall nodded. "She's fine. Doing good."

"They do that keyhole surgery for appendectomies nowadays?"

"Yeah."

"I remember when Joey had an appendectomy," said Wilson. "This is going back . . . twenty years. More. Hell, he was in the hospital for a week. Then another month before he went back to school. Huh? And now it's what? A few days?"

"Becky's going back to school on Monday. She's still a little sore."

"Monday, huh? How long is that. Ten days?"

Gelb grimaced again. He took a sip of his coffee.

"You want to watch that, Lyall. Coffee's a killer if you've got an ulcer."

Gelb nodded. He rubbed his stomach. Wilson watched him uneasily. Stomach pains. He didn't like the sound of that.

"Okay," said Wilson. "Let's think about this. You think the leak came from someone at Dyson Whitney, like it says in the article?"

Lyall shrugged. "What do they get if they kill the deal?"

"That's what I think. What about someone else? Disgruntled employee. They'd have to know the finances. You got someone on your team who might have done it? Someone you let go recently?"

"You know I try to treat everyone decently, Mike."

"Yeah, I know," said Wilson. Good Christian. Such high morals.

Lyall winced again.

"Get the security stepped up," said Wilson. "Review anyone who's got access to your data."

"My team's good, Mike. No one even knows there's a deal except Dave Sagger."

"What about him?"

Lyall shook his head.

"Okay. Will you just review the security, Lyall?"

"Okay."

"So what else do we do?"

"It could be anyone. Anyone with an ax to grind. You're probably right, Mike. It's probably some ex-employee who saw the results and thought, Okay, let's do it."

"Why now?"

"Who knows?"

Wilson nodded. Then his expression changed. "No. They knew about Dyson Whitney. Whoever it is must know there's a deal. We've never used Dyson Whitney before."

"I don't know, Mike. Word gets out. You know the banks. Dyson

Whitney's probably leaked the fact that they're working with us to help them get some other client. Doesn't mean they're saying anything about a deal. The Street picks it up . . . then some journalist gets a call from someone peddling some other story about our revenues, he puts it together, comes out as one. Makes it look like the story came from Dyson Whitney to conceal his source."

"But they still leaked!"

"Yeah, but not this. Not the deal. Just the fact that they're working for us. Realistically, you've got to expect that."

"I'm going to give them a blast," said Wilson.

"Go ahead." Gelb shrugged. "Give them a blast if it makes you feel better."

Mike Wilson shifted disconsolately in his seat. He wanted someone to blame. Someone he could yell at. Someone he could string up and flay.

"Mandy Bellinger says she might have an idea about how to track down the source," he said at last. "I'm going to give the guys at Dyson Whitney a blast in case anything came from there. You know, I got fucking Merrill on my back now."

"I know. I've been dodging calls from Dave Bracks all morning." Gelb winced again.

Wilson watched him anxiously. "You should see a doctor."

Gelb shrugged. "It's the coffee."

"You should try some milk."

Lyall nodded.

Wilson got up and went to the window, looked down at the river. A line of barges made its way downstream. He turned back to Gelb. "What are we going to do about Bassett?"

Gelb didn't reply.

Wilson looked at his watch. Almost eleven A.M. That would make it almost five in the afternoon in London. The board of BritEnergy had conditionally approved the deal the previous day. But a board could withdraw its approval.

"He would have called you," said Lyall, knowing what Wilson was thinking.

"Still might." Wilson checked his watch. "You or me? What do you think?"

"It'd be more courteous for you to call him, Mike."

"No, I was thinking you might call their CFO."

"Finance director, Mike. They call them finance directors over there."

"Whatever. What's his name again?"

"Oliver Trewin."

"You want to call him?"

Lyall was confused. "Sorry, how does that work?"

It was what Mandy Bellinger had been saying. Wilson was just extending the idea. Play everything down. Make it sound so small it wasn't even worth talking about.

"If I call Bassett," said Wilson, "it's a big thing. Like we're panicking. You call Trewin, ask if they've seen it, laugh it off. Huh? Like it's some piece of garbage. You know, say we get this stuff all the time over here. What's he gonna know? Just make it sound like it's not so serious."

"It sent the stock price down twelve percent, Mike. He's going to know it doesn't happen every day."

"All right. That's true." Wilson frowned. "I still think it's better if we play it down. Try Trewin. Let's start with that. If you think it doesn't go down right, I'll call Bassett."

Lyall didn't reply. He shook his head slightly.

"What?"

"What's the point?"

Wilson stared at him.

"What's the point, Mike? They're going to walk. You know they're gonna walk."

"They're not gonna walk."

"Please! Twelve percent down. Jiminy Creeper! We're gone, Mike. We're . . ." Gelb shook his head, face creased in dismay, unable to get the words out. He threw up his hands. "There's nothing left for next quarter. You understand me? Nothing. Twelve percent down. After our next filing, we're gonna wish it was only twelve percent."

"There's not gonna be a next filing," said Wilson. "Not for Louisiana Light. It's going to be for LLB."

"Right. I forgot. We're going to get this done in ten weeks, right?"

"That's right. And when LLB files, no one's gonna know what's our numbers and what's BritEnergy's. If there's anyone who can mix them up so good no one will ever be able to pull them apart, it's you, Lyall."

Gelb didn't reply.

"It's gonna turn out the combined LLB's numbers aren't so great. Why's that? Because BritEnergy put one over on us. They didn't perform as well as they projected. But hell, it'll be okay. Just give us a year or two and we'll work that old Louisiana Light magic on them." Wilson grinned. "Huh? Now, you tell me the market won't buy it. Just let me at 'em. The market always buys it."

Lyall shook his head.

"What?" demanded Wilson. "What the hell's wrong with you?"

"We're kidding ourselves, Mike. It's ridiculous! They're gonna walk. We will not get this done in three months. We'll have to file again as Louisiana Light, and when that happens, we're done. We're finished! So let's just . . ." Lyall gave up, waving his hand in exasperation, grimacing, wincing.

"What? Let's just what?"

"Let's just stop pretending we can do anything about it!"

"And what?"

Gelb smiled in despair.

"And what?" Wilson sat forward, jabbed a finger at Lyall. "We're gonna do this deal. You understand me. We're gonna do this deal in ten weeks flat. Louisiana Light is *never* gonna file again!"

Gelb kept watching him.

"Get a grip, Lyall. You and me are going to make this happen. We can do it and we will. You got that? Because if we don't . . . This isn't some company that's just gonna go bankrupt, Lyall. It's way worse than that. The things you've done . . ."

"It was you, Mike. I never wanted to. You know I never did."

"The things you've done," said Wilson again, slowly, "are gonna put us both in jail. Now, just think about that for a second. It's a witchhunt out there, Ly. Every DA in the country wants to bag him a corporate felon. Hell, there just ain't no sympathy for white-collar crooks no more. Bad Bernie Madoff done gave us all a bad name." Wilson paused. "You take a second to think about your family, Lyall. Think about little Becky. Now, you look me in the eye and tell me we're not gonna get this deal done."

There was silence.

"They're gonna walk, Mike," said Gelb quietly.

"Then we're gonna have to stop them from walking. You think getting this done in ten weeks is gonna be tough? We have *zero* chance if this falls through and we have to start again with someone else."

Lyall took a deep, troubled breath.

"You understand me? Now pick yourself up."

Gelb nodded.

"All right. That's what this is all about, Lyall. Your family. You just remember that. Now, you ring Trewin. Tell him it's just one of those things that happens. Some scut sheet with a rumor. Tell him to watch our stock price and see it come back up. Tell him we're setting up our data room for their due diligence just like we promised. They can see anything they like. Absolutely anything. They can see our petty cash accounts. Make that clear to him, Lyall."

Gelb frowned again.

"Come on, Lyall. We're gonna be helpful." Wilson smiled. "You just put so much damn stuff in there it'll take them a year to figure anything out."

"And what if they do?"

"They're not going to have a year, are they? They're going to have a week. They were happy with that. Tell Trewin we're setting up the data room. We'll have it ready for them on Monday, like we said. Tell him our guys will be in London on Monday to start using their data room. We'll do it just like we talked about it, okay? When you call Trewin, keep it light. Then you come back and tell me how it went, and you let me know if you think I should talk to Bassett." Wilson paused. "We're gonna do this, Lyall. You hear me? We're gonna do it."

Lyall sat for a moment longer. Then he got up. He grimaced again.

"Try some milk for that stomach," said Wilson as Gelb turned to leave.

Wilson watched him go. He was starting to worry about Lyall Gelb. He couldn't do this deal without him. Wilson himself didn't know the details of how Gelb had managed to do what he did, and couldn't have understood them if he had. Only Lyall knew all the secrets, only he could do the financial work necessary to finalize the deal without exposing them. And only Lyall could then use the finances of BritEnergy to quietly dismantle the hidden framework of loans and off-balance sheet vehicles and the other structures that were threatening to collapse from under Louisiana Light. Wilson could do this deal without Stan Murdoch, without Doug Earl, without just about anyone else. But he couldn't do it without Gelb.

Gelb didn't know the half of what Mike Wilson faced if he failed. Lyall Gelb thought that all they had to worry about was getting chased by some DA. That would be nothing compared with owing money to a man like Tony Prinzi.

Wilson gazed out the window, at the long curve of the river below. He followed a barge slicing slowly through the mud-brown water, drifting along until it moved out of sight. He watched it, face calm, composed, his features revealing nothing of what was going on inside him.

But Mike Wilson was on the edge. On the very, very edge, in a way that Lyall Gelb, who had never gambled in his life, could never even have understood.

Mike Wilson had always been a gambler. In life, in business, in everything. At school, he was betting on baseball games in the third grade. His second wife, Aileen, insisted he go through counseling to try to deal with it. That was a condition for her staying in the marriage. For about ten months he hadn't wagered a dime. The most miserable ten months of his life. When he finally decided to quit therapy, he sent the therapist a thousand dollars' worth of casino chips as a thank-you.

In his early days, he hadn't shown much discretion. At InterNorth, in the eighties, he had been pretty wild. But that had been a crazy time all around. The only person in Baton Rouge who knew him from that period was Stan Murdoch, and he never let Stan see him gambling now. With age and responsibility, Mike Wilson had learned to be discreet. He didn't shake the polite society of Baton Rouge. The people closest to him, both in business and in his personal life, would have been shocked to discover what he did when he was away. It was amazing what you could do when you had a corporate jet at your disposal and apparent reasons to visit just about any continent on the globe. He hadn't been to Vegas in years. He played away from home. Hungary, Poland, the Czech Republic. Mike Wilson loved the casinos of Eastern Europe, raw, crude, vulgar. And South America. You could just about chart the electricity plants he had acquired against a map of the casinos of the world.

They were gambles as well, the plants in the old Communist bloc. The truth was, the entire business model of Louisiana Light was one huge bet. It had been his own theory, buy up old Communist plants and turn the operations around. Turned the old theory on its head, which was that dirty old Communist plants could never be efficient. The point was, you didn't need to be efficient, just *more* efficient, to make a heap of money. That was what he said, anyway, and the banks bought the story. Mike Wilson had sold it to them so many times he almost began to believe it himself. It had a nice contrarian ring to it, just the right tone in the years before the crunch when credit was easy and banks couldn't wait to give it away. Long after the credit bubble burst, the market still wanted to believe in the miracle that was Louisiana Light. They'd listened to him sweet-talk them so long they just kept listening. Even after the writedown in January, he'd managed to snow them with the strength of his conviction. There was a lot you could do with a brazen show of bullishness in front of an audience that stood to lose a shitload of the money it had lent you and still wanted to believe that it wouldn't. But there were limits even to that. There was only so long you could keep going before the facts began to show through from behind the tinsel.

Everyone wanted to believe the bets would pay off. For a long time now, Mike Wilson had known they weren't going to. The analysts could have worked it out for themselves, all those analysts who thought they were so smart, if they had bothered to go find out the tariffs Louisiana Light was able to charge in those countries and if they had taken a stab at calculating the cost of production. It wasn't too hard. They might have been smart, but they were lazy. Turned out the old theory was right. It was hard to get money out of those plants. Efficiencies came slowly. The contract terms that he had had to agree to just to get the right to pay top dollar for those plants were extortionate. Not to mention the personal considerations. Millions, sometimes tens of millions. Mike Wilson had had a gutful of corrupt bureaucrats in godforsaken towns in the boondocks of godforsaken countries whose only aim in life was to extract as much graft as they could from the windfalls that came their way. Lyall Gelb's financial wizardry had kept the Louisiana Light growth story going a long way past when it should have ground to a messy, nasty halt. Somehow Lyall had gotten them through the credit crunch when better companies were going down around them. Perversely, the mere fact that they hadn't gone down—not even suffered a serious scare—made them seem all the stronger to the so-smart analysts who tracked them. But even Lyall's wizardry of concealment could only go so far. There was only so long you could keep hiding the truth. And the more you did to hide it, the uglier the truth became.

Wilson was at the end game now. Winner take all. If he pulled off this deal, the elaborate, fraudulent structure that was Louisiana Light, grafted onto BritEnergy's solid foundations, might just hold up long enough to be quietly rebuilt. Wouldn't that be something? Like any gambler, Mike Wilson couldn't resist the idea of the one last, almost miraculous bet that wins against the odds and brings you back from the brink. This was it. It would be like out-bluffing a full house with your last chip on the table and nothing but a pair of deuces in your hand. It would be that good.

And he personally would have twenty-four million dollars at his disposal, the bonus he'd negotiated with the board for executing a major deal in Europe. No one could quibble with that arrangement. It was a little on the generous side, perhaps, but within the range of bonuses that CEOs of major corporations were offered when tasked with doing a major deal. Fortunately, when it came to executive pay, the Obama age of austerity hadn't extended beyond the banks the government had bailed out, and even there it hadn't lasted long. Twelve million would come to him in the form of options, which he wouldn't be able to sell right away. But twelve would come in cash, which would solve his biggest problem.

Mike Wilson's lifestyle was a facade. The truth was, he had nothing. Less than nothing. For months now, he had been gambling on credit, if that was what you could call the debt he owed to people like the Prinzi brothers. That debt was the only thing he could truly call his own. The jet, the house in Baton Rouge, the chalet in Aspen, the apartment in Manhattan, and just about everything else were on the company account. Take Mike Wilson away from Louisiana Light and he had nothing but the clothes he stood up in. And most of those had been bought with company money. That was fine, he knew, as long as Louisiana Light continued its apparently inexorable rise. No one was going to look too hard at where the petty cash was going. But if that came to an end, he knew he would be on his own. No one was going to stand up and defend him. Especially not from the Prinzis.

He had told the Prinzis he was going to do a deal by the end of the year and a large sum of money would be coming his way. He had no idea what they would do to him if he couldn't pay. Tony Prinzi made jokes about breaking his legs. His brother, Nick Prinzi, a big man with a reputation for violence, apparently looked after that side of their activities. Would they really do that? Most of what Wilson knew about mobsters came out of B-grade movies. Sleep with the fishes? Mario Puzo made up the stuff in *The Godfather,* didn't he? Did they really do that kind of thing? Surely they wouldn't do it to him, the CEO of a major American company?

That made him shiver, when he thought that. He knew it was wrong. He sensed that people like the Prinzis had no respect for reputation or position. He'd have no immunity from them.

And in the meantime, they kept lending to him on the strength of the money that was supposedly coming to him. And he kept taking it, building up the debt, building up the pain that lay in store, which only this deal could take away.

Mike Wilson was on the edge, at a place where someone like Lyall Gelb had never been, couldn't even imagine. All his chips were on the table. The last card in this particular game, which might be the ace he needed—and might not—was already leaving the dealer's hand, sliding facedown over the table toward him. And yet, despite the horror of what lay in store for him if he failed, Wilson still felt that familiar thrill of pleasure, that sense of desperate, almost unbearable anticipation as you wait for the card to reveal its secret. When you think your nerve is going to fail you. When fear itself makes the thrill almost too intense to bear. When you know you cannot, *cannot* afford to lose. And yet you might.

He closed his eyes, imagining it. Imagining the unknown card coming toward him across the table. Seeing it.

For a moment, he froze the image and held it in his head.

Then he opened his eyes.

Dyson Whitney, he thought.

Mike Wilson went to his desk and picked up the phone. He hoped Pete Stanzy was quaking in his miserable banker's boots.

19

The *Herald* lay open on a desk. The offending article was like a tense, reddened abscess, throbbing with pain.

Phil Menendez had been in first thing and chewed them out thoroughly. Then he had to go to a meeting with Louisiana Light's lawyers and accountants to coordinate the due diligence that was supposed to start in London on Monday, and when he came back he chewed them out some more.

Then Pete Stanzy arrived.

That morning, Stanzy had been in Cincinnati, taking part in a pitch to the board of a gas turbine manufacturer that had decided it wanted to go public. They were talking to just about every Wall Street bank that could be bothered going to Cincinatti for the sake of a $300 million listing. The first Pete had heard of the *Herald* article was in a message from Phil Menendez on his cell phone. It wasn't until he got back to New York that he saw the paper for himself.

He looked carefully in turn at Sammy, Cynthia, and Rob.

"I've just gotten off the phone with Mike Wilson," he said.

The atmosphere in the room got tenser, if that was possible.

"He'd like to know how this happened." Stanzy glanced at the article on the desk, then looked back at them. "So would I."

There was silence.

"A lot of people would like to know," said Stanzy.

Silence again. Phil Menendez stood a foot behind Stanzy, arms crossed, glaring belligerently.

"Did we leak this?" demanded Stanzy. "That's what I want to know." He picked up the newspaper, held it for a second, then threw it down on the desk. "Huh? Did this come from anyone in this room?"

Stanzy waited.

"Okay, I'm going to ask each one of you individually. Be honest now, because we will find out. Did any of you speak to a journalist and tell them we were working with Leopard? Sammy?"

"No," said Sammy Weiss.

"Cynthia."

"No. Definitely not."

"Rob?"

"No."

All morning Rob had been searching his memory, replaying the encounter. Did he say anything to that woman? He couldn't remember telling her anything but his name. Nothing about the client. She was the one who had mentioned Louisiana Light. But had he confirmed it? Maybe she was fishing and something about him had confirmed it. What? Something he said? He refused to comment. The look on his face?

Maybe he should own up about the encounter, he thought. He hadn't done anything wrong. If anyone had leaked anything, it was the other person the journalist had mentioned. John Williams. He was fairly certain that was the name she had mentioned. But he had already checked the Dyson Whitney directory and found that there was no one at the firm by that name. So what exactly would he be owning up to? Having had a conversation with a journalist who claimed to know about Louisiana Light from a nonexistent person at Dyson Whitney? He glanced at Phil Menendez, who was staring at him suspiciously. From the look in Phil's eye, Rob didn't think an admission like that was going to do much to help him.

"Maybe it was someone else here," said Rob cautiously.

"Like who?" demanded Menendez.

"I don't know."

"Then what the fuck are you talking about?"

"It's just a possibility."

"They'd have to know about the deal, wouldn't they? You been telling anybody?"

"Maybe he's right," said Stanzy. "Someone else could have leaked. Has anyone here talked about Leopard with anyone else at the bank? Outside this room?"

Once again, Pete Stanzy glanced at each of them in turn.

They shook their heads.

"Think."

Stanzy knew that if the source was from someone else in the bank, it was a whole different ball game. There were a number of other people at Dyson Whitney who knew the identity of Leopard. The mandates committee, for a start. If one of them had leaked, or gotten someone else to leak, then they were trying to spike the deal. There was no other possible reason for it. That would mean he was fighting someone inside the bank. Pete Stanzy had a pretty good idea who it might be. But it would be a huge risk for that person to take. If anyone was trying to spike a deal this size, and the Captain found out about it, they'd be toast. He didn't think even John Deeming would take that chance.

"What about girlfriends?" demanded Phil Menendez. "Boyfriends? Huh? Bit of pillow talk?"

Stanzy looked at them expectantly.

No response.

Stanzy and Menendez exchanged a glance. Stanzy nodded.

"Rob," said Pete Stanzy. "I want to see you in my office. Ten minutes."

• • •

Rob walked around the edge of the bullpen. He had a horrible feeling in the pit of his stomach. He didn't know what Stanzy was planning to say to him, but he didn't think it was going to be good.

Stanzy sat behind his desk. He pointed at a chair.

He paused, after Rob sat down, holding him in his gaze.

"You don't like this client very much, do you, Rob?" said Stanzy suddenly.

Rob stared at him in confusion.

"Well?"

"I don't know what you mean. How could I not like them? I've never met a single one of them."

"Oh, I think you know what I mean. I think you know very well."

"I'm sorry, Pete. I don't."

Pete Stanzy sighed, as if this whole thing were very painful. More painful for him than it was going to be for Rob. "You didn't like what they offered. Am I right? I heard about that. You thought it was a little too high."

"It was above our range."

"So you thought it was too high."

"I thought maybe we should ask some questions."

"What kind of questions?"

"They're paying us forty bips. They go above our range. They've got this weird writedown in revenue back in January . . ." Rob shrugged. "I just think, you know, to me, when you put them together, those things look like red flags."

"So you think we should ask some questions?"

"I guess so."

Stanzy nodded. "And that means you assume I haven't. Right?" Pete Stanzy folded his arms. "Don't you think that's a little arrogant, Rob? I've been in this business fifteen years. Don't you think it's a little arrogant for you to come in after . . . how long exactly?"

"Eight weeks," murmured Rob.

"Eight weeks. Don't you think it's a little arrogant for you to come in after eight weeks and tell me I ought to ask some questions?"

Pete Stanzy's voice rose. "Didn't it occur to you that I might already have asked those questions? Or did you just assume I wouldn't have figured it out for myself?" Stanzy stared at Rob with an intense, contemptuous gaze.

Rob looked down. "I'm sorry." Stanzy was right. He hadn't stopped to consider that Stanzy might have already checked things out for himself. That was arrogant, just as Stanzy said.

"Damn right you should be sorry! Do you know what happens to a deal when you pull a stunt like this? Do you know what—"

Rob looked up. "I didn't pull a stunt! Maybe I was wrong to question you, but I didn't—"

"Didn't you? Are you seriously telling me you didn't leak that story? Isn't it about time you started to tell me the truth?"

"I am—"

"Leopard's share price was down five-point-two last time I looked. This deal only works if the stock price stays up. Do you understand that? Maybe eight weeks isn't long enough for you to get a grasp of that, so let me lay it out plain for you, just in case there's any confusion. Most of the acquisition price is being paid in Leopard stock. Remember? So the thing that holds this deal together is Leopard's stock price."

"I know that."

"Well, if you know that, you can figure out what effect a dip in the stock will have. Mike Wilson is going crazy! Absolutely crazy! And I don't blame him! You know what, I should put you on the phone and let you deal with him! Now, you tell me what the fuck you were thinking when you spoke to that journalist."

Rob took a deep breath. "I did not speak to any journalist."

Pete Stanzy stared at him.

Rob returned his gaze. As steadily as he could. The last notion of owning up to his encounter with the journalist—if he ever really had any notion of it—evaporated.

Stanzy continued to watch him.

"Okay, you listen to me," said Stanzy eventually. "You may think you know everything after eight weeks, but I'm going to tell you a couple of things. Me, I'm an investment banker. That means my first responsibility is to my client. My only responsibility is to my client. That's why he pays me—to make sure I'm on his side. One hundred percent. I don't see why that's so hard for you to understand. You were a lawyer before you joined us, right? It's the same. If your client's a crook, you still do the best you can for him, right? That's your duty as his lawyer."

Rob frowned.

Stanzy corrected himself hastily. "I'm not saying Mike Wilson's a crook. I didn't mean that, right? Don't get it out of context. What I meant . . . what I *said* is that you do your best for your client, whoever he is. He's your number-one priority. He's your only priority."

"Pete," said Rob. "You don't need to say this stuff. I did not leak this story. I didn't do it."

"Let's say he's done a few things. Like any businessman. Some sail close to the wind, some sail closer. Okay, let's say Mike Wilson's sailed closer than most. That's what it takes sometimes to make a company great. Are we going to punish him for that? What's wrong if this deal brings them back on an even keel? Say it does. You don't think that's ever happened before? You don't think that's ever been the reason a deal's been done? Fundamentally, Louisana Light is still a great business. It's a great platform. Okay, maybe it needs some shoring up. Do the deal, and you've done that. You've saved it. You've saved a business, you've saved jobs, you've saved a great American name. Do we need another Enron? Do we need another Stanford Bank right now? Fuck that! That's for politicians. That's for slimebag lawyers who wanna make a name for themselves. What the fuck do they care? The economy's gone to hell in a handbasket and it's only halfway back. It's not gonna come back by putting more companies in the fucking doghouse. Do we need any more of that crap right now?"

Rob stared at Stanzy in genuine surprise.

Stanzy frowned, breathing heavily. He looked away, as if suddenly embarrassed at what he had just said.

"Pete," said Rob. "I did not leak this story. I can only say it so many times. I didn't leak it. You've got to believe me."

Stanzy looked back. "I'm not going to ask you again, Rob."

Rob smiled helplessly. "Pete, what else can I say? It's the truth."

Pete Stanzy nodded. He gazed at Rob for a long moment.

"Rob," he said at last, "I'm taking you off the engagement."

Rob's mouth dropped.

"I just can't have anyone I don't trust on the team."

Rob stared.

"I have to be able to trust my team, Rob."

"You can trust me."

"Can I?"

"Yes! I haven't done anything!" Rob was staring at the end of his career. Right here, right now. After eight weeks. If he got thrown off a team because the MD didn't trust him, who'd ever want him on their project? He'd be out the door at Dyson Whitney. And who'd want him then? This was it! Wasted. The MBA. The time, the money, the effort. Everything. "Don't do this to me. Please, Pete. Don't do it."

Pete Stanzy shook his head. "Sorry, Rob. Someone's on my team, I have to be able to trust them a hundred percent."

"You can!"

"Can I? I don't think so."

"Yes! You can!"

Pete Stanzy sat back in his chair. Rob watched him anxiously, hardly daring to breathe.

"Well, your output has been good," murmured Stanzy. "Sammy's happy with you. I will say that."

"He hasn't seen anything yet! I can work twice as hard."

Stanzy shook his head. "It's not the work, Rob. It's trust. We're gonna send you over to London to do the due diligence. Do I trust you enough to do that? Do I?"

"Yes! You should. There's no issue, Pete. Leopard—that's all that matters. I've told you. That's all that matters to me, getting this deal done. Just like a lawyer, Pete. You said it yourself. Doing the deal for my client."

"I don't know, Rob." Stanzy grimaced. "Trust, you know . . . trust is everything."

"Come on, Pete."

Stanzy frowned. Rob gazed at him imploringly. His whole life, it seemed, was teetering on the knife edge of the other man's decision.

"Please, Pete . . ."

Pete Stanzy sighed. "I really shouldn't . . ."

"*Please,* Pete."

Stanzy watched him for a moment. Then he took a deep breath. "All right. I'm going against my own better judgment here, but. . . . Okay, Rob. You're back in. You've got a second chance."

"That's all I'm asking!"

"But if there's any hint of anything . . . you've got to be whiter than white, Rob. I'm telling you, if there's anything—"

Rob jumped up. "There won't be, Pete. I promise!"

"Go on, then, get back down there."

Rob nodded. "You won't regret it, Pete."

"Yeah, well . . ."

"You won't. I'm telling you, you won't."

Rob marched out of Stanzy's office and back around the edge of the bullpen, half full of disbelieving relief, half full of rampant triumph.

He was back from the dead.

20

The doors to the elevator opened. Immediately, Pete Stanzy wished they hadn't.

"Hey, Pete," said John Deeming, who was standing inside.

Stanzy acknowledged him with a nod and got in.

"I heard things are getting a little rocky in Baton Rouge," said Deeming.

Stanzy didn't respond.

The elevator began to drop.

"Thing like that in a newspaper can upset everything."

"Nothing that won't blow over," said Stanzy.

Deeming laughed. "Hurricane season down there, is it?"

The elevator stopped and the doors opened. John Deeming was still chuckling as Stanzy got out.

John Golansky was on the phone. He beckoned Stanzy into his

office and motioned to a seat. It was almost nine o'clock at night but Stanzy hadn't been able to coordinate a time to meet with him any earlier.

"Yeah, Bob," John said into the phone. "Yeah, I hear what you're saying." Golansky glanced at Pete and rolled his eyes. *"Just a minute,"* he whispered to Stanzy, holding the receiver away from his mouth.

Pete nodded.

"Yeah, Bob. Yeah, I'm listening. We've been through this a million times. You come back to me with the prospectus and we'll start talking. Bob? Bob . . . don't say that, Bob. All right . . . Bob . . . Bob . . . Bob, listen to me. I've got to go. I'll talk to you Thursday. All right? Bob? Thursday."

John put down the phone.

"Fucking time waster," he said to Stanzy. "You know, before I got into this business I never would have guessed how many fucking time wasters there are."

"Tell me about it," said Pete.

"So?" John Golansky kicked back. He stretched himself out, hands behind his head. He was tall, well-built. A college football player. That was some twenty-five years ago, but he still had the look. "How we doing?"

Pete Stanzy grinned ruefully.

"What's their stock price?"

"Forty-seven-point-three at the close," said Stanzy. "That's only three bucks down. They recovered half the drop."

Golanksy nodded. "This doesn't make it any easier for us."

"Yeah," said Stanzy. "Look, on Monday it'll be back. No one's going to believe what's in the *Herald*. They've got nothing. They know they've got nothing. The Street knows they've got nothing."

Golansky nodded again. He seemed to be thinking about something. Pete waited.

Golansky took his hands out from behind his head. He sat forward. "Citi's not gonna give us the four-point-two billion as a bridge."

Stanzy took a moment to take that in. "Because of this?"

Golansky shook his head. "They were saying that to me yesterday."

"How much will they give?"

"Half. Maybe. If we find someone else to match it."

Stanzy smiled. "You can do that, right?"

Golanksy didn't reply.

Pete Stanzy laughed in disbelief. "Come on, John. We don't get the loan, there's no deal. You know how important this deal is."

"I know how important it is," said Golansky. "I just don't want to end up going junk."

Pete laughed. "No way we're going junk."

"Don't be so quick to say it. We might not be able to get it even if we wanted to."

Junk debt meant high-interest loans for perceived high-risk investments. They could command a five, ten, fifteen percent premium on the interest rate. But with credit still in short supply after the crunch, you couldn't necessarily raise junk debt even if you were prepared to pay for it. In any event, the BritEnergy board wouldn't likely approve a deal with $4.2 billion of debt financed with junk. The interest would be crippling.

"This is Louisiana Light," said Pete. "Come on, John. It's not some two-bit startup. This is a great company. This is a growth story."

"With a balance sheet I wouldn't use for toilet paper."

True, thought Pete. "John, we're borrowing against the integrated company. Has Citi seen the integrated balance sheet once we put Leopard and Buffalo together?"

John looked at him as if he wasn't even going to bother answering that.

"Then I don't see the issue," said Stanzy. "I can't see what Citi's problem—"

"Is there something I should know about this client?" asked Golansky abruptly, cutting Stanzy off.

For a second, Stanzy just looked at him. Then he smiled. "Like what, John?"

"Like anything you think I should know," said Golansky evenly.

Stanzy shook his head.

"Look, Pete. I've got Bruce Rubinstein on my back. After the thing with the stock price this morning, I had him in here for a half hour. Now, I don't know why, but he doesn't like this deal."

"Bruce doesn't like any deal," said Stanzy. "If he had his way, we'd never make a dime."

Golansky shrugged, conceding the point. "Look, I'm going out on a limb here, Pete. Way out. So I need to know if there's anything I need to know."

"John, as God is my witness. There's nothing I can tell you."

"Okay." John Golansky grimaced. He squeezed the bridge of his nose between thumb and forefinger. "Okay. Look, Pete, I've been hearing things."

"What things?" asked Stanzy quietly.

"I've been hearing there are maybe some tricky things that have been going on inside that client of yours. Creative things. A bit too creative, if you know what I mean."

"Like what?"

Golansky shrugged. "No one seems to know how much debt they really have."

"What are you talking about? It's all there in the filings."

"Some of it's off–balance sheet."

"Yeah, but that's listed. They've just gotta read the notes when they look at the balance sheet."

"*More* than in the notes." Golansky gazed at Stanzy knowingly. He raised an eyebrow. "Stuff that no one can see."

Pete Stanzy shook his head as if the idea had never occurred to him. "How much more?"

Golansky sighed. "No one knows."

"So it might be nothing," said Stanzy.

"No one knows," repeated Golanksy.

"So it might be nothing," repeated Stanzy.

"Listen, Pete . . ."

Stanzy shook his head. "No, this is bullshit, John. Someone's trying to spike this deal. First there's this thing in the *Herald* and the stock price takes a hit. Now someone's telling you the Leopard's got a bunch of debt they can't even see. You gonna believe that? Come on, John. You gonna believe that crap? Who is it, huh? Who's telling you that?"

"Pete, I want this deal as much as you do."

You couldn't, thought Stanzy.

"I said it from the start. This is a great deal for the firm. You wouldn't have gotten it past Bruce without me. Remember?"

"And it's still a great deal, John."

"And I'm still out on a limb. You know their CFO down there at Louisiana? What's his name?"

"Lyall Gelb."

"He's a smart guy."

"Yeah."

"Excellence Award winner from *CFO Review*."

"Yeah?"

"Two years running."

"Well, there you go," said Pete. "I'll be sure to congratulate him."

"That scares the crap out of me," said Golansky. "You understand? I don't want some fucking smartass CFO who's been playing games with the financials—"

"What the fuck is this, John?" Pete stared at him, eyes blazing with anger. "You're gonna tell me you don't want to do the deal because their guys are too fucking smart?"

"Okay. Look, Pete, I've been talking to Jay Hartson. You know Jay?"

Pete Stanzy shook his head.

"He's at Merrill. Jay says—"

"He's at *where*?" Stanzy exploded. "Jesus, John! Fucking Merrill? They're pissed because Wilson came to us for this deal. Come on! You can't believe a thing they fucking say!"

"I know Jay."

"Yeah, right. You know Jay. So now there's a code of honor?"

"Hear me out, Pete. I backed this deal from the start. Hear me out. You owe me that much."

Pete rolled his eyes.

"All right?"

"All right," muttered Stanzy. "I'm listening."

"Jay says there have been some things going on. He wouldn't tell me exactly what. That's a hungry company you've got down there, Pete. It's chewed through a lot of capital in the last five years, and it's still hungry. Last time, Merrill drew a line. They refused to do what Gelb wanted. Some kind of loan facility, Jay wouldn't tell me what it was. He figures that's why they came to us when they wanted to do this deal."

"That's bullshit. That's bullshit right there."

"Maybe it is bullshit that that's why they came to us. But Jay wouldn't lie to me about the other stuff."

"Come on, John. If there was a problem with Louisiana Light on the debt side, they would have gone down in the credit crunch. You know that. Everyone knows that. It's obvious. And what happened? Nothing! The crunch didn't touch it. In fact, they managed to raise capital. How many companies did that?"

Golansky didn't reply.

"Merrill got its own money on the line?"

"Some, I think. Jay didn't say exactly."

"I bet he didn't. And when was this with this loan facility? This supposed thing they wouldn't do?"

"About three months ago," said Golanksy. "I don't think Merrill was the only one who turned them down, either."

Pete Stanzy shook his head.

"Pete, I believe Jay Hartson. And you know what? Merrill's pissed, like you said."

"Mother*fucker*." Stanzy shook his head in disgust. He knew what that meant. Whatever they were saying to Golanksy, they'd be saying to the market. And worse. "You think they leaked the *Herald* story?"

"No. Sounded to me like Jay had just found out we were working with them."

Pete Stanzy shook his head again, thinking about the effect this kind of badmouthing would have. He'd have to do something about it, maybe start saying a few things to the market about this Jay Hartson guy. Maybe put out some kind of rumor that Hartson's job was under threat because he hadn't been able to hold on to the Louisiana Light account.

"You got any idea where the article came from, Pete? What about your team?"

"No."

"What about that analyst you told me about. The one who was saying we bid too high?"

"No. He didn't do it. I had a talk to him."

"You sure?"

"Yeah. It was a long shot. I scared the crap out of him, though. Made him think I really thought he'd done it. I pretended to fire him." Golansky grinned.

"Why not? Teach him a lesson. You should've seen him, he was shitting his pants. Begged me to keep him on the team."

They looked at each other for a second, then they both laughed.

"He won't step out of line again, that's for sure," said Stanzy.

Golansky nodded, still grinning. They both looked out into the bullpen, where a good number of analysts and associates were still at work. Pete Stanzy had a wife and two kids to go home to. John Golansky had a wife, his second. Neither of them seemed to be in a hurry.

John Golansky stretched back again. He put his feet up on his desk. "Okay, what are we gonna do?"

"The stock price'll come back," said Stanzy, still gazing at the bullpen. He turned back. "It's the *Herald*. No one believes that crap."

"Why don't they hold off with the deal until their next filing? Reassure the markets they didn't pump the results this time around. Make the lenders happy."

"Hold off?" said Stanzy in disbelief. "They're hot for it. What are you saying? You want me to tell Wilson to hold off?"

Golansky nodded.

Stanzy stared at him, speechless.

Golansky broke into a grin. "That's what that moron Rubinstein suggested to me."

Pete Stanzy laughed, more out of relief than amusement. Hold off on a deal? You never did that. You never, ever, ever let a deal go cold. No matter how good it was, no one would come back to it. People did deals because they were hot for them. Every other reason—synergy, strategy, whatever you wanted to call it—was secondary.

"Fuck Rubinstein," said Golanksy. "If he had his way, we'd never do a deal."

"So we're gonna do it, right? You're gonna get the bridge?"

"I told you, Pete, I want this as much as you do. We need this deal. This bank doesn't execute something like this soon, we're all screwed."

"So?"

"We got half from Citi," said Golansky. "I've still gotta find two-point-one. I'm just telling you, Pete, it's not gonna be a walk in the park."

"But you'll get it, right?"

Golanksy didn't reply to that. He frowned, squeezing the bridge of his nose.

Pete Stanzy watched him. He wondered just how close Golansky actually was to telling Stanzy to go look somewhere else for the debt, which would kill the whole thing as far as Dyson Whitney was concerned. In the long run, Golanksy had to live with Bruce Rubinstein. If Bruce was whispering in the Captain's ear against Dyson Whitney getting involved in funding the deal, John would carry the can for anything that went wrong with the debt further down the line. The charges would be laid against him personally. No matter how much Golansky wanted to fund the deal—and he did, Pete Stanzy truly believed that—there would be a point at which the personal risk became too great, and he'd walk away.

"Pete," said Golansky, "you know the firm was going to raise part of the bridge on its own account?"

Pete Stanzy nodded. "A hundred million, right?"

"Is there anything I should know? Really?"

"Nothing." Pete smiled, and he watched Golansky, trying to figure out how close the other man was to walking away.

21

Rob let himself into Emmy's apartment.

"It's Saturday," she said, watching him come in. "What's wrong? You work on Saturdays now, remember?"

"I thought I'd come back and catch you with your lover," joked Rob.

"If you left it much longer, you probably would have."

Work in the war room had finished early. Sammy had needed Rob and Cynthia to crunch some numbers to go in the loan document he was preparing for John Golansky. Other than that, he just wanted to be sure they knew what they would be looking for when they got to London for the due diligence. By noon, Rob was done.

"Had lunch?" he said.

Emmy shook her head.

"Don't tell me. You were gonna have corn chips, right?"

Emmy grinned. Corn chips were her staple. There was always a cupboard full of them.

"Come on," said Rob. "I'm buying."

They went to a deli and got a couple of bagels. Then they headed for the park. It was a warm, breezy October day. For a while they just walked, holding hands. It felt like a long time, an awfully long time, since they had had the time together to do that.

A group of joggers went past, unbunching into a line as they went around them.

"So, what's been happening in your world?" said Rob.

"Ah, well, no multibillion-dollar deals, funnily enough."

"Okay," said Rob. "I guess I had that coming."

"We lost out in the auction."

"Oh." Rob looked at her. "I'm sorry."

"We found out yesterday. That novel's going to be huge. Honestly. Caitlin and Andrea both agree, but Fay wouldn't bid up past fifty thousand, which was way too low."

Caitlin and Andrea were two other editors who shared Emmy's office.

"So that's what you bid? Fifty?"

"Forty-five, actually. Doesn't matter, anyway. We lost it to Harper-Collins."

"How much did they offer?"

"Not sure. Possibly six figures. We can't compete with that, but the author really liked us. If we could have gotten some way toward it, she might have gone with us."

"That's a real shame," said Rob.

"Fay's too timid. You've got to have faith in your convictions.

Sometimes you've got to be prepared to go a little further when you really think you've got something special. That's how you build a great list."

"But she's built a list."

"Yeah, but . . . we miss out on stuff. Not only because we can't pay top price, but because sometimes we're not even prepared to offer what we can afford. I mean, I know this must sound like peanuts to you. You're talking in millions, and for us it's a few thousand here or there."

"Well, that's the business," said Rob. "That's what it is. Doesn't matter what the size of the sums is."

"It's not about money," said Emmy. "I wish it wasn't, anyway." She shook her head. "I would have loved to edit that book, Rob. I know exactly what I'd do. Damn it! It's honest, it's real. It's what I want to be in publishing for."

"Is there any chance it might come back?"

Emmy shook her head. "It's done. It's gone now. Those things don't come back."

They walked on in silence.

"So, what about your world?" said Emmy. "Nowadays, I don't seem to hear anything about it."

Rob shrugged.

"Nothing?"

He didn't reply. He had spent a long, fitful night thinking about what had happened in Pete Stanzy's office the previous afternoon. It was still eating away at him.

Emmy looked at him knowingly. "What is it? There's something, isn't there?"

He hesitated. "You ever read the *Herald,* Emmy?"

Emmy laughed. "If you want to insult me, just tell me I've got a big ass."

"You don't have a big ass. You have a perfect ass."

"I'd rather have a big ass than be known as a *Herald* reader."

"There was a story in it yesterday," said Rob.

"Well, that'd be a first."

"About us."

Emmy glanced at him. "What do you mean?"

"There was a story about how Dyson Whitney's working with my client."

"Is that bad?"

"It's meant to be a secret."

"Doesn't sound like much of a story," said Emmy. "Must have been a slow day."

"It said more. It said our client isn't very sound. It implied there's some fancy footwork going on. The stock dipped quite a way. That's a problem when a deal's going on. That can really hurt them. It's the kind of thing that could stop the deal cold."

"Do you believe it? This story?"

Rob didn't reply.

Emmy stopped. "Rob? Do you?"

"I'm not sure."

"You mean you think there really is something going on?"

"It's possible. I don't have any proof. It's just a suspicion."

"What makes you suspect it?"

"Things. There are a few things. Red flags, they call them. Things that are supposed to make you suspicious."

"And they do?"

Rob hesitated. "Yeah."

"Well, if that's what you think," Emmy said, "you need to bring it up with your boss."

"I did."

"And he said . . . ?"

"He said, 'Yeah, right.' Emmy, these guys . . ." Rob thought of Pete Stanzy. And Phil Menendez. "You've got to see these guys. When this story appeared yesterday, you know what they thought? They thought *I* leaked it!"

"Why would they think that?"

"Because of those things, those red flags, because I dared to say something about them. That's the way they think. I was the one who mentioned it, so I must be the one who went and leaked this stuff about the client's honesty. That's their logic."

"And did you leak it?"

"Of course not!" Rob looked at her in surprise. "What do you think? I wouldn't even know how to do it."

"You'd just ring up a newspaper, I guess. It couldn't be too hard."

"Well, I didn't ring up any newspaper. I just . . ."

"What?"

"Nothing." He hadn't said anything to that journalist. Whatever she knew, she knew before she spoke to him.

They sat down on a bench facing an area of open grass. People were having picnics. There wouldn't be too many warm days left this year.

"They were going to fire me," said Rob.

"*What?*" Emmy stared at him.

"Pete Stanzy, he's the MD, he was going to pull me off the team. Said he couldn't trust me. Said he couldn't have someone he couldn't trust a hundred percent. Who's going to want me after that? That happens, I'm dead in that firm. I'm dead in the business. I get kicked out after eight weeks, who's gonna want me?"

"Could they do that? Could they fire you just like that?"

Rob shrugged. "Why not? What was to stop them?"

"So are you still on the team?"

"Yeah. I told him I didn't leak the story. I told him I'd never do that. I told him he can trust me to the hilt, all I care about is the client. It's like being a lawyer. I'll do whatever it takes to do the best for my client."

Emmy nodded.

"I tell you, Emmy, I begged. I'm not proud of it."

"Why didn't you tell me last night?"

"You were asleep."

"You don't tell me anything, Rob, do you realize that?"

"I'm sorry. It's all meant to be secret."

"From me?"

"You wouldn't say anything, I know that."

"Then why don't you tell me anything? What are you doing? Protecting me? If you can't even . . ." She stopped, shaking her head in frustration.

"I don't know. I don't know, Emmy. I've been working so hard, I don't know if I can even think straight."

There was silence.

"I'm telling you now, aren't I?" Rob paused. "It wasn't pretty, Emmy. Seriously, I'm not proud."

Emmy watched him. Eventually she sighed. "Rob, you've worked for this. God knows how hard you've worked, everything you've sacrificed. Two whole years. I don't care if you begged for your job. You did the right thing. You don't deserve to lose it over some ridiculous suspicion."

"The other night you said you didn't think this job would satisfy me."

"I had no right to say that. It's what you want and you worked to get it. You deserve it. So what are you going to do, walk away and let them destroy you? You stood up for yourself."

Rob wasn't so sure he had stood up for himself. "Rolled over" might be a better description.

"I'm proud of what you did," said Emmy. "You understand? I'm proud you fought for your job."

She wouldn't be so proud if she had been there to see it, thought Rob. He wished he could blank it out. He couldn't think about the conversation in Pete Stanzy's office without cringing. Physically cringing. And to think about the way he had come out of there, as if he had won some kind of big victory, as if he had come back from the dead . . . he wished he could put it out of his mind, draw a curtain over it, put it someplace and forget it had ever happened.

But it had happened. He had spent a long, sleepless night replaying the conversation, every word he had said and everything he had done, as if he had to keep punishing himself for it and the only way he could punish himself enough was to replay it over and over and over in his head. And each time, he felt physically sick at the thought of it.

He didn't think of himself like that, like the person who had sat in Pete Stanzy's office the previous afternoon and begged for his job. That wasn't the image he had of himself. He'd let go of everything. Principle. Decency. Self-respect. It had taken him all of a minute. In another minute he would have been down on his knees.

It was disgusting. Craven, cringing capitulation. When he thought about it, he felt as if he were seeing himself in a mirror for the very first time—his true self, his real self—and what he saw was enough to turn his stomach.

And yet, he was almost certain now that something really was wrong at Louisiana Light. It wasn't the way they had pumped their revenues to get their stock price up. And it wasn't the level of the bid, or the size of the fee they were willing to pay, or any other red flag. More than any of those things, it was that speech Pete Stanzy made. All that stuff about the great American business that had gone wrong but could still be put right. All that stuff about not needing another Enron, another Stanford Bank. It had forced its way out from inside of Stanzy, from whatever warped sense of morality was left within him after fifteen years in the business. That's how it had seemed to Rob, when he was lying open-eyed in the darkness, thinking about it. It came out against Stanzy's will.

Why? Because Pete Stanzy knew something about Louisiana Light, or at least suspected it strongly. He must. There was no other way to understand his need to say those things.

Pete Stanzy had sold his soul, and when he said those things, he was looking for a way to rationalize it.

But was *he* any better? It had taken Stanzy fifteen years. It had taken him all of eight weeks. The very first time he had been required to take a stand, he had failed. All that mattered was his job. At that moment in Stanzy's office, he would have done anything, said anything, promised anything to keep it. Nothing else counted.

And was he still going to do nothing, just quietly go about his work, even though he was almost certain now there was something wrong with this client? Wouldn't that make him as bad as Stanzy? Was he really going to do nothing?

But what could he do? He had already spoken to Stanzy, and Stanzy had almost kicked him out.

He watched one of the families having a picnic on the grass. The father was kicking a soccer ball with his two kids while the mother sat on the picnic blanket peeling fruit. One of the kids, Rob could see, had Down syndrome. The two kids took turns kicking the ball.

"Rob, what is it?" said Emmy.

He watched the dad with his kids. The little kid with Down syndrome kicked and missed and fell over, and the other kid and the dad laughed. But warmly. The kid himself laughed as well. The mother looked up and smiled.

"What if there is something going on with this company?" said Rob. "With our client. What if they really are doing some bad stuff?"

"I thought you said you didn't know for sure."

"But what if they are?"

"But it's just a suspicion, right?"

"Emmy . . ."

"You raised it with your boss. What else can you do? Did anyone else even do that? Anyone else on your team?"

"I don't think so."

"See? Rob, honey. Listen. You're the most junior person there. You've done what you can. You talked to your boss and told him what you thought. Now it's up to him."

Rob frowned. Wasn't this just another way of getting out of it? If Stanzy wouldn't do anything, did that absolve him of responsibility just because Stanzy was his boss? He remembered the big speech he had made at Donato's, when Greg was talking about joining the corporate crime team. How you had to follow the signs, how you had to go on and on and on and not let anything stop you. And what was he doing now?

"Maybe I should go higher."

"Higher than your boss?" asked Emmy doubtfully. "Over his head?"

Rob nodded. It wasn't exactly the most appealing prospect. If he did that, he would need to be a hundred percent certain of his facts. Stanzy wasn't the kind of guy to forgive something like that. If he was wrong, he was finished.

"But you're not *sure* there's a problem, are you?" said Emmy, thinking the same thing.

"Not completely."

"Well?"

"You don't think I should do something to try to prove it?"

"What could you do?"

"I don't know." Rob frowned. "There's nothing I can think of."

Emmy took his hand. "Rob, it doesn't always have to be Robert Holding against the world. You know, there are other people out there as well. Sounds to me like you've done exactly what you had to do. You had a concern, you raised it. No one else on your team even had the guts to do that. You're way too hard on yourself, honey."

Rob shook his head.

"Yes, you are. That's why I love you."

"Because I'm too hard on myself? Now I know you're just trying to make me feel good."

Emmy smiled. "It's one of the reasons. A very small one."

"I hope so."

Rob was silent again. Then he glanced at Emmy, smiling despite himself. Emmy moved up close against him on the bench. Rob put his arm around her. They watched the family having its picnic. The dad and the kids had stopped playing. They were all sitting on the blanket now, eating the fruit the mom had peeled.

"You still going to London tomorrow?" asked Emmy.

"I guess so. Unless Pete Stanzy changes his mind about me again. Their data room's ready. We've got to get the due diligence done."

"What is that, anyway?"

"Due diligence? It's when you check that everything's as it should be, that it all stands up. You look at their data, their financials. This isn't stuff you can get publicly. It's their confidential information. You need to check it all."

"Sounds like fun."

"Do you think so?"

Emmy laughed. "No."

"Yeah. Right." Rob smiled, but a moment later he was lost in thought again. So was that really it? He'd done what he had to do and now he was going to forget about it?

Emmy watched him, as if she knew what he was thinking. "Rob, you just go in there and show this Stanzy guy what a mistake he almost made. That bastard wanted to fire you? You go in there and do that due diligence and show him what you've got."

British Airways Flight 178 from JFK boarded at nine o'clock on Sunday morning. When it touched down at Heathow seven hours later, it was nine P.M. on a wet London night, and it was heading toward eleven by the time Rob and Cynthia traveled across town and checked into their hotel in the Docklands area, the section in the old East End of London that had been redeveloped into a high-rise business district. They went to their rooms. Rob called Emmy, then he dozed for a short time, and then he was awake for most of the night, finally falling asleep only about an hour before his wake-up call came through.

He met Cynthia in the lobby. BritEnergy had set up their data room in the offices of Stamfields, their law firm. The concierge in the hotel looked at the address and gave them directions to a tower a couple of minutes' walk away.

Sammy had made sure they knew exactly what they needed to find. A data room is a repository of information that a company makes available to authorized parties during the course of a transaction. In other words, a room full of documents. The material can't be taken away or copied, so the only way to use it effectively, without getting caught in the sheer mass of information available, is to enter the room with clear objectives and to know what you're looking for. For Dyson Whitney, the point of gathering information from the data room was to refine the financial model Cynthia had constructed for the accounts of the combined company and to test their own valuation of Buffalo. In order to do this, they would need Buffalo's budgets, business plans, data underlying the plans, and any work done by Buffalo on different business scenarios. All the other stuff that would be checked during the due diligence process—leases, contracts, financial statements, audit papers, legal matters—could be left to Leopard's lawyers and accountants, who would be in there as well during the time that the data room was accessible. Some of Leopard's executives might also be in there to check on various things. Sammy had warned Cynthia and

Rob to say as little as possible to anyone. In a situation like this, it was impossible to know how much any given person knew about various aspects of the deal, client executives included. The agreed allocation of the top jobs, the timetable for the deal, and all kinds of other extremely sensitive matters might be known to some but not to others. The safest thing, Sammy told them seriously, was to say nothing at all.

Cynthia knew all that already. She had worked her way through a dozen data rooms on previous deals. She just wanted to get it over with.

The morning was bright and blustery. They got to the address across a wide, windy square. Stamfields's reception was on the twenty-second floor. When they told the receptionist who they were and why they were there, she checked her screen and asked them to take a seat. They went to a pair of leather armchairs at a glass table in the waiting area. The receptionist made a call.

Rob glanced at the front page of the *Financial Times,* which was lying on the table. The headline was about a takeover of a British bank.

"What do you think Leopard stock will open at?" he said to Cynthia.

"Fifty bucks."

"You think it'll blow over that quick?"

"Yeah. Who believes the *Herald*? It's a storm in a teacup."

Rob smiled.

"What?"

"You sound more English, that's all. Your accent's stronger."

"Are you saying I have an American accent when I'm in New York?" Cynthia seemed offended at the idea.

Rob laughed. "No. It's just . . . it's gone a little more English, that's all."

Cynthia gazed at him for a moment, then looked away.

Rob watched her, amused. There never seemed to be anything to Cynthia but work. No feelings, no humor. Just work and her overwhelming ambition to get a great review at the end of the project.

"So you think the stock price drama is over, huh?"

Cynthia gave a quick nod. She looked around impatiently. "Let's just get this done," she muttered. "Data rooms are so tedious."

A couple of minutes later a woman stepped out of an elevator and came toward them. They both got up. The woman verified who they were.

"I'm terribly sorry," she said. "But I've just checked, and apparently we haven't received authorization for you to enter the data room."

"Isn't it ready?" asked Cynthia.

"It's ready," said the woman.

"Well, I don't understand," said Cynthia. "We're here to use the data room."

"I know that," replied the woman.

"Listen," said Cynthia, "I'm not sure if you understand the situation. We're under extreme time pressure here and I can assure you that BritEnergy will be very upset if they find out—"

"Miss Holloway," said the woman, interrupting her. "I think it's you who doesn't understand the situation."

"How so?" retorted Cynthia.

The woman gave her an icy smile. "Let me put it another way. You're from Dyson Whitney, aren't you?"

"Yes."

"Well, BritEnergy doesn't want you in their data room."

23

Lyall Gelb rubbed at his belly. The pain was there again. It was six-thirty on Monday morning and he was already in Mike Wilson's office. Wilson had called up and woken him an hour earlier and told him to get in right away.

He wondered whether he'd be able to get away again. It was Becky's first day back at school after her appendectomy and he had promised to drive her. It was important to him. Right now, it seemed a lot more important than what might or might not be happening in a data room on the other side of the Atlantic.

"Could be a mistake," said Lyall. "They might have forgotten to give the clearance."

Wilson shook his head. "They're up to something."

Lyall winced.

"You all right? You had something to eat? Maybe you should eat something."

"No, I'm all right."

Wilson watched him uneasily.

"When did you find out about it?" asked Lyall.

"Just before I called you. Stanzy rang me. His people in London were turned away. They waited until six in New York to wake him." Wilson shook his head in disgust. "I tell you, Lyall, something's going on. I want you to get on the phone with Trewin. Take it easy, see what he says, find out what's going on."

"What are you going to do?"

"What do you think I'm gonna do?" Wilson pushed the phone toward him. "I'm gonna listen!"

Lyall pulled out his cell phone and found the number for Oliver Trewin's direct line. He punched it into the speakerphone on Wilson's desk. A voice-mail message responded in a woman's voice, saying it was Oliver Trewin's office. Lyall left a message asking Trewin to call back.

He and Wilson sat in silence, waiting for the phone to ring. Wilson stared out the window at the river, which was a kind of purple color in the early light. Lyall glanced at his watch. A quarter of seven. If Trewin rang back, if he could clear this up relatively quickly, he might still get back to take Becky to school.

"Try again," said Wilson.

Lyall punched the numbers again. This time Trewin answered.

"Lyall!" he said. "I was just about to call you back. Just picked up your message. Can you give me a few minutes?"

Lyall glanced at Wilson. Wilson rolled his eyes. He shook his head and whirled his hand quickly, telling Lyall to keep going.

"Ah . . . Oliver?" said Lyall. "This isn't going to take long. We just need to get something covered off."

"All right . . . hold on a second . . ." There was a shuffling of papers from the other end of the line. "All right, that's better. What can I do for you, Lyall? Heavens, it's awfully early for you, isn't it? What time is it over there? Quarter to eight?"

"Quarter of seven," said Lyall.

"Of course. Sorry. You're an extra hour behind the East Coast, aren't you?"

Wilson rolled his eyes again and motioned to Lyall to speed things up.

"Oliver, I've got you on speaker. That okay? I've got my hands full here."

Trewin laughed. "Haven't we all?"

"Okay, Oliver, you know we have a couple of people from our investment bank over in London this morning for the due diligence."

"Oh. Really? Already? You don't hang around, do you?"

Oliver Trewin's voice sounded genuinely surprised. Mike Wilson scowled. That's what all the Brits were like, actors. Like those characters in their situation comedies the Brits all found so funny. You never knew what they were actually thinking

"Yeah, the guys from Dyson Whitney are there," said Lyall. "I believe our lawyers will be there tomorrow."

"Excellent. Get it all moving, eh? We must get over to your side of the pond."

Lyall glanced at Wilson, who shook his head impatiently.

"Oliver," said Lyall, "we have a problem."

"Oh?"

"Only a small problem. I was wondering whether you could help fix it."

"I certainly will if I can, Lyall," said Trewin cheerfully. "What is the nature of this problem, if one may ask?"

Like "one" didn't know already, thought Wilson in disgust.

"Oliver, your lawyers won't let our bankers into the data room."

There was silence on the line. Lyall and Mike Wilson glanced at each other.

Trewin's voice came on again. "That doesn't sound very sensible. How are they supposed to do their work?"

"That's what we've been wondering," said Lyall.

"Did they give a reason?"

Lyall looked at Wilson questioningly. "No authorization," whispered Wilson.

"Apparently they didn't have authorization," said Lyall.

"How odd," said Trewin. "Well, I'm sure this is just a mistake. Lawyers!" he chuckled. "A law unto themselves, if you'll excuse the pun."

"Oliver," said Lyall, "our guys are sitting there doing nothing."

"And costing you a pretty penny, I shouldn't wonder. This is no good, this is no good at all. We'll have to get this sorted out for you. Look, give me a couple of minutes and I'll call you back. Are you on your office number?"

"Yes."

"Okay. Give me two minutes."

The line went dead. Wilson picked up the receiver and put it down again to make sure the connection was cut.

"You think he knew?" asked Lyall.

Wilson shrugged. "Brits! Who knows what they're fucking thinking."

"I don't think he knew," said Lyall.

Wilson didn't reply.

They sat in silence. The view from the window was growing brighter by the minute. Lyall glanced at his watch. And again, thinking about Becky.

They heard a phone ring down the corridor. For an instant they looked at each other, then they both realized they were sitting in Wilson's office. They bolted down the corridor to Lyall's room.

"Lyall?" said Trewin.

"Yeah." Lyall was panting.

"Sounds like you've been running, Lyall. You don't have one of those awful treadmill things in your office, do you?"

"No."

"Very good. Get out in the fresh air, that's what I always say. Best thing for you."

Wilson took a deep breath, just wanting Trewin to get on with it.

"By the way, Lyall, I might go on speakerphone as well, I think."

"Sure," said Lyall, glancing at Wilson. "So, what's happening?"

"Well, this . . . can you hear? Is that all right?" Trewin's voice now had a hollow quality.

"It's fine, Oliver."

"Good. Well, this data room thing, Lyall. Now, the thing is, I'm afraid there's been a bit of a . . . how would you chaps put it? A bit of a glitch."

Wilson's eyes narrowed.

"What kind of a glitch?" asked Lyall.

"Well, I'm afraid Andrew's asked them to hold off for a little while."

"Andrew?" said Lyall. "You mean Andrew Bassett?"

"Yes."

Lyall glanced at Wilson, who was shaking his head in disbelief.

"Asked who?" said Lyall.

"The lawyers," replied Trewin. "He's asked them not to let anyone in just yet."

Lyall could see Wilson getting angrier by the second. Wilson motioned brusquely for Lyall to continue.

"Why is that, Oliver?" asked Lyall evenly.

Mike Wilson cocked his head, listening intently for the answer.

"Well, Lyall, all of this kerfuffle last week . . ."

"Kerfuffle? Oliver, I don't follow."

"Well, that awful article that came out . . ."

Wilson clenched his fist. Lyall half-expected it to come slamming down on the desk. Wilson was bursting to say something, but he managed to stay silent, jaw set, eyes narrowed, as he continued to listen.

"Oliver," said Lyall. "Didn't I explain that to you on Friday? The *Herald*'s a well-known muckraker."

"I know, Lyall. Frightful. Don't worry, we have the same over here. Every day, Lyall, one of them has a young lady on page three who's completely topless. That's what they have to do to attract readers. And the sad thing is, that's the best part of the paper. Only bit worth looking at."

"Oliver," said Lyall, "the article was pure slander."

"I don't doubt it for a second."

"So? What are we saying here?"

"Well, your share price, if I might be so bold . . . it did rather stumble somewhat."

"It was halfway back by the close. I'd expect it to be all the way back up by the end of trading today."

"I wouldn't be at all surprised," said Trewin affably.

"The market will go back and look at the results we put out, Oliver. That's what matters."

"Yes. Excellent results. Excellent! I wouldn't mind being able to put out a set like that myself from time to time."

"Damn right he wouldn't!" whispered Wilson. He was sick of Oliver Trewin with his British understatement and slightly too-smooth agreeableness. He regretted that it had already been agreed that Trewin would leave the company when the deal was done. He would have enjoyed sacking him.

"So?" said Lyall.

"It's just . . . there's rather a lot of volatility, Lyall," said Trewin. "I suppose we'd prefer to see rather less volatility, considering that quite a proportion of what you're offering us is in the form of shares. Up, down, down, up . . . you understand what I mean."

"Ask him who's saying this," whispered Wilson very softly.

"Oliver," said Gelb, "let me ask you straight. Is that your opinion, or is that Andrew's?"

There was a pause. Mike Wilson leaned forward until he was only inches from the phone, trying to hear if anything was being said in the background on the other end of the line. He stabbed at the volume button, turning the sound up as far as it would go.

"Well, we did have some discussions with our chaps from Morgan Stanley over the weekend," said Trewin.

Wilson sat back in his chair violently.

"I can't divulge those, of course."

"Of course not," said Lyall, glancing at Wilson, who looked as if he was going to pick the phone up and smash it to pieces.

"I believe Andrew spoke to our chairman over the weekend. Now, no need to worry, Lyall. I think we're just looking for a short period of calm and reassessment. I don't think we've got a major problem here."

"The hell we don't!" hissed Wilson.

"Lyall? Did you say something?"

"Umm . . . Oliver, this is a little surprising," said Lyall, playing for time and looking at Wilson to see what he wanted him to do next. But Wilson's face was a mask of pure, cold rage. "I mean . . . you know, our guys are over there right now. Perhaps you could have told us . . ."

"I believe Andrew took the decision early this morning," replied Trewin. "Don't quote me on that, but I believe that was the case. And it is still rather early now with you. I imagine he just thought he'd leave it a little longer before calling. I think he was planning to call Mike Wilson at . . . ah . . . nine o'clock your time. That would be three o'clock here. Would that be right?"

"Yes," said Lyall.

"Do you think Mike will be around then?"

Wilson nodded. Then shook his head in disgust. Then nodded violently again, seeing that Lyall didn't know what he wanted him to say.

"Probably," said Lyall. "Yes, I'm pretty sure he will."

"Excellent. I wonder if you could let him know?" said Trewin, and Lyall wasn't sure he couldn't hear a note of amusement in Trewin's voice as he said it, as if he knew that Wilson had been sitting there all along.

Wilson got up as soon as Lyall had cut the connection.

"They're fucking with us." He paced violently around Lyall's office, then threw himself into a chair. He said it again, more loudly this time. "They're fucking with us!"

Lyall watched him.

"They figure they've got a chance to screw us."

"Possibly," said Lyall. He glanced at his watch.

"What is it?" demanded Wilson. "Why the hell do you keep looking at your watch? Somewhere else you got to be, Lyall? You got something that's more important than this?"

Lyall shook his head.

"Damn right you haven't!" Wilson stood up again. "Come with me."

He opened the door to Lyall's office. It was after seven now. Other people were arriving for work. From somewhere along the corridor, they heard the voices of a couple of junior executives bantering about what they had done over the weekend.

Back in his own office, Wilson got Pete Stanzy on the phone.

"Pete, you were right," said Wilson, without any preliminaries. "They're fucking with us."

"What happened?" asked Stanzy.

"We talked to Trewin, their finance guy. Lyall here talked to him."

"Hey, Pete," said Lyall.

"Hey, Lyall. What did he say?"

"They're worried about the stock price. They want to wait and see—"

"They've been talking to Morgan Stanley!" interjected Wilson. "They've been talking to them all weekend. Then fucking Bassett spoke to his chairman and they've shut down the data room."

"Until when?"

"Who knows? Bassett's calling me at nine. According to Trewin, he was going to do it anyway. I bet he was listening in on everything we said."

"Wait," said Stanzy. He was in his office on the thirty-fourth floor. In New York, it was after eight. "Let me get this straight. They're saying they've reacted to the stock price. But at the close it was only three bucks down from where it was before the article came out. And that was *up* a dollar eighty with your results. So it's only *one-twenty* down from where it was when you agreed the deal with them. And our projection is it's easily going to be back up to that point by the close of trading today."

"I told them that," said Lyall. "It's the volatility they don't like."

"Yeah," muttered Wilson. "And if it wasn't the volatility, it'd be something else."

"So they've put things on hold and Bassett's calling you at nine. Is that what you said?" asked Stanzy. "Is that nine o'clock your time?"

"Jesus Christ, Stanzy, let's get to the point! What difference does it make what fucking time he calls me?"

"Yes," said Lyall. "Nine o'clock our time."

"They're shopping themselves around," said Wilson. "Huh, Stanzy? Right? That's what they're doing."

"Possibly." Pete Stanzy gazed out through the glass wall of his office at the associates hunkering over their computers in the bullpen. His mind was working fast, crunching through the possibilities. "That's one possibility. Their bankers will be telling them they can get more."

"More than twelve-point-five? Plus our break fee?"

"That's what they'll be telling them," said Stanzy, who had done precisely the same thing himself dozens of times, and had sometimes even gotten clients to believe him. "They'll be saying they can get more. They'll be looking for five to ten percent of the difference as a success fee, so they'll be pushing that line hard."

"You fucking investment bankers!"

"That's how it is, Mike."

"Jesus!" said Wilson. "Bassett would have to be a hell of a lot dumber than I thought to fall for that. They'll never get it! That's why we went in at twelve-point-five, right? To stop them from doing this."

"Morgan Stanley's got nothing to lose. If they can get a bidder to come up with another billion, that's a hundred million for them. It's all upside. You've gotta expect them to try it."

"Morgan Stanley may have nothing to lose," retorted Wilson, "but Andrew Bassett sure does."

"What's that, Mike?"

"Us!"

In his office, Pete Stanzy nodded. That was precisely the point, and he was glad Wilson had gotten there himself. "Exactly. Mike, that's what we've got to use. That's our strength."

"What else?" demanded Wilson hungrily. "Come on, Pete. Hell, you're an investment banker. You know how you bastards think. What else might they be doing?"

"Well, they might not be shopping themselves around. They might just be trying to get more out of us."

Wilson laughed incredulously. "Do they really think . . . ?"

"We've gone in high; they might think we can go higher."

"Their board's approved it!"

"No, Mike," said Stanzy, "their board's approved it conditionally. They might be treating it as a floor."

"See, I told you these bastards were screwing us!" muttered Wilson to Lyall Gelb.

Stanzy gazed at the bullpen. What else did Wilson expect? Buffalo was trying to screw Leopard, but that was only because Leopard was trying to screw Buffalo. That's what deals were about. That was what made them fun. In addition to the fee. And this was one fee Pete Stanzy wasn't going to let go of. He was going to hang on to it with his fingernails, if necessary. Or with Mike Wilson's fingernails, to be more accurate.

"Again, say they are trying to jack up the price," said Stanzy. "What do they stand to lose, Mike? Us, right?"

"Damn right."

"Whichever way you look at it, that's our card. They can shop themselves around, they can try to jack up the price, but there's a cost. They'll lose us. And do they *really* think they're going to get a better deal? That's what they'd have to believe, right? That's what it comes down to. Because they'll *lose* us. You gotta call their bluff, Mike. Do they really think they're gonna get someone to come in and put more than twelve-point-five on the table? Do they really, really believe that?"

"They couldn't," said Wilson. "They'd have to be fucking crazy."

"Exactly."

"Hold on," said Lyall. "What if they're telling the truth?"

There was silence on the phone. Wilson stared at Lyall as if he'd just landed from Mars.

Pete Stanzy's voice came over the speakerphone. "What are you saying, Lyall?"

Gelb glanced at Wilson. "Let me play devil's advocate. What if they really are just worried about the stock price? What if Morgan Stanley's said to them, You know what, this is a great price, but it's got a whole bunch of stock in it, and right now that stock's going up and down like a yo-yo, and maybe you'd better just . . . have another look at it."

"Bullshit," muttered Wilson.

Pete Stanzy thought about it. That was the soft point in the deal, as it is in any acquisition that isn't paid for with a hundred percent cash. There's always going to be room for dispute over the true value of the acquirer's stock in relation to the stock of the target. Even when the stock price stays steady, a deal can fall apart over that. Stanzy had seen it happen plenty of times.

He thought about what John Golansky had said to him. Why don't they wait until they put out their next set of results, reassure the market? That was Bruce Rubinstein talking. Stanzy wouldn't dare even raise that question with a client. What if the client said yes?

"We could increase the cash component," said Wilson.

"No," said Stanzy.

"We could push up the cash some and see if that makes them happier."

In his office, Stanzy stared at his phone in horror, as if he could hardly bear to hear what was coming out of it. He was just thankful John Golansky wasn't there to hear it. Four-point-two billion was enough. More than enough. It was already looking hard to get.

"Mike," he said, "hold on. Just . . . keep it in perspective. You're the one in the position of strength here. You've offered them a price they're never going to get from anyone else. Right? Never! You're the one who holds the cards. No more cash. You don't need it. Same stock-to-cash split, two to one. They procrastinate, they lose you. Let's stick with that. That's our line. They delay, you're out of there."

"Yeah, okay," said Wilson.

"Did you hear me, Mike?"

"I heard you!" retorted Wilson in irritation.

"Okay. All right. Just don't talk about any more cash." Pete Stanzy paused, wondering whether he should tell Wilson about the difficulties Golansky was having in getting the bridge loan set up. But Wilson didn't sound in the mood for that right now. "He's going to lose you, Mike, that's what you've got to remind him. For Bassett, it's now or never. That's how you'll hook him. Trust me."

"Yeah," said Wilson.

"Why is it now or never?" asked Lyall.

Wilson looked at him sharply. Lyall Gelb knew the answer to that better than anyone. But Lyall didn't return Wilson's glance.

"I mean, if I'm Bassett, why?" said Gelb. "Why can't we wait a few weeks to see what happens with the stock price? In fact, why can't we wait until the next set of results?"

Because you never, ever, *ever* let a client go cold, thought Stanzy. He waited to hear what Mike Wilson was going to say.

There was silence on the phone.

Eventually Stanzy spoke. "Look, just remind them how good the price is. Just remind them he's going to lose it. Keep Bassett thinking about that, Mike. It's a bird in the hand. A very, very attractive bird."

"Yeah," said Wilson.

"Don't talk about raising the cash component. Mike? You hear me? Whatever you do, don't talk about cash." Stanzy tried to control the urgency in his own voice. You could only tell a client something so many times. Stanzy knew if he kept saying it, Wilson would get irritated. He might even decide to do the opposite. "He hesitates, he loses you. That's the line."

"Yeah," said Wilson.

"Call me after you've spoken with him," said Stanzy.

"Sure," said Wilson.

Stanzy put down the phone. There was no particular God Pete Stanzy believed in, but he closed his eyes and prayed, prayed that Wilson would hold the line and stick to it.

In Baton Rouge, Wilson turned to Lyall Gelb. "What the fuck was that about, Lyall? 'What if they're telling the truth?'"

Lyall shrugged. "What if they are, Mike?"

Wilson watched him. Then he nodded. "You're right," he said quietly. "He's going to ask. That's the kind of guy he is. Bassett's going to ask exactly what you said. Why can't we give him a few more weeks?"

Lyall nodded glumly.

A thick silence hung between them. They didn't have a few more weeks to give Bassett. Not even a couple of weeks. At best, without a single delay, they'd get the deal down with only days to spare before the next filing was due.

Mike Wilson glanced at Lyall. Lyall didn't meet his eyes. Gelb didn't dare think what the numbers were going to look like if they had to file for Louisiana Light alone at the next quarter. Yet he couldn't stop himself. The figures danced through his mind, had done so for weeks, day and night, like a nightmare recurring.

The silence was heavy. Suffocating.

"I don't know, Mike," said Lyall eventually. "Maybe they are trying to jack the price up or shop themselves around. If they are, Stanzy's right. We stick to that line and it'll work. When Bassett calls you at nine, tell him we'll walk away and they'll lose everything."

"But what if they're not like you said?"

Lyall didn't reply.

Wilson was silent for a moment. Then he nodded curtly to himself. "I'm gonna get this settled. They are *not* gonna fuck with us like this."

Lyall glanced at his watch.

"What is it with you?" demanded Wilson angrily. "Go on, get out! Get the hell out of here!"

24

There was a holdup on the corner of North and Twenty-second, where a water main had ruptured. Lyall waited in line, almost bursting with impatience. Eventually he inched past the spot, the car wheels churning through six inches of water. When he finally turned into his street, his heart was pounding. He pulled up in front of the drive just as Margaret's car started to back out.

The car stopped. One of the doors opened and Debbie and Josh jumped out yelling. They came racing toward him. Then out came Becky, more gingerly.

Margaret got out as well. She and Lyall exchanged a glance. She smiled.

Lyall knelt down. "How's my Becky?" he said.

Becky nuzzled up against him. She had been clingy since the operation. Lyall hugged her.

"I thought you weren't gonna come, Daddy," she murmured.

"Of course I was gonna come," said Lyall.

"Then why did Mommy put us in the car?" demanded Josh.

"Mommy was tricking," said Lyall. He hugged Becky closer. "Didn't I say I'd take you to school, honey?"

"Come on, Josh. Debbie," said Margaret, "get in Daddy's car."

"Let's go, huh?" said Lyall to Becky.

They got to school with about a minute to go.

"Okay, guys," he said to Debbie and Josh, and he gave them each a hug and pushed them away gently. "Go on. Don't wanna be late." They ran in.

He crouched down close to Becky.

"Okay, honey?"

Becky nodded.

"You just be a little bit careful, and you'll be all right."

Becky nodded again.

"Mommy called Ms. Elkins. She knows all about it."

Becky didn't say anything.

He hugged her. "I love you, Becky."

"I love you, too, Daddy."

He looked at her. "Now you go on inside. I'll see you tonight."

"Yes, Daddy."

"Good girl."

She smiled at him, and then she went through the gate.

The playground was just about empty now. One of the teachers stood at the door and waited for the stragglers to come in.

Lyall watched Becky walk gingerly across the yard. She stopped just before she went in and gave him a wave. He waved back. His heart was so full of love for her, it was bursting.

Then Becky was gone. The teacher closed the door behind her.

One of the parents came past on her way back to her car and smiled at Lyall. Lyall smiled back mechanically. He stood outside the gate a little longer, gazing across the yard at the building where his three children would be sitting down to their lessons.

He walked back to the car. He began to go over it all, as he had been doing a lot recently. Each step on the path that had brought him to this point, how it had happened. That first little deal in Hungary. "We could use the joint venture," he had said jokingly when Wilson was fretting about raising more cash. And he outlined it for him, the way you could do it, given Hungarian tax law and the way it lined right up against a loophole in the U.S. accounting requirements. It was like a magic window, like an escape hatch between two different worlds that was perfectly aligned and you could jump right through it. And no one else had realized it, no one but him. But when he said it, it was like an exercise. Like a kind of game. We *could* use the joint venture. Not that we ever would, but we *could*. That's how he meant it. But that wasn't how Mike Wilson took it. "Explain it to me," said Wilson, and Lyall Gelb had.

It wasn't strictly illegal. It just pushed the envelope. After that, there were other things that weren't strictly illegal, things that pushed the envelope further. He was so much smarter than the auditors. They weren't even in the game. That was what he had really enjoyed, slipping though crevices in the rules that the auditors didn't even know existed, thinking up intricate new structures and balancing them delicately within visible frameworks in such a way that the structures themselves remained completely invisible, knowing they were so subtly designed that no one else would be clever enough to see them even when they were staring them in the face—and then watching as the auditors and analysts looked right past them. And he was careful, of course, to make sure that from the outside everything looked right. Picture perfect. He shunned the obvious little tricks every other CFO used and, consequently, he got a reputation almost for excessive rectitude. He avoided anything that might even give an appearance of malpractice. He insisted on having an external auditor approve every one of the company's charitable donations, both in the United States and abroad, to avoid the imputation that the company might be using them to curry favor. In one of the early ventures, he wanted to refuse a Catherine Gelb as a director, even though she had been nominated by one of the partners, in case someone mistakenly thought she was a relative. The other party insisted for its own reasons and he had had to accept it. But that was how meticulous he was. Nothing was allowed to give the slightest hint of being dubious.

Yet under that perfect appearance, what he had done wasn't just dubious. "Dubious" didn't come close to describing it. Exactly at what point his creation turned into the monster that it had become, that was difficult to say. It wasn't possible to pinpoint any one individual step that was clearly illegal, at least not at the start, and yet after enough steps had been taken, something illegal had clearly been created. The financial statements he was putting out bore no relation to the reality of the finances that he was managing. The profits he claimed were no profits. The balance sheet was no balance sheet. It was as if he had stepped not through a magic window, but through the looking glass into a place where nothing meant what it said, nothing said what it meant, into some kind of parallel universe, and to keep the whole thing from imploding around him he had to keep going farther and farther in.

But all he wanted now was to get out. He was exhausted by it, weary, ravaged, scared by what he had done and how it had grown. And was it possible that there was a way to get out? That's what Mike Wilson said, and BritEnergy was that way, the door that was going to lead them back into the real world. But Lyall didn't really believe it. You couldn't get out that easily. It didn't work like that. God didn't let things like that happen.

Lyall didn't know if he could bear it if everything was ever revealed. He didn't know if he could bear the way Becky and Debbie and Josh would look at him. If not now, when they were old enough to understand. That would be the worst of it. And Margaret? Maybe, in a way, Margaret would understand how it could have happened, how one thing had led to another and he had ended up doing the things he'd done. But the kids, how could the kids ever forgive him for what it would do to their lives? How could he expect them to?

No, Margaret would never forgive him, either. Not for her own sake, but for the kids'.

If it came to that, it would be better if he wasn't there. He had thought that for a while now. It would be better for all of them.

He got back to the car. His cell phone rang. Lyall looked at the number.

His stomach contracted in pain.

25

Rob had spent a week in London with Emmy during the summer before last. He liked the place. Given a day to himself, there were lots of things he would have done in the English capital. Sitting in a hotel and waiting for a call to come through from New York wasn't one of them.

The day passed in a series of receding deadlines. First Cynthia said she'd have to wait until eleven, which was six A.M. in New York, before she could start calling people. At a quarter past eleven she called Rob in his room to say she had spoken to Sammy, and Sammy had spoken to Pete Stanzy and Pete was going to sort it out and let them know when they could go in. Rob couldn't go anywhere in case authorization for them to use the data room came through. By twelve-thirty, Rob hadn't heard from Cynthia and he called her up and she said she was still waiting, and he should sit tight. Rob ate lunch in the hotel. At two she rang to say that Phil Menendez had called and they were going to get the go-ahead any minute. At three Rob rang her back and she said Phil hadn't called. Then nothing happened, and it was pretty obvious the day was shot. But it was still only the middle of the day in New York, and apparently Menendez was saying they might still get the go-ahead to go in that night. He had told Cynthia to wait around a couple of hours more and get the last flight out of London that night if there was still no news, so Cynthia organized seats. At six, just as they had checked out of the hotel and were about to head for Heathrow, Sammy Weiss rang to tell her to cancel the seats and hang on to see what happened in the morning.

They checked in again.

"What do you think's going on?" Rob asked as they headed back to the elevators with their bags. They had wasted the whole day, and there was no certainty that anything better was going to happen tomorrow.

"No idea," said Cynthia. "Could be the deal's still on. By tomorrow, could be it's off."

"Just like that?"

"Could be anything. That's how it is in this game, Rob. If you want to stay sane, don't try to read the runes. You'll always get it wrong. Just be ready to move when someone tells you. I'll give you one piece of advice: Always have your passport, your credit card, and your cell phone in your pocket. That's all you need, they'll cover you for anything." Cynthia shrugged. "Great life."

They waited for the elevator. It was taking a while to come.

Suddenly Cynthia looked at him. "How do you think I'm doing?"

Rob looked at her in surprise.

"What do you think?" she asked.

"On this project?"

Cynthia nodded.

"Isn't that something you should ask Sammy?"

"You're a straight guy," said Cynthia. "You're honest. That's more than you can say about most people at Dyson Whitney. Tell me what you think."

"I think you're doing fine. I think Sammy thinks you're doing a great job."

"And Phil? You think Phil likes me?"

Rob laughed. "Cynthia, Phil doesn't like anyone."

Cynthia watched him for a moment, then she walked quickly away. She sat down at a chair in the lobby, head bowed.

Rob followed her with their bags and sat down beside her.

"Cynthia, Phil's a psycho. You must have known that before you started."

Cynthia nodded.

"You okay?"

She nodded again. Then she shook her head. "I'm fucked, Rob. This is it."

"That's not true."

"It is. I only did this project because Bernard Fischer told me Phil asked for me specifically. I wouldn't have gone near it, otherwise. I don't know why he did, though. He seems to hate me." She looked at Rob, smiling bitterly. There were tears in her eyes. "Last time, I only just managed to hang on. I know what's going to happen. Phil's going to kill me in the reviews." She threw her head back, trying to hold back the tears. She took a deep breath.

"Don't you think you're exaggerating a little? Your work's great."

"Doesn't matter. I know what's going to happen." She looked at him, trying to smile again. "You know, I've been at the firm three years, and when they tell me they don't want me anymore, what am I going to have to show for it? Three years of hundred-hour weeks and quite a large shoe collection."

"Well, that's something."

Cynthia laughed a little, wiping at a tear.

"Is there anything I can do?" asked Rob.

"No." Cynthia took a deep breath. "You know, the best way to get some money out of this place is to get them to pay you to go away. There was a guy last year, Jeff Estevez, they paid him two million bucks to go. That's the rumor, anyway. Two million bucks because some of the senior guys had made a bunch of remarks about Latinos and they thought he was going to bring a case."

"What about Phil Menendez?"

"Menendez was one of the guys who made the remarks!"

Rob couldn't help laughing. "And I guess no one's been making anti-British remarks?"

Cynthia shook her head. Rob wasn't sure if she was laughing or crying. Probably both.

"It's Catch-22," she said. "Estevez didn't want to go. If they think you want to go, they won't give you anything. And if you don't, like Jeff, what's a couple of million bucks compared to what you might earn over a career?"

"So why did he go?"

"What else could he do? Bring a court case that he might not win? And who's ever going to employ him again?"

"Is that what you really want, Cynthia? A career at Dyson Whitney?"

"No, I want a career at Goldman Sachs. But Dyson Whitney would do." She shrugged. "Anyway, that's not going to happen. None of it's going to happen."

"You never know," said Rob. "Phil mightn't kill you in the reviews.

I think it's hard to predict what a guy like Phil's going to do. All you can do is keep doing your best."

Cynthia looked at him and smiled. "You're a nice guy, Rob." She kept looking at him. Their eyes met.

Rob got up.

She got up as well. She checked her watch. "I told some friends I'd meet up with them if I had time tonight."

"Sounds like a good idea."

"Looks like you're going to have to eat by yourself again." The way she was looking at him, it seemed as much of a question as a statement.

"Forget about it," said Rob.

Cynthia didn't reply immediately. "Okay," she said at last.

They went back to the elevators with the bags.

"So you think I'm doing a great job, huh?" said Cynthia.

Rob grinned. "Best analyst I've ever worked with."

He ate alone in the hotel restaurant. He thought about Cynthia, the way her facade had cracked. She was brittle, way more brittle than he had imagined. And she was probably right about Menendez. Rob didn't know exactly what you would have to do to get Phil Menendez to support you, but whatever it was, there was nothing to show that Cynthia was doing it.

Afterward he went back upstairs and called Emmy at work. He told her what had been happening with the data room.

"Is this normal," she asked, "to go all that way and find you can't do anything?"

"You're asking me? The deal could be off."

"What? Just like that?"

"Apparently. I guess we'd be the last to know. Emmy, I have absolutely no idea what's going on."

"If it was off," said Emmy, "what would happen to your team? Do you keep going or do you split up?"

"They'd wind us up. You don't keep the team together if there's no deal."

"Well . . ." Emmy paused. "Maybe that wouldn't be such a bad thing after everything that happened. You know, with your boss. You'd get to have a fresh start with some other team. Maybe it wouldn't be such a bad thing if this deal didn't go ahead."

Rob thought about that. Maybe it wouldn't. It would solve his dilemma, that was for sure. He wouldn't have to worry anymore about Louisiana Light and its red flags and what might or might not have been going on there. That was an appealing prospect.

But not as appealing as being on a team that successfully executed a deal, a multibillion, forty-bip deal the likes of which Dyson Whitney had never seen. You didn't have to be a rocket scientist to figure that out. If it were successful, Rob knew, the deal was what everyone would remember, and any little glitches along the way would be forgotten. Anyone on the team that brought that deal home would be a legend. But if it stopped here, he'd be just another guy on another deal that fell through. At best. At worst, he'd be the guy Pete Stanzy almost threw off his team. And that was probably all that anyone would ever want to know about him as they declined to staff him on their projects.

"No, honey," said Rob. "That wouldn't be good for me."

"No?"

"No. We've gotta hope this deal keeps going."

"Then that's what I hope," said Emmy. "So, when are you likely to be back?"

"Depends what happens."

"I miss you."

Rob laughed. "It's only been a day."

"I can still miss you."

"True. I miss you, too."

They talked a while more. As he hung up, Rob looked at the time. Eleven o'clock. Six in New York. He wasn't sleepy. It would be hours before he could get to sleep. He turned on the TV.

At about the same time, to the northwest of London, the lights of a Learjet appeared out of the darkness of the night sky. The plane was on its final descent. Shortly afterward it roared low over a highway, crossing the white and red streams of moving car lights, and landed. The airfield where it touched down was RAF Northolt, the military airfield where the body of Princess Diana, on a sultry day in 1997, was brought back after her death in a Paris motor tunnel. Northolt also offered commercial landing facilities, noted for their efficiency and discretion, which were popular with celebrities and anyone else with a private jet and a reason to avoid the congestion of Heathrow, six miles to the south.

The jet taxied. When it stopped, three men got out. A drizzle was falling, and an official led them briskly to a low office block where they presented their passports. The three men then exited the office block. A car was waiting for them. They got into it and the car headed for the gate. It swung onto the highway over which their plane had landed and turned toward London.

The night receptionist at the Mandarin Oriental on Hyde Park didn't see too many guests checking in on his shift. He tended to remember them.

"Mr. Brown," he said. "Back again? And Mr. Leopard?"

Mike Wilson nodded.

"And your name, sir?" asked the receptionist, glancing up from the screen at the third man.

"This is Mr. Green," said Wilson. "You should have a room for him."

"Mr. Green . . . Mr. Green . . . ah! Here it is. Mr. Green. Will you be staying for just the one night like the other gentlemen?"

Stan Murdoch nodded.

26

Mike Wilson had made the decision as soon as Gelb left him that morning, even before Andrew Bassett rang. There was only one way to handle the situation. You couldn't expect to win a game of poker without being able to see your opponent's face. When it came to talking turkey with Andrew Bassett, Wilson didn't want to be listening to some disembodied voice on the other end of a phone, and he didn't want Bassett to be doing that, either. He wanted the other man to feel his presence in the room. He wanted to be looking straight into Bassett's eyes.

When Bassett called at nine o'clock, the Englishman gave no sense of wanting to talk turkey. He talked about the stock price as if he really was concerned by the volatility, as if that weren't so much baloney to cover up what was really going on. His board was nervous about taking an offer to the shareholders, he said, when there was so much stock in it and the stock price was bouncing. Wilson listened. But it was nothing like being in the room with the man, being able to see his expression, forcing him to say those same things to his face. That's when his real agenda would show through. It just confirmed what Wilson had already decided. Talking over the phone like this was making it too easy for Bassett.

"All right," said Wilson at last.

"You understand my position?"

"Sure, Andy. It's a tough one. I apologize again for putting you in it. The press in this country . . . what can you do?"

"Oh, we're no better over here, Mike. I assure you."

"Say, Andy, we need to get this figured out."

"Absolutely," said Bassett. "I thought we might just wait a couple of weeks and—"

"I'm coming over."

Silence. Wilson liked that. Exactly the effect he wanted.

"I'll be there tonight," he said. "You have your guys ready to meet with us tomorrow."

"Mike, I'm not absolutely sure that's—"

"Andy, I am."

Wilson could hear the silence again, Bassett trying to think. Wilson didn't want to give him time to do that.

"My secretary will be in touch with the details. See you tomorrow, Andy."

"Yes. All right. You don't think—"

Wilson put the phone down.

He had already decided he would be taking Lyall Gelb with him. If the discussion got deep into numbers, he'd need Lyall there. But that was only part of the reason. Every time Wilson saw him, Gelb worried him more. He needed to keep him fully committed. Gelb had to be in that room.

He had decided to take Stan Murdoch as well. Wilson was satisfied he had taken the sting out of Stan's opposition by the severance offer he had made. And he had decided that Stan would be leaving. Wilson had had a word with Gordon Anderton about doing a search for Stan's replacement, and Gordon already had a couple of names on the short list. Good guys, too, operations guys Wilson knew about. Since seeing their names on the list, Wilson had begun to think that maybe it wouldn't be a bad idea to have a change anyway. Bring in some fresh thinking, not have someone who hankered after a bunch of plants that had been taken away from him. But it was still critical to keep Stan happy until the deal was done. The best way to do that, Wilson figured, was to get him involved. Let him sit in on some of the discussions. Ask him to handle some of the due diligence. Make him feel important. Make him think it would still be up to him whether he left when the deal was done.

The meeting was scheduled for nine-thirty the next morning. A few minutes before that time, Andrew Bassett arrived at the Mandarin Oriental. Two men were with him, Oliver Trewin and the company secretary, Anthony Warne. Bassett asked for Mr. Leopard's suite.

"Who shall I say is here?" inquired the receptionist.

Bassett felt like a fool saying it. "Mr. Bison."

"Buffalo," said Trewin quickly.

Anthony Warne poked his head around from the other side of Bassett. "No, I think Andrew's right, Oliver. I think Mike's secretary said it was 'Bison.'"

"It was Buffalo," said Trewin.

"Oliver, you'll find they call it Bison in the States."

"No, Anthony, *we* call it Bison. They call it Buffalo."

"I suspect you'll find it's Bison."

"Buffalo," said Trewin.

The receptionist raised an eyebrow.

"Buffalo Bill," said Trewin to Warne. "What about that? It's not Bison Bill, is it?"

"Who's Buffalo Bill?"

"Haven't you ever heard of Buffalo Bill?"

"Buffalo Bill?"

"Oh, for heaven's sake!" snapped Bassett impatiently. He turned to the receptionist. "Just ring Mr. Leopard. I'm sure any bovine will do."

• • •

One of the rooms in Mike Wilson's suite had been fitted out with a conference table. The usual niceties were exchanged as they milled around it, how lovely it was to see one another again, how nice it was to meet Stan Murdoch at last, jokes about the tedium of crossing the pond, which they would all soon be doing a lot more often, ha ha! Bassett was an overweight man of below middle height, with remnants of thin, sandy hair and a red complexion. He lamented the loss of "poor old Concorde."

"We came in the jet," said Wilson curtly, and with that, the niceties stopped. The air was tense. Exactly as Wilson wanted it. He wanted these guys under pressure. He wanted these guys to realize what they were about to lose.

Wilson noticed with satisfaction the uneasy, questioning glances that the BritEnergy executives exchanged.

"Gentlemen, shall we sit?" he said.

They sat, leopards on one side of the table, buffalo on the other. Wilson waited for everyone to settle. Then he let the silence go on just a little longer.

"Let me summarize the position as I understand it," he began.

Warne, BritEnergy's company secretary, got ready to take notes.

"Gentlemen," said Wilson. "We made you an offer last week that you agreed to take to your board. Twelve-point-five billion dollars, eight-point-three billion in Louisiana Light stock at a swap ratio of five-point-one to two, and four-point-two billion in cash. Our board approved the deal, as did yours. Due diligence was due to start yesterday, with a joint announcement in two weeks presuming all was found to be in order. Our data room in New York is now open and available for your use. Over the weekend, however, you decided to put a stop on the due diligence from your side. I am unaware how long this stop lasts or what needs to happen before you lift it. If this deal is to go ahead, we need to clear these things up right now. That's why we're here." Wilson paused. "Is that a fair summary?"

Bassett looked right and left at Trewin and Warne. Then he turned back to Wilson.

"Mike," he said, "the first thing I'd like to say, again, is to apologize for the way you found out. We didn't make the decision until early on Monday morning, which would have been the middle of Sunday night for you. I was planning to call you as soon as you got into the office. Unfortunately, your people were already on the ground and they beat me to it."

"Accepted," said Wilson. "That's not the issue. I understand that."

"Still, I just want it to be clear," said Bassett. "That's not how I do business. That's not my style, and I want you to know that."

"Okay," said Wilson. "Let's put that behind us. Where are we now?"

"Well . . ." Bassett paused. "This is rather delicate for both of us. I don't know how to put this nicely . . ."

"Just spit it out, Andy."

"There's concern about your share price."

"Because of Friday?"

Bassett nodded.

"Lyall," said Wilson, "what was the closing price in New York yesterday?"

"Fifty-point-four-five," said Gelb.

Just as Pete Stanzy had predicted, the stock price was back up to where it had been after the results. In fact, it was a few cents higher. Amanda Bellinger had done her work well. There was barely a journalist or an analyst of note she hadn't reached over the weekend.

"Which makes it . . ." Wilson prompted Lyall, just to make sure that Andrew Bassett thoroughly grasped the point.

"A dollar thirty up on the price when we reached agreement last week," said Lyall.

Wilson spread his hands. "A dollar thirty up. A dollar thirty *up* from where we were."

"That's equivalent to an extra two hundred twenty million on the acquisition price," added Gelb, in case the men on the other side of the table couldn't work it out for themselves.

Bassett frowned. Wilson watched him closely. The frown seemed genuine. It got deeper. Bassett looked as if he were in some kind of actual pain. From their previous meeting and phone conversations, Wilson had already gotten the feeling that Bassett was the kind of guy who disliked confrontation, who hated being in a position where he had to disappoint someone. The kind of guy who was more comfortable sharing a joke about the loss of poor old Concorde, and can't we just pretend there's no conflict between us? Now Wilson could see it confirmed in front of him. It was the right move, to come over to London and face him physically at the table. Absolutely the right move. A guy like that had to be confronted. Once he was, he could easily swing to your side just to get the comfort of conciliation.

"We still have a problem, Mike." Bassett said it reluctantly, not looking at Wilson. Then he glanced up at him.

On the other hand, maybe he was simply a very, very shrewd negotiator.

"What's that?" asked Wilson coolly.

"Mike, I said to you yesterday . . . it's the volatility." Bassett shrugged, as if he wished he didn't have to say it. "We would have been happier—I mean, my board would be happier—if the share price had stayed flat. This way, it's gone up and down fifteen percent in three days. When the offer price has this much stock in it, that's an issue."

Wilson stared at him. He had to stop himself from slamming the table in frustration. Even after the *Herald* slur, the price was up on where it had been before the quarterly results. So what was Bassett saying? That he would have preferred the price to be lower? It was a dollar thirty up. How could anyone, anywhere, figure that was a bad thing? It was an extra $220 million for his shareholders, right there, sitting in his hand!

"Mike, look at it from our side," said Bassett plaintively.

"You can have a collar," said Wilson. "We can do that, right, Lyall?"

Lyall nodded. They had discussed this on the flight over, and since it didn't involve any more cash, Pete Stanzy had agreed. "Sure. Let's say ten percent. If our stock price goes down more than ten percent, we renegotiate the stock swap."

Bassett didn't say anything.

"Andy?"

"If we announce, Mike, we'll be in play."

"Yeah, but with a floor of twelve-point-five billion! Twelve-point-seven, actually, with the extra one-thirty on the stock price."

"With respect, not if your share price falls," said Oliver Trewin. "Say it goes down ten percent between now and completion of the deal? Our floor is eleven-point-six."

"No, it's not. We renegotiate the swap. We just told you that."

"Say it goes down fifteen percent, our floor is—"

"Jesus, it's not *going* to go down!" yelled Wilson, and this time he did hit the table. "You've had one scurrilous, anonymous report, possibly concocted by someone to do exactly this—to put a hit on the stock price and make you block this deal—and you fall for it. Hell, you just fall straight in!"

Bassett and Trewin glanced at each other. "With respect," said Trewin again. "This isn't the first hit, as you call it, that your share price has taken. There was another at the beginning of the year."

Wilson stared at Trewin, as if to ask who invited him to the meeting. But the other man didn't flinch. Oliver Trewin was a tall, distinguished-looking man whose every word was a study in charm and civility. But rewind forty-five years, and he had been an officer in the SAS. Borneo. He knew a thing or two about playing rough. Besides, one way or another, either with a deal or without, he was leaving BritEnergy. He had nothing to lose.

"Listen," said Wilson, and he talked straight at Andrew Bassett, trying to cut Trewin out of the conversation. "You should ask yourself why this article appeared. You should ask yourself who it's aimed at. If you ask me, it's aimed at you, Andy."

Wilson paused, letting the point sink in. He could see that he had Bassett thinking now.

"You're being suckered, Andy. Think about it. Someone does this, you walk away, you want to know what's going to happen next? The very same person leaks that you were about to cut a deal. You know what? You're still in play, but this time you've got no floor. Hell, forget twelve-point-five. Forget eleven-point-six. You've got nothing."

"We're not walking away, Mike," said Bassett. "We never said—"

"No? You may be a lot closer to that than you think." Wilson stared pointedly at Bassett, making sure he got the message.

Bassett glanced uneasily at Trewin. Anthony Warne, taking notes on the other side of him, put down his pen.

"Now, I'm going to ask you something," said Wilson, still gazing straight at Andrew Bassett. "I'm going to ask you straight, Andy. Because I want to do this deal. I'm here to do it, understand? So I'm going to ask you. Are you shopping yourself around? Is Morgan Stanley out there shopping you around?"

"No," said Bassett.

Wilson kept his eyes fixed on him. "This deal is not going to sit here stewing while your investment bankers go looking for a higher bid. You understand me? This is not an open offer. It's not indefinite. You think about whether you want to lose that. Twelve-point-five billion. Think about it. Twelve-point-five billion. Do you really think you're going to do better than that?"

"Mike," said Bassett. He took a very deep breath and let it out slowly. "This is a very attractive offer. We understand that. We appreciate it. And I promise you, we are not looking for anybody else. We do not want to be put in play. Before you approached us, we weren't looking for a deal. You know that."

"Are you telling me that's not what Morgan Stanley's telling you?" demanded Wilson. "You telling me they're not saying they can get you a higher offer?"

"I don't think we should discuss Morgan Stanley," said Trewin.

"Andy?"

"I think, if we can just have a few more weeks . . ."

"A few more *weeks*?" said Wilson incredulously.

"If we can just let things settle down for a few weeks . . . so the board can see that the volatility's gone, everything's stable, then I think there wouldn't be any—"

"Forget it," said Wilson. He got up. "Come on, Lyall. Stan."

Bassett looked at him in shock. "But . . ."

"You don't have a few more weeks."

"All I'm saying—"

"You don't have it! You've got today!"

Lyall Gelb looked at the men on the other side in alarm. Wilson had gone too far, he was sure.

"But . . . why?" asked Bassett.

Lyall froze. That was the question, the one they didn't have an answer to. Not one they could give, anyway. He waited to see what Wilson would say. Like everyone else. On the other side of the table, the three men were watching Wilson intently.

"You can't keep the secrecy together that long," said Wilson.

"But no one outside this room—"

"I'm not a patient man. Right or wrong, that's not how I am. You're not the only company we're looking at. The fit's great with you, you know it is, but there are others. So if you're not interested, get out of the line. Now, you have twelve-point-five billion on the table." Wilson leaned forward. He tapped the table with the flat of his hand a couple of times, as if the money were sitting right there in front of them. Then he looked at his watch. "It's here until twelve noon today, then it's gone. If you think you can get a better offer elsewhere, I suggest you get up and leave right now."

Bassett and Trewin exchanged a glance.

Wilson watched them closely. He had them, just about. Or did he? Maybe he shouldn't have said they had until twelve o'clock. Suddenly he sensed that if Andrew Bassett and Oliver Trewin got up and walked out, as he was daring them to do—even if they said they just wanted to go away and think about it until noon—they were gone. He had to keep them here. And Trewin, he knew . . . Trewin would want to get up. And Bassett . . . Bassett . . .

Bassett was about to say something.

"However, I do think your board is going to need reassurance," said Wilson abruptly. "After the volatility, I can understand their concern. Andy, I want to make sure you're in a position to give them that." Mike Wilson sat down. "This deal is exceptionally strong. I don't think there's any question that the price we've offered is very generous."

"Mike," said Bassett, "this isn't about trying to get more—"

"I am, however, prepared to raise the cash component of our offer."

Lyall Gelb stared at Wilson. Along with everyone else in the room.

"Our original offer was four-point-two in cash and the rest in stock. I think we can raise that to fifty-fifty, don't you, Lyall?" As he said it, Wilson turned calmly to Lyall Gelb.

"Umm . . . ahh . . ." Gelb was lost for words. Fifty-fifty? That was 6.25 in cash—$6.25 billion in cash that they were going to have to raise.

"Andy?" said Wilson, turning back amiably to Bassett, like a man who knows he's just offered something too good to be refused.

"I think that would make a considerable difference to our board's view," said Bassett slowly.

Trewin's expression remained set. Mike Wilson glanced at him and saw it.

Wilson stood up. "There's a couple of things I'd like to discuss privately with Andy," he said. "I wonder if you could give us a few minutes. Lyall? Stan?"

Lyall and Stan got up.

Trewin shook his head. "I believe we were going to have until twelve—"

"Andy?" said Wilson, cutting across Trewin's protest.

Bassett nodded. He looked pointedly at Trewin. Anthony Warne stood up. Slowly, Oliver Trewin got up from the table as well.

They stood in a small, uneasy group outside the closed door of Mike Wilson's suite.

There was an awkward silence.

Trewin looked at Lyall Gelb. "Doesn't have any inhibition letting people know what he thinks, does he, your Mr. Wilson?"

"Mike usually gets what he wants," replied Lyall guardedly.

"Yes," murmured Trewin. "I shouldn't wonder that he does."

Silence again.

Anthony Warne whispered something in Trewin's ear, and Trewin nodded, and they moved off down the corridor. They stopped farther away and began to talk about something.

"You didn't know that was coming, did you?" said Stan Murdoch. "Raising the cash stake?"

Lyall Gelb didn't reply.

"No. Didn't think you did."

None of them knew how long they'd be waiting, so they stayed in the corridor, Trewin and Warne at one end and Lyall and Stan at the other. Lyall and Stan felt awkward. They had never been close—they were too different in their outlooks—and the role Gelb had played in the deal had eroded the small amount of trust Stan did have in him.

Soon Murdoch pulled out his cell phone and started talking to one of his plant managers in Europe. Gelb got out his phone and gave his finance director in Hungary a call.

Almost half an hour had gone by when the door to Wilson's suite opened again.

"Come in, guys," said Mike Wilson.

They filed in, wondering what they were going to find.

Bassett was sitting where he had been when they went out. Wilson gestured at the table. "Take a seat," he said to them. "Sorry about asking you to wait like that. Andy and I had a few things to run over."

Bassett nodded. He looked very pleased about something.

"To summarize," said Wilson, when they were sitting, "we're at twelve-point-five, fifty-fifty cash and stock, and we announce Friday week."

"Friday week?" said Anthony Warne in surprise. "But we were going to announce on the following Monday. And we've lost two days!"

"Anthony," said Bassett. "It'll be perfectly all right. We'll manage."

"Any other points?" asked Wilson. "Any questions?" He looked around.

"Gentlemen?" said Bassett, avoiding Oliver Trewin's eyes.

They waited.

"Good," said Wilson. "Then the only question I have is whether it's too early for champagne."

27

Anthony Warne sat in the front passenger seat of Bassett's Bentley. Bassett and Trewin were in the back. There was silence between them all the way to the office on account of the driver.

When they got back, Oliver Trewin followed Bassett into his office. Uninvited, he sat down.

"You think you'll enjoy working for that man?" he asked.

"It won't be forever," said Bassett. He leaned on the edge of his desk, as if to make clear to Trewin that he needn't bother settling in for a long conversation. "Besides, I think Mike Wilson is a very prag-matic man."

Trewin wondered what had been said during the time when Bassett and Wilson were closeted together.

"You seem very confident about this deal, Andrew."

"Why shouldn't I be?" replied Bassett. "The logic is sound. Just as sound as it was when we agreed to it last week."

"Call me old-fashioned, but I do rather take a step back when someone ups the price they're offering before I've even said no."

"They didn't up the price."

Trewin looked at Bassett knowingly. Increasing the cash compo-nent was just as meaningful. "I only hope the combined company can service the debt," said Trewin.

"Well, that won't be your concern, Oliver, will it? Their finance man seems relaxed about it."

Trewin laughed at that. "Could have knocked him over with a feather! Did you see the look on his face? He hadn't the slightest idea that was coming. No more than you or I."

Andrew Bassett didn't join in the laughter. He didn't welcome this conversation and wished Oliver Trewin would go away.

"Well, yes, I'm sure he was quite relaxed," said Trewin, and chuck-led to himself. "I think they really did believe we were going to put ourselves on the market! See, Andrew? I told you dropping Morgan Stanley's name into the conversation yesterday would spice things up."

"Yes," said Bassett drily. "Very clever. Almost lost us Wilson's trust altogether."

"Nonsense, Andrew! Brought him running. In fact, don't you think Mr. Wilson was in just a little too much of a hurry? Again, call me old-fashioned, but when someone bangs on the table and says I've ten minutes to decide and then offers me more even before I've had a chance—"

"Maybe you are a little old-fashioned, Oliver," said Bassett point-edly. "We talked about a number of things when you were out of the room."

"Really? And may one inquire . . . ?"

"Mike asked how long you had been with the company."

Trewin smiled. He had been with BritEnergy before it had that name, or even existed. The organization he had originally joined was the British national electricity supplier when it was still in public ownership. BritEnergy was one of the companies that had been carved out of it during privatization. Mrs. Thatcher had seen to that, as to so many other things in the British economy.

"He thought you ought to have some special recognition when you leave," said Bassett. "Over and above what you'd normally be getting, of course. Something extra. So many years of service, et cetera."

"All in the line of duty," murmured Trewin.

"Don't be modest, Oliver. We were thinking something in the order of . . . a million, perhaps? Plus a handful of options. A rather large handful. Might come in handy, eh?"

Trewin raised an eyebrow.

"If the deal goes through, of course," said Bassett.

"Ah . . . yes . . ."

"Don't fight this, Oliver," said Bassett quietly. "What's the point? It's going to happen. May as well make it a pleasant experience for everyone, eh? Yourself included."

Trewin watched him.

Bassett smiled. "The due diligence, Oliver. We're going to need to do it rather quickly. With fifty percent in cash, I don't think we need to get caught up in the details, do we?"

"I'm sure we don't, Andrew," murmured Trewin. "I'm sure it will be very straightforward."

"Good. I'll leave that to you. Why don't you talk to the lawyers? Let them know."

Trewin nodded. "If you like."

"Good." Bassett rubbed his hands. "Well, rather a good morning's work all round, I think. Two billion more in cash. The shareholders can't complain."

"I was going to ask you, Andrew . . ."

Bassett smiled, waiting to hear Trewin's question.

"What were you about to say when Wilson offered you the extra cash?"

The smile stayed on Bassett's lips. As if stuck there, frozen.

"He'd asked whether we wanted to leave," said Trewin. "Remember? You were just about to answer him."

"Was I?" said Bassett. "I'm sure I can't remember."

"Ah," said Trewin. He smiled. "Must be mistaken."

"Yes, you must be," said Bassett.

Trewin got up to go.

"Oliver?"

He stopped.

"Better make sure our data room is open. Let them know. Straight away, if you wouldn't mind. We wouldn't want to keep their people hanging about any longer. It's not polite."

"Of course, Andrew."

Oliver Trewin went back to his office.

He sat down at his desk. A million pounds, he thought, plus options. For a deal that was going to happen anyway. Why fight it? Why indeed?

He smiled wryly to himself. Andrew Bassett, he thought, that man will eat you alive.

Lyall Gelb was still in shock. He had taken a single sip of champagne, if that, when Wilson toasted the deal. He had raised the glass for appearance's sake. The fluid burned his lips.

"Mike," he said when the BritEnergy executives were gone, "where are we going to get the money?"

"We'll get it," said Wilson.

"Did you clear this with Stanzy?"

Wilson didn't reply. He turned to look out the window at the view of Hyde Park. The trees were golden with autumn foliage.

"Two billion more, Mike. Two billion!"

"Leave it to me," growled Wilson, still staring at the park.

"What do you mean, leave it to you?" Lyall clutched at his belly. "Where are we going to get it? Two billion! You heard what Stanzy said. No more cash. Jiminy Creeper, Mike!"

"I said leave it to me! I'll speak with Stanzy. They'll raise it. Hell, you think those greedy bastards won't? They've got no deal if they don't."

Lyall looked at Stan Murdoch. Stan didn't respond.

Pain sliced through Lyall's stomach. This was madness. An extra two billion? This was out of control.

"Lyall," said Wilson coldly. "Get on a plane back to the States. Go home to your family."

Lyall shook his head in disbelief. He dropped into a chair.

"Stan, you stay here. Go take a look at their data room tomorrow. See if there's anything we should know about. From tomorrow, you can talk with Anthony Adams, their director of operations. You're both cleared."

"Anything you want to know in particular?" said Stan quietly.

"I'll leave that to you," replied Wilson, hoping that would make Stan feel valued. "You're the expert. Just make sure you talk to me first about anything you find."

"What about you?" asked Stan.

"I'm taking the jet on to Hungary."

"You got business there tonight?"

Wilson looked at him sharply. "Yeah," he said. "I got business there."

28

It was going to be a hell of a call. Even for Mike Wilson, this one was going to take some chutzpah.

The phone was on a small mahogany table under the window. Beyond it, through the glass, were the gold-tinted trees of the park. When he picked up that phone, he knew, he was going to have to go in hard. Not show the slightest doubt about what he'd done. Not concede for a second that he'd given away any more than was absolutely necessary.

One more piece of acting, he thought wearily. One last effort before he could get on the jet and forget about everything. For a night. He closed his eyes, imagining the casino in Budapest. Imagining how he'd feel when he took his seat and watched the first hand going down on the baize in front of him.

He opened his eyes, took a deep breath, and picked up the phone.

"Say that again, Mike," said Pete Stanzy in New York when he had heard what Wilson had called to tell him.

"We've gone fifty-fifty cash and stock on the deal."

"No, Mike." The words came out of Pete's mouth automatically. He was gazing at the bullpen, still trying to take in what he had just heard. What he still hoped he hadn't heard.

"What's wrong with you, Pete?" demanded Wilson. "Can't you hear me?"

"Mike, Mike . . ." Stanzy shook his head in bewilderment. "You were going to tell Bassett he had to make up his mind, the offer wasn't indefinite. Isn't that what we agreed? He delays, you walk. That was the line, right?"

"Yeah," said Wilson.

"Well?" said Stanzy, almost begging, almost pleading for Wilson to start over and say that was what he had done.

"Bassett was holding out on me, Pete. He was looking for a kick in the price. I had to make a decision. I'm not going to give him any more on the price, right? But—"

"How could he be seriously asking more on the price?" demanded Stanzy. "Twelve-point-five! Jesus Christ, Mike. How could you seriously believe that? What the fuck are you—"

"You gonna tell me how to negotiate?" yelled Wilson down the phone. "I was there, you understand me? You weren't! I was the one in the room!"

Stanzy was silent, too angry to say anything. There was no need to have given Bassett anything, price or cash. Nothing. Under no circumstances.

"Now listen to me, Pete," said Wilson. "He was holding out on the price. Believe me."

"How do you know?"

"He said it! Right upfront. His chairman said the price wasn't enough, what with their attractiveness in the market. Starts talking about their portfolio of assets and all this crap. So I said, that's it, we can't do anything on price, you've got the best deal you're ever gonna get. Make your mind up, the offer closes today. And what does he do?"

"What?" inquired Stanzy mechanically. It was beyond belief.

"Bassett gets up. He physically gets up from the table. He's walking. So I say, Listen, there's no way I can budge on price. But it's a strong deal, a good deal, and I want to do it. So let's see whether we can't put some more cash into it. And he sits down again."

"Does he?" muttered Stanzy. "Isn't that a surprise?"

"Sits down, and I say, Okay, let's see what we can do. So he sits down and says he wants sixty-forty. I say there's no way we can do that. So he's about to get up again. So I say, Let's do it fifty-fifty."

"And he accepted that?"

"He did."

Stanzy bet he did. He shook his head in disgust.

"So, that's where we are," said Wilson. "I had no choice. Fifty-fifty. We announce Friday week."

"Fifty-fifty," murmured Stanzy, thinking of what John Golansky was going to say when he told him. "Mike, that's six-point-two-five billion. Do you realize that?"

Wilson laughed. "Hell, Pete. I negotiated it. Of course I realize it."

Stanzy didn't see what was so funny. "Don't you think you should have spoken to me about this before you offered it?" He was no longer thinking about what John Golansky was going to say. He couldn't even imagine how he was going to tell him.

"Come on, Pete," said Wilson cajolingly. "You guys can cover it."

"Mike, I don't think you understand. That's a full two billion more than we agreed."

"I can do the math, Pete."

"Then maybe you can tell me where it's coming from?"

"Same place the rest is coming from," replied Wilson amiably.

"No, it's not!" Something in Pete Stanzy snapped. "We are struggling to get the four-point-two, Mike. Do you understand that? We are struggling. I'm gonna tell you something. For some reason, your name as a debtor isn't exactly pure and virgin out there in the market. You understand what I mean?"

"I don't need you to tell me—"

"Well, you fucking need someone! We are *struggling* to get you four-point-two! You are *this* far above junk! I want you to understand that. People are talking about you, Mike. Merrill is saying things."

"Fuck Merrill!" Wilson yelled back. "You believe what they're saying?"

"Doesn't matter if I believe them! What matters is what other people believe!" Pete Stanzy was beside himself with anger. He could see the deal slipping away because of this ludicrous offer Wilson had just made, this offer that was utterly unnecessary. There were simply no circumstances he could imagine that could have required Wilson to do that. The deal was going to slip away because they weren't going to get the cash to finance it. This big, beautiful deal with the big, fat forty bips waiting for him at the end of it. His deal. If Wilson had been standing in front of him, Stanzy probably would have tried to throttle him.

"Come on, Pete," said Wilson again, jocular.

The lightheartedness in Wilson's tone just aggravated Stanzy even more. "You don't understand, do you?" he yelled. "We're going to be getting you junk, Mike! Junk! If you're lucky! If we can even find it. Is that what Buffalo wants? Is their board gonna go for that?"

"Pete, relax. Combine the balance sheets and it's still strong. Even with the extra two billion."

"It's not the balance sheet people are worried about! It's what's not on the balance sheet!"

Wilson was silent.

"You hear me, Mike? You hear what I just said?"

"What's not on the balance sheet?" said Wilson quietly. "What do you mean, Pete?"

"You tell me, Mike."

"It's all in the filings. Everything we've got that's off the balance sheet. We've got three billion of debt in special-purpose entities. It's there in black and white. Everyone knows it."

"And that's it?"

"That's it."

"Are you prepared to sign a document to that effect?"

"Jesus Christ, Pete! What are you accusing me of? Everything's audited. Everything's—"

"Are you prepared to sign a document to that effect?" demanded Pete Stanzy again.

"What is this?" retorted Wilson. "Is this a condition of you continuing as my banker?"

"Yes," said Pete Stanzy. "It is."

There was silence. In London, Mike Wilson stared at the autumn trees in the park. In New York, Pete Stanzy stared down at the traffic on Forty-fifth Street.

Stanzy didn't quite know how he had reached this point. He desperately wanted this deal. It was the biggest deal he'd ever done or even come close to doing. Yet he had just demanded his client's personal statement of honesty in the bluntest terms possible, and threatened to walk away if he didn't get it. He had never done anything like that before, never even considered doing it. Or anything remotely approaching it. But he just couldn't go back to John Golansky, not after their last conversation, and ask for another two billion. Not without something to back him up. Although what a piece of paper with Mike Wilson's personal guarantee was worth wasn't clear. Even as he stood there with the phone in his hand, waiting to hear what Wilson was going to say, Stanzy realized the absurdity of asking for it. He couldn't believe the story Wilson had just told him about the meeting with Bassett. Why should he believe anything Wilson signed?

In London, Mike Wilson was still thinking about it. Swallowing his pride. "All right," he said.

"I appreciate that, Mike."

"I won't be back in the States until tomorrow."

Stanzy didn't say anything to that. His silence was pointed.

"Jesus Christ!" said Wilson. "All right, I'll speak to our counsel and get him to draw something up. He'll fax it to me here and I'll sign, then I'll fax it to you." Mike Wilson paused. "Will a fax do?" he asked, and Stanzy could hear the belligerency creeping back into his tone.

"That'll be fine, Mike."

"You're screwing things up for me here, Stanzy. I'm meant to be flying out of here right now."

"I'm sorry, Mike. If you just do it like you said, that'll be great."

"Yeah." Wilson laughed sarcastically. But his mind was already moving on. Let Pete Stanzy humiliate him if he dared. It was a small price to pay, and once this deal was done, just let Dyson Whitney try to get any more business from him. Right now, he still needed them to raise the loan or the deal wouldn't go through. Everything else was set. After this morning, he had Bassett in his pocket. Oliver Trewin had looked like he might make things difficult, but Wilson was confident he had disposed of that threat as well. He didn't like the man, but he would happily give him a payoff if that would buy his cooperation. The boards of the two companies were lined up. Nothing else stood in his way. The loan was the last remaining obstacle, and if his signature on a piece of paper meant he was going to get over it, that was one signature he could certainly provide.

"Mike," said Stanzy, "I really appreciate it."

"Yeah," replied Wilson, and he slammed the phone down.

Pete Stanzy took the fax up to John Golansky's office.

"I've been speaking with Mike Wilson," said Pete. He didn't know any easy way to say it, so he just went ahead. "He wants another two billion."

John Golanksy started laughing.

"He recut the deal, John. Fifty-fifty, stock and cash. They announce Friday week."

Golansky stopped laughing. "You're serious, aren't you?"

Pete Stanzy nodded. He put Wilson's fax on the desk.

"What's this?" asked Golansky.

"It's the best I could do, John."

Golanksy read it. "What? I'm supposed to frame this?"

"Come on, John. We don't get this loan arranged, we don't get the deal. We don't get the deal, we get nothing. And we both look like jerks."

Golansky read over the fax again, a look of distaste on his face. "Anyone who signs something like this, it just makes me think he's an even bigger crook than before. Bruce Rubinstein's gonna love it. You want to go show him?"

Pete sat down across the desk from Golansky. "He's not a crook,

John. He's just given away a little more cash than we agreed. We've got to help him raise it."

"He's not a five-year-old, Pete. He ought to have—" Golansky stopped. His eyes narrowed. "You didn't tell him he could offer more cash, did you?"

"Are you out of your mind?"

Golanksy continued to watch him suspiciously for a moment. Then he sat back in his chair. "Bruce Rubinstein's gonna love it," he murmured to himself again. He shrugged. "What do you want me to do, Pete? Tell me. You want me to go to junk? You want me to raise this money whatever the cost? He's gonna be paying fifteen percent on this debt."

"Just get the money," said Stanzy.

"Just get the money," murmured John Golansky. "Even at fifteen percent, I don't know if I could. We were hitting the wall at four-point-two, Pete. Now you're looking for half as much again."

"You can't get it?"

"Their balance sheet stinks. Every day I look at it, it stinks more."

"Yeah, but BritEnergy's strong."

"Brit Energy's strong . . ." Golansky sat forward. "Let me tell you what I think. I think your boy and his whiz kid of a CFO have been up to a few tricks. I think the market's starting to figure it out, and they don't like it." Golansky glanced at the fax from Wilson again. "You think that's possible, Pete?"

Stanzy shrugged.

"Tell me," said Golansky, "what do you really think about this deal?" He looked Stanzy straight in the eye. "Level with me, Pete."

Pete Stanzy and John Golansky liked each other. They pretty much trusted each other—to the extent that any two people can trust each other in a world where a multimillion-dollar bonus may depend on one person not letting the other know all of what he knows, even if they're supposedly batting for the same team. And from the very start, they had both wanted this deal. But they wanted different parts of it. Stanzy wanted the acquisition to be made, the money and stock to be handed over to BritEnergy's shareholders. When that happened, the bank would earn its advisory fee and the bulk of his bonus was safe. Golanksy wanted the debt, not just the bridge loan that would finance the deal in the first instance, but the bonds he would then sell to investors over six months to pay back the bridge. When the bonds were sold, the bank would earn the other part of its fee, and his bonus was secure. Pete Stanzy needed the combined Louisiana Light and BritEnergy company to last all of three minutes. Golansky needed it to survive six months.

They both knew it. And they both knew that each one's trust for the other had its limits.

"Huh, Pete?" said Golansky. "What do you say? Really?"

Stanzy thought about it carefully. "From my client's perspective, I think this is one of those deals. . . . If it happens, everything's great. And if it doesn't, maybe everything isn't."

"Can you be more specific?"

"Honestly, John, I can't. I don't *know* anything. It's just a feeling."

"So it's like a kind of Hail Mary deal?" said Golansky, who had been a football player.

Stanzy nodded. "Something like that."

"Really?"

"Yeah. I think so."

Golansky considered it.

"A Hail Mary deal with a fucking big fee for us on the end of it."

"That's a point," murmured Golansky.

They looked at each other.

"Bruce Rubinstein's gonna love this," muttered Golanksy again.

"Fuck Rubinstein."

"Yeah," said Golanksy. "Fuck him."

Stanzy got up to go.

"Pete," said Golansky. "You know the stake the firm was going to raise on its own account?"

Stanzy nodded.

"We might not do that. Huh? Maybe it's not such a great idea."

29

A shutdown in a Lousiana Light plant in Argentina had hit at around eight A.M. local time. In London, Stan Murdoch spent the afternoon on the phone in his hotel room trying to help resolve it. He was given ten different reasons before he received what sounded like a sensible explanation, involving a faulty heat gauge that had tripped the system. But that might just be another false lead, or another lie someone was telling to shift the blame from themselves. By then, Ernesto Poblán, his deputy for South America, had arrived on location, and Stan left it to him.

Stan Murdoch wasn't ready to retire. He loved what he did. But he was sixty-one. If Mike Wilson got rid of him after he did this deal, who was going to take him? Who'd hire an operations director at sixty-one?

It wasn't a question of money. Money had never been a big factor for Stan. The older he got—and the more he had of it—the less important it was. By his own standards, he had plenty, anyway, more than he could ever have imagined when he enrolled for engineering at state college in Wyoming back in 1967. It had been a big subject of discussion in the family, whether he should go to college or stay on the ranch. Those were the days when you could still make money running cattle on a family ranch. But he was the smart one. His two brothers, Max and Art, didn't even finish high school. They needed the ranch more than he did. So Stan went to college, but the lean, Spartan ethos of the Wyoming rancher was in his blood.

How much money did he need, anyway? His wife, Greta, was happy. They had a nice big house in Baton Rouge and a cabin at Breaux Bridge where he went summers to fish. They had a good pension coming, when that day arrived. Maybe when Stan retired they'd sell the place in Baton Rouge and buy a farm somewhere and have a couple of horses. They'd talked about it, kind of go back to the way of life from which they'd both started. Their kids had gone through college and had their own families. Sometimes Stan helped them out, but they weren't in need.

For Stan, that was probably the most insulting thing about this whole sorry tale. Not the way Mike Wilson had kept the deal secret from him for so long, or the way Lyall Gelb and even Doug Earl— Doug Earl, who wasn't anything more than a jumped-up country lawyer sitting in a big fancy office down the hall from Mike—knew about it before him, but the way Wilson had offered him a fistful of cash to get out of the way. Like that was all he was, an obstacle that a couple of million bucks could remove. It was sad. Showed how much Mike Wilson had changed. Time was when he would have known better than to make an offer like that to Stan.

Nine years before, when Mike Wilson called up and asked Stan to come over and head up operations at Louisiana Light, he would have known. Stan agreed to come to Baton Rouge because he figured he'd be able to go out there and build a great operation and he figured that was Mike Wilson's idea as well. At first it panned out like that. They bought a couple of good plants and added them to the portfolio. But things changed. Mike lost interest in the day-to-day operations. He got big ideas, he wanted to buy all kinds of things. Then Lyall Gelb appeared and suddenly they were buying god-awful plants in Colombia and Europe and God knows where, and they were creating all kinds of companies in all kinds of places and Stan didn't know where the money was coming from or where it was going. Stan didn't understand Lyall Gelb. He was sure he was a finance whiz, as Mike kept saying, but he just didn't understand what made him tick. Lyall was a city boy; Stan came from a ranch in Wyoming. They could have been two different species. The installations Mike kept buying were dirty, almost derelict old plants that you couldn't run properly no matter how much money you threw at them. But no matter how often Stan told him, Mike would laugh it off and go buy something else. "I'll buy 'em, you run 'em," Mike kept saying. Stan sweated blood to get those plants up. He was proud of what he achieved, but he had it in perspective. He knew just how bad these plants were even after he'd gotten all the improvements out of them that were humanly possible. But it was as if Mike didn't care; all that mattered was the next purchase, and the next one, and the one after that. Stan just didn't know how the company could go on. Mike laughed it off. "The stock price doesn't lie, Stan," he would say. "Just look at the stock price."

Mike was right about that. The stock price kept going up. Stan didn't know how that could happen when the plants were so poor and the operations so bad. He didn't understand how these things worked. He figured somehow it must have something to do with Lyall Gelb and all the financial stuff he was doing, but he didn't trust that, either. When you came right down to it, if your operations weren't good, how could the value of your company keep going up? Stan didn't understand much about finance, but he figured he knew enough to understand that. There came a point where he decided to sell every Louisiana Light share that he owned. After that, he exercised every option the day it vested. Wilson didn't like it. It didn't look good, the operations director bailing out of the stock at every opportunity. "You're crazy, Stan," Mike would say, trying to persuade him to hold some stock. "Don't you want to be rich?" And it was true, if he'd held on to his stock, and if he'd sold it a year, or two years, or three years later than he had, he'd be a wealthier man. But Stan didn't understand what was happening at the company. And he didn't trust what he didn't understand.

Over the years, the company had changed. It went from the head down, as it always does. First, there was the company jet. With the new international plants, they needed one, Mike said. It would save the company money. But the jet went a lot of other places as well. Mike's wife at the time, and then his girlfriends spent plenty of time onboard. Stan knew for a fact that on more than one occasion it had been used to fly Mike's kids to Europe on vacation. That was plain wrong. Mike bought a corporate chalet in Aspen. To entertain clients, he said. And there was the company apartment in Manhattan. The kind of executives had changed as well. Young, greedy, only worried about the number of stock options they had in their pockets.

For a while now, Stan hadn't known what kind of a place he worked in anymore. It wasn't the same place as the one he arrived at nine years earlier. Not his kind of place. He had seen the same thing happen at InterNorth back in the eighties, the same excess, the same greed, all coming from the top. And InterNorth had fallen like a ripe apple to the grasping hand of Ken Lay.

In the InterNorth days, Mike Wilson had been at any poker game going. Spent weekends in Vegas. Back then, he was open about it, almost boastful. Now, you never heard him talk about gambling. But that only made Stan suspicious. Gamblers don't just stop, he knew. He was pretty sure Mike was gambling again. A couple of times, when they had been abroad together, Mike disappeared for the night. In Budapest. In Bogotá. What was in those cities that was so attractive to him? A woman? Or one of the casinos? More often, Mike found a reason to go on somewhere in the jet and told Stan to catch a commercial flight home. Like today, when he said he had to go to Hungary. For business.

If Mike was secretly gambling, it just made Stan feel more nervous, more uncomfortable with the place Louisiana Light had become. It seemed to him it was a house built on sand. Stan didn't know how or where or what would make it happen, but he feared that anytime now it might creak, lean, and come crashing down.

Somewhere in the back of his mind he had begun to wonder if the British guy, Bassett, might be able to restore some sanity to the madhouse that had become Louisiana Light. Maybe he could work with him. But now Murdoch had seen the other man and he wasn't impressed. Mike Wilson was going to walk all over him. As Stan sat watching the two of them, he wondered how he could ever have imagined it might be otherwise.

Nothing was going to change. With a bigger company for Wilson to play with, it was probably going to get worse. Deal or no deal, Murdoch felt, the house on sand was coming down. Wilson's desperation to do the deal only made it seem more certain. But it would take two companies with it, rather than one, if the deal went ahead.

That night he called Greta. They talked about stuff. Not business, other stuff. Family stuff. He told Greta he'd be staying over in London the next day, probably back on Thursday. She wanted to know if he was all right. She must have heard something in his voice. How long had they known each other? Forty-plus years. High-school sweethearts. If Greta didn't know his mind, who did? She knew when something was troubling him. But she knew if he wasn't ready to talk, there was no point asking.

He didn't sleep much that night. Thoughts kept going through his head. Sometime during those long dark hours in a London hotel room something happened to Stan Murdoch. He faced up to the truth. Something was seriously wrong with Lousiana Light, and he had known all along. Not the details, but that something bad was happening. Yet he had put on a pair of blinders, pretended that all he had to worry about were the operations of the company's plants and that he had no responsibility for anything else. And the truth was, he did have responsibility. He was a director. He should have asked, not just signed whatever documents Mike or Lyall Gelb or Doug Earl put in front of him, telling himself no one could expect him to understand them. It wasn't good enough to say he couldn't understand. It was his duty to understand, or keep asking until he did.

There were names in his mind, names that had been there a long time. Subsidiaries, joint ventures, entities that had been set up for reasons he never understood or wanted to know. Nothing to do with operations. The truth was, Stan Murdoch didn't know the first thing about the intricacies of the financial structures that Lyall Gelb had been creating at Louisiana Light over the past six years. He didn't know how Lyall had managed to park the company's excess debt, but he guessed that Lyall had. And he could guess where the bodies were buried. Some of them, anyway. There were names that had kept coming back over the years, names mentioned in documents that referred to other documents that he never got a sight of. Two names in particular. There was something about the way Mike and Lyall spoke whenever they mentioned them.

It would be going too far to say that during that sleepless night Stan Murdoch decided what he was going to do. It would be going too far to say that he had consciously decided he was going to do anything at all. Everything in his mind was still confused, disjointed. But he had crossed a certain threshold, and crossing that threshold had freed him to confront the reality of Louisiana Light, of the sick place it had become, and of the way it would infect another company if Mike Wilson got his hands on it. It forced him to confront his own responsibility. And for a man like Stan Murdoch, once you owned up to a responsibility—even if it was years after you should have—you couldn't just ignore it. You had to do something. He just didn't know what it was yet, or how he was going to do it.

The next morning, Stan Murdoch got up troubled, tired, and unhappy, and headed for the Stamfields office building. He was ushered from the reception area to the BritEnergy data room. As he left the elevator and walked toward it with the woman who was accompanying him, he was unaware that it had been open to Dyson Whitney since after the meeting with the Buffalo executives the previous day and that Cynthia Holloway and Rob Holding, having worked there all night, were just getting ready to leave.

30

They had gone in at noon, shortly after the Leopard-Buffalo meeting had broken up and the message had bounced from London to New York and back to Cynthia Holloway in London to let them know the data room was open.

The same woman who had turned them away the previous day came to the Stamfields reception to get them. She smiled icily at Cynthia, who smiled icily back. Rob shook his head. Brits! The woman gave them a pair of visitors' passes and took them down to the twenty-first floor and through a code-controlled door. The data room was a large, windowless meeting room. On the way in, the woman showed them where there were bathrooms they could use without having to go through any access points. She gave them the numerical code to get into the data room. When they were ready to leave, she said, they should ring reception and someone would come to get them. Every part of the building was access controlled, and under no circumstances were they to try to go anywhere else unaccompanied. They would be immediately ejected if they did. If they needed anything, they should call reception. It was staffed twenty-four hours and they could work as late as they liked.

"What if there's a fire?" asked Rob, only half jokingly. "Do we call reception then?"

The woman pointed seriously to a floor plan tacked to the back of the door, with the fire exit marked in red. "Study your exit route. You'll be able to get out that way. Anything else?"

"No. Thank you," said Cynthia. Her accent had gotten more and more English over the past couple of days. Especially now, as if she were in some kind of Englishness competition with the Stamfields woman. "This is confidential data. Please leave us so we can get to work."

The woman looked at her archly. "Ring reception when you're ready to leave. Dial zero," she said, and she left.

Rob wouldn't have been surprised if she were heading straight to reception to tell them to ignore their calls.

Three sides of the data room were taken up with shelves holding row after row of box files, each with a handwritten label. Other boxes of files stood in stacks inside the door. In the middle of the room four desks had been placed together to create a large table, with ten seats around it. A single telephone sat in the middle of the table, its cord running down through the crack between two of the desks to a hatch in the floor, where there was a clutch of electrical points.

"Not bad," murmured Cynthia, glancing around at the shelving, as if she were a connoisseur of data rooms. She hoisted her computer bag onto the desk. "If we're lucky, we'll have the rest of the day to ourselves. The lawyers and accountants aren't here yet so they're probably still in New York. This place will be like Piccadilly Circus tomorrow."

"Sorry?" said Rob.

"Like Grand Central Station. Let's see if we can get out of here today."

Cynthia was all efficiency and practicality again. She had said nothing that morning about the conversation with Rob the previous evening, behaving as if it had never happened. Rob let it go. He understood. She probably regretted confiding in him.

"We need the budgets and business plans, right?" he said.

Cynthia nodded, unpacking her computer at the desk.

Rob went to the shelves.

"They could be anywhere," said Cynthia. "If they want to make life difficult for us, they'll put one part of the budget somewhere, and another file on the other side of the room. And others somewhere else. And of course they'll accidentally mislabel some of the boxes. Might take hours to find them."

And it might not, thought Rob. In front of him, at eye level, was a box file labeled BUDGETS. A half-dozen other boxes had the same name. He hauled them off the shelf.

"Great!" said Cynthia. "I'll start with those. You look for the business plans."

Under the harsh fluorescent light, Cynthia sat down and began working through the files. Pretty soon, she had piles of paper all around her.

Rob found the business plans. Pretty soon he was sitting at the desk with piles of paper around him as well.

At two o'clock they called down to reception and asked to be let out. They brought sandwiches and coffees back to the room. The desk was covered with files. Rob could see why Cynthia hoped to make it out today. With another eight people in here, the place would be a madhouse.

They kept crunching through the data, hoping no one else would turn up. Rob lost track of time. Could have been morning, evening, or night; it was all the same in that windowless room as his body clock wandered around like a lost soul somewhere out in the mid-Atlantic. At eight o'clock they went out for more food and came back with supplies. At midnight they were still going. They were both on New York time, five hours behind, so they were still pretty fresh. At three in the morning they estimated they had another two hours to go, and decided to keep going. At six they realized they'd underestimated. It was now one A.M. New York time, neither of them had had much sleep in the last couple of nights, and they were flagging. But if they stopped now, they knew, they'd crash and probably wouldn't be back until noon, when the place would be like Piccadilly Circus. Or Grand Central Station. They decided to crunch on.

At eight o'clock they were almost done. There were papers all over the desks, the chairs, the floor. Rob began packing them back into their boxes.

"How long are you going to be?" he asked.

"A few more minutes," said Cynthia.

"Can I take those?"

Cynthia nodded. "Just leave this one."

Rob packed up a set of files beside her. Cynthia kept working at the file she had open. At last she closed it.

"That's it," she said, shutting down her computer. "We're done. Let's get out before everyone else arrives."

As she spoke, the door opened. The woman who had shown them into the room the previous day had come in with a tall, lean man.

The woman stared at them for a moment, surprised to see that they were still there. Then she began to give the man the same set of instructions she had given them.

His face seemed familiar, thought Rob.

"Excuse me," said Cynthia, as the woman turned to go. "We're almost ready to leave. I wonder if you could take us down. We'll just be another couple of minutes."

The woman glanced at the number of box files that were still on the table, yet to be returned to the shelves. "I haven't time to wait."

"Well, we're just going to have to ask you to come back."

The woman looked at Cynthia impatiently. Then there was a chime from the phone she was carrying in her hand, a cordless internal phone that allowed her to be contactable from anywhere in the building.

"Trowbridge," she said curtly. She listened. "All right. I'll be down." She left the room.

Cynthia began to pack her computer away. "Everyone's going to want to see those ones," she said, pointing at a set of files that Rob was about to put away. "Make sure you put them where they can find them."

The man who had come with the Stamfields woman watched them. Rob glanced at him. He had blue eyes, leathery skin. The face was familiar, thought Rob again, he just couldn't quite place it.

He nodded at the man. Rob hadn't said a word. Sammy had told him not to say anything to anyone. Cynthia hadn't said anything to the man, either. It was obviously normal practice in a data room when you didn't know who you were with.

The man was just standing there. Not talking. Not moving. Just standing.

There were only a few files left on the table. "I'll call reception," said Cynthia.

But there was no need for Cynthia to call. The door opened, the woman from reception reappeared, and a half-dozen people poured in behind her. Suddenly there were loud American voices in the air, Grayson Arpel lawyers and DeGrave Peterhouse accountants who had flown in on the red-eye from New York. The woman from reception vainly tried to explain the rules. But the lawyers and accountants were already swarming around the table, grabbing places and unloading their computers.

Cynthia picked up her bag and went to the door. "You can take us out now," she said, trying to get the woman's attention. "We're finished."

Rob turned to a shelf to put the last file away. The noise of the others who had just arrived filled the room.

Suddenly he heard a voice right beside him in his ear, low, murmuring.

"If you want to know where the truth is, look at ExPar and Grogon."

Rob looked around. The man was next to him, pretending to be looking at the shelf, his hand on a file.

His voice dropped lower. "I'm the Deep Throat. You know about Deep Throat? If you want to know the truth about Louisiana Light, tell your guys to check out ExPar and Grogon when you do your due diligence. That's where the bodies are buried. Got it? ExPar and Grogon."

"Rob!" said Cynthia. "Come on! What are you waiting for?"

Rob nodded at her hurriedly. He looked around again. The man had stepped away.

Cynthia walked out the door. The Stamfields woman was looking at him impatiently.

Rob grabbed his computer bag and headed out. He glanced back as he left. He caught a glimpse of the man looking at the shelves, and then the door to the data room, full of jabbering lawyers and accountants, closed behind him.

Inside, Stan Murdoch let his head rest against a shelf. The metal was cool against his forehead. He felt weak, drained, yet with an enormous sense of calm, as if he had just made some kind of confession.

He hadn't known what he was going to do that morning when he came into the data room. Hadn't had a plan. He only knew that he hated this deal. He hated Wilson and Gelb and what they had done to the company. He hated himself for letting it happen, watching it all these years and not saying a word. It was too late to do anything about that now. But it wasn't too late to stop another company from being dragged down into the same pit.

Yet he hadn't decided anything. He was just full of guilt and anger and self-recrimination and a bunch of other powerful emotions.

And then the Stamfields woman opened the door to the data room and there were these two people inside stacking files on the shelves, and when one of them spoke it was obvious from her accent that they were Brits, and it was obvious they weren't from Stamfields because they had to be asked to be let out, and so Stan Murdoch drew the obvious conclusion. They were from BritEnergy, sorting out the materials in their data room. And then everyone else poured in and there was this moment of confusion, distraction, and suddenly it seemed to Stan that he knew what to do, someone had put the solution right in front of him, as if a way had been opened up for him just when he could see no exit. As long as he didn't hesitate.

Stan knew where the bodies were buried. Some of them. The chances of someone finding them in a week of due diligence in Louisiana Light's books were close to zero. But not if that person was told where to look.

He didn't know why he said he was Deep Throat. That was kind of corny, but it just came out. And then the names, the two names, they came out as if it were the most natural thing in the world. And the agitation and trouble he had felt went right out of him with them.

Stan closed his eyes as the lawyers and accountants jabbered behind him, still feeling the metal of the shelf against his brow. He felt a kind of peace. It was done now. He had done what he had to do. Now let whatever would happen happen.

31

The flight landed at JFK. They got a cab straight to the office and were there by three. Sammy and Phil Menendez were waiting for them.

"Well?" demanded Menendez. "What's the story?"

"Looks okay," said Cynthia. "No big surprises. They're rather bullish on the British and Australian markets, and they're expecting to double their cash flow on their Indian plants in the next three years, which is probably somewhat too optimistic. I can't see why it's going to happen."

"Fucking data room business plans," muttered Menendez.

"It's no big deal," said Rob. "The entire Indian operation is less than fifteen percent of their revenue. The overall variance is only a couple of points."

Sammy glanced at Menendez. "We'll run scenarios."

"What else?" demanded Menendez.

Cynthia shook her head.

"Nothing? You sure? Nothing I should know about?" Menendez looked at Rob. "Huh?"

"Nothing," said Rob.

Menendez glanced at Sammy. "Check this out, right? You know what to do. Make sure they get on with it."

Menendez left.

"What's been going on, Sammy?" asked Cynthia. "What was the holdup?"

Sammy explained as much as he knew, although he wasn't aware of the exact details of what had been happening, and he realized it. "Anyway, looks like they've agreed now. Announcing Friday week. Mike Wilson raised the offer to fifty-fifty stock and cash."

Rob and Cynthia stared at him.

Sammy nodded. "You should've heard the Shark when he found out."

"I'm glad I didn't," muttered Cynthia.

"No one's happy about it," said Sammy. "Wilson didn't need to do it."

"Why did he, then?" asked Rob.

"Who knows? Funny things happen to people when they want to cut a deal. The need takes over. Deal fever. Gets the better of them. They lose perspective."

It didn't get the better of Andrew Bassett, thought Rob. He had just walked away with an extra . . . what was it? Two billion in cash.

It just kept getting better, he thought. It just kept getting better and better.

But by now Rob knew more than to say what he was thinking to Sammy. He was pretty sure Sammy was aware of what had happened between him and Pete Stanzy. Something in the look Sammy had given him the morning after that encounter suggested he'd been informed. Menendez had probably told Sammy to let him know if there were any more problems. Rob figured there was nothing Menendez would have liked more than to hear that there were.

Just focus on your work, that's what Sammy would say. Just as Sammy did himself. Do what you've been told to do and don't ask questions that don't concern you. Besides, Sammy didn't have the answers. Not to the questions Rob had.

"You guys look beat," said Sammy.

Cynthia nodded. "We worked all night. I'm glad we did, though. The lawyers were all over the files when we got out of there."

"Rob?" said Sammy.

"Yeah, I'm pretty tired. But I'm okay."

"Okay. Listen up. The priority for you guys over the next couple of days is to recut the models using Buffalo's data. That's a scenario with their data on the upside, their data on the downside, as well as our base case and our scenarios. Cynthia, the model's yours. I suggest you use Rob to get the data together to create the assumptions for the scenarios and anything else you need."

"But they're still doing the deal, right?" said Rob. "This won't affect it."

"Not unless you found a nasty surprise."

"And it's not going to affect the price? That's already agreed, right?"

"Right."

"So why are we doing this?" Rob knew this kind of question was safe. This was the kind of rookie-type question, Rob had learned, that Sammy liked to hear.

Sammy explained. "Leopard's board will need to see this before they commit. It's part of the due diligence process, shows we've tested our assumptions against the target's. Also, we need to show projections in our document for the bridge loan. I've got the ones we've done already, but it helps if we can say the scenarios include Buffalo's own figures."

Rob nodded.

"I'm going to leave it to you. It's your call. Work as much as you think you need today, then go home and get some sleep. Just make sure we've got a first cut of the scenarios by end of day tomorrow."

Cynthia looked at Rob. "Keep going?"

"Sure."

They worked until about nine. By then, they were both fading.

When he left, Rob took his computer with him.

Emmy's voice on the phone sounded hurt. "I thought you were coming here."

Rob had gone back to his own apartment.

"You've got nothing to eat there," said Emmy.

Rob sighed. "I'm beat, Emmy. I couldn't eat anything anyway. We got off the plane and went straight to the office. Honestly, I haven't slept in forty hours. I'm going to bed."

"You could have gone straight to bed here. I made you some food."

"Honey, please. I'm beat. I'll come over tomorrow. I promise."

"Like when? Midnight?"

"Please, Emmy. I'm beat. I've got to be in the office at seven. I can't keep arguing."

"I'm not arguing."

"Emmy, I'm going to put the phone down."

Emmy didn't reply.

"Emmy, I love you. I'll see you tomorrow. I promise."

Emmy sighed. "Okay. I love you, too. I just wanted to see you to-night."

"I know. See you tomorrow?"

"Yeah. All right."

Rob put the phone down. He reached for his computer. The phone rang again. Rob picked it up wearily, thinking it was going to be Emmy.

"Hey," said a voice.

Rob didn't recognize it for a second, the tone was so flat. "Greg?"

"You got a minute? It's not too late, is it?"

"Well, I'm just back from . . ." Rob stopped himself. "No, it's not too late."

"Okay," said Greg. His voice was listless. He was by himself, he said. Louise and he were breaking up.

"Where is she now?" asked Rob.

"She went away for the week. Went to stay with a friend in Boston. We agreed I'd move out by the time she gets back on Sunday."

"Greg. I'm sorry to hear that, buddy."

"Yeah."

Rob wasn't really sorry to hear it, but Greg was in pain and Rob felt for him. He'd do whatever he could to help him through it. But it was necessary pain. In the long run, Greg would be better off without Louise.

Rob knew it was too early to tell him that now.

"You okay?"

"Yeah . . . kind of . . ."

"Listen, you know you can stay here, don't you?"

"Actually, that's why I was calling," said Greg. "Did you mean that when you said it?"

"Absolutely. This is like the first time I've been here in a week."

"It's just . . ." Greg paused. "I think I'm going to need a week or two to get my head together before I can think about finding somewhere new."

"It's fine, Greg. I'll make sure the place is ready." Rob looked around the living room as he spoke. The place hadn't been cleaned since the subletters left. On the other hand, it had hardly been lived in, either.

"Don't do anything," said Greg. "I'll fix it up."

"No, it'll be fine. Listen, we'll get together on the weekend and I'll give you a key. When did you say you have to be out?"

"Sunday?"

"You need help?"

"I can manage."

"I'll help. Okay, that's settled."

"Thanks, Rob."

"One thing, though."

"What?"

"Don't thank me, huh? That's a condition. You don't need to thank me." Rob paused. "Okay, we'll talk. Sunday, right?"

"Right."

Rob put the phone down. He opened his bag. Finally, he pulled out his computer.

Rob didn't know exactly what the man in the data room that morning had been trying to say. He didn't even know who that man was yet. But he knew where he had recognized him from. He had seen his picture somewhere in the pages of Louisiana Light's annual report. And whatever the man had said to him, Rob knew it was meant to be secret. That's what he meant by "Deep Throat," wasn't it? Deep Throat, the guy who told the Watergate reporters where to look. That's what the man in the data room that morning had been doing. Telling him where to look.

He hadn't had any time on the plane. For seven hours, Cynthia had been sitting beside him. She went to the bathroom once, but that was it. She didn't even sleep. And Rob didn't want to do anything to remind her of the man who had spoken to him in the data room.

The computer booted up. He opened a copy of the latest Louisiana

Light annual report. The familiar image of the report's front cover—the yellow and black Louisiana Light logo taking up the top half, a color picture of a cooling tower at sunset taking up the lower half—appeared.

Rob didn't know why the man had chosen him, but he had. And now he could either ignore it or take the hint.

He gazed at the cover image on the screen. He didn't have to go further. He could still shut the computer and put it away. It wasn't too late. He could forget what he'd heard in that room in London and just concentrate on doing his work, like Sammy would have told him.

Why couldn't he let it go? Why couldn't he be like Sammy or Cynthia? He had already raised concerns, which was more than either of them had done. Why did he have to do more?

If he scrolled down into the report, he knew, he was taking a step he couldn't reverse. At the very least, even if he did nothing afterward, he was admitting to himself that he truly believed Louisiana Light was rotten. He would never be able to pretend that he didn't. A person who didn't believe that wouldn't sit here, dog tired, after a day that had started forty hours earlier on a different continent, and check an annual report.

He gazed at the cover. He didn't *have* to scroll down. For a minute longer, he continued to tell himself that, as if it were true.

And then he scrolled.

He stopped on the directors page. There was the face staring out at him from the screen, the man who had come into the data room. Rob read his name: Stan Murdoch. He'd heard the name before. Stan Murdoch, director of operations. He read his bio.

"ExPar and Grogon," whispered Rob to himself. If they existed, where would they be? He had a pretty good idea.

He moved rapidly toward the back of the report and came to the page listing Louisiana Light's subsidiaries. He ran through them, name after name after name. The small print on the screen swam before his exhausted eyes. They must have more subsidiaries than Procter & Gamble. And there it was. Grogon. Suddenly the print was very clear, as if he were seeing it through some kind of a magnifying glass. Grogon, incorporated in Hungary.

He felt a terrible sense of dismay. Even now, even until this very second, he had hoped that he was wrong.

There were maybe eighty subsidiaries listed on the page. What were the chances that anyone was going to decide to check the details on precisely this one?

Eighty subsidiaries. Say they were using only one of them to take their debt off the balance sheet and hide it. One needle in a haystack. You'd never find it unless someone told you exactly which one it was. Even then, you'd need an expert to figure out how it was being done.

He looked for the name of the other company. He went on to the next page. More names of companies. Joint ventures.

There it was. ExPar.

32

Sammy Weiss leaned forward, hands clasped under his chin, gazing at the screen. He was going over about the tenth draft of the document for the bridge loan. Every draft came back with comments from John Golansky, Pete Stanzy, and Phil Menendez, often contradicting one another, all of which he was supposed to incorporate. Rob stole a glance at him. Sammy punched in a couple of words on his keyboard and then read over what he had written, rubbing his chin, frowning thoughtfully.

Sammy's phone rang. He picked it up. Rob could hear Phil Menendez's voice on the other end of the line. Sammy saved the work on his computer, closed the file, and left the room.

Rob glanced at Cynthia. She kept working. He glanced at her again. The minutes passed. Rob got up and said he was going to the bathroom, hoping that would make Cynthia want to go to the bathroom, too. He came back. She was still there. Go, he thought. Go to the bathroom!

Cynthia turned around. "I'm going to get a coffee. You want one?"

Rob shook his head. Then he nodded. It would take her longer if she had to get two.

As soon as the door closed, Rob grabbed the phone and called up the library. He got through to Libby, who was always the most helpful librarian whenever he had to put in a request for data that he couldn't get for himself on the Net. He could feel his heart pounding. Any second, he expected Sammy or Cynthia to open the door. He told Libby he had an urgent request.

"What is it, Rob?"

"There are two companies I need to find out about. I only have their names. One's Grogon . . ." Rob spelled the name for her. "The other's ExPar."

"Grogon and ExPar," said Libby.

"That's right. I need you to get me anything you can find on them as quickly as possible."

"Can you tell me anything about them?" asked Libby.

"No. Just send me anything you can." Rob was speaking fast. "This is absolutely crucial, Libby. I know it's short notice, but—"

"It's okay. That's what I'm here for. Do I charge this to your engagement?"

"Yes," said Rob quickly. "And Libby, this is ultraconfidential. I've been asked specially to do this. . . . If you get someone else on this number here, no matter who it is, don't let them know about it." There were some advantages to working in a place where just about everything was top secret, he thought.

"Sure, Rob. How do you want this? E-mail all right?"

Sammy opened the door.

"Yes, e-mail's fine. Thanks. I owe you."

"Well, we'll just have to see how we can make you pay," said Libby.

Rob laughed, a bit more heartily than was strictly warranted by Libby's joke, and put down the phone.

Libby called back during the afternoon. Sammy and Cynthia and Phil Menendez were there. Rob told her he'd call back. Menendez left, but Rob didn't get another opportunity when Sammy and Cynthia were out of the room together. He left it as late as he could before he took a chance.

"I was just about to go," said Libby. "I didn't know whether to call again."

"No, thank you," said Rob. He tried to sound natural, in case the others were listening, but he felt wooden.

"I didn't find much, which is why I didn't e-mail."

"Yes," said Rob.

"Rob, can't you talk?" asked Libby.

"Not really."

"Shall I just tell you what I found?"

"That would be a good idea."

"Okay," said Libby. "The only Grogon I could find is some Hungarian company. I believe it's connected in some way with a company called Louisiana Light here in the States. Do you know that company?"

"Go on," said Rob.

"Well, there does appear to be something that looks from the description like a prospectus, but I think it's in Hungarian. It's from a few years back. Took a lot of digging to find it. I couldn't find any accounts, though. Would the prospectus be of any use to you? I could try to get it, but I couldn't guarantee it."

"If you can," said Rob. He glanced around at Sammy and Cynthia. They appeared engrossed in their work. "What about the other one?"

"I found a company registration by that name out of Delaware. Nothing else, I'm afraid, just the bare minimum. I don't think it'll be of much help. It's online, so I could e-mail it if you like." Libby laughed. "At least it's in English."

"That would be good."

"You want me to e-mail it?"

"Yes."

"Okay, I'll do that now."

"Thanks," said Rob.

"That's it?"

"Yes. Thanks."

Rob put the phone down. The others were still working.

The e-mail hit his in-box two minutes later. He didn't dare open it there in the war room. When he left that night he took his laptop with him.

He got in a cab and gave the driver Emmy's address. As the cab started moving, he opened the laptop. He had left it on, but for some reason now it shut itself down. Rob fired it up again. He watched it as the cab took him uptown, impatiently waiting for it to start.

Finally he was able to open the document Libby had sent him. He scanned it, all concentration, oblivious to the city going past outside the cab window. It was as uninformative as Libby had intimated. Just a basic document of registration. Date, place, list of directors.

He read the names of the directors.

He stared. No, thought Rob. That would be too much of a coincidence.

Catherine Gelb. Gelb? That was Leopard's CFO's name, wasn't it?

"Hey, mister," said the cabdriver. "Here we are."

Emmy opened the door. "Hey, baby," she said, and put her arms around him.

Rob gave her a kiss. "I just need a minute, Emmy. Do you mind?"

He sat down and pulled out his computer. Working quickly at the keyboard, he opened the file for Louisiana Light's annual report, then went to the directors page. Lyall Gelb *was* the CFO. He opened the document Libby had sent him on ExPar. Catherine Gelb. There was the name, one of the ExPar directors. That had to be Lyall Gelb's wife. His wife? You don't have your wife on the board of a company unless for some reason you want to avoid having genuinely independent directors.

He remembered Murdoch's voice in the data room. Grogon and ExPar. That was where the bodies were buried. Murdoch would know. He was on the Louisiana Light board, the same as Lyall Gelb.

Rob still couldn't work out why Murdoch had chosen him, but that didn't matter. He had.

Rob read the document on ExPar again, going through it carefully, hoping to find something he had missed. There was so little in it, so little to go on. He studied every word.

He wasn't even aware of Emmy's voice the first time she spoke.

"I said, would you like me to leave?"

Now Rob looked up. "Sorry, Em. What was that?"

Emmy was standing where he had left her, arms folded. "Do you want me to leave? I don't want to get in your way. Maybe I'll just go to bed so you can get on with your work. Help yourself to food, by the way."

Rob saw the way the table was set. Candles glowed. A bottle of wine stood open. He had been so caught up with his own thoughts, he hadn't noticed it before. Emmy had gone to some trouble.

"Emmy, don't be like that."

"Like what, Rob?"

"There's just some stuff I'm trying to work out."

"That's what I said. Go ahead. I'll get out of your way. I'll go to bed. Actually, you can let yourself out."

"I don't want to let myself out."

"Then what do you want, Rob?" She stared at him, eyes narrowed in anger. "You go off to London, you come back, you're too tired to see me last night—which is okay, I understand—then tonight you come over, but you've got stuff you're trying to work out, so maybe, actually, it would just be better if I got out of your way and you can deal with your stuff and that's just great."

"Emmy, don't." He got up and tried to take her hand.

She pulled away.

"What am I, Rob? Since you do happen to have a moment right now, why don't we just look at that? What am I, huh? Your girlfriend? Your partner? Maybe I'm just someone you fuck every so often. When you can find the time. When we happen to be in the same city. When you don't have anything better to do. When there's no *stuff* you have to work out."

"Emmy . . ."

"I missed you, you know, over the last few days."

"I missed you, too."

"I was looking forward to seeing you."

"I was, too."

"Were you? I don't think you were. Is this a chore for you, Rob? Tell me if it's a chore because I'd *hate* to think you have to do something you don't want to do."

"Emmy, Jesus, it's not a chore. How can you—"

"Then what is it, huh? What is it exactly you planned for us when you came back from Cornell? You gonna live in your own apartment forever? You at your place, me at mine? Is that how it is, Rob? Is that the kind of relationship you want? How long does it go on like that? How long do you expect me to wait? Another year? Two years? Five?"

Oh God, thought Rob. Oh God, oh God. Not now. Please, not now.

"Well, Rob?"

"Emmy, I can't deal with this now. I've got too much on my mind."

"So have I!" yelled Emmy, and she stormed into the bedroom and slammed the door with a bang that sent a tremor through the wine and the food and the candles she had prepared so carefully before Rob arrived.

33

"Emmy," he said.

She was lying on the bed in the dark. Curled up. Facing away from the door.

"Emmy."

"Leave me alone."

He went farther into the bedroom.

"Emmy, don't do this. I feel terrible."

"How do you think I feel?"

"I was preoccupied. I'm sorry. I didn't think."

There was silence.

"Emmy, come on. I need you. You know I do."

"Do I? I'm not sure about that anymore, Rob."

"Emmy." He sat down beside her on the edge of the bed. He reached out and touched her hair. Her long, dark, lovely hair.

"Don't," she said. *"Don't!"*

"Okay." He drew back his hand. "Will you at least listen to me?"

Silence.

"Will you?" said Rob.

Still silence.

"There's some stuff I've discovered—I mean, stuff I've been told. That's what I was trying to figure out."

"You don't need to tell me. It's none of my business. You've got a right to do whatever you want. You want to look at your computer, that's fine."

"Please, Emmy. Don't."

Suddenly she turned to him. Her eyes blazed with anger. "I don't need anything from you, Rob! Understand me? Don't do me any favors. I don't need your protection, I don't need your help. If you don't want to be here, go! Who's stopping you?"

"I do want to be here."

"Then behave like you do!"

Rob nodded. "You're right. I'm sorry."

Emmy stared at him. "I'm angry. Do you understand? I feel like I have to pretend nothing matters to me, where you live, what's happening with us, anything. And it does matter to me. I can't pretend anymore. I just can't do it. We need to deal with this!"

"We will. I promise."

"Now."

"I can't. I just . . . not tonight, Emmy. Please. I'm too tired. I can't do it. I've got too much to deal with."

Emmy looked at him. She shook her head disbelievingly.

"Please, Emmy. We will. I promise we will."

"When?"

"As soon as I can."

"That's a copout. That's what guys say, Rob. It's a copout."

"It isn't. I swear."

She continued to watch him. Then she turned away again.

Rob sat on the bed. She had a right to be angry, he knew. He had evaded the question. But he just couldn't deal with it now. He didn't know when he would be able to deal with it—maybe when this thing with Louisiana Light was over. But he couldn't do it now.

He waited, hoping that her anger would lessen.

"Can I tell you about it?" he said eventually.

Emmy didn't reply.

"What I found out in London."

There was silence.

"You know my client, Louisiana Light—"

"You don't need to tell me their name," said Emmy.

"I want to."

"Why? Why now? Why not before? You don't tell me anything, Rob. I don't know what to expect from you anymore."

But he did want to tell her. He wanted her to know.

"Emmy, will you listen to me? Please. I need you to listen."

There was silence for a moment. Then she turned around. "We'll deal with it? You promise?"

"I promise."

"And not like in another ten years?"

"Not in another ten years. Five max."

Emmy stared at him coldly. It wasn't the time for jokes.

"Soon, Emmy. Soon. I promise."

She nodded. "Okay. I just can't pretend anymore. Okay? You understand that?"

Rob nodded.

"All right." She paused. "So, what is it, this thing you found out in London?"

"This client of mine, Louisiana Light—well, we call them the Leopard."

"The what?"

Rob shrugged. "It's a code. We're Leopard, they're Buffalo."

"You guys . . ." Emmy shook her head. "What kind of a world do you live in?"

"Yeah, I know. Remind me to introduce you to Phil Menendez one day. Or should I say, the Shark? Anyway, the Leopard, I think it's been doing some bad things."

"You told me that in the park," said Emmy bluntly.

"No, now I'm pretty sure."

"Because of something that happened in London?"

Rob nodded. He told her about the data room, about Stan Murdoch, about what he had said. The way he had said it.

Emmy listened. "What do you think they've been doing?"

"Whatever they could. Booking revenues they haven't actually got yet, or one-offs as repeatables. Claiming operating expenses as capital expenses. Hiding debt." Rob shrugged. "Those are just the things a novice like me could think up. There's any number of things you could do if you know what you're doing. It can be unbelievably complex, Em. I don't know enough about this stuff even to tell you what I don't know."

"And you think these two companies you mentioned are related to all that?"

"I think so. I'm sure they are. You need to have entities, companies, to do this stuff."

Emmy frowned. "I don't understand. If they're in such trouble, what's this deal about? How can they buy another company?"

"They have to. That's their only way out. Buffalo has a strong balance sheet, so—" Rob stopped, seeing Emmy's uncomprehending look. "What I mean is, Buffalo's hardly got any debt. That means when you put the two companies together, Leopard's debt doesn't look so out of proportion, even with the extra debt they have to take on to actually buy them. And if they're expecting more debt to come back from wherever they've hidden it, they need the strength of Buffalo's balance sheet to absorb it. If they don't, they could go bankrupt."

Emmy looked at him doubtfully.

"Seriously, Em. The banks get skittish, start to call in their loans . . . they're finished. It can happen overnight. It can happen in a matter of days."

"So, they're not a solid company? They're not making a profit?"

"No. It looks like it, but the profit isn't really there. It's all on paper. They only look solid because people are prepared to keep lending them money. And people are only prepared to keep lending them money because they've lied about how much money they've already borrowed and how much they earn. They've used a bunch of tricks to hide the truth. I'm guessing a little here, but if that's true, and the banks realize it, they'll be calling in their loans faster than you can imagine. That'll be it. Curtains. Unless, of course, the Leopard can find another company that has hardly any debt on its balance sheet and manage to get hold of it."

"Like Buffalo?"

"Exactly. They can go back to their banks and renegotiate. And here's the other thing. They do a deal, and it's like no one can see exactly what's going on. A big deal like this, it's hard to compare the companies before and after. Say the Leopard's income is about to go south, they're about to book a big bunch of losses—they do this deal and suddenly no one can see it anymore because it's mixed in with the Buffalo's numbers. Mike Wilson can say, you know what? Our operations are still fine, but the Buffalo's haven't been going as good as we expected. And the market won't know. You don't have to be that specific in the filings, you don't necessarily have to give that much detail in the breakdown. So no one will know from the numbers where the problems lie."

"So this deal's like camouflage? Like a diversion from the problems?"

"It's a solution and a diversion at the same time. It acts as a diversion to buy time for the solution to work."

"Then why would Buffalo want to do it?"

"Because they don't know."

"But you know."

Rob thought about that. He tried to see it from the BritEnergy perspective. They'd know about the weakness of Leopard's balance sheet, but nothing else. They wouldn't have seen the red flags. They wouldn't know Mike Wilson had never used Dyson Whitney before. Or that he was paying forty bips. Or that he had offered a price above the top of the valuation he had received. Or that Stan Murdoch had said to look into Grogon and ExPar. Especially that Stan Murdoch had said to look into Grogon and ExPar.

In fact, there was only one person who knew every one of these things.

Emmy was watching him. "Are you going to say something?"

"To who? Pete Stanzy already just about fired me for asking questions. I say something now, what happens then?"

"Wouldn't he want to know?"

"If I've seen the red flags, Emmy, you can bet he's seen them as well."

"But he doesn't know everything you know. He doesn't know what you were told in London."

"He's knows enough. He knows enough to have done something. I go back to him now, it's like rubbing his nose in it. Emmy, you weren't there when he tried to fire me. I go back to him again, I won't get to finish the first sentence before he sacks me."

"Last time you said you might go higher up."

"I could, but . . . the minute I do that, what'll he do? He'll say he's already on to it. He'll say we've already had a conversation about it. He'll make me look like an insubordinate. The junior guy never wins in these situations."

Emmy frowned. "If the guys at this company have been doing the things you say, they deserve to be exposed."

"I can't be certain of this without seeing their books. And I can't see their books. I don't have access."

"But you're pretty sure. More than pretty sure. Rob, if they've ruined one company, they'll just do the same to the next one they buy."

"Jesus, Emmy! The other day you were telling me I should protect my job. Now what are you saying?"

"I'm saying something's wrong here." Emmy gazed at him. "The other day you didn't know what you know now."

"It's still not proof."

"It's close. It's a lot more than you had before. I don't want to tell you what to do, but you asked me. You have to do something about this. I'm sorry. That's what I think."

Rob took a deep breath. "I know I do. I just don't know exactly what the best way is to do it. All I've got now is a pointer about where to look. Without actually seeing their books, without actually seeing the figures, I can't say a hundred percent that I know what's going on."

Emmy nodded. She reached for his hand.

There was silence.

Suddenly Emmy glanced up at him. "Were you the one who talked to that journalist?"

Rob looked at her in surprise. "No. Why do you ask?"

Emmy shrugged. "I just thought you might have."

"She bumped into me. The day before the article came out. She asked me some questions. I didn't tell her anything. I just said 'no comment.'"

"You know her?"

"No. Never seen her before in my life." Rob thought about it for a moment. "I still have her card."

"That's odd, don't you think, that she just bumped into you? Just like that? The day before the article came out."

Rob shrugged. "She must have already got hold of the story and been looking for someone to confirm."

"But you didn't?"

"No."

Emmy frowned. "I don't know, Rob. I don't know what to tell you. It's unfair that you've been put in this position. You've worked so hard for this, it's taken you so long . . ." She shook her head. "It's so unfair."

Rob nodded. That's how it seemed.

Emmy's brow furrowed in concern. "You're not in any danger, are you?"

"What do you mean?"

"Well, you know all these things . . . someone's told you this stuff, secrets. You don't think you're at risk?"

Rob smiled. "Emmy, these are businessmen. Fat, middle-aged businessmen. What are they gonna do? Call out the mob?"

Emmy shrugged. "I guess not." She paused. "Isn't there anyone who can help you? Someone you can talk to about it?"

"I've tried that."

"Someone else?"

"Like who? All of this is ultraconfidential. Even the fact that there's a deal is confidential."

"There must be someone. It doesn't always have to be you against the world, Rob."

Rob smiled.

"What?" said Emmy.

"I just had a thought. I could call up that journalist and give her the scoop. Last time the Buffalo ran a mile and the deal almost collapsed. And they had nothing compared to what I've got now. I wouldn't even have to mention the deal. I could just say I've got information that there's problems with these two companies that Leopard owns, Grogon and ExPar. They print that, the Buffalo will take notice. They'll ask the Leopard what it's about. The Leopard won't have a choice. Either they produce the figures to refute the charges or it shows them up for what they are."

"What if they found out it was you?"

"How? Confidentiality, right? A journalist never reveals her sources. It's the best of both worlds. The information gets out and I'm protected."

Emmy frowned. "Well, maybe . . ."

Rob laughed. "I'm only kidding. It'd never work. It's too good to be true."

"Yeah." Emmy laughed, too.

But they soon found themselves looking seriously at each other.

Actually, when you thought about it, why wouldn't it work?

34

It was the paltriness of the sum that was the hook. Sandy Pereira knew it as soon as she heard the message on the Groanline. Jealousy, outrage, accusation, and counteraccusation—over a measly five hundred bucks. A "No, New York!" classic.

The only problem was that the lady on the phone was refusing to admit it.

"I never said it," she claimed. "Never, never! Will I say such a thing? To my own niece?"

"Mrs. Torres, I know you did," said Sandy Pereira.

"Who? Who tells you such a thing? Such a terrible thing!"

"I can't tell you, Mrs. Torres."

"People have dirty tongues. People are jealous."

Jealous of five hundred bucks? According to the accusation on the Groanline—anonymous, of course—Mrs. Maria Torres had told her niece that she would withhold the money she'd promised her on her wedding if she married a certain boy called Felipe. She wanted the niece, Corazón, to marry Umberto, who was the son of one of Mrs. Torres's friends. Needless to say, Corazón didn't love Umberto. She didn't hate him, she just didn't love him. Umberto himself would marry Corazón, according to the Groanline, but this was because he had no scruples, as he had shown many times, for instance when he visited his mother in the hospital every day only to make himself seem better than his brother, Alejandro, who was unable to visit so frequently because his job as a debt collector kept him working late at night. . . .

The Groanline message had been a long and detailed one, with numerous diversions, worthy of an episode of a soap opera, if not an entire series. Mrs. Torres herself was childless. The "dowry," as the anonymous female informer called it, that she had promised her niece was the sum of five hundred dollars. She had promised it ever since Corazón was a little girl. It was probably Corazón, thought Sandy, who had left the message.

If it had been a hundred thousand dollars, it would have been different. You would have been on one side or the other. You would have felt sorry for the niece, or you would have thought, Serves her right if she wants to go her own way, she has to take what's coming. But at five hundred dollars, it made you cringe. You couldn't sympathize with either side. It made you want to shout out, "You, for God's sake, give her the five hundred bucks! And you, for God's sake, if she doesn't, forget about it!"

Sandy sighed. Five hundred bucks. She rolled her eyes. This was what she had to deal with.

Mrs. Torres was crying now. She was obviously guilty, guilty as sin. It was only a question of whether Sandy would use her name in the article. The readers liked to see names. But if she couldn't get Mrs. Torres to admit it on the phone, which was being recorded, it would be safer not to. Not that Mrs. Torres was likely to sue, but you never knew. It could be a setup. Mrs. Torres might be recording the call as well, and she and Corazón could be in it together. Corazón leaves the message, Mrs. Torres denies it, the *Herald* publishes, then— bang—you've got your lawsuit.

"Mrs. Torres, it's true, isn't it, that you promised you'd give Corazón five hundred dollars on the day she gets married?"

"Is true!" wailed Mrs. Torres.

"And it's true as well that you said she'd get nothing when she told you she was marrying Felipe."

"Is such a horrible boy! Thoughtless, careless. Will he be good for her? You tell me this."

"I don't know, Mrs. Torres," muttered Sandy in exasperation.

"Listen. Umberto, he is nice. He cares. When you get out from the car, he opens the door for you. This is nice, no?"

"It sounds nice. Mrs. Torres—"

"And when his mother is sick, he goes every day to visit her in the hospital."

"Mrs. Torres—"

"Not once does he miss. You think Felipe will do this? If his mother is in the hospital, you think he will visit? For a *histerecto-mía*. You think a *histerectomía*. Imagine. For a man, a *histerectomía* is not something he likes to think. But every day, Umberto goes. His brother, Alejandro? Does he go? No. But Umberto, every day, not one day does he—"

"Mrs. Torres!" interrupted Sandy. "You refused to give her the money, didn't you? I know you did. Admit it."

There was silence.

"Admit it!"

"Maybe I say . . . maybe I am upset. . . . Corazón, she will never think I will not give it to her."

"But you're not going to, are you?"

"Who says this?"

"You told her you wouldn't."

"Was not serious. My Corazón . . ." Mrs. Torres began to cry again. "*Ai!* She is like my own daughter."

"You don't have a daughter," said Sandy coldly.

Mrs. Torres wailed.

Sandy had had enough. "You said you wouldn't give it to her, Mrs. Torres. I know you did."

"I will give it."

Great, thought Sandy. There goes the story.

"Thank you. I will give it."

"What about Umberto?"

"Ah, it is Corazón I love. She is my light. If Felipe make her happy, I am happy."

"But he won't make her happy!"

"Who can tell? Life. Love. These are strange, no?"

Sandy listened to her in disgust. Suddenly the old tyrant had gone all philosophical.

"Thank you, miss. Is a very good talk we have. Why do you call me? Does someone tell you we must have this talk?"

Yeah, thought Sandy, and she felt like telling her exactly who.

"Thank you."

"A real pleasure," said Sandy.

She put the phone down. She thought about it, looking over the notes on her pad. She'd still write the story. No names, though.

She looked up. Marvin Koller was standing over her desk. Leering into her cleavage.

She straightened up.

Marvin ran his hand over his thin, oily hair. "Cracking another big story?"

"What do you want, Marvin?"

"I want a little action."

Sandy rolled her eyes.

"I'm serious. A week ago, you give me this rumor about Louisiana Light. Come on, where's the follow-up?"

Sandy shrugged.

"What about your source? You said he had proof."

"Look, it's very . . . you know, he's . . ."

"What? This was some bullshit thing you picked up on the street, wasn't it?"

"No."

"You never had a source," said Marvin. "You just heard something."

Sandy didn't answer that.

"Don't try to put one over on me, honey, because I've seen it all."

Marvin shook his head in a great show of disgust. In reality, he never really thought Sandy had had a reliable source. At most, he figured it was barroom bravado from some Wall Street type trying to impress her. But he was disappointed with the outcome of the story. He'd expected at least some kind of a response from Louisiana Light, which he could then use to push the story along a couple more issues. Make that the story, at least. But all he got was a call from Amanda Bellinger. He said he'd go off the record, expecting her to tell him something. But all she did was try to find out about his source and then threaten him with litigation if he published anything else. She didn't give him anything, not a crumb for him to use, off the record or not. The whole thing, in short, was very disappointing. When Marv Koller was disappointed, he liked to share the pain around.

"Marvin," said Sandy, "if I get anything else, I'll tell you right away."

"Yeah? Real stories don't just come to you on the Groanline, Sandy. They don't just walk up to you while you sit here on your fat ass. You gotta go out and get 'em. You gotta make 'em. Didn't they teach you that at Columbia?"

"NYU," muttered Sandy.

Marvin snorted. "You get out there and find me something on this. You let me know when you do." He stared at her for a moment longer, then walked away.

Sandy turned back to her notes. She opened a new document on her computer and began typing.

How low can you go when two people fall in love? In Queens, an aunt who shall remain nameless has decided to show us. When her niece, 24, fell in love with

Sandy stared at the words. NYU, she thought resentfully. This is what they were preparing her for at NYU.

She backspaced.

When her beautiful young niece, 24, fell in love with

The phone rang. Sandy picked it up.

"Is this Sandy Pereira?"

"Rich?" Sandy giggled. Rich was a guy she'd been with a couple of nights before.

"No. Is this Sandy Pereira?"

Suddenly Sandy recognized the voice. Her expression changed. "Yes," she said. "This is Sandy Pereira."

Rob had gone to a pay phone. He couldn't have taken the risk of calling from the war room even if no one else were there. And his cell phone bill went to Dyson Whitney, so they would have a record of his calls. It was a long shot they would ever check them, and an even longer shot they'd identify the number he was calling, but it was possible.

He had also taken the precaution of walking a few blocks from the office. He didn't know if that was overkill, but if anyone saw him using a pay phone, it was going to be pretty hard to explain what he was doing there. He felt as if he'd stepped into a walk-on role in a thriller.

The journalist sounded surprised to hear from him when she answered the phone.

"You gave me your card," said Rob.

"That's right. I remember."

Rob hesitated. He was about to cross a line, he knew. "This has to be strictly anonymous, all right? Do you understand that?"

"Yes," said the journalist. "We do this all the time."

"A journalist doesn't reveal her source, right?"

"Never."

"Do you promise me?"

"Yes."

Rob hesitated again. He hadn't crossed the line yet. "Can I trust you?"

"Yes. You can trust me."

Rob took a deep breath. He looked around. A woman came toward the pay phone and glanced straight at him as she headed past. Rob turned away and put his hand up against his face, trying to shield himself from being seen.

"All right," he said at last. "You were investigating Louisiana Light, weren't you?"

"Yes." On her notepad, Sandy wrote *Louisiana Light* and underlined it.

"For a long time?"

"For quite a while," said Sandy.

"I have two names for you. You may already know them."

"What are they?"

"Grogon and ExPar."

"Can you spell those, please?"

Rob spelled them.

Sandy wrote. *Grogon. ExPar.*

"I need to know everything you know about them," she said.

"It isn't much."

"Tell me what you do know."

Rob told her. It was so little, he felt foolish. He added a few of his own thoughts about how the companies might be used to park debt off Louisiana Light's balance sheet.

"And you're sure this is reliable?" asked Sandy.

"Yes. Very sure."

"How do you know about it? Did someone tell you?"

"I can't say. But I can tell you why this is coming out now."

I should have asked that one, thought Sandy.

"They're doing a deal."

Rob waited, expecting to hear some kind of reaction. Nothing.

"Did you hear what I said?" he demanded.

"Yes," said Sandy. *Doing a deal,* she wrote, wondering why that made such a difference.

Suddenly Rob had the sense he was wasting his time. "Do you understand what that means?"

"Of course I do!" snapped Sandy.

"Okay. I can't tell you who they're doing the deal with. It's a foreign company. In Europe."

Foreign company in Europe.

"Do you know where?"

"I can't say. But I can tell you when."

"When?"

"The announcement's next week."

"Next week!" said Sandy, sensing that she was supposed to be surprised.

"That's right. Next Friday. So you'll have to act fast."

"Right," said Sandy. "That is fast."

"That's all I can tell you."

"Is there anything else? Anything else at all you can tell me?"

Rob thought.

"The more you tell me," said Sandy, "the stronger the story I can write."

"Isn't that enough for a story?" said Rob.

"Yes," replied Sandy hurriedly. "Excellent. It's exactly the break we were looking for. This is just great."

"You got those names I gave you, didn't you?"

"I got them."

"You going to use them?"

"Absolutely. If you get anything else, let me know. The more information I can get, the better."

"I can trust you, can't I?"

"Yes, you can trust me."

"This is confidential, right?"

"Absolutely. Rob, I need some kind of data so I can verify who you are."

"You've got my name."

"I can't just have a name."

"You know where I work."

"I need something else. It's not me. Those are the rules. What about your address? What's your address?"

Rob hesitated.

"This is all confidential, Rob. It's for internal purposes. I can't publish this story without it. If we get challenged on this, I can't say to my editor that I got it from some guy with a name."

"You sure about that?"

"I'm sure."

Rob thought about it. If this leaked, it wouldn't matter if the journalist had his address. His name alone would be enough to sink him. "One-oh-three West Thirty-ninth Street," he said. "Apartment twelve."

"Okay. Rob, you've got my number. Anything else you find out, you let me know. Call me right away."

"Okay."

Rob put the phone down. He looked around. People continued to walk past. He backed away from the phone. A moment later, he had mixed in with everyone else on the sidewalk.

In the *Herald* newsroom, Marvin Koller stopped on the way back to his desk. He ran his eyes over Sandy. She smiled.

"You tell me when you get anything, right?" he barked at her. "You get off your fat ass and get out there and find something."

"Sure, Marvin," said Sandy, edging her elbow forward to cover her notepad. "I'll let you know the minute anything comes in."

35

The call had been scheduled two days earlier. Stanzy wanted an end-of-week review to cover off progress on a number of fronts. In reality, there was only one major area of concern, which was why John Golansky was sitting in Stanzy's office when he dialed the number.

On the other end of the line, in Baton Rouge, Wilson was with Lyall Gelb.

"First of all," said Stanzy, "I want to cover off the due diligence."

"You guys happy at your end?" said Wilson.

"Yeah. So far, so good. Our team's crunching the scenarios. We'll have it ready for the review on Monday."

"Nothing I'm going to have trouble with for the board?"

"No, as far as we can see, you're fine, Mike. What about you? You hear anything yet from the lawyers?"

Wilson laughed. "They're gonna be there all weekend. So far, they're saying it looks all right. With about a thousand qualifications. They're lawyers, right?"

Pete laughed. "Don't worry. We'll sort them out for you on Monday."

"And you'll have the report finalized Tuesday?"

"Absolutely. What about Buffalo's due diligence? You hear anything?"

"Their guys are starting today," said Wilson.

"They're leaving it kind of late, aren't they? That only gives them a few days."

"I don't think they're going to be looking too hard," said Wilson. "Lyall's got four big rooms of files all ready for them, haven't you, Lyall?"

"That's right," said Gelb.

Stanzy glanced at Golansky. Golansky rolled his eyes.

"Okay," said Stanzy. "Now, we still okay for the announcement?"

"Yeah," said Wilson. "You guys are writing the presentation, right? My people are going to want to see it. And the Buffalo's going to want to see it as well."

"Absolutely," said Stanzy. "We'll have a first draft to you Monday, Mike."

The announcement was scheduled for Friday, exactly one week away. Louisiana Light was listed on the New York Stock Exchange and BritEnergy was listed in London, so the announcement would be made simultaneously in both places. It was timed for ten A.M. in New York and three P.M. in London. Mike Wilson and Andrew Bassett would start talking at their press conferences at precisely the same moment, using identical prepared scripts.

"Now what about PR? I was thinking—"

"I'm gonna let Mandy Bellinger know about it today," said Wilson. "I've kept her in the dark till now. She's gonna handle the PR for us."

"I thought your corporate affairs department would do that," said John Golansky.

"No, John." Wilson laughed. "Hell, I wouldn't trust them with something this big. We want to make a splash."

Stanzy and Golansky glanced at each other.

"Mike," said Stanzy, "when you say you want to make a splash, we wanted to talk to you about the kind of PR you want to do. There are pros and cons to—"

"Now, you just leave that to me and Mandy, Pete," said Wilson, cutting right across him. "You know Mandy?"

"No."

"Well, she knows what she's doing. Let's not waste any more time on this, huh? What about the loan?"

In New York, John and Pete simultaneously leaned closer to the table. From their perspective, this was what the call was really about.

"We do want to talk about that," said Stanzy.

"At the moment," said Golansky, "we're looking at about four billion."

"What was that?" said Mike. "Did I hear you say 'four billion'?"

Pete glanced at John. John nodded. "That's right, Mike. I said four. We're at four-point-one, to be accurate. Which, incidentally, is more or less the amount of cash we originally agreed that you'd offer."

"Well, that's great!" said Wilson, either ignoring or not picking up on John's sarcasm. "We only need six and a quarter. What's that, another two-point-one? You've still got five days to find it."

No one on the call knew whether Wilson was being serious or sarcastic. Not even Lyall Gelb, sitting across the table from him in Baton Rouge, could tell.

"Mike," said John Golansky, "that's a lot to find."

"Two-point-one?" replied Wilson, as if he were in the habit of walking around and picking up a couple of billion dollars every day of the week.

John Golansky glanced at Pete.

"Two-point-one-five, Mike," said Stanzy. "To be accurate."

"Come on, John. You guys raised the Alesco loan in two days. What was it? Five billion or something? Isn't that what you guys always say? Isn't that your pitch?"

Yeah, thought Golansky. But people *wanted* to invest in Alesco.

"Lyall's got something to say," said Wilson. "Lyall?"

"Ah . . . yeah. I think I can find maybe three hundred and fifty million."

Golansky and Stanzy glanced at each other.

"Where's this coming from, Lyall?" asked Pete, writing *350 million* on his pad.

"Umm . . . we had a couple of disposals we were looking at. I've been seeing what I can do and I think we may be able to bring them forward."

"That'd be good," said Stanzy encouragingly.

Golansky raised an eyebrow.

"Lyall's being modest," said Wilson. "We'll have four."

"Lyall?"

"Yeah, Pete. Call it four."

"That's four hundred million?" said John Golansky.

"Yes, John."

"Does Buffalo know about these disposals?"

"It's all in the due diligence documentation," replied Wilson. "These aren't new disposals. We've planned them for a while now. We'll just be bringing them forward so they're done before the deal's complete."

"It's not . . . we'll still be operating the assets," said Lyall. "It's just the ownership, which—"

"It's complicated," interjected Wilson. "Right, Lyall?"

"Yes. Fairly complicated."

Wilson laughed. "Boys, when Lyall says something's fairly complicated, there's no one else in the world who can understand it!"

John and Pete were supposed to laugh, they knew, but neither of them did.

"Where are these assets?" asked Stanzy, trying to ignore the look John Golanksy was giving him.

"Hungary," said Wilson. "We have a number of assets in Hungary. You ever been there?"

"No," said Stanzy.

"You should. Great little place. World of opportunity."

Pete looked at Golansky. He shrugged. If Mike Wilson said they had assets to dispose of in Hungary, they had to take him at his word.

"Pete? John? You guys still there?"

"Yeah. We're still here," said Golansky. He shook his head and pinched the bridge of his nose for a second. "Okay. Look, four hundred million will help. Can I definitely count on that?"

"Yeah," said Wilson's voice. "You got it."

"Lyall? Is it definite?"

"Yes," said Gelb.

"You sure?"

"Lyall," said Wilson. "We're sure, aren't we?"

"Yes." There was a pause. "I'm sure."

"So that makes the total loan we need to raise five-point-eight-five billion? Is that what you're saying? I need to be absolutely sure."

"Yes," said Wilson impatiently. "Hell, how many different ways do you want us to say it?"

"Okay," said Golansky. "We've got four-point-one, so that leaves our shortfall at one-point-seven-five."

"So, how are we looking?" asked Wilson.

"Well," said Golansky, "looks like we're looking for one-point-seven-five."

Wilson laughed. "Come on, John. You know what I'm saying."

Golansky turned to Pete. He moved each hand up and down a little, as if it were an even money bet whether they could get the rest of the cash.

"I think we're looking pretty good," said Pete.

"John?"

"I'm not saying we're there, Mike."

"You two, you're like Laurel and Hardy." Wilson laughed. "What do I have to do to get a straight answer?"

Pete left it to John.

"We're not there," said Golanksy. "All right? I've gone to the majors, and Citi and Bank of America are giving me four-point-one between them. From here, I don't know. I could go down a tier or two, but you're gonna be paying a premium, Mike. We're talking two, three percent minimum."

"How about a little help from you guys?"

John Golansky frowned. "What was that?"

"Come on, John," said Wilson. "We just put in another four hundred million. I raised, you match."

Golansky stared at Pete in disbelief.

"How about it?"

"Mike," began Pete, "I don't know if that's—"

"Where's the commitment?" There was no humor in Wilson's tone now. "Huh? We're having trouble getting over the line. You telling me you guys aren't gonna push a little?"

"Mike, we're not that kind of bank. We don't have the kind of balance sheet that allows us to provide loans from our own funds. That's why John's gone to—"

"Pete, don't give me that crap! Now tell me, how much are you guys putting in?"

"Now, Mike, you really have got the wrong idea about—"

"Whatever it is," said Wilson, "double it!"

Pete didn't respond to that. On the other side of the table, John Golansky was getting angry.

"How much is it?" persisted Wilson. "Come on, how much are you guys putting in. Two hundred? Three?"

"Mr. Wilson," said John Golansky quietly, "I'm not sure we can take this business further."

"What?" demanded Wilson.

Pete stared at Golansky.

"I don't know whether we have anything further to talk about," said Golanksy.

"The fuck we don't!"

"I'm going to tell you something, Mr. Wilson. Your company is not well regarded in certain sectors of the investor community. In fact, that's putting it mildly."

"What the fuck?"

"Do you understand me, Mr. Wilson? Or do I need to spell it out? Now, if you think you know how to get the funds for the ridiculous amount of cash you offered your target, I suggest you take your little deal and go elsewhere and get them. Because I sure as hell can't."

"John . . ." said Pete.

"No, Pete. Mr. Wilson should know what's going on out there. Now, it's very nice that Mr. Gelb has found a further four hundred million, but right now that's about as useful to me as a bite on a rat's ass. When you find another billion and three quarters, Mr. Wilson, give me a call."

There was a deathly silence on the line.

"Pete," said Wilson at last. His voice was quiet. "Is that your attitude as well?"

Stanzy looked at Golansky. Golansky didn't return his glance.

Pete didn't know what to say.

"John," said Wilson. "Okay. Listen. You're right. What you put in is your business. I was out of line."

"I don't think you've been listening to me," said Golansky. "There's a smell about your company."

"John, John, come on." Wilson laughed. Even across the phone line it sounded desperate. "You guys can do this. Right, Pete? You guys can do this."

Stanzy didn't say anything. He was in the middle. He had the sense that he had better just shut up at this point and leave it to Golansky or Golansky really might walk.

"Come on, John," said Wilson. "Think of the fees. Think of the business you'll get in the future. You do this for me, who do you think I'll be coming back to? Merrill? Fuck Merrill!"

"There are some things that are more important than money, Mr. Wilson. That's how a firm like Dyson Whitney builds its name."

Pete stared at Golansky.

"But you'll do it, right?" said Wilson.

"How much did I say we still needed?" said Golansky.

"One-point-seven-five billion."

"Well, I've told you. I'm not saying we're there. I'm not saying we're going to get there."

"But you're saying we might, huh?"

Golanksy paused. He let the silence go on until it was almost intolerable. "We might," he said at last.

"You know the timelines," said Wilson. "You have the due diligence review Monday, right? I go to my board Wednesday. Bassett goes to his board the same day. We've got to have the loan set up by then."

"We're aware of the timelines," snapped Golansky. "If I were you, Mr. Wilson, I'd be more concerned about the premium you're going to be paying for this loan if I do manage to get it."

"Well, let's just see you get it."

"I'd be more concerned about what your board is going to say."

"You just do your job, Golansky. Just worry about getting your fee. I'll handle my board."

Pete Stanzy could feel the hostility mounting again. He wanted to get this call finished before any irreversible damage was done. "Mike," he said hurriedly, "we'll talk Monday after the due diligence review. I'll call you when it's finished."

"Fine."

"We're done. Have a good weekend. You, too, Lyall."

"Yeah," said Wilson irritably. "You guys have a good weekend as well."

Stanzy killed the line.

He glanced at John.

Golanksy shook his head. "Fuck Wilson. He can keep his fucking deal."

"You don't mean that," said Stanzy.

Golansky shrugged. "You like that guy? He's a king-size prick."

"Yeah. But you'll get the money, right?"

Golansky shrugged.

Stanzy smiled. "Come on, John."

"What?" said Golansky. There was no smile on his face. "We're not there, Pete. Nowhere near there. I'm serious. I wasn't kidding."

In Baton Rouge, Wilson noticed the way Lyall Gelb was looking at him.

"What?" he said.

Lyall Gelb didn't say anything.

"You were worried about that?" Wilson forced a smile. "That was banker's bullshit, Lyall."

That wasn't what had shocked him. It was the look on Wilson's face in that first moment when John Golansky told him to forget the deal. Desperation. Panic. Lyall Gelb had never seen a look like that on Mike Wilson's face before.

"What is it?" Wilson laughed. "All they care about is the fees. They're prostitutes, Lyall. They're all the same. They'll get the money. You'll see. It won't be a problem. You watch. They'll get it easy."

There was silence.

Wilson grinned. "Listen, Lyall, if we need to, we can get another few hundred million, right?"

Lyall stared at him.

"Huh?"

Lyall began to laugh.

"What?"

"Mike, do you think I've got some kind of bottomless piggy bank of cash where you can keep going every time . . . every time . . ." Lyall gave up, grinning in utter, despairing disbelief. "This last four hundred . . . Jiminy Creeper, Mike! We are so overloaded out there, we're pulling in debt from so many places, even the Hungarian authorities are going to start asking questions."

"Yeah, and my grandmother's going to play for the Jets."

"Mike. You don't get it, do you? There's nothing more! Do you understand? Nothing! I can't get another cent."

"Take it easy . . ."

"No!" Gelb jumped up. "You don't understand! We're done! We're through!"

"Lyall, get a grip!"

"Get a grip? Get a what? Mike, you're—"

Wilson grabbed him by the shoulders. "Get a fucking grip!" he said, and he shoved him back into the seat.

Lyall fell silent. He clutched at his belly.

"Now, listen to me. You've got to get a grip." Wilson watched him. "Okay? Listen, Lyall. We're gonna be all right. We're going to do this deal, and we're going to be all right. Lyall, you hear me? We're not through. This is only the beginning."

Lyall had closed his eyes. Only the beginning? He just wanted it to end. He felt as if he were wrapped up in coils, as if a giant snake were wrapped around him, squeezing tighter and tighter.

He opened his eyes. Wilson was watching him.

"Okay?"

Lyall nodded.

"We're gonna be all right. And guess what? Your contract says there'll be a big bonus for you when we do it as well. Remember?"

Gelb wished he could forget. The thought of the bonus that was waiting if the deal went through just made him feel even more sick. It made everything seem even more wrong, if that was possible.

"Can I go now?" he said.

"Sure, Lyall."

Gelb got up.

"You seen a doctor yet? About that ulcer?"

"No."

"I'm surprised Margaret hasn't driven you down there herself. You give her my love when you see her tonight, Lyall."

"Sure."

"And the kids. How's little Becky?"

"She's fine."

"Good. You going to get any rest this weekend? I bet the kids keep you busy, huh?"

Lyall nodded. He looked ill.

"Get some rest, Lyall. We're gonna be okay."

Lyall closed the door behind him. Mike Wilson sat down at his desk. He looked at the pictures of his own kids. No wives, just the kids. He hadn't seen them in a while. Especially the older two. When this was over, maybe he'd get them all together. Maybe fly them all down to the chalet in Aspen.

When this was over . . .

Wilson stared out the window, face set. Very calm. Very blank. Just as if he were sitting at a poker table, deep into an outrageous, almost inconceivable bluff.

He had almost blinked, just now, when John Golansky came back at him. Hell, he had blinked. And in front of Lyall Gelb.

That was bad. Lyall wasn't the man he'd been. Right now, Lyall had to be bluffed just as much as anyone else. More than anyone else. He was falling apart. Wilson had to keep him together, and the only chance he had of doing that was if Lyall saw nothing from him but the strongest, most unshakable belief that this deal was going through. That's what everyone had to see.

Wilson thought over what he'd said to Lyall after they'd gotten off the phone. He hoped he'd done enough to repair some of the damage. He'd go talk to him again later.

It was sad, the way Lyall was unraveling. Wilson doubted Gelb would ever have the nerve to be any good again. He'd keep him for a couple of years, treat him with kid gloves as Lyall quietly unwound the structures he had created. No one could do that but Lyall himself. Then he'd have to get rid of him. Give him a big payout and send him off.

Maybe he would let Bassett step up to CEO. Wilson thought about it. No, Bassett was useless. He'd get rid of him as well. In a couple of years he'd need replacements for both of them, Bassett and Gelb. That meant it wouldn't be more than a year or so before he'd have to start looking. A conversation with Gordon Anderton, the head of the recruitment consultancy who sat on the board. Very private.

Wilson brought himself back to the present. The deal wasn't done yet, he reminded himself. He couldn't afford to let anyone see him blink again.

He ran through the elements in his mind, everything that still had to fall into place. For a start, raising the loan. He had overreacted. As far as walking away over some matter of the bank's reputation, Wilson was almost certain Golansky was all talk. If he wasn't, he'd be the first banker Mike Wilson had ever heard of who'd done such a thing. The fee at stake was too large. As long as the money was there to be had, Golanksy would get it. Pete Stanzy would see to that. Wilson knew there was nothing he could do now on that front but hold his nerve and wait for the bankers to deliver. Next, there was the issue of BritEnergy's due diligence on Lousiana Light's data. He didn't think that was going to be a problem. There was so much information in that data room in New York, they wouldn't know where to start. Besides, they weren't going to be looking too hard. What did that leave? Getting the final terms of the deal past his own board, whose members hadn't been told about the increased cash he had put into the offer. He thought about Ed Leary and the other members of the board. There were ways of managing that.

Actually, everything was on track. The conversation with Golansky had unsettled him, but when you took it piece by piece, everything was as good as it could be at this stage. Now he just had to keep it all going. Everyone had to believe that he believed it was a certainty. In the middle of it all, that was the thing that held it together.

One more week of bluffing. One more week to hold his nerve.

The phone rang.

"It's Ms. Bellinger, Mr. Wilson," said Stella.

"Put her through." Wilson composed himself. "Mandy!" he said ebulliently when she came on the line. "You've saved me a call."

"Really?"

"Do you remember I told you there was something big I'd need you to work on? Well, I was just about to call. I'm going to need your help with an announcement."

"Don't tell me," said Amanda. "Louisiana Light is doing a deal."

Wilson laughed. "You're smart, Mandy. I knew you'd guess."

"I didn't guess. I know."

"Confident, aren't you?"

"No. I *know*, Mike. That's what I rang to tell you."

Wilson laughed again. "What are you talking about, Mandy?"

"I know already. You're doing a deal with a company in Europe. You're announcing Friday."

In an instant, the ebullience drained out of him. Mike Wilson felt a horrible, cold contraction in his stomach. Then the sensation spread through his body, as if infiltrating down his veins in icy tentacles. Like the feeling he got when he saw a winning hand go down on the table against an enormous stake that he knew he should never have bet, couldn't afford to lose.

"And I believe a pair of companies called Grogon and ExPar are of interest."

For an instant, Mike Wilson couldn't breathe.

"I got a call from our friend. You have a leak, Mike. A hostile leak. And make no mistake, this leak wants to scupper your deal."

"Where's it coming from?" whispered Wilson. He could barely form the words.

"Your bank. Dyson Whitney."

Wilson closed his eyes. "Who is it?"

"Don't worry, Mike. I've got his details."

36

Stella knocked on Mike Wilson's door. She waited for a moment, then went in.

"Mr. Wilson?" she said. "Are you all right?"

Wilson was sitting at his desk, gazing blankly at the window. Slowly, he turned and focused on her.

"Mr. Wilson? You didn't answer the phone."

"Didn't I?"

"Are you all right, Mr. Wilson? Can I get you something?"

"No, Stella."

"I have Mrs. Rubin here to see you. That's what I just called you to say."

"Does she have an appointment?"

"Yes. It's on your daily itinerary, Mr. Wilson." Stella took a couple of steps closer to the desk. "Shall I find it for you?"

"No, Stella. What does Mrs. Rubin want?"

"I believe it's about the company's annual donation to the Livingston Young Entrepreneurs' Association." Stella paused. "Do you want to reschedule?"

"No." Mike Wilson shook his head. "Send her in."

"Are you sure, Mr. Wilson?"

"Please, Stella."

Stella nodded quickly. She watched him for a second longer and then went out.

Jackie Rubin came in. She was a big woman with a habit of wearing sleeveless dresses and a lot of makeup. "Looks like that nasty business with the *Herald* has gone away," she remarked as she sat down.

Mike Wilson almost wanted to laugh.

He had meetings through the rest of the afternoon, routine stuff that had been building up with all the time he had been spending on the deal. Don Lepore, the sales and marketing director, briefed him on a new contract they had designed for their top corporate customers. Hannah Grainger from personnel came in with a couple of her people to talk through a new training program for management inductees. Then there was another marketing thing and Don came back with one of his people. Then there were a couple of IT people who gave him an update on a project he couldn't remember anything about. One of the Mexican plant managers was visiting and he had half an hour with him and Ernesto Poblán, the operations guy for South America. Then it was something else. And something else. All the crap a CEO had to sit through. But Wilson didn't mind. He was grateful for it. Grateful to have his mind taken off the other thing and what he was going to have to do.

But it didn't really take his mind off it. Not really.

At the end of the day, Doug Earl came by and asked if he could have a few minutes. There was some legal stuff relating to the deal he needed to go over and the lawyers in New York had asked him to get back to them before the weekend. They sat at the coffee table in Wilson's office and Doug took him through a bunch of documents. Wilson listened mechanically, nodding when he was supposed to nod. Doug left.

Wilson slumped in the armchair. Outside, over the river, the sun was setting. He stayed there, staring, as the room got darker.

There was a knock. The door opened a fraction.

"Come in," said Wilson.

It was Stella. "Don't you want a light in here, Mr. Wilson?"

"I guess so."

Stella looked at him quizzically. She turned on the lights in the office.

"Just a few things to go over," she said. She came to the table and set down a portfolio of letters for him to sign. Then she sat down and went quickly through the notes she'd made during the day, dealing with the matters that needed to be cleared, requests for appointments to be scheduled or denied, e-mails addressed to him that he needed to look at, messages she'd taken that she had decided could wait for the end of the day. It took about fifteen minutes.

"Shall I wait while you sign those?" she asked, nodding at the portfolio on the table.

"No, Stella. You go on home." He looked at his watch. "You should have been gone an hour ago."

"It's no problem, Mr. Wilson."

"You go on home, Stella."

Stella stood up. She was looking at him again with concern. "Are you sure you're all right, Mr. Wilson?"

"Yes, Stella."

"I could stay a little longer . . ." She shook her head questioningly.

Wilson smiled. "Go on home."

"Well, don't forget, you have the State Orchestra board of trustees dinner tonight. Ms. Mendelsson rang to make sure I reminded you."

"How many times?" asked Wilson.

Stella smiled. "Three."

Mike Wilson sighed wearily.

"She said—"

"I'm sure I know what she said, Stella."

Stella nodded quickly. "I'm sorry, Mr. Wilson."

"Oh, shoot! I'm sorry, Stella. I didn't mean to snap. You go on home now. You've done more than enough for one day."

"All right, Mr. Wilson."

"Stella?"

Stella stopped and turned back. "What is it, Mr. Wilson?"

"How long is it you've worked for me now?"

"Four years, Mr. Wilson. Four years last September."

"And . . . it's okay, isn't it?"

"What do you mean, Mr. Wilson?"

"I mean, you don't mind . . . it's not too bad, is it?"

"It's a very good job, Mr. Wilson. I enjoy each day. I just hope I do it well enough for your satisfaction."

"Oh, no . . . that's not what I mean. I mean . . ." Mike Wilson frowned. "Working for me. You don't think I'm such a bad guy, do you?"

"Oh, Mr. Wilson." Stella shook her head. She even blushed a little. "You're fine, Mr. Wilson. Better than fine. I'm very happy working for you."

Mike Wilson nodded. "Well, that's good to hear," he murmured. He nodded again and sighed. "Thank you, Stella."

There was silence.

"Is that all, Mr. Wilson?"

"Yeah, Stella. Thanks."

"Good night, Mr. Wilson."

"Good night, Stella. You have yourself a fine weekend."

"Thank you, Mr. Wilson."

Stella closed the door. Wilson opened the portfolio and started signing the letters. When he had finished, he tossed the portfolio back on the table.

And then there was nothing left, nothing to distract him from his own terrible thoughts. They came out, as if from the recesses of his mind, and ran riot.

He was finished if the deal fell through. That was clear. Finding another one would be impossible. Even if he found another target, even if he had one selected right now, there wouldn't be time to complete it before the next quarterly filing. So this was it, make or break. The only hand in the game. Everything was riding on it.

And it had all seemed to be falling into place until the phone call had come through from Mandy Bellinger. Even that stuff from the bankers about the loan, that was just talk. But now something had gotten in the way. Someone was apparently talking. An analyst who had names. Actual, accurate names. And he was telling people. Journalists.

He couldn't just ring up Pete Stanzy and tell him to shut the analyst up. He'd talk even more if he did that. And if he had those names, he must have details. Wilson shuddered to think what those details might be.

So what was he meant to do?

Mike Wilson didn't regard himself as an especially good person. He had done some bad things in his time, he knew. In business and in his personal life. Things that he never thought he would do, if you had asked him when he was younger. But like everyone, he found ways to rationalize them. There were reasons, explanations. When there was nothing else, he could always remind himself that there were still some things he wouldn't do. If he wasn't exactly a good person, he wasn't utterly bad. He had boundaries. He had limits. Didn't he?

The phone rang. His cell phone. It was on the desk. Wilson got up and looked at it. The display showed Dot Mendelsson's number. Mike Wilson ignored it.

It was dark outside now. Wilson turned off the lights in the room. Down by the river, the lights of the factories glittered cold, blue-white. The river itself was a deep, inky strip of darkness.

What choice did he have? There was no other way out. And no time to lose. It was as stark as could be, black and white, a zero-sum game. It was him or this analyst, one or the other. And whose fault was it? Who asked this analyst to get involved? Why had he decided to start talking?

Yet it gave Wilson a cold, nauseating feeling. He felt as if he were going to throw up, just thinking about it.

And yet, what choice did he have?

Mike Wilson picked up the phone. He knew that he was going to make the call. He had known, at some level, from the moment he heard Mandy Bellinger tell him what she'd heard. Maybe he just had to wait for night to fall before he could bring himself to do it.

37

The voice on the phone was impatient. "Yeah?"

"Tony? It's Mike. Mike Wilson."

The tone changed. "Mike Wilson. This is a pleasure. How are you, Michael?"

"Not bad, Tony."

"I heard you didn't have such a good night in Budapest the other night." Tony Prinzi chuckled. "And in London the other week. You been busy, Mike. All over the world."

"Yeah. I've been busy."

"So, how is this big deal of yours going, Mike? When am I going to see my money?"

"You'll get it," said Wilson. "Everything. As soon as the deal's done."

"I know that, Michael. You think I'd keep bankrolling you if I didn't? Mike, I have to tell you, if not, you would have had a visit by now. Not from me, you understand?"

Mike listened to Tony laugh.

"It's all right, Michael. I'm just talking."

Was he? Wilson still didn't know if this gangster talk was for real or if it was just the stuff you saw on *The Sopranos*. He was about to find out.

"Listen, Tony, there's some advice I need."

"How can I help you, Michael?"

"This deal of mine, Tony . . ."

"What is this deal, anyway, Mike? I've been patient, and I believe what you have told me, but I'm not sure I understand how this works. You tell me you'll pay me everything you owe when this deal is done. All right. What are you doing in this deal?"

"It's confidential, Tony."

"I understand, Michael. Confidentiality in my business also is something we take seriously."

"I'm buying another company."

"You?"

"My company is buying the other company."

"You see, this is what I don't understand," said Prinzi. "Your company buys another company. But your company isn't *your* company. You work for this company. Am I right?"

"You're right, Tony."

"So it buys another company. Where from do you get the money out of this?"

"They pay me for doing the deal."

"Who?"

"My board."

"How much?"

"Twenty-four million."

There was a long whistle on the phone.

"Let me get this straight. You buy a company, and your board gives you money? Just for doing the deal?" Prinzi laughed. "Mike, that's easier than stealing candy from a baby. And let me tell you, I've done that."

"That's how it works," said Wilson. He was getting impatient.

Prinzi was still chuckling in amusement.

"Tony, listen to me. I need some advice. There's someone who's making trouble."

"There's always someone making trouble, Michael. This is a fact of life. You gotta ask yourself, how bad is this trouble?"

"Bad, Tony."

Prinzi sighed, as if it disturbed him deeply to say what he was going to say. "Then you must take away the source of this trouble."

"That's not so easy."

"There's always a way, Michael."

Wilson hesitated. He frowned, almost as if he were in pain. "Tony, I think I might need to ask you for a favor."

"I must tell you, Michael, favors I don't do so much."

"This person, Tony, the kind of trouble he's making could make my deal very hard to do."

"That doesn't sound good for you, Mike."

A rare moment of understatement from Tony Prinzi, thought Wilson.

"Tony, no deal, no money."

"Michael, if I don't get my money, unpleasant things are going to happen. You understand me? I don't dislike you. It's not personal, it's business."

"Yes. But that doesn't get you your money, does it?"

"Listen, I'm not a cruel man, Mike, but if I don't get my money . . ."

"Tony, what I'm saying is, you want this deal to happen, too. If it doesn't happen, it's your money that doesn't get paid."

"Yeah, but it's your kneecaps, Mike."

"But it's your money, Tony. What do you prefer to have, my

money or my kneecaps? What good are my kneecaps going to do you?" Wilson waited for Prinzi's response. He had been involved in hundreds of negotiations in his business career, but this one was unlike any of them. It was possible, he thought, that Tony Prinzi would say he'd take the kneecaps.

Prinzi laughed. "I understand, Mike."

"So, is there any way you can . . . you know, scare this guy?"

"Scare him?"

"You know," said Wilson. "Stop him talking."

"Michael, you been watching too many gangster shows."

Wilson nodded to himself. For a moment, despite everything, he felt a sense of relief. Of course, Prinzi was all talk.

"You want to stop someone talking, you don't scare him. Who knows what such a person will do? Go to the police, maybe. Make things worse. You want to stop someone talking . . . you have to stop him. Period."

Wilson was gripped by a clench of cold, clammy nausea.

"Michael? Are you still there?"

"Isn't there any other way?"

"If you ask my opinion, no."

Wilson really did think he was going to throw up. He breathed deeply.

"Michael, who is this person? He's important?"

"Not really."

"People know him? He's some kind of a public figure?"

"No, Tony."

"Then what are you worried about?"

"So, you can . . . you can do it?"

"Mike, please. Who are you talking to here? I'm putting my trust in you. You're not a violent man, right? You're not a thug. You wouldn't ask this thing if it wasn't important."

"No," said Wilson hoarsely.

"I respect this. So I say to you, we can do this."

Wilson shut his eyes. Was it really this easy? It seemed even easier than in the movies.

"But Mike, it'll cost you. You want to know how much? He's no one special, right? No one anyone's going to notice? Let's say, twenty grand. On account of I'm partly doing this for myself, as you pointed out. But I've still got expenses, you understand. All right? Twenty K? And listen, interest on this, I won't charge you."

"Fine," whispered Wilson. Twenty thousand. Less than he spent on the corporate jet in a week.

"What was that?"

"Fine, Tony. Add it to the bill."

Prinzi laughed. "'Add it to the bill.' I like that. Add it to the bill. All right. So, who is he? Where are we talking about?"

"New York," said Wilson

"New York? That's convenient. You got an address? Makes it easier if you can give me an address."

"It's on West Thirty-ninth Street."

"Oh, Hell's Kitchen. We cleaned that up, you know. Long time ago now, back in the eighties. The Westies, they were making life hell for everybody. No class. You been there recently, Mike? It's amazing how the area's improving."

Tony Prinzi, the civic father, thought Wilson in revulsion.

"Where on West Thirty-ninth Street? You want to tell me? I'll get a piece of paper."

"Tony . . ." Wilson grimaced. "How do you . . . you know . . . what do you do?"

"Mike, you don't want to know the details. Trust me, we know how to do this. Every case is different. In the city, we make it look like a burglary maybe. That's a very good way of doing it. Does he live alone? If he lives alone, you just knock on the door, go inside . . . then it's done. A knock on the door, it's done. Make it look like a burglary. But there are other methods we can employ. You must leave this question to us. Now, who is he?"

"It's not . . . it'll be quick, right?"

"Jesus Christ, Mike! You want a video of it?"

"Christ, no!"

"Then what the fuck are you worried about? Excuse me for cursing."

"I just don't want it to be bad."

"It's bad. Michael, this is not a good thing. On the other hand, it can be worse. You want us to hurt him first?"

"No!" cried Wilson. "Christ, no!"

"All right, we'll do our best to make it quick. I'll see to it. But no guarantees. It's not a science, Mike, it's an art. Now, I haven't got all night. You want to keep talking about it or you want me to do something?" Prinzi paused. "You want this done quick?"

"How quickly can you do it?"

"Tonight, I'm not sure if we have availability. This is something Nick will know. Michael, to be on the safe side, if not tonight, I would say by tomorrow night definitely. Will that be quick enough for you?"

Wilson shuddered. "Yes," he whispered.

"Okay. So, who is it?"

Wilson picked up the piece of paper with the details Mandy Bellinger had given him.

"Hold on, Mike. Hold on. I gotta write this down."

Wilson heard Prinzi take a few steps. He imagined a dwarflike, barrel-chested man waddling across a room.

"Ahhh. Okay. Shoot."

Wilson stared hard at the piece of paper in his hand.

"Michael, what is it? You wanna do this or not? What's his name?"

Mike Wilson hesitated for one last moment. "Robert Holding."

38

Rob opened his eyes. Emmy was watching him.

"What?" he murmured.

"Nothing."

"You hear something?"

She shook her head. Rob listened. The noise of New York early on a Saturday morning. Emmy was still gazing at him, propped up on her elbow. Rob smiled blearily, sheepishly.

Emmy turned over, with her back to him, and nestled close. Rob kissed the back of her neck. He ran his hand over her arm. Then over the curve of her hip. Then lower.

"Mmmm . . ." murmured Emmy. She reached back and let her hand wander. "Ooh!" she said in a tone of mock surprise, then giggled as she got on top.

Afterward they lay side by side, hands entwined. Rob gazed at the ceiling, not thinking about anything in particular.

"How are you feeling?" said Emmy.

Rob smiled.

Emmy smiled for a second as well. Then she was serious. "Well?"

For a moment, Rob didn't know what she meant. Making love with Emmy had driven it out of his head completely.

"I mean about what you did yesterday."

"Oh," said Rob. "Yeah. Fine. I'm all right, I guess."

"You don't regret it?"

Rob thought. Did he regret talking to the journalist? No. Not yet, anyway. He might feel differently by the end of the day, when the shit had really hit the fan.

He looked at the clock. Six-forty. He had to be in the war room again today. Saturdays and Sundays didn't seem to mean anything anymore. But Sammy had gone easy on them this time. Told them to be in at nine.

"Shall I go get the *Herald*?" said Rob suddenly.

"Yeah. Go on. Go get it. I'll make breakfast."

"What will you make?"

Emmy frowned. "I may have a couple of eggs in the fridge . . ."

"No corn chips?"

"Funny."

"Let's go out," said Rob. "The *Herald* and a champagne breakfast. What do you think?"

"Rob, the *Herald* doesn't go with a champagne breakfast."

"You're right. The *Herald* and . . . pancakes."

"Better," said Emmy.

At the first newsstand they came to, Rob bought a copy of the *Herald*. He stopped to open it.

"Come on," said Emmy, grabbing his hand. "It's freezing!"

The wind was biting. They half-ran to a diner a couple of blocks away. Rob turned to the financial page of the paper. Emmy blew on her hands to warm them.

"Well?" she said.

"It's not here."

"Don't look in the middle of the paper. It's a big story!"

The waitress came. Emmy ordered coffee and pancakes for the two of them. Rob leafed through the paper.

"Well?"

"I can't find it."

Emmy sighed. "Hand it over."

She went through the paper, page after advertisement-filled page. "Where's the news in this thing?" she murmured. By the time the pancakes arrived, she had reached the same conclusion as Rob.

Rob frowned. "Why didn't they print it?"

"Maybe this is an early edition."

"I spoke to her at lunchtime, Emmy. How early can it get?"

"You want maple syrup?"

Rob didn't want anything at that moment except to see the story in the paper.

Emmy waited a second, then poured maple syrup over her own pancakes. "They're probably holding it back a day or two. You said yourself they'd been investigating for months. It's a big story, right? They're gonna make sure they get it right." Emmy chewed on a piece of pancake. "You know what?" she said, waving her fork. "I bet they're holding it back for tomorrow. It's a great Sunday story."

Rob grunted. "Maybe."

"Eat!" said Emmy, waving her fork at him again.

He reached out for the maple syrup and drizzled the pancakes until they were soaking. He took a piece. Then he slurped a sip of coffee and ate more. Emmy was leafing through the paper.

"Look at this," she said, shaking her head. "Some lady's refusing to give her niece five hundred bucks because she's marrying someone she doesn't like. And she promised it to her from the day she was born."

"Who does she want her to marry?"

Emmy frowned. "Some cripple. But with a heart of gold."

"Yeah," said Rob. "Isn't that always the way?"

"She won't give her the money."

"How much did you say it was?"

"Five hundred bucks."

Rob laughed. "Get a life!"

Emmy nodded and kept reading the column.

Later, they walked back to the apartment.

"You going to be working all day?" asked Emmy.

Rob shrugged. Since the story hadn't been published, work in the war room would continue. "I really thought the story was going to be there."

"It will be. Look, if you're so worried, call up the journalist."

Rob thought about it. It was less than twenty-four hours since he had given the information. Emmy was right. They probably had some checking of their own to do before they published something like that.

"Well?" said Emmy.

"No. It'll be there."

"Okay. So, is it all day today?"

"Sammy says we're in good shape. A few hours' work this morning on our section of the due diligence report, maybe early afternoon, we'll be done."

"Isn't Greg moving into your apartment today?"

"No, that's tomorrow."

"And you're going to stay . . . where, exactly?" said Emmy.

"Well, there's this young lady I know."

"Isn't that rather presumptuous, Mr. Holding?"

"She likes presumptuous."

Emmy laughed. "Does she just?"

"That's what I've heard."

Emmy slapped him on the arm.

"Thanks."

"You deserved it!"

Their eyes met. Suddenly there was more to that slap than a mock rebuke over Rob's presumptuousness. There was more to everything now. It was out in the open, the question that had been buried between them for months. Rob had promised to deal with it and Emmy's gaze told him that she had decided to give him a little more time and see if he did. But he didn't know how long she would wait. At some point, he knew, it would burst out again. If he was lucky, she would wait until this deal was over, until he had some time to think. If he wasn't lucky, it would be tonight.

But not this morning. She huddled close to him as they walked into the cold breeze.

"Will Greg need any help to get his stuff to your place?" asked Emmy.

"Don't know." Rob thought about it. "That's a good question. I'll find out."

39

Sammy was right. They were in good shape. Until Phil Menendez walked into the war room at eleven o'clock and told them that with the extra two billion of debt, the banks were asking for all kinds of covenants and triggers and they were going to have to rework the loan schedule and model a whole new bunch of scenarios. Soon they were deep in the work. At first Rob felt a little false, thinking how all this effort was going to be wasted once the *Herald* published his story. But then the numbers took over and he was absorbed in the work as well. They ordered in sushi and worked through lunch. At about three o'clock, Rob got a phone call. It was Greg.

"You set for tomorrow?" asked Rob, realizing that he had forgotten all about him.

"Actually," said Greg, "I was wondering if I could get over to your place today."

"Umm . . . sure," said Rob.

"Were you planning to be there?"

"No, not at all. Only, I haven't cleaned it and I won't have a chance—"

"Don't worry about that," said Greg. "That doesn't matter. You don't mind, right? You'd tell me if you minded?"

"Absolutely."

"You're not using it?"

"No, I'll be at Emmy's."

"Turns out Louise is coming back tomorrow morning. I thought it was tomorrow night. I mean, I could stay tonight and get out early tomorrow, but right now I just want to get out. I just want to get it done."

"Sure. Greg, listen, the place is yours. I wanted to ask you, you need help with your stuff?"

"No, it'll take a couple of trips, that's all."

"All right, well, why don't you go pick a key up from Emmy. You know where her apartment is?" He gave Greg the address and told him he'd call to let Emmy know he was coming. "The place is yours. There's sheets and towels and . . . it's yours, just use it."

"Thanks, Rob."

"Wait till you see the state of it before you thank me."

Greg laughed, a little sadly.

"Hey, you going to be all right?" said Rob.

"Sure."

"Really?"

"It's just one of those things, right?" said Greg. "You've got to go through it. It's life. No downs, no ups."

"That's right."

"What doesn't kill you makes you stronger."

"At least your appetite for clichés hasn't suffered."

Greg laughed again, in the same way.

"You know we're here for you, Greg."

"Sure. I know that, Rob."

"Both of us. Me and Emmy."

"Yeah."

"Okay. Well, make yourself at home when you get there. If you can find any liquor, it's yours. Drink yourself into a stupor if that'll help. I'll call you later to make sure everything's okay."

"You don't have to do that."

"I'll call you later."

At about six o'clock, Phil Menendez came back. He was on his way somewhere, head freshly shaved, reeking of fragrance and dressed in a tux. Blue velvet jacket with big lapels and a big velvet bow tie. Very tasteful. He looked like a shiny, blue, bullet-headed beetle.

Sammy had a set of outputs of the loan scenarios ready for him. Menendez grabbed them and sat down. Rob watched as Menendez ran his eyes over the pages, wondering what it was like to be inside that belligerent head, what the world looked like from in there. What it was going to look like tomorrow after the *Herald* came out.

Menendez was happy with the outputs, even Rob could see that. He was struggling not to let it show.

"They're not complete," said Sammy. "We have a couple more scenarios to run."

Menendez threw the sheets back at Sammy. "We'll see what John Golansky says when he sees them," he said, as if that were the only threat he could think of. "He wants the complete set five P.M. tomorrow." Menendez got up.

"Hey, Phil, where are you going?" asked Rob on some kind of wild, disinhibited whim.

Menendez looked at him incredulously. "What the fuck difference does it make to you?" He shook his head. "Little fuck," he muttered as he left the room.

"Like I fucking care," muttered Rob as the door closed.

"He's going to a dinner function with his fiancée, if you want to know," said Sammy. "At least, I believe that's what he's doing."

Cynthia and Rob glanced at each other incredulously.

"Dressed like that?" said Rob.

"He has a fiancée?" said Cynthia.

Emmy was having a glass of wine when Rob got home. It was after eleven.

"I've taken to drinking alone," she explained.

"That's nice," said Rob.

"But you're going to join me."

"I don't know, Emmy. I'm kind of tired . . ."

Emmy was already pouring him a glass.

"But on the other hand, how can I say no?"

"Cheers," said Emmy.

They clinked. Emmy sat down on the sofa and beckoned to Rob. He wondered just how many glasses she'd already had.

"How was your day?" she asked.

"Yeah, okay. Cut a loan schedule," he said, as if he did it every day of the week.

"How interesting," said Emmy, as if she cared. "Greg came for the key."

Greg! Rob had forgotten all about him.

"He didn't look too good. I decided to go with him. Helped him move his stuff in."

"Thanks, Em. I really appreciate it. Did he have much stuff?"

Emmy shook her head. "Couple of suitcases. A few boxes. He said he was leaving the bigger stuff until he had a place of his own. We had coffee afterward at that little place you like on Tenth."

"What did he say?"

"Not much. That's okay. I think he just welcomed the company. He didn't need to say anything. If he'd just wanted me to sit there, that would've been fine." Emmy sighed. "He's a really nice guy. He deserves someone way better than that Snookums bitch."

"I'm not going to lose you to him, am I?" said Rob.

"Well, you never know. Me and the bottle, we get lonely sometimes."

Rob looked at her. She shrugged.

He glanced at his watch. "I said I was going to call him."

"Yeah?" said Emmy. "You should."

"It's not too late?"

Emmy shook her head.

Rob wasn't sure. Hugging her wineglass, Emmy didn't look like a woman whose judgment was at its peak.

"Honey, if you said you would, you should. This isn't the time to let him down. Call his cell phone. If he's asleep, he'll have turned it off."

Rob nodded. He rang Greg's cell. Greg answered.

"You're still awake?" said Rob.

"Apparently."

"Sorry I'm calling so late. I got held up."

"No problem."

"Anyway, I just wanted to check. Everything all right?"

"Yeah, there's just—"

"What's that you're listening to?" Rob laughed. "You having a party over there?"

"No, it's this radio you've got in here. I've been fiddling with the alarm."

"You work out how to use it?"

"Yeah. Look, there's this blind here in the bedroom. I've been trying to get it down . . ."

"There's kind of a trick to that. I should've told you." Rob explained how to do it. The mechanism for the cord was broken and the only way to get the blind down was to manually release it.

"Wait a second," said Greg. "Let me see."

"Be careful, because if you push the whole thing, it's gonna come down. It's just the release you want to push."

"Okay."

"Can you see it? Get a chair."

"Okay . . . hold on . . . give me a second. . . . Okay, yeah, I see it."

"You just kind of push it to the right."

"Okay, I can do that. Yeah, I see. I'll be fine."

"Everything else all right?"

"Yeah, it's great. Emmy came over with me. Made it a lot easier. It would've been kind of depressing to have to move everything in without anyone else around."

"Listen," said Rob, "I was thinking, if I finish early enough tomorrow, maybe we can get together." Rob glanced at Emmy as he said it. Emmy nodded.

"Yeah, that'd be good," said Greg.

"I'm not sure what's happening, though. I think we're going to be done by about five. So maybe after that. Huh? I'll give you a call."

"Okay," said Greg. "Don't worry if you can't."

"No, well, I'll see. It's just this deal's getting hotter and—"

"Hey, whatever happened with that company?" said Greg. "You were saying it was shaky."

"Read the *Herald* tomorrow, Greg."

"The *Herald*?"

"Yeah. You'll know what I'm talking about when you—"

"Hey, Rob. Sorry. Someone's knocking."

Rob laughed. "That'll be Mrs. Angelou from twenty-four."

"This late? You sure I should answer?"

"It's fine. She's kind of demented. She's always knocking on people's doors, asking for milk for her cat. She doesn't have one, by the way."

"So, am I meant to give her any?"

"Opinion's divided. Just wait . . ." Rob glanced at Emmy. "Mrs. Angelou's knocking," he said softly.

Emmy laughed.

"Greg, is she still knocking?"

"Yeah."

"Well, you'd better answer. She'll knock all night, otherwise. Say you've run out of milk and she can come back tomorrow if she wants some. Don't worry, she won't remember you said it. Just be nice to her and she'll go away."

The next day, Sammy faxed the loan document to John Golansky's home at five o'clock. They waited for Golanksy to okay it and they all went home.

There had been no article in the *Herald*.

"It's only Sunday," said Emmy.

"The whole point is for them to publish."

"But the announcement's Friday, right? You told the journalist."

Rob nodded.

"So there's time. They're probably working it up into a big splash." Emmy smiled. "Come on, you've got a night off! That doesn't happen every day. Or every week, for that matter. What do you want to do?"

"I told Greg we might hang out with him."

"Sure," said Emmy. "Call him up."

There was no reply on Greg's cell. Rob left a message, saying he and Emmy were free for dinner if Greg wanted to do something. Greg didn't call back.

"Maybe we should just go over there anyway," suggested Rob.

"He'll know you've called. If he's there and he wants to be by himself, let's let him do that. Maybe he needs a little space."

"I've got to get some fresh clothes," said Rob.

"Can it wait until tomorrow?"

"I guess so."

"Then go tomorrow," said Emmy.

40

The Louisiana Light due diligence review meeting was scheduled to kick off in the Sixth Avenue offices of Grayson, Arpel, Madden & Lamb, Louisiana Light's lawyers, at one o'clock Monday afternoon. The lawyers and accountants would present their findings. So would the investment bankers, who would also run the meeting. Their main interest was to make sure the lawyers and accountants didn't put any language into the final report that would give the Louisiana Light board a reason to reject the deal.

Pete Stanzy and Phil Menendez took Sammy Weiss for backup on detail. The minute they walked out of the war room, Cynthia and Rob shut down their computers. Neither of them planned to stay around. Once Sammy was back from the meeting, they knew, the work was going to start again. The due diligence report had to be finalized by the following morning, which meant they were probably going to be working all night.

Particularly since the *Herald* still hadn't published the story.

Rob waited for Cynthia to go and then called Emmy.

"They didn't print it."

"I know," said Emmy. "I saw."

"I'm going to call that journalist. Where are you now?"

"At work."

"You want to grab lunch? I've got a couple of hours."

"Oh, honey, we've got a working lunch with Fay." Fay Pride, the editorial director at Lascelle, was famous for her so-called working lunches. According to Emmy, they consisted of drink, food, and work. In steeply descending proportions.

"Can't you get out of it?"

"I shouldn't, Rob."

"You don't love me, that's why."

"On the contrary, my darling."

"You're all sweet words."

"I'm an editor." Emmy laughed. "I'll see you tonight?"

"I doubt it. They're at the review meeting. When they get back, it's all going to start. Actually, I should go by my apartment and pick up some clothes. Might be the only chance I get." Rob thought for a moment. He could call the journalist from there.

"Did you hear back from Greg, by the way?" asked Emmy.

"No."

"Well, I'm sure he's fine. He just needed some space."

"Yeah, it's always the same," said Rob. "You give 'em your apartment and they don't want to know you."

"I've got to go," said Emmy.

"Sure. I'm just talking."

"See you tonight."

He rang his apartment, on the off chance that Greg hadn't gone to work, and got through to his own answering machine. Then he rang Greg's cell phone. The phone rang and went to voice mail. Rob hesitated, then didn't leave a message. Then he wondered whether he should have, so he texted Greg to let him know he was on his way over, just in case Greg was at the apartment after all.

He left the office. Outside it was breezy, cool, but the sun was shining. It was good to be outside, out of the war room and away from it all. He started walking.

Less than ten blocks. It didn't take long.

Rob knocked. Along the corridor, a door opened and Mrs. Angelou put her head out.

"Hello, Mrs. Angelou," said Rob.

Mrs. Angelou stared at him for a moment. Then she smiled. She waved her hand slowly. Rob waved back. Mrs. Angelou nodded and disappeared.

Rob knocked again. Then he put his key in the lock and opened the door.

The place was a mess. Greg, he thought. He went in. Then he stopped. It wasn't just a mess. The DVD player was gone. And DVDs. He looked around more carefully. He didn't move. The apartment had been burgled.

He became aware of something else. Music was coming from somewhere inside the apartment. He listened. It was coming from around the corner. From the bedroom.

The radio? The radio was on.

"Greg?" he called.

The music kept playing.

Rob didn't want to move. He really didn't want to move.

"Greg?"

Rob pulled out his cell phone. His mouth was dry now. He called Greg's number. There was no ring. Thank God.

Then he heard it.

His heart almost stopped. Greg's phone was ringing around the corner, where the music was coming from.

Rob didn't want to go around that corner. More than anything in the world, he didn't want to go around the corner.

He stepped forward through the littered, burgled room. Fear and dread physically weighed him down, as if each of his feet were made of lead.

He got to the corner. He was breathing heavily. His pulse raced, he was clammy.

He looked.

Greg lay facedown in the bedroom doorway, dressed in jeans and an old sweater, a huge dark stain on the carpet beneath him.

41

His cell phone rang.

"You have to answer that?" asked the cop.

Rob shook his head, looking at the number. It was Sammy Weiss. "I'll turn it off," he murmured.

There were two detectives with him. They had introduced themselves as George Nabandian and Steve Engels. Engels had short dark hair and looked about Rob's age. Nabandian was older, rounder, and almost bald, with a thick mustache. There were other cops around as well, more coming all the time. Rob and the two detectives were standing in the corridor. Over their shoulders, Rob could see one of the cops looking around his apartment, dressed in white coveralls and a mask. From time to time, he caught the flare of a camera flash through the door.

Mrs. Angelou was staring at them from her doorway. The cops had already told her to go inside, but she kept coming back.

"She's probably scared," said Rob. "She's a little demented."

"It's all right, lady," yelled Engels, as if that would calm her. He turned back to Rob. "So, this is your apartment?"

Rob nodded. "I spend most of my time at my girlfriend's. Greg was—"

Someone pushed past them, coming out of the apartment. The detectives took Rob a little farther down the corridor.

"What were you saying?"

"Greg's a good friend . . ." He was distracted by someone else going into the apartment.

The two detectives waited.

"Umm . . . what was I saying?"

"Greg was a good friend."

"Yeah, that's right. We went to law school together. He split up with his girlfriend last week. I told him he could use the apartment until he found his own place. See, he was living with her, in her apartment . . ."

"You have his girlfriend's name, Rob?"

"Sure. Louise . . . Louise . . . Jesus, I've forgotten her last name." Rob shook his head. He'd gone blank. "I'll remember it. Give me a second."

"You got the address?"

"Yeah. It's down in the Village. Umm . . . Effers!"

"What?"

"Her name. Effers. Louise Effers."

Engels was writing in his pad. "All right, Rob," said Nabandian. "That's fine. We'll check it out. Now, coming back to Greg, you say he moved into your apartment. When was that?"

"That was Saturday," said Rob. "I was at the office, so he picked up the key from Emmy—she's my girlfriend. I called him up on Saturday night to see how he was doing."

"He was here?"

"I guess so." Rob frowned. "I called on his cell phone, but he said he was here. He was having trouble with the blind in the bedroom."

"And then? When did you talk to him after that?"

Rob thought. "I didn't. That would be the last time I talked to him."

"On Saturday night?"

Rob was staring at the ground.

"Rob?" said Nabandian gently. "That was the last time you talked to him? Saturday night?"

"Sorry. Yes. That was the last time. It would have been . . . it was sometime after eleven. I got back to Emmy's after work and I can remember thinking it was kind of late to call him. But I said I would. I guess you can check the exact time from my phone records, huh?"

Engels glanced up at him from his pad.

"What did he say when you talked to him?" asked Nabandian.

"Not much. I just asked him how he was and how he was settling in." Rob shrugged. "Like I said, he was having trouble with the blind. See, there's this blind in the bedroom that doesn't work, I mean there's kind of a trick to it. I can show you. You want me to show you?"

"Not now," said Nabandian quickly. "It's all right. We'll check it out."

"Okay."

"You said you asked how he was settling in."

"Yeah. That's right."

"And then?"

"That was pretty much it. He had to get the door. Someone was knocking."

Engels looked up. "At eleven o'clock on a Saturday night?"

"She's awake all hours," said Rob, and he nodded toward Mrs. Angelou, who was still watching from her doorway. "It wouldn't be unusual. She thinks she has a cat."

The cops watched him. They had both been inside the apartment, and they had both seen enough corpses in their years on the force to know that the body lying in there had been dead for some time. Over a day, maybe closer to two. Eleven o'clock on Saturday night? Could have been around then, the coroner's report would tell. Right now, it sounded very much as if the individual in front of them was trying to fix that time in their minds by saying the victim had said there was a knock on the door—while he, Rob, had been elsewhere. And of course there was no one who could refute that story, because the victim had supposedly told him about a knock on the door in a phone conversation that no one else had heard. And Rob had already told them to check the phone records to see when he had spoken to Greg. To a detective, that automatically sounded suspicious. Put it all together, and it sounded as if the individual in front of them had already spent some time figuring out how his alibi could be established.

Rob shrugged. "She likes to borrow milk for the cat."

"So she'd be able to tell us if she knocked," asked Nabandian.

"You can ask her," said Rob, "but she won't remember. She can tell you all about Harry S. Truman, but she can't tell you a thing about what happened ten minutes ago."

The two detectives exchanged a glance.

"What about yesterday?" asked Nabandian. "You didn't talk to him?"

"I was working most of the day."

"You sure work a lot," said Engels.

"I'm an investment banker. I called him when I finished work."

"What time?" asked Nabandian.

"Some time after five. We were going to hang out."

Engels looked at him sharply. "Was that something you'd arranged with him?"

"Kind of."

"When?"

"When we talked on Saturday."

Engels looked at his notes. "I thought you said you asked him how he was and you talked about the blind and then he had to go get the door."

"Yeah, well, I talked to him about hanging out as well."

The two detectives exchanged another glance.

"Anything else you didn't tell us about when you talked to him?" asked Engels.

"Take a moment to think about it," cautioned Nabandian.

Rob frowned. He shook his head.

"So you called him on Sunday," said Nabandian. "What happened?"

"I told you, I didn't talk to him. I got put through to his voice mail. And today as well, before I came over."

"He call you back after your message yesterday?"

"No."

"Is that unusual?"

Rob frowned. "I don't know. Maybe."

"But you didn't do anything about it?"

"Look, I don't know," said Rob. "I guess it didn't worry me at the time."

"You didn't think you should come over and see if he was okay?" said Engels.

"No."

"Not even after he had this supposed knock on the door late on Saturday night?"

"It just didn't . . ." Rob glanced toward Mrs. Angelou. "She's around all the time."

Engels watched Rob for a moment. Then he glanced at Nabandian.

"Okay," said Nabandian. "You know we need to check everything, Rob. Just routine, make sure we've got the times right. Is there
anyone who could corroborate what you're telling us?"

"My girlfriend, Emmy," said Rob. "Emmy Bridges. She was there
when I called Greg. And at work, there's two associates I work with.
You want their names?"

Nabandian nodded.

"Sammy Weiss and Cynthia Holloway."

"You want to spell those?" said Engels.

Rob did.

"What bank is that?" asked Engels, writing the names.

"Dyson Whitney."

"Tell me, Rob," said Nabandian. "You know any reason anyone
would want to kill Greg?"

Rob frowned. "This is a burglary, right? There was a burglary in
another apartment in the building a few months ago."

"Anyone get killed?"

"No."

"Anyone get hurt?"

"No one was at home."

"So you think this was a burglary that went wrong?" said Engels.

"Wasn't it?"

Engels didn't reply. Whoever was responsible for the murder of
Greg Ryan hadn't gone to that apartment to commit a burglary.
Even a cursory examination of the crime scene was sufficient to
show it. The bedroom was untouched, a radio had still been playing.
The bed was unused, the victim was in his clothes, so he hadn't been
asleep at the time of the intrusion. Yet in the living room, just about
everything that could be moved had been uprooted or smashed,
whether or not it could conceal valuables. Even the chairs at the table
had been knocked over. If it was an interrupted burglary, with the
victim, who had been awake at the time and now lay dead in front of
the bedroom, coming out to investigate the noise, surely he would

have been alerted before so much damage had been done. Which meant the murderer must have killed him, then continued to trash the room. If a burglar was that cool, cool enough to keep going after he'd been surprised and had killed someone, he'd step over the body and check out the bedroom to see what he could get from there as well. He wouldn't just leave it.

"We just need to cover all the bases," said Nabandian. "Think about it again. Is there any reason anyone would want to kill your friend?"

"I can't think of any reason." Rob thought. "I don't know. He was a DA. Maybe there's someone with a grudge. I'm just guessing. Must happen all the time, people get grudges against DAs."

"But you don't know of anyone in particular?"

"No."

"He didn't mention anyone with a grudge? No death threats?"

Rob shook his head.

"What about you, Rob?"

Rob looked at Nabandian in incomprehension. "Why would I have a grudge against him?"

"No. I mean, any reason anyone would want to kill you?"

"Me?"

"It's your apartment," said Nabandian. "Maybe they thought it was you."

Rob shook his head. "Me? . . . That's crazy."

"No one?"

"Not that I can think of."

"No old girlfriends?" said Nabandian.

"No debts?" said Engels.

"No threats?"

"No fights with anyone?"

Rob frowned. "No. Nothing. I can't think of anything."

"Okay," said Nabandian. He looked over his shoulder. Behind him, a stretcher was being wheeled into the apartment.

Rob looked as well. "Are they taking him out now?"

"It'll be a little while yet. You got somewhere to stay tonight, Rob? For the moment, this is a crime scene. We're still looking for evidence."

"I'll stay at Emmy's."

"We'll let you know when you can come back. It'll probably be tomorrow. You'd better give us Emmy's address and phone number."

Rob gave it to them.

"You mind if we talk to her? It's routine, like I said."

"Sure. Go ahead."

"Where would we find her?"

Rob looked at his watch. "She'll still be at work."

"Maybe we'll leave it until she gets home."

"Can I ask one thing?" said Rob. "I'd like to tell her before you speak with her. So she hears it from me first."

The two detectives exchanged a glance.

"Sure, Rob," said Nabandian. "You haven't spoken to her already on the phone since you found Greg?"

Rob shook his head.

"Okay. You know what, maybe we'll go find her right now at work. Why don't we drive you over there?"

There was a kind of kitchen that doubled as a meeting room at the offices of Lascelle Press. It wasn't exactly the way Rob would have chosen to tell Emmy the news, with a cop standing on either side of him. Then he was asked to wait outside while they spoke with her. He didn't know where to go, so he stood in the corridor outside the room.

Rob couldn't hear what was being said behind the door. When the cops asked him to step outside, Emmy had looked at him in dismay. She was in shock. She had had barely a moment to take it in.

He looked at his watch. Almost five-thirty. He took his cell phone out of his pocket and switched it on. There were a couple of messages from Sammy. There was one from Phil Menendez as well, laced with obscenities. Sammy's second message sounded urgent: "Rob, we're in the war room. The review meeting went well, but there's a whole bunch of work to do. We're really going to be crunching here. We need you back right now."

Rob returned the call.

"Sammy," he said. "It's Rob."

"What's happening, Rob?" Sammy's voice was even, not flustered, not punishing. Yet.

Rob heard Phil Menendez yell something in the background.

"I've got a problem," said Rob.

"We're crunching here, Rob." Sammy's voice was becoming a little more imperative, a little more threatening.

"Sammy," said Rob, "I've been with the police all afternoon. My best friend's been murdered."

There was silence. Rob heard Sammy's voice, muffled, saying: "He says his best friend's been murdered." Then he heard Menendez reply: "Tell the little fuck we're sorry and to get his ass back here."

"Rob?" said Sammy, coming back on the line. "Are you still with the police?"

Rob didn't reply.

"Rob?"

"Tell the big fuck he can shove his head up his ass!" said Rob. And he almost held on to hear how Sammy was going to translate that.

He looked around. A couple of people were staring at him. He frowned. "Sorry," he murmured. A couple more people arrived. Rob recognized Caitlin and Andrea, the two editors who shared Emmy's office. Word was going around that Emmy's boyfriend had arrived with two cops and they had taken her into the kitchen.

"Rob," said Caitlin, "what's going on?"

"Something's happened."

Caitlin looked at him anxiously. "Is Emmy okay? I heard the police are here."

"She's okay."

"Then what is it?" said Andrea.

Rob gazed at them. There were half a dozen people around him now. The only ones he knew were Caitlin and Andrea. He couldn't talk about it like that, as if it were some kind of a story to entertain a crowd. It was his best friend. He heard the words he had said to Sammy: "My best friend's been murdered." Suddenly it was real. Greg was dead. It was a fact, and it would be a fact for the rest of his life.

"I can't say," he said.

It hit him again. His best friend was dead. Murdered. In his apartment. And then all the things the cops had been saying. Was it really a burglary? Was it an accident or was it on purpose? Was it meant to be Greg, or was it meant to be him? He couldn't get it straight. What if it *was* meant to be him?

The crowd outside the kitchen watched him disbelievingly. He saw the way they were looking at him. Blaming him. As if it were his fault, in some way, that Emmy was inside that room with the cops.

"Excuse me," he said. "Excuse me. Can you just . . . can you get out of my way!"

Inside, the cops were almost done. When you give people news like that, you've got a certain amount of time, a few minutes, when they're in shock, off balance, and as long as they hold it together, they'll answer anything you ask. Then their thought processes kick in and you lose them until they've had a chance to cry or scream or question or shout, to vent their initial feelings of horror and disbelief. The two cops had gone straight for the key time markers, the ones that would cover the time points Rob had given them. Those were the essential things they wanted to get out of Emmy before she had the chance to talk to anyone else or even think about what she was saying.

Now she was getting increasingly agitated, not addressing the questions, starting to ask questions of her own. But they had what they needed.

"I think we're done for now," said Nabandian. "Thank you very much, Ms. Bridges. I know this has been a shock. We may need to talk with you again, if that's okay."

"But how could it happen?" demanded Emmy. "What's happened to the body? My God, who's going to tell Greg's parents?"

"We'll take care of that," said Nabandian.

Emmy stared at him in anguish.

"Let's go out and get your boyfriend," said Engels.

The two detectives stood up. They waited. Emmy got up. Nabandian opened the door for her.

The corridor was full of people. But Rob was gone.

42

Kelly Tan had worked the afternoon shift at the Bean of Content coffee shop on Second Avenue for two years. She'd seen a bunch of weird characters come in over that time. Normally they didn't worry her, but there was something about the customer down in back that was spooking her out.

She stole a glance at him as she unloaded the cups out of the dishwasher, stacking them still hot and moist over the coffee machine. There were only another couple of tables occupied in the whole place and her boss had stepped out for an hour and told her to hold the fort. There was something plain wrong about the guy in back. Ever since she had taken his latte over, he had sat at the table and stared. His cell phone was on the table, and even when it rang he just continued to stare.

The cell phone rang again. Kelly watched him. He didn't touch it. The phone rang until it stopped.

Kelly came out from behind the counter. She hesitated for a moment and then went closer to him. He didn't look around, seemingly unaware that she was there.

"Everything all right, sir?" she said, and she stole a glance at his coffee to see if he'd drunk any.

Slowly, he turned and nodded.

Kelly smiled nervously and retreated back to her counter.

She watched him. He was just staring again. She wished he'd go. She was starting to get a little scared. Maybe, she thought, she should call the cops.

At his table, Rob was utterly oblivious of the effect he was having on her.

He needed to think. He needed to get it straight.

He knew when it had happened. Saturday night. It had to have been. He was no pathologist, and he only saw the body for a few moments, and he didn't touch it, but the blood on that carpet was dry. And there was a lot of blood, so that would have taken time. And the radio was still on, just as it was when he spoke to Greg. And Greg hadn't answered his call the next day. So it had to have been then. It made Rob ill to think about it. That knock on the door that Greg had heard—that knock on the door that had cut short their conversation—it had been them. The burglars who had killed him.

And Rob had told him to answer it, told him it was only Mrs. Angelou.

He kept thinking about it, seeing an image of Greg opening the door. Opening the door, pulling it back. His mind focused on that, wouldn't let it go. What if Greg hadn't opened the door?

And what if Greg hadn't moved in until Sunday? Or what if he hadn't moved in at all? What if he hadn't broken up with Louise? What if? What if? Too many what-ifs, one after the other, all leading to Greg's death.

And what if Rob had told him not to answer the door? What if he had never stood there, as Rob could see him in his mind's eye, opening it?

Rob couldn't bear to think about it. But that's all he had been thinking about since he sat down. His cell phone must have rung half a dozen times and he hadn't once answered. Didn't even look at it.

What were burglars doing knocking on a door? That was the thing he couldn't figure out. Burglars don't knock on the door. All right, maybe they knock on the door to see if anyone's home, but they don't go on in if someone answers. Murderers do that, not burglars. A burglar would run away. And Greg had answered, hadn't he? That's why he cut the conversation. That's why he put down the phone. He answered the door.

Maybe it wasn't a burglary. The cops obviously doubted it. Maybe someone had deliberately intended to kill the person who opened the door. But if that were the case, as the cops said, how did he know they expected it to be Greg who was standing there?

Rob stared into the coffee, deep, deep into the pale brown liquid.

It was his apartment. But they might still have wanted Greg. Or they might have wanted him.

That was another what-if. One that was more unbearable and

guilt-inducing than all the others. What if Greg had died in his place? What if he told Greg to open the door to his killers, and what if he died because they thought Greg was *him*?

It was too agonizing to think about. He couldn't. He shook his head. He buried his face in his hands. He just couldn't think about it.

Kelly was getting really spooked. She came out from behind the counter and backed away. She stood by the door. The other people in the place looked at her quizzically, but Kelly didn't care. She wasn't going to get trapped behind the counter when that guy in the back pulled out a carving knife or something.

Rob felt as if he were going to hyperventilate. He stopped himself. He put his hands on the table and pressed down hard, to feel something solid. He stared at his hands, still pressing, until he breathed slower. Slower. That was better. Try to be rational, he thought. Try to be analytical. There were two possibilities. They wanted Greg, or they wanted him. Greg or him, he thought. Greg or him . . . If they'd wanted Greg, they'd gotten him. That was the end of it. If they'd wanted him, they hadn't gotten him. That meant they would still be looking.

But only if they knew they hadn't gotten him. They might not know that. They might think they had, because they'd gone ahead and killed Greg. So they probably thought the person who answered the door . . . the person who answered the door . . . who opened it . . .

Rob frowned hard. He had lost his train of thought. For an instant, it had all seemed so clear. But now, all he could see was that image of Greg standing at the door, opening it.

His gaze shifted to his cell phone. It was still sitting there, next to his coffee, where he had put it. He stared at it.

Suddenly he reached into his pocket.

Kelly jumped. She was ready to run out the door. But all he pulled out was a small white business card.

Rob put the card on the table beside the phone. He had meant to call, he remembered. He had a feeling that if he had called, if only he had called, none of this would have happened. It was irrational, he knew. The two things weren't connected. He wasn't thinking clearly. He was angry, frustrated. His friend was dead and it shouldn't have happened. His story should have been published and that hadn't happened, either. Why not? What was stopping them? He should have called already. He should have called yesterday or even the day before.

Abruptly, he punched the numbers on his phone.

He heard her answer. There was noise in the background.

"Why haven't you published?" he demanded.

"Who's this? I can't hear you. Wait a minute . . ." Rob heard the background noise diminish. "Okay. Who is this?"

"Why haven't you published?" repeated Rob in a low, deadly tone.

Standing on a sidewalk outside a bar twenty blocks away, Sandy Pereira froze.

"Answer me!"

"Is that you, Rob?"

"Don't use my name! Why haven't you published?"

"Have you got more information?"

"I told you everything I know. You said you were going to publish."

"Rob . . . Rob, listen. My editor . . . he said we need more proof."

"That's not what you told me!"

"Well, I didn't think we did. But we do. He says we can't go with the story until we know for certain. We can't go with one source. We need proof. I've been trying to get it."

Rob held on. He didn't know whether to believe her. "You said I could trust you."

"You can."

Rob didn't reply.

"Rob?"

"That other story you published," he said, "that was nothing. What did you have? Nothing! Innuendo!"

"That's the problem. If we put out anything else now that isn't a hundred percent right, they'll sue us."

"How do you know?"

"They've told us."

"I've given you hard facts. I've given you names."

"Just names, Rob. Not facts. I need more."

"Go check."

"I have."

"And?"

"I can't get anything."

Rob shook his head. "You're shitting me."

"No, Rob. I'm not shitting you, I swear. I swear I'm not. You won't find a newspaper in the country that would publish on the basis of what you've given me. I need more. Give me more. Keep digging. When you get more, we'll publish, I promise. I just need to have—"

"My best friend's dead."

There was silence.

"Did you hear me?" demanded Rob.

"What do you mean?"

"He's dead. Murdered. In my apartment."

Sandy didn't speak.

"Can't you hear me?"

"I hear you."

"Two days ago. I found him this afternoon. In a pool of his own blood." Rob waited. "My best friend. In my apartment."

"What was his name?"

"What difference does it make? Greg Ryan. He's dead. Go check."

Sandy shook her head. His name made no difference. She hadn't been able to think of anything else to say. "Have you called the police?" she asked quietly.

"No!" retorted Rob. "I thought I'd call the fucking *Herald* first."

"Okay, Rob. What did they say?"

"They said he's dead. Aren't you listening to anything I've been saying?" Rob was boiling with rage. "Maybe I was lucky, huh? Maybe they got my best friend instead. Maybe they meant to get me."

Rob waited.

"Rob—"

He pulled the phone away from his ear and disconnected. He stared at it. The phone shook in his hand. He was physically trembling.

He put it down. He had to get control. He put his hands on the table again, pressed hard.

Two possibilities, he said to himself. Two possibilities. He kept repeating it. Kept trying to get some clarity. Two possibilities. But he couldn't get past those words, couldn't figure out what they implied. Every time he tried, he kept seeing Greg, standing at the door of his apartment, opening it.

The phone rang. He looked at the number. Sammy Weiss. He let it ring and go to voice mail.

He got up. For some reason, the waitress was over by the door. He went to the counter to pay. She didn't move.

"Two dollars," she called out.

Rob looked in his wallet. "I've only got five. You want to come over here and give me some change?"

"Forget about it," said the waitress. "On the house."

Rob stared at her quizzically.

"Happy hour."

"For coffee?"

The waitress nodded.

The other people in the coffee shop looked around in surprise.

Rob headed for the door. Kelly circled away from him as he approached. "Thanks," he murmured.

He left the Bean of Content. His phone rang. He pulled it out and checked the number. Sammy again. He didn't answer it. He couldn't go back there today. Tomorrow, maybe.

He switched the phone off. He headed randomly up Second Avenue, trying to get the image of Greg out of his head.

43

Amanda Bellinger sat behind her desk and watched the two people who were sitting on the other side. One of them was a boyish-looking music star whose face was vaguely familiar to her. The other was his small, balding, worried-looking manager. Behind them, a full-wall window gave a view down Fifth Avenue. The lights of the cabs were beginning to glint in the gathering dusk.

The man-child in front of her wasn't a major star, but his manager feared that he had just booked himself a one-way ticket to has-beenhood. A video clip had appeared on the Internet showing him snorting cocaine. Actually snorting it. Through a hundred-dollar bill.

"I don't know what this shit is," said the star. "I'm a rock star. I'm supposed to do drugs."

He had said this a number of times, possibly, suspected Amanda, because he had done what a rock star is supposed to do when he stepped out to go to the bathroom shortly after he and his manager had arrived.

"Well?" said the manager anxiously, ignoring him. "What do you think?"

"You can deny or admit," said Amanda.

The manager nodded quickly, waiting for more, hanging on every word.

"Is it true?" asked Amanda.

The manager glanced helplessly at his client.

"I don't know what all this shit is . . ."

"I'd be inclined to admit. Never compound an offense with a lie unless you know absolutely that you'll get away with it."

"We won't get away with it," said the manager.

"Then the lie will kill you quicker than the offense. If there's one thing we can thank Richard Nixon for, it's for teaching us that. Now, if you admit, you can show contrition or bravado."

"What do you mean by bravado?" asked the manager quickly.

"You can be upfront and proud," replied Amanda. "He's right. He's a rock star. Rock stars do drugs."

"See, I don't know what all this shit—"

"Shut up!" snapped the manager.

"But I'm—"

"You're not a rock star! Hendrix was a rock star. Jagger's a rock star."

"Who?"

"You sing pop. Not even pop. Pap!"

The pap star stared at him, eyes slightly unfocused.

"Most of his audience are girls of twelve," explained the manager to Amanda.

"Are they? No, Arnie, come on—"

"Shut up, I said!" The manager, whose name was Arnie Klein, looked as if he were going to hit him.

Amanda coughed discreetly. "Contrition," she said, "can be done in a couple of ways. You can say you repented. Or you can say you're going to repent. The choice depends on a number of factors. Now, how long ago was this clip taken?"

"Three days," said Arnie Klein.

"Ah." Amanda nodded. "I think we're going to repent."

"Damn right we are," muttered Klein.

"We're in crisis," said Amanda, expanding on the theme. "We realize we've come to a turning point. We know we have to change our ways. We don't want anyone else to make the mistakes we've made."

"What mistakes have you made, Arnie?" the pap star asked.

"You, you moron!" yelled Klein.

"Me? Am I at a turning point? Is that good? That sounds really positive."

"We want to be an example," continued Amanda, ignoring the subject of her exposition. "We go into therapy. We emerge reborn. Our next album is poignant, deep, meaningful, reflecting the trauma we've suffered."

Arnie Klein, who had been nodding enthusiastically to every point, scratched his head. He glanced at his client. Poignant? Deep? Meaningful?

"We start with a statement acknowledging the pictures."

"They've just appeared," said Klein doubtfully. "Maybe we should wait—"

"Perfect! We get to make an admission even before pressure builds up on us. Excellent. Honesty. Remorse. Put it all out upfront. We get big points for that, owning up before we're forced to. Then we set up a TV interview, someone soft, sympathetic. Let me think about it. Print media, we're looking for publications that like redemption stories, the fallen hero and his heartbreaking climb back to decency, nothing hard-ass. . . . We'll announce he's going in for detox, of course. Might even let slip which clinic."

The star looked at her in alarm.

"Don't worry," said Amanda smoothly, "at most of these places it's quite easy to keep using. Think of it as a vacation. Now, timing. Today's Monday. We go with a statement first thing tomorrow. Then we play hard to get for a day, say it's all private, there won't be any further statements, whip up interest. Wednesday I'll be trailing the interview—"

The phone rang. Amanda stopped. She picked up the receiver. "Yes?" she said brusquely. "I'm in a conference."

"Ms. Bellinger, I'm sorry to interrupt you." It was Saskia, Amanda's PA.

"What?"

"I have a Sandy Pereira on the phone."

For a second, Amanda struggled to place the name.

"She's says it's urgent."

"Tell her I'll call. Get a number."

"She really does sound very—"

"Tell her I'll call," snapped Amanda.

The cab lights twinkled. It was dark outside by now. Amanda Bellinger watched the lights moving down Fifth Avenue.

Arnie Klein and his coke-snorting boy-client were gone. Right about now, Amanda was due at Lincoln Center for the National Petroleum Association's annual dinner. Part of the program was the launch of the association's social responsibility report. For the third year running, Hill Bellinger was publicizing it. But Amanda hadn't even changed into her dress yet.

It took a lot to shock Amanda Bellinger. That was what she liked to think, anyway. Like most PR practitioners, she affected an air of worldly experience, as if she had seen and heard just about everything under the sun. This was partly because it encouraged people to talk, imagining that nothing they could say could shock her. And it was partly because Amanda Bellinger really did imagine that she had seen and heard just about everything under the sun. But in reality, the everything of which she had seen and heard such a large part was a limited, sanitized, controlled, and very small segment of the larger whole. The coke-snorting escapades of a man-child singer, the illicit love tryst of a Hollywood B-lister, a bribe paid by a supposedly upright corporation to a supposedly honest senator, or any of the other so-called crises that Amanda Bellinger was called upon to defuse were tame little affairs compared with the reality she could have seen had she just chosen to glance out the window of her limo from time to time. Her world, which she imagined to be so encompassing, was like a tiny, fragrant, privileged corner of a big, dark jungle. Violence wasn't part of it, not real physical violence. Not a fist smashing into a face, a boot in a groin, a knife sinking into flesh.

Not a man dead on the carpet in someone's apartment.

Sandy Pereira had been almost hysterical on the phone. And for once, Amanda Bellinger didn't know what to say. The only thing that had saved her from a moment of hysteria herself was the journalist's babbling incoherence and the need to get control of it.

Somehow, she had calmed her down. But now Amanda was left with her own suspicions and doubts, as if the journalist had infected her with fear. Three days earlier, Pereira had given her the details of the person who was leaking rumors about Louisiana Light. Not only his name, but his address. And Amanda Bellinger had passed on that information to only one person.

She looked at her watch. Time was ticking. Downstairs, her driver was waiting.

Amanda picked up the phone and dialed Mike Wilson's number.

He didn't answer. Amanda left a message. She sat behind her desk, watching the cabs going down Fifth Avenue, the thoughts in her mind getting darker and darker.

She glanced at her watch again. At Lincoln Center, the waiters would have started circulating cocktails.

The phone rang. Amanda grabbed for the receiver.

Wilson was cheerful, effusive. Didn't let her get a word in edgewise. Things were going well. He'd just heard that the due diligence was complete. What did she want? Questions about the announcement? He had been planning to call her tomorrow to go over the details, but tonight would do.

Amanda broke in. "Mike," she said, "I need to tell you something."

"Sure. Shoot."

"I had a phone call from our friend."

It took a second for Wilson to respond. His tone changed. "What did she want? More money, huh?"

"No."

"Has she got something else?"

"No, Mike. But she got a phone call from her source."

"Her source?"

"Yes, Mike." Amanda paused. She was alert for every sound, every nuance.

There was no reply from Wilson.

"You know the one?" said Amanda.

"The analyst? Is that who you're talking about?"

Was his tone more guarded now? More careful? Was he hiding something?

"He was very angry that she hadn't published the story." Amanda waited again.

"What did she say to him?"

"She said what I told her to say. She needs more proof. Her editor won't pass the story without another source. You'll sue them if they put a foot wrong."

"Did he buy it?"

Amanda tried to read the tone of Wilson's voice. It was cautious. But there could be all kinds of reasons for that. Bribing a journalist was enough to put you on your guard without having done anything else. She would have to come right out and say it.

"She told me something else, Mike."

"What was that, Mandy?"

"There'd been a murder."

"A murder?"

The words came out cold, flat. Unsurprised? Or just unemotional?

"His best friend, Mike."

"Whose best friend? The analyst?"

"That's right. Found dead in his apartment."

"What's that got to do with it?"

"In the *analyst's* apartment."

"Oh . . ."

Amanda Bellinger listened. The silence went on for a long time. Too long? She waited. She wasn't going to say anything. She wanted to hear what Wilson was going to say.

"What was he doing there, in the other guy's apartment?"

"I don't know," said Mandy.

"Wrong place at the wrong time, huh?"

"What did you say?"

"What? Oh . . ." Wilson laughed. "I mean, that's what you're saying, right? It was supposed to be the analyst. . . . He was . . . that's what you said, isn't it, Mandy?"

"I didn't say anything, Mike."

"Well, I just thought . . . hell, Mandy! You know what I thought!"

Amanda Bellinger was trying very quickly to work that out. She frowned. Could it be an honest conclusion he'd reached from what she'd said? Had she led him? Or had he said it too quickly, with too much knowledge? She wished she could remember exactly what she had said and how she had said it. She wished she could rewind. She wished she could start over and do it again.

"Mandy," said Wilson, "if you've got a problem, come right out with it. Don't beat around the bush."

Amanda took a deep breath. "All right, Mike. This isn't easy to say. Did you . . . ?" She stopped. It was absurd. Was it even possible that she was going to ask him the question she had in her mind?

"Mandy, talk to me. You know I'll be straight with you. You've known me long enough to know that."

"Okay. Mike, you didn't . . . you didn't somehow organize for him to be killed?"

There was silence. Amanda winced.

"You mean, like put out a hit on him?"

"Yes," she said. "I guess that's what I mean."

"Mandy." Wilson began to laugh. "Mandy . . . are you . . . you *are* serious, aren't you? All right, no, I did not put out a hit on him. I swear to you . . . Jesus Christ, Mandy!" Wilson's laughter began again. "I don't even know how you'd do something like that."

"Mike, I gave you his name . . . I gave you his details . . . who else knew who he was?"

"But you said it wasn't our source who was killed, right?"

"No, but the man who was killed was in the source's apartment. His best friend."

"Look . . . it's okay. Mandy, I guess it's scary, huh? Maybe it was some kind of burglary or something. Poor guy. What was he doing there? Coincidence. Wrong place, wrong time. Isn't that what I said?"

Amanda nodded.

"Huh, Mandy?"

Already, Amanda could barely believe she had asked Mike Wilson that question. It was crazy, thinking he could have done something like that. "I'm sorry, Mike."

"It's okay, Mandy." Mike Wilson laughed. "Hell, I've been accused of most things in my time, but this is a first."

Amanda cringed. "Jesus, I'm sorry, Mike." Now she really couldn't believe it. What had come over her?

Wilson laughed.

"Oh, Jesus, Mike."

"Okay. Look, Mandy, let's not worry about that now. Let's think about what we've gotta do here. The journalist. Let's make sure we're still okay on that front. What did she say she was going to do?"

Amanda nodded, grateful for something concrete to focus on. Sandy Pereira. That was who she needed to think about.

"Mandy? You think she's going to do something?"

"I don't think so," said Amanda. "Nothing's changed. Why should she do anything?"

"You sure about that?"

"Well . . ." Amanda thought about it. "She's scared. And she's not very smart."

"Is she chasing this murder thing, like a story?"

"I doubt it."

"And the analyst, when he called her, he didn't tell her anything else? He didn't make up any more lies about us?"

"No. She said he didn't have anything for her."

"Well, that's one good thing, at least," said Wilson. "My theory is he's being paid by another bidder to blow the deal."

"Why would they need to use him to do that?"

"I don't know."

"Why can't you talk to his boss at the bank?"

"Jesus, Mandy! I'm under enough pressure here. I got some guy running around out there trying to blow up my deal and now you're giving me the third degree again."

"Sorry, Mike."

"That's okay. . . . All right, listen, here's what I think you should do. Call up the journalist and say you've been thinking about it and it's probably a coincidence."

Amanda nodded. "I think she could do with some reassurance. I think that's definitely what she needs."

"Good. Well, reassure her. Tell you what. Say you've talked to someone you know in the police department and they think it's a burglary that went wrong."

"I'm not so sure about that," said Amanda. "It might make her think she should investigate it herself."

"All right, you're the expert."

"I'll think about it."

"Offer her some more money."

"No," said Amanda quickly. "That'd be a mistake, Mike. She'd think we're hiding something."

"Why? We're just grateful for what she's done."

"What has she done? Trust me. In this business, you give something because you get something. We haven't gotten anything new from her, so why would we give her more? She'll think it's hush money. She'll think she's hiding something new for us. She'll start asking herself what it is."

"Nothing," said Wilson. "She's not hiding anything new."

"Exactly. So we don't give her any more." Amanda was feeling more like herself again, back in control, the PR queen who had seen everything. "You've got to trust me on this, Mike. I know how these people work. Besides, what's she going to do? Who's she going to talk to? She doesn't look too good herself if this comes out."

"That's a good point."

"Exactly. After what she's done, basically, she says anything, she loses her job. Any job. She'd never get a job again. I might just give her a gentle reminder."

"How much did we give her again?" asked Wilson.

"Twenty thousand dollars."

"Jesus Christ." Wilson laughed. "Twenty thousand. The great American press, huh? Wonder of the free world."

Amanda Bellinger smiled. It had been remarkably easy to suborn Sandy Pereira. She had come cheap, too. Amanda was prepared to spend a hundred thousand of Mike Wilson's money, but it was clear that Sandy Pereira's price was a lot lower than that. She was unhappy, disillusioned, and it had been simple for Amanda to play to her resentments. Amanda had taken her to lunch a few days after the original *Herald* article appeared and they hadn't even finished their cocktails before Sandy admitted she had provided the information for the piece and told her how she had happened to come by it. They weren't finished with their entrées before Amanda had bought her loyalty. It didn't take much to persuade her that this wasn't going to be the scoop she hoped it might be, that it wasn't going to be her big break out of the *Herald,* that Marv Koller was going to take the credit for anything that did come out and, at best, she'd be seen as some junior little assistant who'd done a bit of the groundwork along the way. Not to mention hinting that if she cooperated, there might be a place for her in the wonderful, shiny world of PR at Hill Bellinger. Now, wouldn't it make a lot more sense to let Amanda Bellinger know if she came by any more information, and earn a little something for herself, rather than handing the information to a lech like Marv Koller and get absolutely nothing in return? Apart from a pat on the ass. Literally.

"You want to talk about the announcement now?" said Wilson.

Amanda glanced at her watch, thinking of Lincoln Center. "Actually, Mike, I'm already late for something."

"What? Another client? I'm jealous, Mandy."

"Save it, Mike."

"Call me tomorrow. We need to talk about the announcement."

"Sure," said Amanda.

"Have a good night, Mandy."

"You, too, Mike."

Amanda got up and went into the private bathroom off her office. She shuddered as she changed into her dress for the evening. *What* had come over her? A moment of madness that could easily have killed a very important client relationship. And another kind of relationship, potentially. Luckily, Mike Wilson had seen the lighter side of it.

She thought about him as she got changed.

He wouldn't have forgiven just anyone for accusing him like that, would he? He was too proud, too strong. There was definitely something between them. With anyone else, he would have blown up.

She freshened her makeup. She put new lipstick on. She pouted, pressed her lips, and scrutinized her mouth in the mirror.

It couldn't be her imagination. It was real. She let her thoughts linger. There was a chemistry between them. That conversation proved it.

Sin changes a man. Each rung down the ladder makes it easier to descend the next. Three days earlier, the thought of procuring a man's death had nauseated him. Now that a man had actually been murdered, Mike Wilson felt nothing but rage.

When he got Tony Prinzi on the phone, he exploded, just as he would at one of his executives.

"You fucked up, Tony!" he yelled. "Your guys fucked up!"

"Excuse me, Mike . . ."

"You told me it'd be easy. You fucking tell me it's gonna be a simple fucking thing to do and—"

"Excuse me," interjected Tony. "I think you forget who you're talking to."

Prinzi's tone had hardly changed, and yet somehow there was a powerful, naked menace in his voice. Even in the midst of his anger, Wilson heard it.

"That's better," said Prinzi. "Let's talk like gentlemen. If we have a problem, let's resolve it in a civilized manner."

Wilson took a deep breath. "You told me you were going to get this guy."

"I'm informed the job was done very successfully, and you should be very satisfied."

"Yeah? Well, whoever informed you informed you wrong. You got the wrong guy."

For a moment, there was nothing on the line but Prinzi's breathing. "Are you sure of this?"

"Yes," said Wilson.

"Well, that is very unfortunate. I apologize."

"It was someone else in his apartment."

"Oh, that's not good. They're supposed to ask. If not, some kind of identification."

Wilson shook his head incredulously. He almost wanted to laugh.

"However, sometimes circumstances don't permit. Things happen in these situations. Nick's employees are very good, I can vouch for them. But even in the best of hands, these things can be unpredictable, Michael. This is the reality. And remember, when we spoke, you yourself could not give me a description of the gentleman in question."

"Well, we've got a problem," said Wilson.

"*You* have a problem," Prinzi corrected him. "However, I'm not a man to shirk my responsibilities. When I say I'll do something, it will be done. This is a matter of honor for me. Like paying my money, Michael, must be a matter of honor for you."

Wilson grimaced. It would be two deaths now instead of one. "This is bad, Tony. It feels like it's getting out of hand."

"Now, Michael. Let me reassure you. Once you set a course of action, you must stick to it resolutely. Those who waver are lost. Surely I don't need to tell this to you, a captain of industry."

Wilson didn't reply.

"I have said to you, Michael, this is a matter of honor for me. That is enough."

"Okay, Tony," said Wilson quietly.

"Good. So now we must find this gentleman. Usually, this isn't too difficult. You got a picture of him? I don't think we want any more mistakes."

"No. I don't have a picture."

"Tell me again where he works."

"Dyson Whitney."

"That's a bank?"

"Yes, it's an investment bank."

"Spell it for me, please. We want to be sure."

Wilson spelled it.

"Not so fast, Mike."

Wilson spelled it again. He imagined Prinzi holding the pen in his fist like some kind of ape.

"Whitney with an H?" said Prinzi. "English is funny, don't you think? Who would think of such spelling? It's an interest of mine, the spelling of English."

Wilson didn't respond.

"Okay," said Prinzi. "Now, another thought. Many organizations today have pictures of their employees on the Internet. Not my own, I should add."

Very funny, thought Wilson.

"We might find one. We'll check. Mike, very likely he won't be staying at his apartment now. There'll be police involved. If you can find out anything about his whereabouts, that would be helpful."

Wilson nodded wearily.

"Did you hear me, Mike? Each of us must do what he can."

"What if he suspects something? What if he disappears?"

Tony Prinzi chuckled. "No one disappears, Mike. They just go somewhere else. So we have to look. Usually, it isn't too hard to find them. People are very predictable, Michael. Sadly predictable. When you strike a man, he cries out. When he runs, where does he go?"

"Where he thinks no one will find him?" said Wilson.

"That's what you would expect, is it not? But this is a very interesting thing. Most people, when they are frightened, go where they will get comfort. This is not necessarily the smartest thing. It's not necessarily the hardest place to find them. But this is what they do. This is their need, comfort. And the human being, like any animal, seeks to asserge its needs."

"And where do they get comfort?"

"Where?" Prinzi laughed. "Where would you go, Mike?"

Wilson didn't answer.

"No, don't tell me. One day, I may need to find you." Prinzi chuckled. "Think, Mike. Where would you go? You're a man. Think about where you would go." Prinzi waited. "Now, I'll tell you. Michael, most men go to their woman."

Wilson nodded.

"Predictable, isn't it?"

Predictable, thought Wilson.

"He has a girlfriend, our boy?"

"I don't know," said Wilson.

"You want to ask?"

"Who would I ask?" demanded Wilson irritably. "The bank?"

"Forget about it. This, we can find out easily enough. A couple of phone calls, it's done. You ask me, he's with a girl. Nowadays, sometimes, it's a boy." Prinzi laughed. "Modern times. Mike, leave this to me."

"Tony, you're sure this is necessary?"

"Michael, you want this done or not done? Either way, you pay me my money. You don't want it done, I can finish now. So what do you want? Yes or no?"

"Yes," said Wilson.

"Yes. Good. Good-bye, Mike."

The line went dead.

Wilson went to his desk. He clicked on Google and did a search and got the Dyson Whitney home page up on the screen. There was a button labeled About Dyson Whitney. Wilson clicked. There was another button labeled Our People. Wilson clicked again. A series of faces came up on the left of the page, the name and a few lines of biography beside each one on the right. Wilson scrolled, scanning the names.

He stopped.

Robert Holding, analyst

Prior to his MBA at Cornell, Robert R. Holding graduated in law from Columbia University and spent two years in the corporate law practice of . . .

Wilson's gaze shifted to the picture. A handsome face. Young. Hopeful looking. Nice smile. About the same age as Joey, his oldest son. Just a boy.

Wilson felt the nausea welling up inside him. Until that last conversation with Amanda Bellinger, he had thought he couldn't go any lower.

He imagined Tony Prinzi, at that very moment, gazing at that same picture on the Net. And then picking up a phone and telling someone to find the boy's girlfriend.

44

Emmy heard a key turn in the lock.

She watched the door open.

"Where have you been?" she demanded.

Silently, Rob closed the door.

"Where? It's ten o'clock."

"I had to think," said Rob quietly.

"Fuck you, Rob! You had to think and you couldn't even tell me? Why didn't you answer my calls?"

Rob shrugged. "I just . . . I'm sorry. I needed some time."

He sat down on the sofa beside her. Emmy's gaze remained fixed on him, angry, confused.

Rob stared at the rug. Eventually he shook his head. "I keep seeing him, Em. I just keep seeing him opening the door. It was that night, when I rang him. Remember? When I said it was Mrs. Angelou who was knocking. It wasn't Mrs. Angelou. And when I called him on Sunday, when he didn't answer . . . he was dead, Em. That's why he didn't answer. He was already dead." Rob paused. He looked at Emmy. "The radio was still playing."

Emmy stared at him.

Rob told her about going into the trashed apartment, about hearing the radio, about ringing Greg's phone. About finally going around the corner to the bedroom and finding him. About the moment before he went around that corner. About the moment after.

Tears ran down Emmy's cheeks. She reached for Rob and buried her face in his neck.

Rob frowned hard, trying to hold back his own tears. "Emmy," he said. "Emmy . . ." He pried her loose. "I'm sorry. Are you okay?"

She nodded.

"The cops didn't give you a hard time?"

"No. I don't know, they just asked about where you were. You know, on the weekend. It didn't take long. Then I came home."

"I'm sorry I wasn't there."

"It's all right." She smiled sheepishly. "I called my mom. You weren't here and I had to talk to someone. She asked if she should come down."

"Your mom?" Rob looked at her in alarm. Emmy's parents lived upstate in Rochester. He liked them, but dealing with Emmy's mom was about the last thing he needed right now.

"It's all right. I told her I was fine. I said I'd call if I wanted her to come down."

Rob nodded. "Listen, Emmy. There's something I've got to talk to you about. Did the cops say what they thought happened?"

Emmy shook her head.

"When I went in, I thought there'd been a burglary. But I'm not sure if that's what it was. I think that's what it was made to look like."

Emmy gazed at him, not understanding.

"They knocked on the door, Em. You don't knock on someone's door and then kill them when they answer it, not if you're just trying to steal their iPod."

"Why not? Some crackhead . . ."

"Emmy, come on. The radio was still playing. And the place was really trashed. Think about it. They must have trashed it after they killed him. They made it look like a burglary. That's what the cops think. I can tell from the things they asked me."

"So someone . . . what? I don't understand."

"Someone went there with the intention of doing what they did."

"You mean someone wanted to kill Greg?"

"I'm not sure it was Greg they were trying to kill."

"Well, who—" Emmy stopped. Her eyes went wide. She shook her head. "No! What? You're saying . . . no. Come on. No."

"Greg moved in that same day. How would anyone have known where he was?"

"Maybe he told someone."

"Someone who wanted to kill him?"

"Maybe they followed him. Rob, he was a DA. There must have been hundreds of people who had a reason to hate him."

"When was the last time you heard of a DA getting killed?"

Emmy shook her head again. "No. I don't believe it."

"What if they made a mistake?"

"No. This is crazy, Rob. You're saying someone wanted to kill you?" She stared at him in incredulity. "Why? Why would they? What could they possibly expect? No. You're wrong. It's ridiculous!"

Rob grabbed her hands. He leaned close to her, looking into her eyes. "Emmy, let's say it wasn't really a burglary. It's a possibility, so let's assume it for a second. If it wasn't, then they went in there to kill someone. And if that's what they were doing, it's a lot more likely they were looking for me than Greg. It's logic. It's gotta be a possibility."

"Have you told the police?"

"Emmy, it was the cops who suggested it to me."

"And they let you go?" demanded Emmy in horror. "They're not gonna . . . protect you or something?"

"It's just a theory to them. As far as they're aware, there's no one who'd want to kill me."

"Exactly! Who would want to—" Emmy stopped. Something in Rob's gaze struck her cold. "You mean this deal?"

Rob nodded. "What else could it be? I've thought about it. What I told that journalist is enough to stop this deal cold. The paper prints that and it's over."

"But they didn't print it."

"Someone must have told someone."

"A journalist doesn't reveal her sources."

"It might not be the journalist. There's probably a bunch of people at the *Herald* who know about this by now. Editors, secretaries. It wouldn't be too hard to get my name if you tried."

"But it's just business. You said it yourself. They're not gangsters, they're businessmen. Fat, middle-aged businessmen."

"Chasing twelve billion dollars' worth of deal, Em. That's what this is worth. You don't think someone might kill for that kind of money?"

"Jesus, Rob . . ."

"For us alone, Dyson Whitney, it's sixty, seventy million in fees."

"How much did you say?"

"Sixty or seventy million."

Emmy's eyes went wide at the sheer scale of the numbers. "Rob, you've *got* to go to the police."

"And tell them what, exactly?"

"That this deal's wrong."

"And how do I know that?"

"You've got the proof."

"No, I haven't. You know what I've got. A couple of names. Circumstantial evidence. No detail, Emmy. And no one anywhere is going to back me up. No one in the bank, and sure as hell no one at the Leopard."

"What about the guy who gave you the names?"

"The guy who gave me the names gave them to me because he doesn't want to be identified. He'll deny it just like everyone else will, and I'll look like an idiot. I simply haven't got enough. I spoke to the journalist tonight. Yeah, I gave her a call. You know why they didn't publish? Not enough evidence. Not enough proof. If a shitty paper like the *Herald* isn't prepared to use that stuff, I don't think the cops are going to be too impressed, do you?"

Emmy watched him, eyes full of concern. "So, what are you going to do?"

"I don't know. I need to figure that out."

"Rob, maybe you should talk to the police. Really."

Rob didn't reply.

"Have you been back to the office?"

Rob shook his head.

"Have they been calling you?"

"About a million times. Lucky they don't have the number here."

Emmy nodded. She took his hand. "Well, you're safe with me. No one knows you're here, right?"

Sleep didn't come easily. After a while, Emmy fell into a kind of drained, exhausted slumber. But Rob couldn't sleep. He lay awake in the darkness, staring, and there was nothing to distract him from the what-ifs in his head.

They came back, one after the other. What if? What if? What if? What if he hadn't told Greg to answer the door? He saw him in his mind, opening it. He imagined what happened in the moments that followed. But how could he imagine it, how could he even begin? Maybe that was why his mind kept sticking with that image of Greg opening the door, because it didn't want to go any further. He thought of the cops turning up at Greg's parents', giving them the news. What if he had been in the apartment, as anyone would have expected, instead of Greg? He thought of cops turning up to his own parents'. To Emmy. His mind rebelled at that as well. It went around and around, looking for something it could bear to think about, moving on to the next thing, and the next.

He had to stop. He had to think. There were things he had to work out. Be rational, he thought. Like when he was in the coffee shop. Be rational. Be analytical.

He kept saying that to himself. He *had* to get a grip. Feelings could come later. There would be time to grieve for Greg, to feel the guilt in knowing that he had died in his apartment, to try to explain it to Greg's parents, to tell them how Greg happened to be there that night, to ask for their forgiveness, or at least their understanding. Later.

He frowned, forcing the what-ifs and the images and everything else into some closet in his mind. It was almost a physical effort, pushing them in there, closing the door against them. Locking it.

He stared at the ceiling. Okay. Be rational, he thought. Be analytical.

He could go to the police with his suspicions, but where was his proof? Louisiana Light wasn't some two-bit pawn shop. Allegations about a company like that had to be backed up with evidence. Where was it? Not even enough for a scandal sheet that was a national disgrace to publish the story. It was an allegation without any evidence, without foundation. A couple of names he really knew nothing about and now a theory that someone was trying to kill him because of them. He thought about the two cops. If he came to them with a story like that, what would they do?

He tried to see it from their point of view. It would sound unbelievable. They'd think he was trying to . . . what? Put them off the scent? Divert them? From what? He'd turn himself into a suspect.

In fact, he probably was a suspect.

He thought about it. He was, he had to be. He went over the questions the two detectives had asked him, the looks on their faces when he answered. And Emmy had said all they asked her about was where he had been over the weekend. Of course he was a suspect. When could he have done it? It was obvious. On the way back from work on Saturday night, before he got to Emmy's. There was a time gap there when no one was with him to say what he was doing. But when they got the phone records they'd see he didn't have time. But what if it looked as if he did? Desperately, he tried to remember how long he had been at Emmy's before he made the call to Greg. That would be the only fixed point the cops would have, from his phone records. It couldn't have been more than a few minutes, could it? What if it were ten minutes, fifteen? When exactly did he leave the office? He tried to remember. Sammy and Cynthia had left at the same time. What if they didn't remember? What if they said it was earlier than it was?

And now, what if he came to the cops with this unbelievable story, backed up with no evidence at all? What were they going to think?

And even if they believed him, they'd leave him waiting while they investigated it. Waiting, hanging out in the open, while whoever killed Greg came looking to correct his mistake. Or say they took it seriously, put him under some kind of protection while they checked it out. Say they did that, at best. What would they do then? Go and ask Louisiana Light if there was any problem with Grogon and Ex-Par. And what would Lousiana Light say? No. What would they do then? Send in a bunch of accountants with a search warrant? Yeah, right. Two cops like Engels and Nabandian? Or they'd go and ask the journalist and a bunch of people at the *Herald* if they gave his name to anyone. And what would the *Herald* say? Of course not.

And then what? Then he'd be a bigger suspect than before. They'd take the protection away, and whoever killed Greg would still be waiting for him.

Then go back a step, he told himself. Was he really sure he was the intended victim? Maybe not. It was just a theory. Was that important? He thought about it. It was as he had told himself in the coffee shop. There were two possibilities. One, they wanted Greg—end of story. Two, they wanted him—which meant the story was still unfolding.

Rob stared at the ceiling in the darkness, trying to keep that thought clear in his head. Two possibilities. Be analytical, he told himself. Pretend like it's a case back in business school. A strategy case. You've got two possibilities, two scenarios. In the first, the process is finished—there are no further implications, not for you, anyway. In the second, the process is continuing and the implications for you are catastrophic. You don't know which scenario is the real one. You're in a state of uncertainty. So it's about probabilities. That was the core question. How low would the probability of the second scenario have to be before you ignored it, before you chose to do nothing about it and take the chance that it was wrong?

Low, thought Rob. Very low. Given the severity of the conse-quences, zero.

He couldn't ignore the chance that the second scenario was true while there was even the slightest probability that it was. And if he couldn't ignore it, that meant he had to behave as if it *were* true. If you're faced with a potentially catastrophic scenario, but you don't know whether it's actually happening, you act as if it is. Don't you? Obviously, you do.

So that's what he had to do. He made a decision. From that moment, until he knew for certain otherwise, he was going to act on the assumption that Greg's killers had been after him.

And that meant it had to be related to the deal. It couldn't be anything else. And that meant he needed hard evidence of what Louisiana Light had been doing. Evidence that a bunch of cops who needed a suspect couldn't ignore.

But where could he get that? Only from inside Louisiana Light itself. That kind of evidence would be buried deep under layers and layers of documents and camouflage. No one found out what had really been going on inside Enron until the company went bankrupt and its innards were exposed to outsiders. But the Leopard's innards were tightly packed and sealed. The only way to get the evidence was to get inside them.

It was ironic. If it were the Buffalo, he could have gotten on a plane and walked into the data room in London and found whatever he wanted. There was exactly the same data room for the Leopard right here in New York, not more than forty blocks from where he was lying at that very moment, and yet he couldn't go into it because it was open only for people on the other side of the deal. Yet it was only the fact that he didn't have access that prevented him . . .

For a moment, Rob didn't breathe. Louisiana Light *was* open. It was vulnerable. For the space of just a few days, no more, its belly was slit and its innards were on show. Whoever was examining them just needed to know which parts to look at.

It just needed the right kind of due diligence.

The Buffalo could do it. Its people were doing their due diligence. It could get inside the Leopard. If the Buffalo knew where to look, it would do the job for him. It would find the evidence he couldn't get himself. It only had to be told where to start.

How? He had to be credible, otherwise they'd ignore him.

There was a way, but it would take time. How much time? Rob calculated. A day at least. Maybe a couple.

And in the meantime, he had to act as if the second scenario were true. He had to act as if Greg's killers had been looking for him. As if they were still looking for him.

They had found where he lived. How long until they tracked him here? He had to assume they would. Maybe he had a head start. Maybe they didn't know they'd gotten the wrong guy yet. But how much longer did he have?

He wasn't safe here. More important, Emmy wasn't safe, not while he was with her.

Rob turned to look at her. She lay, back toward him, dark hair streaming over the pillow, the blanket showing the curve of her body. Her breathing was even, regular.

He watched her form in the shadow. He'd die if anything happened to her.

He knew what he had to do. There was only one way to get to the Buffalo and keep Emmy safe at the same time.

He reached out to touch her cheek, but didn't dare. Right now, he was Emmy's worst enemy. As long as he was here, she was in danger.

For a moment longer, he watched her. He had never loved her so much as now, at the leaving of her.

He had to go. Right now. He eased himself out of bed and gathered up his clothes. Emmy stirred. He froze. She murmured something. Rob waited. Then he picked up his shoes and left the bedroom, silently closing the door behind him.

He went into the living room and turned on a lamp. He looked at his watch. It was a little after four. He dressed and checked that he had everything he needed. Cell phone. Credit card. Passport. Always have them with you. Cynthia was right. Good advice.

He sat down to write a note.

Em, he wrote. *You'll be safer without me. I've gone. I'm safe. I'll come back.*

He added another line.

I love you. Trust me.

He read it over. Then he suddenly thought: What if they come?

What if they tracked him down here and he was gone and they turned up and found Emmy by herself?

The thought sent a shiver down his spine.

He didn't want to wake her. She wouldn't let him go.

But he couldn't leave her here.

He went back into the bedroom. "Emmy," he said quietly. He touched her shoulder. "Emmy, wake up."

She stirred. He turned on a light. She blinked, her eyes adjusting. Then she stared at him.

"What time is it? Why are you dressed?"

"Emmy, we've got to leave. It's not safe here. They can find us."

She sat up in the bed. "Where are we going?"

"You need to go somewhere safe. Maybe go to your folks'."

"My folks'?" She smiled, despite the situation. "You want to go to my folks'?"

"Not me. You."

"What are you doing?"

"I'm going somewhere else."

"Then I'm coming with you."

Rob shook his head.

"Where are you going?" Emmy waited for a moment, then repeated the question.

"It's better if you don't know."

"I am not going to my folks' to sit around in Rochester not knowing what the hell's going on with you. Now you tell me where you're going!"

Rob glanced at his watch. They weren't safe here, either of them. Every minute added to the risk.

Emmy folded her arms. "I'm not leaving unless you tell me where you're going."

"All right," said Rob. He told her as briefly as he could, feeling the seconds ticking away.

"I'm coming with you." She got out of bed.

"No, Emmy. This is something I've got to do. You don't need to be involved."

She stopped, standing in front of him in her T-shirt. "You don't get it, do you, Rob? I am involved. If something's happening to you, it's happening to me. It doesn't stop *here*, or *here*, or *here*. It's everything. It's the whole lot, the good and the bad. It's all or nothing, Rob. All or nothing!"

No, thought Rob. Not now. Please don't start now.

But she had no intention of starting. This wasn't the time for it, and she knew it. She was immediately practical. "What do I need to bring?"

Rob shook his head. "Emmy, it's too dangerous. They're going to be looking for me. Doesn't matter where I am, they're still going to be looking for me."

"Oh?" said Emmy. "And I hadn't worked that out?" She pulled on a sweater over her T-shirt.

"You don't understand—"

"No, *you* don't understand." Emmy's head came out through the top of the sweater, her face covered in hair. "You do not have the right to do this." She brushed her hair away, trembling with anger. "Do you understand me? You do not have the right! Just reverse the tables. Imagine me saying this to you. Imagine me saying, 'Go to your folks', Rob, and I'm going to go out and do what I have to do.' Imagine it! What would you do?"

"It's different."

"No, it's not different! You always think you need to protect me, don't you? Well, you don't. Not if I can't protect you."

"Emmy," said Rob, shaking his head, "you're the most precious thing I've got."

"And you're the most precious thing I've got! Think about it, Rob. What if the tables were turned and I said the same thing to you? Think about how it would feel. Tell me. Would you do it? Would you just leave me and go off quietly to your folks'?"

Rob was silent.

"No. Never." Emmy shook her head. "You don't need to do everything by yourself. It doesn't always have to be Rob against the world. You're allowed to have some help." She paused. "Even if it's only from a book editor."

Rob gazed at her. "Book editors can be quite fearsome, I see."

"You're damn right we can." Emmy turned to the wardrobe and pulled on a pair of jeans. "I say: Fuck 'em! *Fuck 'em!* If they get one of us, they get us both."

Rob couldn't help smiling. Emmy put out her fist. Rob bumped it.

Emmy put on a pair of sneakers. Then she looked back at him. Her gaze was serious. "All right?"

Rob nodded. He couldn't do anything but. She was amazing, a force of nature.

"Good. What else do I need?"

"Not much," said Rob. "Have you got your passport?"

45

Phil Menendez sat across the table from Pete Stanzy, marking up Stanzy's changes to the due diligence report. They couldn't touch the final drafts of the legal and accounting sections, only the executive summary and the financials they had produced themselves. But Stanzy was happy.

"I'd buy this fucking company," he said, closing his copy of the report.

"For twelve-point-five billion?" said Menendez.

Stanzy laughed. He was feeling pretty good. The loan pledges were coming together. Wilson didn't seem to care what premium they were paying anymore. Suddenly, junk was okay. Golansky, who had used every contact he had on the Street, was beginning to say it might fall into place.

"Go," he said. "Fax it once you do the changes. We don't want Mike Wilson doing anything tricky with an electronic copy." Stanzy paused. "By the way, Phil, what happened to the analyst?"

Menendez's face darkened. "Holding? He's still not there."

"What do you mean?"

"He hasn't shown. Pete, we gotta fire that little fuck."

"Hasn't anyone called him?"

"No. Like a million times." Menendez had worked all night with

Sammy Weiss and Cynthia Holloway to get the draft of the report in final shape, spending half the time on the phone yelling at Grayson Arpel lawyers and DeGrave Peterhouse accountants, who had been up all night themselves, sending over reworked drafts of their own sections.

"So he's just disappeared?" Stanzy frowned. "What did you say happened? His friend got murdered, right?"

"Yeah. And my gerbil died when I was in the fourth grade, but do you see me crying?"

Phil Menendez couldn't remember an analyst going AWOL. Simply disappearing without even trying some pathetic excuse about being sick. He took it personally. It was an affront to his dignity. It was insulting. People were going to laugh at him behind his back. This you didn't do to the Shark. Menendez could hardly wait for Rob to show up so he could give him what he had coming.

"I'd better talk to him when he comes in," said Stanzy. "Let me know."

"What?"

"When he comes in, Phil."

Menendez snorted.

"All right," said Stanzy. "Go and make the changes. Send it to Wilson's private fax. Wait till I call you before you start."

"Right."

"I want to be absolutely sure Wilson's there to receive it himself. Don't fax before you hear from me, right?"

Menendez rolled his eyes.

"Get out of here," said Stanzy.

Menendez left.

Stanzy got Wilson on the phone.

"Mike," he said, "the due diligence report's done. We're about to fax you a copy. We'll send the finance document as well. Can you be by your private fax? That's the eighty-two twenty-eight extension, right?"

"It's right here in my office, Pete. I'm looking right at her."

"Okay. We're going to start sending in a few minutes. When you've had a look at it, call me back and we'll talk through anything you want to change."

"Am I looking for anything?"

"Absolutely not. She's clean, Mike. This is about the best due diligence I've ever seen. I was just saying to my VP, I'd buy this company myself."

"Find your own one, Mr. Stanzy!"

Pete laughed.

"You know, Pete, I really appreciate all this," said Wilson.

"You're paying for it, Mike."

"Still, your guys are putting in. I'm guessing they didn't get too much sleep last night."

"All part of the service."

"Hell of a job. How are they holding up?"

"Fine," said Pete.

"Sure?"

"Yeah."

"No problems?"

"No."

"Really? Nothing?"

Stanzy didn't answer right away. Mike Wilson had never shown any interest in the team before. Suddenly he had a feeling that Wilson wasn't asking now purely out of concern for them. He wondered if Wilson had heard something. Clients always get spooked if they think there's trouble with the team, but if they find out you've been holding out on them, it's even worse.

Wilson seemed pretty happy, thought Pete. Everything was falling into place. He could take the chance.

"One of our young guys, Mike, one of the junior guys on the team . . . he's had a bit of a personal problem."

"What's that?" asked Wilson.

"One of his friends was found dead yesterday."

"Oh. I'm sorry."

"Murdered, apparently."

"Hell, that sounds pretty horrible. How is he?"

"He's okay."

"Sure?"

"I think so."

"Is he at work?"

"Mike, don't worry about him. He's a very junior guy. The main thing is, everything's going to run smoothly from your perspective. Whatever resource we have to put in, we'll put in. If we need to bring someone else onto the team, that's what we'll do. Whatever it takes. This deal is our number-one priority. No question. That doesn't just go for me and John Golansky, it goes for the whole firm. Now, when you've had a chance to have a look at the—"

"Your analyst," interjected Wilson, "is in possession of very sensitive information."

Stanzy stopped, pulled up short by the sudden change in Mike Wilson's tone. The amiability had gone right out of it.

"This deal is not done, Pete. It's not close to being done." Wilson paused. "Let's remember where we are. Until we announce, Bassett isn't locked in in any shape or form. He can walk away from the table and you know what? No one will even know he was there. And if this thing leaks . . . all bets are off. Now, I'm sorry about what happened to your analyst, I really am, but I need to know if this guy's okay. Have you talked to him?"

"Mike . . ."

"I want to know where this guy is. Have you talked to him, Pete? Yourself?"

"No. Not myself."

"Why not? Don't you think you should?"

Stanzy shook his head, wondering what to say.

"Pete? Level with me."

"Mike, we do have a problem with this analyst. He's . . . look, we don't actually know where he is."

"Jesus Christ, Pete! What's his name?"

"Rob Holding."

"Is he stable? How long has he been with you? What do you know about him?"

"Mike, calm down. This thing . . . this incident . . . has obviously upset him. I assume he's just needing time to work through it. Look, it's not ideal, I know. When I talk to him, we're going to have to have a serious look at the way he's behaved. But it's got nothing to do with the deal. It's a personal issue. There's absolutely no reason he should tell anyone anything. The deal is safe, Mike. That's what matters."

"Are you telling me," said Wilson slowly, "that you have absolutely no idea where he is? I want you to be straight with me, Pete. You have no idea at all?"

Pete Stanzy took a deep breath. "We don't. I'm not going to try to kid you. We don't know. He's not answering his phone."

"When was the last time anyone saw him?"

"Sometime yesterday, I believe."

"And you have no idea where he is? Absolutely none?"

"No."

There was silence.

"I'm sorry, Mike. It's not ideal, I know. But . . . what can I say? I'm as unhappy about it as you are. And believe me, I'm doing everything I can to deal with it."

"Okay. Okay, I understand. I'm glad you leveled with me."

"I really don't think there's an issue with the deal, Mike. This is a personal problem our guy's got."

"Yes. I'm sorry for him. Listen, it must be hard on the rest of your team, making up for someone like that. Let them know I appreciate it."

"I will," said Stanzy. "They'll appreciate that. They're a great bunch of guys."

"Let them know there'll be a little something extra for them when it's all done."

"No, Mike. That's not necessary. Everything we have to do for this deal, we'll do it. I guarantee that. Whatever it takes. We're two hundred percent committed. Mike, we're going to send that fax down in a couple of minutes. Give me a call when you've checked it over. I'll be right here."

"Okay. Pete, when your guy does turn up, as soon as you know where he is, I want to know. I want to know when you've found him and I want to know where he is. You call me, right?"

"Sure," said Stanzy.

"All right." Wilson's tone was peremptory. "Make sure you do. As soon as you know."

• • •

Mike Wilson watched the pages coming out of the fax machine as he dialed the number. He waited as the phone rang. Then he heard the familiar, nasal voice on the line. It was too familiar, like something you've carried with you for too long and just wished you could get rid of.

"I just spoke to someone at Dyson Whitney," said Wilson. "Apparently he hasn't turned up for work. They don't know where he is. I thought I should let you know."

"Thank you, Michael."

"He's not answering his phone. They've got no idea at all what's happened to him." Wilson paused. "Tony, it sounds to me like he's figured out someone's after him. Sounds to me like—"

"Michael, we'll find him."

"What if he talks to the police?"

"What will he say?"

Wilson didn't want to imagine. He had no idea how much Holding knew.

"Michael, you ask me, I don't think you need to worry that he talks to the police."

"How do you know?"

"Because he would have done it already. Let's be calm. We'll find him. I told you, there are not so many places a person goes. And if we don't find him there, we find someone who can tell us where he is. It's very simple."

"Have you found her? His girlfriend?"

"It's in hand."

Wilson closed his eyes.

"Michael?"

"What?"

"Thank you for this call. You'll let me know if you hear anything else, yes?"

"Yes."

"Good. Good-bye, Michael."

Wilson heard the line click dead. His eyes were still closed. On the other side of the room, the drone of the fax machine continued.

He was deep, deep in self-revulsion. Now he was hoping that Prinzi's thugs had gotten hold of the girl. Every time he thought he'd reached bottom, he found himself sinking lower.

He heard a knock. He spun around. The door was open. Lyall Gelb was in the doorway.

"How long have you been there?" he demanded sharply.

"Just a second."

Wilson stared at him suspiciously.

Lyall came into the room. "You all right, Mike?"

"What do you want?" demanded Wilson.

"I just got off the phone with Trewin. Their due diligence is done."

"And?"

"They're happy."

Wilson stared at Lyall Gelb a moment longer. Then he pulled himself together. He grinned. "That's great. Come over here. Come on, let's call Bassett."

Wilson punched the speaker button on the phone. A moment later, he had Bassett on the line. They exchanged jokes about their due diligence, about each not being able to find the skeletons the other party had buried.

"Andy, laughs aside," said Wilson, "I want you to be absolutely one hundred and ten percent happy that you've seen everything you wanted to see. We gave you all the data we thought you could possibly need."

"Oliver's team said they'd never seen so much data in one place."

"Good."

"Said they could have used another six months, actually."

Wilson winked at Lyall. "Andy, I wish I could have given it to them."

"Absolutely, Mike. One must do one's best in the time, eh?"

"Exactly my philosophy. There'll be no reservations on my side when I recommend this deal to my board tomorrow, and that's how I want you to feel as well. You still talking to your board as scheduled?"

"Absolutely. Eleven o'clock tomorrow. There'll be no reservations on my part, either, rest assured."

"Well, we may just have a deal!" said Wilson.

"I think we may," responded Bassett.

"Great. I'll tell my guys they can shut down the data room and file all that stuff away," said Wilson.

"Ahh . . . technically, Mike, I think we should just keep it open for the moment."

Wilson glanced questioningly at Lyall. "Why's that, Andy?"

"Well, if the board were to ask for clarification on any point, I wouldn't want to say we don't have access anymore. Wouldn't look good."

Wilson glanced at Lyall again. Lyall didn't speak.

"Sure, Andy. We'll keep it open. Let those lawyers get another couple of days' room rent out of us. You can shut yours down. We're happy."

They arranged to speak again the next day, after their boards had met. It would be evening in London by the time the Louisiana Light board finished. Bassett told Wilson to call him on his home number.

Mike Wilson looked at Gelb after he cut the line. "How much stuff did you put in that data room?" he asked.

"Everything I could find."

Wilson laughed. "You want someone to miss the tree, put him in the forest. A big, fat, Hungarian forest."

Lyall Gelb nodded. But there was a part of him that had almost wanted that tree to be found. He didn't realize it until now, when he knew it hadn't been.

"I've got things to do," he said.

"Sure, Lyall." Wilson watched as Lyall got up and walked out. The door closed behind him.

Mike Wilson leaned back in his chair. It was close now. Close enough that he could almost touch it.

But not close enough that he could afford to celebrate. Three days to go. Three more days of bluffing.

He was thoughtful again, calculating. He went through the elements in his mind. The due diligence was done now. The bridge loan was more or less finalized. The board meeting tomorrow was the last obstacle. The extra cash that he had offered to Bassett, and the structure of the loan that was necessary to raise it, was going to be an issue. The board didn't know about that yet. Even the friendliest board would be bound to ask questions.

Wilson began to go over his strategy for the meeting. He had arranged to have dinner that night with Ed Leary to get him primed. Carefully, methodically, Mike Wilson went through what he was going to say to Leary in eight hours' time. He thought through the angles, how Leary might react, how he was going to play it.

Robert Holding and his girlfriend and what was going to happen to them at the hands of Tony Prinzi had slipped entirely from his mind.

46

Sammy Weiss leafed impatiently through the draft of the due diligence report. He was waiting for Mike Wilson's corrections to come through. Cynthia was proofreading the other document that would be going to the board, which outlined the structure of the bridge loan and the financial arrangements for the deal. They had both worked through the night. Once Wilson's corrections arrived and once Menendez had vetted them, they would only have to make the changes, print out the hard copies, and address them for the courier, and finally they could get out of there.

The phone rang. Sammy picked it up. It was Menendez, wanting to know if Sammy had seen the corrections. He was calling about every ten minutes to find out, and just as Sammy had told him ten minutes earlier, the answer was still no. Sammy didn't know why he kept calling anyway. The corrections were going to go to Stanzy first, and Stanzy would send them to Menendez. Phil was going to see them before they got anywhere near Sammy.

A few minutes later the phone rang again.

"Oh, give us a break!" muttered Weiss. He grabbed the receiver. "Yes?" he said.

It wasn't Menendez. "Is Robert Holding there?" said a voice.

"No," said Sammy, trying to repress his irritation. "He's not here."

"Do you know where I can find him?"

"Who is this?"

"I'm calling from the Eighteenth Precinct. Sergeant Berry. What's your name, son?"

"Sammy Weiss."

"Listen, Sammy." The man coughed. "We're looking for Robert because of a certain crime—"

"I heard about the murder," said Sammy. "I've already spoken to a detective."

Cynthia looked around.

"Of course you have. There's certain things we need to follow up. We're actually looking for Robert's girlfriend and I'm trying to find someone who can help us." He coughed again. "Excuse me. You don't know where his girlfriend lives, do you?"

"No," said Sammy.

"The information seems to have gone missing."

"How could it go missing?"

"Tell me about it. I'm just following up. What's her name, his girlfriend?"

"Emmy."

"Her last name?"

"I don't know her last name." He looked at Cynthia questioningly. Cynthia shook her head.

"Emmy. Okay. You know her address? Her phone number?"

"No," said Sammy. "Hold on." He turned to Cynthia. "You know where she lives? Rob's girlfriend?"

Cynthia shook her head again.

"What about where she works?" said the voice on the phone. "Do you know that?"

"She's an editor at a publishing company."

"Lascelle Press," said Cynthia. "I lived in a street with almost the same name."

"Lascelle Press," said Sammy into the phone.

"Lascelle Press. She's an editor there? Very good. You've been very helpful. Sammy Weiss, right? How do you spell that?"

Sammy spelled his name.

The man coughed. "Thank you, Sammy."

"No problem. Listen, if you find Rob—"

Sammy stopped. The phone was dead. He looked at it in surprise, then put it down.

"Police again?" said Cynthia.

Sammy nodded. "Apparently some information's gone missing. The police, for Christ's sake. You'd think they could get things straight the first time."

Caitlin and Andrea exchanged a glance. "I'll get it," said Caitlin.

She pressed a button on her phone and raised the receiver. The phone on Emmy's desk in the office they all shared stopped ringing.

It was Nicole, the Lascelle Press receptionist. "I've got someone asking for Emmy."

"Emmy's not here, Nicole," said Caitlin.

"I know, but they're very insistent. It's the *police*." Nicole whispered the word, as if it were too scary to say it out loud. "Perhaps you can help them."

Caitlin glanced at Andrea and rolled her eyes. Nicole was way too much a pushover to be a receptionist. She had been known to give out private cell phone numbers in her efforts to be helpful.

"Nicole," said Caitlin, "I can't make her appear out of nowhere."

"Please, Caitlin . . ."

Caitlin rolled her eyes. "All right, put them through." She waited. "Emmy Bridges's phone," she said.

"Is that Emmy Bridges?" asked a male voice.

"No. Emmy's not available, I'm afraid."

"Do you know when she will be available?"

"I'm afraid I can't say that. Can I take a message?"

The man coughed. "This is Sergeant Berry from the Fourteenth Precinct. Who am I speaking with?"

"This is Caitlin Jones, Sergeant. I work with Emmy."

"Well, Caitlin, I'm not sure if you're aware, but there was a certain crime—"

"Yes," said Caitlin quickly. "I'm aware. I'm very aware."

"Well . . ." The man coughed again. "Excuse me. We need to find Ms. Bridges, but we've had some information get kind of lost or something and I'm trying to follow up."

"She's not here, Sergeant."

"No, I understand. Do you have her address, please?"

"Umm . . ." Caitlin looked questioningly at Andrea.

"What?" whispered Andrea.

"We're not supposed to give that kind of information out," Caitlin said to the man on the phone.

"I realize that. This is urgent, Ms. Jones. Let me make sure I've got your name right. That's Caitlin Jones. Can you spell 'Caitlin' for me?"

Caitlin spelled it.

"I hope you're going to cooperate, Ms. Jones."

"Can you hold on a second?" Caitlin put her palm over the receiver. "It's a policeman," she whispered to Andrea. "He needs Emmy's address. Should I give it to him?"

"Give it to him."

"You sure?"

Andrea nodded.

"Sergeant . . ."

"Berry."

"Sergeant Berry, I'm not supposed to do this, but you did say it's urgent?"

"It is."

"Okay. I know she lives on West Seventy-sixth Street. I think it's one forty-four."

"I think it's one forty-two," whispered Andrea.

"It might be one forty-two. I know it's apartment seven."

"Ms. Jones, I need it exactly. It's very important."

"Okay. Hold on a second, please." Caitlin opened the internal company database on her screen and searched through it quickly. The man on the line coughed as he waited. "It's one forty-two," she said.

Andrea smiled smugly.

"So that's apartment seven, one forty-two West Seventy-sixth? Is that correct, Ms. Jones?"

"Yes, it is."

"Are you sure?"

"Yes."

"Thank you."

"Sergeant Berry, if I see her, do you want me to tell Emmy—" She took the phone away from her ear and looked at Andrea in surprise. "Rude! He just hung up."

"Well, he got what he wanted, I guess." Andrea shrugged. "Like any man."

One hundred forty-two West Seventy-sixth Street was an old brownstone. The two men let themselves in easily, looked around, and moved quickly up the stairs. They stopped outside apartment 7 and slipped on surgical gloves. Then they knocked.

One of the men had the inflamed nose and watery eyes of a cold. He coughed. "Go ahead," he said quietly to the other.

The second man quickly picked the lock. They went in, closing the door behind them.

They stood for a moment, looking around. Then the man with the cold pointed at the corridor that led to the bedroom. The second man moved silently toward it.

He came back a minute later. "No one," he said. "No one in the bathroom, neither."

"You check the cupboards? Under the bed?"

The man nodded.

"Okay." The man with the cold looked around the room. He picked up a letter. It was addressed to Emmy Bridges. "It's the right place."

"You want I should call Nick?"

"I'll call him." He dialed a number on a cell phone. There was a short conversation. He looked back at the other man. "We wait."

"How long?"

"As long as it takes." The man with the cold walked over to the kitchen area. He pulled open the fridge. "Let's see what we got in here," he muttered. "You want a beer?"

"Why not?" The other man came over and pulled open a couple of cupboards.

"What's she got in there?"

"Not much. We might have to send out for pizza."

"Yeah, right." The man with the cold closed the fridge and put a beer in the other man's hand. He looked in the cupboards. "Well, she likes corn chips. There's enough here for weeks."

"I hate corn chips."

The man with the cold took out a bag and pushed it into his hand. "Learn to love 'em."

"So who gets the bed?"

The man with the cold looked at him questioningly.

"If we're here overnight, who gets the bed?"

The man with the cold grinned. "What, Danny, you gone all shy? You telling me you don't wanna share?"

"Get the hell—"

The phone rang. The two men turned to look at it.

The answering machine kicked in. "Emmy? Emmy, it's Mom. I tried your cell phone but I thought you might . . . I'll try your cell phone again, honey. Okay. If you get this, call me, huh? I just want to see if you're all right. Umm . . . okay, I'll try your cell."

The men glanced at each other.

"Sounds like she's not answering her cell."

The man with the cold nodded. "Well, we'll be here if she comes home."

In Rochester, Emmy's mother put the phone down. She looked at her husband in concern. "That's the third time today I've tried to get hold of her, Marty."

"Did you leave a message on her cell?"

"Every time. That's not like Emmy. She always answers when I leave a message."

"She's probably trying to get some peace."

"Are you saying I don't give her peace?"

"I'm not saying that, Rose."

"Then what are you saying?"

"It's a tough thing, what happened. That's all."

Emmy's mother frowned with worry. "She sounded very upset last night, Marty. I couldn't sleep, thinking about it."

Marty nodded.

"I offered to go down."

"I know."

"And you know, things haven't been good with Rob."

"Haven't they?"

"You know they haven't. I told you, remember? I'm just worried she's lying there with the phone turned off, all by herself, just, you know, really upset."

"Honey, that's not like Emmy."

"Maybe they've broken up."

"Did she say they'd—"

"They could have. These things happen at stressful moments. Marty, you didn't speak to her last night. She was really upset. And Rob wasn't there. She didn't know where he was!"

Marty frowned. He didn't know what to say.

"Maybe I should go, Marty."

"She told you she'd let you know if she wanted you to go down."

"Maybe I should go anyway."

47

The night was cold and drizzly, but that was about the only similarity to the last time Rob had flown into London, only a little over a week previously. This time, he arrived economy class and there was no car waiting. And instead of Cynthia Holloway, he was with Emmy.

They had been at JFK before six that morning, but couldn't get on a flight until nine-thirty. They went through passport control and spent three nervous hours sitting at the back of a restaurant, hiding themselves behind newspapers. Rob wasn't taking any chances. Just because they were in an airport didn't mean they were safe. They weren't going to be safe until all of this was over.

He came across a report of Greg's death in the *Times*. A couple of short paragraphs on an inside page. DA MURDERED IN HELL'S KITCHEN. No real details. A police spokesman quoted as saying the investiga-

tion was being pursued with all available resources. Those were the
two detectives, Rob supposed, Engels and Nabandian. He showed the
article to Emmy. She read it silently.

He fell asleep after the flight took off, having slept so little the
night before. When he woke up a couple of hours later, Emmy was
dozing beside him. He watched her. He thought about what she had
said that morning. She hadn't been trying to guilt-trip him, he realized, when she said it was all or nothing, when she said there was
nothing involving him that didn't involve her. She was simply saying
how it was. That was how it was for her. It was a scary thing, to hear
someone say that about you. Not just to hear it, but to actually see it
in action. To see her get out of bed and say, unquestioningly, I'm
coming with you, before she even knew where he was going. To say,
Fuck them, if they get one of us, they get us both. It was awesome,
and scary. Overpowering. He felt he had never really understood it
before. He felt like a kid, as if he never really knew what love was
until that moment. Not just the feeling you have for someone else—
but the ability to let someone else have that same depth of feeling for
you. To surrender to it, to give them that right, as Emmy had said.
And she deserved an answer. Was that what he was prepared to do?
Did his love go that far? Because hers did.

She woke up and looked at him. "What are you thinking about?"

"Nothing," he said.

She was silent. She looked at her watch.

"We've got about three hours to go," said Rob.

"Where will we go when we get there?"

"I want to stay away from the obvious places. You remember
where we went when we were here?"

Emmy nodded.

"We'll stay there overnight. By the time we arrive it'll be too late
for me to make the call. I won't be able to do it until morning."

They left Heathrow on the express that runs downtown to Paddington Station. When they got off the train, they walked through
the station and headed into the darkness and rain of the streets outside. There were hotels nearby, crummy hotels, not the kind an investment banker would go to.

They turned a corner. There they were, hotels, a whole streetful.

They were all the same, converted terrace houses with signs above the doors glowing through the drizzle and mist. One after the other. GREEN HOTEL. BARTLETT HOTEL. FRANKEL HOUSE HOTEL. CORBETT HOTEL.

That was the one where they had stayed the previous summer. The Corbett.

Rob headed for it, then thought better of that idea and they went to one a couple of doors away. They went up the steps. By now it was almost midnight. The door was locked. Looking through the glass, Rob could see the little reception desk at the opposite end of the hall. It was unattended. He rang the bell. Then he rang it again.

After about a minute, the night clerk appeared from a door behind the reception desk. Rob watched him coming toward the entrance. He was a thin guy, with protruding cheekbones and hollow cheeks. The blue tie he was wearing was about six inches wide and rode a good two inches above his waistband. He opened the door.

"You got a room?" asked Rob.

The clerk gave them a strange look. They had no luggage with them, nothing.

"Two person?" he said in some kind of an Eastern European accent.

Rob nodded.

"Eighty pounds."

"Okay."

"With breakfast."

"Fine."

The man stepped back and let them in. He led them down the hall and went behind the desk.

"How long you want room?" asked the clerk.

Rob shrugged. "Couple of days."

"You pay now."

"Yeah?"

"You pay one day. You want more . . . tomorrow . . ."

"I pay then?" said Rob.

The man grinned. He looked at Emmy and she smiled back at him.

Rob had withdrawn a few hundred in sterling on his credit card before leaving Heathrow. He pulled out some bills.

The man took them. He pushed a piece of paper toward Rob. "You fill in."

The man turned around to take a key out of a set of pigeonholes on the wall. Rob hesitated over the form. Bill Smith, he wrote, in the box for his name. Then he thought, That was pretty dumb.

"Where you from?" asked the clerk as Rob was filling out the form.

"The States," said Emmy.

"Ah!" The clerk grinned again. "The States! I will go to States. Yes. Soon, when I finish my study here . . ."

Rob slid the form toward him.

The clerk looked at it. "Bill Smith?"

"That's right," said Rob. He took the key. "You gonna give me a receipt?"

The clerk looked at him blankly.

"A receipt?"

"What?"

Rob sighed. "For the money. For the eighty pounds. So your boss knows I paid."

The clerk smiled and waved a hand dismissively. "She knows."

"How does she know?"

"When person come, I must take money!" The clerk held his finger up emphatically, as if this was an iron rule that could never conceivably be broken.

Rob looked at him for a second. He just about opened his mouth to reply, but then he imagined the argument they were about to have. It was too difficult. He just wanted to get up to the room. "What floor?"

"Top," said the clerk. "Stairs there."

"Elevator?"

"Is not working."

Rob glanced at Emmy.

"It's fine," she said.

"Okay," said Rob to the clerk, and they headed for the stairs.

Up to the first landing, the stairs were in pretty good shape. Above that level, the carpet was stained, rucked, and threadbare, openly torn in places, and the paper on the walls was peeling. The stairs ended at a small landing four flights up, where there were three numbered doors of plain wood. Room 24. It was on the left.

Rob switched on the light. The room was small. A double bed was pushed up against the opposite wall, which sloped inward from about halfway up. There was a small wooden desk with a plain chair next to an old wooden cupboard, and a small TV was attached to the wall above the desk on a bracket.

"Jesus," he said to Emmy. "Was the room we had last year so shitty?"

"I think we had our mind on other things."

"Yeah, but . . . this is definitely worse." Rob closed the door. Emmy went into the bathroom. Rob opened the closet. Three twisted steel hangers hung inside. He closed it. A window was set into the sloping wall above the bed. Rob reached over and pulled back a grimy white net curtain. He looked down on a view along the wet, empty street.

Emmy came out.

"What's it like?" he asked.

"It's okay," she said, which Rob sensed was putting it kindly. "I couldn't find any towels. You happy or you want to move?"

Rob glanced around the room again. It was awful. But it was perfect. Who'd look for them here? "If you can bear it, we'll stay."

Emmy nodded.

There was a knock.

Emmy looked at him quickly. Rob moved cautiously to the door. Another knock.

"Who is it?"

"Is me, Mr. Smith."

Rob opened the door a fraction.

"You have towel?" said the clerk from downstairs.

"I don't think so," said Emmy.

"I check."

Rob let him in. He went into the bathroom.

"No. I come back."

The clerk went out. A couple of minutes later he knocked again. Rob opened the door and the clerk handed him a couple of towels.

"Thanks," said Rob.

"Is nothing. You come from States?"

Rob nodded.

The clerk grinned. "Ahhhh."

Rob sighed. "You? Where are you from?"

"Poland."

"Very good," said Rob. "Well, good night. Thank you for—"

"My name is Waldemar. Here everyone say 'Wally.'" The clerk laughed. "Is funny, yes?"

Rob shrugged.

"I study," said Wally.

Rob sighed.

"What do you study?" said Emmy, coming to the door.

"English. In Poland, I am engineer. Civil engineer. Yes? Road. Bridge." He held his arms out, as if showing the span of the bridges he had built. "Yes? I come here to study English. Is easy for me here. Poland is in EU. I work, I study." Wally grinned. "Maybe after I go to States. Like you."

"Good," said Emmy. "Good for you, Wally."

The clerk nodded.

"I'm kind of tired . . ." said Rob.

"Okay! Sure! Good night, Mr. Smith. Good night, Mrs. Smith."

Rob locked the door again. He tossed the towels on the desk.

"He's nice," said Emmy.

"He talks."

"He's lonely. He's here all by himself working a night shift at some shitty hotel."

"Well, whatever . . ."

"I'm going to take a shower." Emmy grabbed a towel and went into the bathroom.

Rob sat down on the bed. He thought about that knock as he

heard the shower go on. It had put that image back into his head, the one of Greg opening the door of his apartment. Only it wouldn't have been some Polish hotel clerk outside with a towel in his hand.

He got up, trying to drive the thought out of his mind. He pulled back the curtain and looked down on the street again. Rain fell through the light of a streetlamp. He saw someone hurrying past under an umbrella. The footsteps echoed. Rob watched until the figure had passed the hotel and turned out of sight farther down the street.

He let the curtain fall back.

It was okay. They were safe here. Apart from the British immigration service, no one knew they were in London. And if they did, they'd never be able to find them.

He glanced at his watch. Midnight. Nine more hours. At nine o'clock, he would make the call.

Emmy came out with the towel around her. "Refreshing," she said. "You've got about a minute before the water goes cold."

He had a quick shower. When he came out, Emmy was in bed. The mattress sagged as he got in. He turned off the light. Streetlight filtered in through the net curtain. He reached around the window in the shadow and found a curtain and pulled it across. It was dark now. He lay down again.

The faucet was dripping in the bathroom. He got up to try to stop it, but as soon as he got back into bed, it kept dripping. He turned over. The bed creaked.

"Rob, relax," said Emmy. She kissed him and searched for his hand under the blanket. "Good night, honey."

"Good night."

They lay in silence. He tried to ignore the dripping faucet, tried to let it recede into the background.

"You asleep?" said Emmy after a while.

"No."

"I keep thinking about Greg. I keep thinking about you finding him."

Rob didn't say anything.

She was silent again for a moment, and then she turned to him. Her fingers caressed his face. Then her lips searched for his, at first tentatively, brushing him, then pressing hard, demanding, hungry. They made urgent love, the bed creaking under them as if it were going to break.

"I'm sorry," said Emmy afterward. "I don't know why I wanted that. I mean, Greg's dead, and I was thinking about that. . . . It seems wrong."

"No." Rob shook his head. "No." He turned to her, and she nestled into him, face nuzzled into his neck, arm across his chest.

He listened to the faucet, and her breathing, as she fell asleep. Gently, he moved her off him.

He envied Emmy her slumber. She was one of those people who always seem to be able to sleep when they need to. He wasn't. He needed sleep now, if only to release him from the thoughts of Greg that kept coming back. But his body clock was in New York and sleep wouldn't come.

Eventually he checked his watch again. Seven more hours. Seven more hours until he could make the call.

In London it was two A.M. on a cold, wet night. In New York it was only nine in the evening.

48

In Baton Rouge, it was eight o'clock. The piano player at Nagel's on the River was playing a soulful blues number. Mike Wilson and Ed Leary were at a window table. Wilson had asked Stella to make sure that Everard, the maître d' at Nagel's, knew he needed a secluded placing.

Ed was drinking a martini as he studied the menu. Wilson was drinking bourbon.

"You want to try the ribs, Ed," said Wilson. "No one does ribs like Nagel's."

Leary nodded. "What about the . . . ah, steak here, Mike? They do a good steak?"

"You can't ever go wrong with a Louisiana steak, Ed. Alligator, right?"

Ed Leary laughed. He sipped his martini.

A waiter came over and took their orders. The sommelier came for their wine.

"Red good for you, Ed?" asked Wilson.

Leary nodded. "Order whatever, Mike."

Wilson ordered. The sommelier took the wine list and disappeared.

"Thanks for sending the jet, Mike."

"Sure. No problem."

"Made it easier."

"Well, I wanted to be sure we had this time to talk things through. You're a busy guy, Ed, I know that. I wanted to make sure we have everything set for tomorrow."

Leary nodded. He finished his martini.

"You want another one of those?"

Leary shook his head. "I think I'll wait for the wine."

"How's Catherine, by the way?"

A shadow crossed Ed Leary's face. "Not so good, Mike. It's . . ." Leary shook his head. He sighed heavily.

"It's a terrible thing," said Wilson, giving Leary a frank, commiserating look.

"Yeah. Terrible." Leary sighed again. "To see her now . . . Catherine was always so full of life. When the kids were young, she did everything. You know how it is. I was hardly around."

Wilson nodded.

"I think about it now, I don't know where the years went." Leary gazed reflectively into his empty martini glass for a moment. "Well, you've gotta make the best of what you've got, don't you?"

The wine came. Wilson tasted. The sommelier poured.

"Here's to making the best of things," said Wilson, raising his glass.

Leary smiled sadly. He raised and drank.

Wilson swirled the wine in his mouth. It was a heavy, full-bodied cabernet, just the way he liked it. He savored it.

"Speaking of good things . . ." he said. "We have quite a good one on the agenda tomorrow."

"The due diligence checked out?"

"Beautiful." Wilson opened his briefcase and took out a portfolio. He laid it on the table. "I've brought a copy of the report for you. Don't worry about the way it looks—it was faxed down to me this afternoon. You'll get a bound one tomorrow, but have a look over it tonight when you get back to the hotel. Ed, you couldn't ask for anything sweeter. Okay, their projections have been a little bullish, but whose isn't? Don't tell me yours never were."

Ed chuckled, taking the portfolio from Wilson and resting it on the floor against his chair.

"Everything else . . ." said Wilson. "It's looking real good. Their balance sheet is just as strong as we thought. If anything, it's stronger." Wilson leaned closer. "Ed, you wouldn't believe what they've got there. Hell, they've been piling so much cash away you'd think they've been using it to prop up their houses." Wilson laughed. "Things are going to change."

He stopped. The salads arrived.

"What about them?" asked Leary. He crunched into a piece of celery. "They happy with us?"

"Yeah. I spoke to Bassett this afternoon. Their report's fine. Their board's meeting tomorrow, just like we planned. They start at eleven their time."

"Great. Well, I can't see any issues for us tomorrow. Could be a short meeting."

"Yeah, we'll see if we can get you out for a round at Emory Point in the afternoon."

Ed Leary chuckled. "That's one fine golf course."

"It is, isn't it?" Wilson watched Leary for a moment. "The other issue, Ed, about the loan. Good news there as well. Dyson Whitney's just about got the bridge taken care of. When you see the details, I think you'll agree they've done a hell of a job. Six-point-two-five billion isn't a trivial sum."

"Four-point-two billion, Mike."

Wilson shook his head. "Six-point-two-five, Ed."

Leary's fork stopped halfway to his open mouth, carrying a lettuce leaf.

"I had to go to half cash in the offer."

Ed Leary put down his fork. He frowned, genuinely confused. "Didn't we agree on four-point-two when we approved?"

"I said," repeated Wilson slowly, "I had to go to fifty percent cash. That makes it six-point-two-five."

"And you didn't tell me?"

"There wasn't time."

"But you said Dyson Whitney's got it taken care of. If they've had time to—"

"Look, Ed. Is it relevant? Does it matter? I had to do it to get the deal done. I had to make the decision there and then at the table."

Leary shook his head disbelievingly. "Fifty percent in cash? How are we going to—"

"I told you, Dyson Whitney's organized it. When you look at the schedule, you'll see they've done a pretty good job. I had my doubts for a while, but . . ." Wilson nodded emphatically. "They came through."

"Well, that's . . ." Leary's voice trailed off. He didn't know what to say.

"I must admit, some of the covenants are pretty stringent. And there's a premium, of course. But, as you say, it's a lot of cash these guys are handing over."

"A premium?" asked Ed Leary. Almost whispered it. "What kind of premium?"

By way of reply, Wilson opened his briefcase and took out a copy of the loan document that had been prepared for the board. He laid it down on the table beside Ed Leary's salad. Then he sat back, watching the other man as he took it in.

Leary's eyes went wide. "Jesus, Mary, and Joseph, Mike!" He looked up at Wilson in disbelief. "You're putting the whole company in hock."

Wilson continued to watch him. Silent, waiting to see just how far this was going.

Leary was shaking his head quickly. "No, no, no. You can't do it. It's too much. Look at this. And this. We're junk! Mike, no. No. No, no, no—"

"Their balance sheet is strong, Ed."

"Not that strong."

"Strong enough. So are their revenue streams. The banks can have their premium. It's not forever. Over a few years, we pay it down. Ed, we can handle it. This is a deal in a lifetime. Short term, we pay a price. Long term, with the value we'll create, it's a price worth paying."

Leary was still shaking his head. "Fifty percent? You offered them fifty percent? How could . . . Mike, you should've walked away."

"From the deal of a lifetime? Ed, you don't walk away from something like that."

"We can't . . . we can't do this."

"Ed," said Wilson, giving Leary one more chance to get into line the easy way. "You're not listening. Don't look at the short term here. Think about the long-term position—"

"They suckered you, Mike. They suck—"

"No."

"Yes, Mike. Jesus, they suckered—"

"Enough!" hissed Wilson.

Leary stopped.

Wilson glanced around. A couple of people at other tables were staring at him. They looked away.

Wilson leaned closer to Leary across their salads. "You disappoint me, Ed. I hoped you'd be able to see the value of this deal for what it is. The full value of it. I didn't want to have to do it like this."

"Like what?" asked Leary nervously.

"I don't think you understand the situation," said Mike Wilson in a low voice, locking the other man's eyes in a direct, deadly gaze. "Let me put it to you directly. We don't have a choice. We have to do this deal."

"No," said Leary. Suddenly he looked at Wilson as if he understood everything for the first time. "It's your new contract, isn't it? Twelve million in cash, twelve million in options. I never thought that kind of thing was right, giving you that kind of money for doing what you should be doing anyway. It's wrong. It's obscene."

"It's normal practice. There's nothing wrong with it. It's market competitive. Hell, Ed, you took advice."

"From Gordon. Gordon Anderton would do anything you say. He'd recommend us to pay you fifty million if that's what you told him."

"Anderton Doolittle is a respectable human resources company," said Wilson impatiently. "Hell, Ed, it's got a whole fucking remuneration practice."

"Twenty-four million," muttered Leary. "It's obscene. It's immoral."

"Spare me your thoughts on morality," growled Wilson.

"Tell me, Mike. Did you have this deal in your back pocket when we negotiated the contract?"

"You're missing the point," said Wilson quietly.

"Huh? Were you already talking to Bassett? Because if you were, and you didn't make the board aware of it . . ."

"What, Ed?" Wilson stared at him with a cruel, unforgiving smile. "What are you going to do?"

Leary stared back at him for a second, then looked away.

"It's got nothing to do with my contract," said Wilson. "Let's just get that clear."

"You expect me to believe that?" Leary looked back at Wilson defiantly, shook his head. "I'm voting against this deal tomorrow, and I'll be recommending the other directors vote against it as well. We've been friends a long time, Mike, but there are some things I won't do even for friends. I'm not going to let you put the company into the pawn shop for the sake of padding your pockets. I'm sorry, Mike, but Ed Leary does not—"

"Ed Leary will do what he's fucking told!" hissed Wilson. Leary stared, bug-eyed, as if Wilson physically had his hands around his neck. Wilson leaned closer. "It has nothing to do with my contract. That's not the issue. Get it straight. It's the company, Ed. You think I'm putting the company in the pawn shop? Without this deal, there'll be no company."

Leary continued to stare.

"You remember all those things you never wanted to know too much about, Ed? You remember those things you signed off on so happily? Well, those things are coming home to roost. They're right outside the window. They're knocking to get in." Wilson paused. He leaned back, watching Leary with a cool, evaluating gaze.

"There was nothing wrong with anything I signed."

"Wasn't there just? You never had an inkling, did you? Never had the slightest suspicion."

"But you said everything was okay. And Lyall, Lyall said everything was okay . . ."

Wilson smiled pitilessly. "Yeah. And you believed him, right?"

"What about the last quarter? The last quarter results were great!"

Wilson didn't even reply to that. He just laughed.

Ed Leary looked around in despair, as if someone else in the restaurant might offer him a way out. He was like a fish, thought Wilson, flailing on the end of a line.

"What are you going to say in court, Ed? That you didn't know? That you forgot to ask what exactly it meant that you were signing?" Wilson raised an eyebrow. He laughed softly. "Ed, Ed . . . that don't wash no more. Little Kenny Lay done closed that door for us all a long time ago."

Ed Leary looked at him in horror.

"Just imagine the headlines, Ed. Not even when it gets to court. Way before that. When the press starts to get the scent. You were the chairman, Ed. Just what were you doing in return for your emoluments? Your very generous emoluments. Hell, to the undiscerning eye, it might look like you were taking all that money just to look away. You know what the press is like, Ed. You know how they twist things. What'll it do to Catherine?"

Leary flinched. Physically.

"They're knocking, Ed." Wilson knocked on the window pane beside them. "They're knocking just outside."

Wilson watched him. Ed Leary seemed to have aged ten years right in front of his eyes.

"What have you done?" whispered Leary.

"You don't want to know. Besides, it's a little late to start asking questions."

"Is it really that bad?"

Wilson nodded.

"How long?"

"The next filing will kill us."

Leary's hand went to his mouth. "Jesus, Mary, and Joseph!"

"We do this deal, Ed, there isn't a next filing. Not for Louisiana Light. That's the point."

Leary shook his head. He still couldn't believe it.

"Come on, Ed. Don't you sit there and say you didn't have a clue. Every time you signed, what were you thinking? Those stock options of yours just kept going up, didn't they? You liked that, didn't you?"

"Don't say that."

Wilson shrugged.

Ed Leary looked away from him. Out the window.

"There's no such thing as a free lunch," murmured Wilson. "What do you know? It's payback time."

Leary kept looking out the window.

Everard, the maître d', approached. His steps were tentative, and he stopped a full two yards away, leaning forward from the waist.

"Excuse me, Mr. Wilson," he said. "Are your salads all right? It's just . . . I notice neither of you have been eating them."

"They're fine," said Wilson.

"Can I get you or your guest something else instead?"

"Everard, they're fine." Wilson skewered a piece of lettuce. "Thank you."

Everard nodded. "Sorry to disturb you." He backed off a few steps, like a courtier in front of some kind of king, before turning away.

Ed was still staring out the window. Wilson watched him. It would take an exceptionally strong man, exceptionally principled, to stick to his guns in Leary's position. And nothing Mike Wilson had ever seen or heard from Ed Leary suggested that he was such a man. If he were, he wouldn't have been in that position in the first place.

Leary turned back.

Wilson gazed at him questioningly.

"Imogen DuPont will be the problem," said Ed, his jaw set so tight he could barely get the words out.

The both knew what that statement signified. Leary's capitulation was clear.

Wilson smiled for an instant. "How so?" he asked, and he skewered a piece of lettuce on his fork.

"She's new. I doubt she'd understand the imperative even if we explained it."

"Yes, I doubt that as well," said Wilson. He ate the lettuce thoughtfully. "Here's how I think we should handle it, Ed. You give Dave and Mal a call when you get back to the hotel tonight. Give them the heads-up on the extra debt and the premium and let them know just how bad we need the deal. I won't tell you what to say. I'm sure you can handle it better than me."

Leary closed his eyes for a second.

"Gordon . . . well, Gordon's just going to go along with what everyone else says, like he always does. I agree with you, by the way, he is kind of pliable. Now when it comes to Imogen . . ." Wilson paused, crunching a piece of cucumber out of his salad. "I figure Imogen wouldn't know a chunk of junk-rated debt from her own sweet ass. You give the lead, come out strong, say this is a great deal, talk a lot about how strong Buffalo's balance sheet is and don't even mention that there's any issue over the loan premium, and Imogen won't know she even ought to ask about it. Especially if you make sure Mal and Dave stay clear of it as well. And especially if we spend a lot of time going through the legal detail of the due diligence report. A whole *lot* of time. So let's start with that tomorrow, huh? Start with the legal matters. Let her talk about that as much as she likes, the whole day if she wants. Because not only does Imogen want to show all us men that she's the one who knows the law, she also wants to cover her ass. Ed, this is the same ass she doesn't know from a chunk of junk-rated debt, and by letting her cover it, we'll make sure that at the end of tomorrow she still doesn't know it." Wilson paused. "Ed, what do you think about that plan? We may not get you out for a round at Emory Point after all, but it's a pretty good one, don't you think?"

Leary nodded, a kind of nauseated grin plastered across his face.

"Yeah. I kind of like it myself." Wilson skewered another piece of cucumber on his plate. "Go ahead, Ed. Eat. The salad's good."

49

The faucet dripped all night. Rob finally fell asleep and then slept deeply, exhausted. He awoke with a gray light filtering through the curtains and Emmy lying beside him. It took him a moment to remember where he was. Then everything came back.

"What time is it?" he asked.

"Eleven," said Emmy.

He sat up. His mouth felt dry and disgusting. Eleven o'clock. He had been planning to make the call at nine.

"Have you been awake long?" he asked.

Emmy shook her head.

Rob got up. His head felt as if it were filled with lead. He went into the bathroom and splashed water on his face, then came back and sat on the edge of the bed. He just wanted to lie back and sleep again. The phone was on the bedside table. Propped up against the wall behind it was a laminated card. There wasn't much to it: 0, reception. 9, external line. Then a bunch of British and international dialing codes.

Rob rang reception and asked for the directories number. The voice at reception asked if he was staying another day. Not so much asked, told him, or at least that he would be paying for it. Fine, said Rob. And that he'd missed breakfast, which they had stopped serving at ten. Fine. Now could he just have the number for inquiries?

He got it and rang through to get the number he needed. He wrote it down.

He was going to call from the hotel phone. He hadn't turned on his cell phone since leaving New York. Neither had Emmy. The location of cell phones could be traced when they were on, he knew. He didn't know exactly how it could be done, but the last thing he or Emmy was going to do was walk around with a device constantly signaling their location to someone who might know how to trace it.

He paused, thinking through what he was going to say. Then he picked up the receiver and punched the number into the phone.

"Wish me luck," he said as he waited for the call to go through.

"Luck!" said Emmy.

The phone rang twice before it was answered. "BritEnergy," said a voice.

He asked to be put through to Andrew Bassett. The line went silent and then clicked.

"Mr. Bassett's office. This is Georgina."

"Georgina," said Rob, "I'm looking for Mr. Bassett's assistant."

"I'm Mr. Bassett's secretary." The voice on the phone sounded as if it belonged to a woman in her thirties. Maybe forties. "How can I help?"

"I wonder if I could speak with Mr. Bassett," said Rob.

"Mr. Bassett's unavailable, I'm afraid. Who am I speaking with?"

Rob knew that tone. Territorial, guarded. Just about ready to shut the gate. The tone of a million secretaries in a million offices when someone they don't know wants to talk with their boss.

"My name's Robert Holding. I'm from Dyson Whitney. That's an investment bank in New York. Mr. Bassett will know of it. I have something very important to discuss with him and I need to set up a meeting. It's urgent, so if you could let him know who I am, I'll hold."

"I'm afraid Mr. Bassett's unavailable, Mr. Holding. Can you let me know something about the matter you'd like to discuss with him?"

"I'm afraid that's confidential. But I can tell you it's important and Mr. Bassett will want to know about it right away, so I'll hold while—"

Georgina's tone was firm. "I'm afraid he's unavailable, Mr. Holding."

"Can you set up the meeting?"

"Certainly, if you tell me what it's about and I can check with Mr. Bassett first."

Rob glanced at Emmy and rolled his eyes. "Does he have a voice mail I can leave a message on?"

"If you give me your contact number, I can pass your message on to him."

"I can call back," said Rob. "Can you let me know what time—"

"Mr. Holding," repeated Georgina, "if you leave me a contact number, I will pass your message on."

It didn't sound negotiable. If they were going to do it, they were going to do it Georgina's way. Rob hesitated. His cell phone was on the table. If he gave the number, he'd have to have it on all the time.

"Mr. Holding?"

Rob grabbed the card with the phone directions. The hotel's number was at the bottom. "I'm at the Bartlett Hotel." He gave the number. "And I'm Robert Holding. That's H-O-L-D-I-N-G. From Dyson Whitney." Rob spelled that as well.

"What room?" asked the secretary.

"Excuse me?"

"What room number at the hotel?"

"Twenty-four." Suddenly Rob remembered he'd given a different name when he checked in. "Room twenty-four," he said again to Bassett's secretary. "Make sure he asks for room twenty-four. That's very important. They've already had one mixup here. Apparently there's another guest with the same name. He just has to ask for room twenty-four. It's very unlikely he'll get to me if he doesn't ask specifically for that room."

"Room twenty-four . . ." said the secretary.

"Georgina, this is a really urgent matter," said Rob. "I just want to make sure you understand."

"I understand, Mr. Holding. Room twenty-four."

"I need to speak with Mr. Bassett as soon as I can."

"I'll pass your message on, Mr. Holding."

"Georgina—"

"I'll pass it on. Good-bye, Mr. Holding."

The phone went dead. Rob put down the receiver. He lay back on the bed and looked at Emmy.

"Well?" she said.

Rob shook his head. That hadn't gone well.

There was a knock on the door.

Emmy got it. It was a maid. Emmy told her they didn't need anything done and came back to the bed.

"He wasn't there?" she asked.

"Not available," said Rob. "Could mean anything."

Rob thought about it. It was likely Bassett really had been unavailable. Eleven o'clock. He should have rung at nine. He was much more likely to have gotten him at nine. Or maybe it was standard practice for Bassett's secretary to take messages and tell everyone he'd get back to them. He might have been right inside his office, just a few yards from the secretary Rob had been speaking to.

In which case, Bassett might call back any minute.

Rob examined the phone. There was no answering facility on it. And the chances of reception at a place like this taking and successfully delivering a message, he figured, were small. If Bassett even went to the trouble of leaving one.

He glanced at Emmy. "I'm going to have to wait here."

50

The board meeting at Louisiana Light ran for four hours. Mike Wilson, Ed Leary, Stan Murdoch, Lyall Gelb, Dave Ablett, and Imogen DuPont were in the boardroom in Baton Rouge. Gordon Anderton and Mal Berkowitz hadn't been able to get down and were hooked in from different locations by phone. After the preliminaries, they dived into the due diligence report and were soon deep in the legal section. Imogen DuPont took them deeper and deeper, putting numerous clarifications, caveats, and qualifications on the record. Doug Earl dutifully noted them all down. Mike Wilson couldn't have been happier. From time to time he glanced at Ed Leary. Ed seemed to have trouble meeting his gaze. After they finished with the due diligence report, they moved on to the loan schedule. Again, Leary avoided Mike Wilson's eyes. He had spoken to Mal and Dave, just as Wilson had told him to. They were as subdued as Ed. For the sake of the record, Mal asked whether Mike and Lyall thought the combined company could service the debt. Mike said it was his belief that the company could, and for the sake of the record he asked for Lyall Gelb's opinion. Lyall said it could as well.

Stan Murdoch watched it all happening. He knew the way Mike Wilson operated, he knew the vote at the meeting would have been fixed in advance. But he was surprised the deal had gotten this far.

Every day for the past few days, he had been expecting to hear the noise of the explosion that would go off when BritEnergy saw the data on Grogon and ExPar. Now he was expecting it by the end of the day. Not from in here. It would happen in the BritEnergy board meeting—which was already under way in London when their own meeting kicked off in Baton Rouge—when the BritEnergy board looked at their due diligence on Louisiana Light. That was what he was waiting for.

By now it was almost two o'clock and a number of people in the room were wondering when they were going to get lunch. Wilson had purposely told Stella not to organize any food so as to discourage drawn-out discussion. Ed Leary called on him to present the takeover schedule, if there were no further questions from the board. Wilson presented the timetable. Then Ed asked again if there were any questions or last points. There were none. Ed Leary called for a vote. Hands went up. Imogen DuPont accompanied her vote with the usual caveats, which Doug Earl dutifully noted down. Approvals came over the phone from Gordon and Mal. Wilson fixed his gaze on Murdoch and eventually Stan's hand went up as well. The acquisition of BritEnergy PLC was unanimously approved by the legally constituted board of Lousiana Light, Inc.

Mike Wilson sent Ed Leary back home to Boston on the company jet. There would have been time for a quick round at Emory Point, or at least nine holes, but for some reason, Ed didn't seem keen to get out there.

When he got back to his office, Mike Wilson picked up the phone to Andy Bassett. It was midafternoon in Baton Rouge, late evening in Britain. Bassett was at his home in Berkshire, outside London.

Wilson sat back with his feet up on the desk. "Andy," he said, "I'm calling with good news. Our board meeting has just broken up and I'm calling to say we have unanimous approval to join Lousiana Light with your fine company."

"Mike, I've got good news as well," said Bassett. "We had a very positive meeting here and we have overwhelming support to proceed."

"That's great," said Wilson. "Andy, when you say overwhelming . . ."

"We did have one dissenter. Sir Charles Kitson. I think I mentioned to you he'd be a problem. Doesn't like debt, our Charlie. Civil service man originally. Permanent secretary to the Department of Trade in a former life."

"Board member of BritEnergy in a former life."

"Quite," said Bassett. "Couldn't agree more."

"All right, Andy," said Wilson. "I believe we have approval."

"I believe we do. If your data room's still open, Mike, you can shut it down."

Wilson paused for a second, savoring the moment. With the BritEnergy board's approval, the last big hurdle had gone down. He was on the home stretch, with nothing but clear turf ahead of him. Once the announcement was made, the BritEnergy board would be locked in and the focus would shift to the PR effort to make sure the share price stayed up and the shareholders of BritEnergy approved the deal. Given the quality of the offer, Wilson expected that to be time-consuming but relatively straightforward. He'd spend as much time as needed in England to keep the authorities, shareholders, and analysts happy. It was the BritEnergy board's public, irreversible commitment to the deal that was the key ingredient. So it wasn't time to celebrate yet, not for another two days. Keep focused, he told himself. And keep Bassett focused as well. Keep him working, not thinking.

"Andy," he said. "You got a copy of the draft for our announcement on Friday from Mandy Bellinger?"

"I have," said Bassett. "She e-mailed it through today. To be honest, Mike, I only saw it after the board and I haven't had much of a chance to look at it. I'm getting together with Oliver and Anthony tomorrow to go over it in detail."

"Okay, I'll have my secretary set up a conference call with you and me and Mandy tomorrow to finalize it. If we do it at, say, ten o'clock here, that'll be four your time. How's that? Will you have time to have seen it?"

"I'm sure we will. I'll get my secretary to let yours know."

"Okay. Well, good work today, Andy. I kind of like the way we're working together already, don't you?"

"Yes, it's going very smoothly," said Bassett. "Must get you out to the house here next time you're over, Mike."

"I'd like that, Andy. You ski, by the way?"

"I have been known to try the piste," said Bassett self-deprecatingly.

"Well, I don't know about *piste*," said Wilson, and he laughed. "But we have one hell of a chalet at Aspen."

"Indeed?" said Bassett.

"Didn't your boys find that one in the due diligence?" Wilson tutted. "Andy, I'm disappointed."

Bassett laughed. "Must have a word to Oliver."

"Yeah, you do that. Okay, well, I guess—"

"Oh, Mike?"

"Yeah?"

"There was one other thing I meant to mention to you."

"What's that, Andy?"

"I had rather an odd phone call today."

"What was that?"

"It was from one of your chaps."

Wilson frowned. "I'm not following you, Andy."

"Chap from Dyson Whitney," said Bassett. "That's the bank advising you, isn't it?"

"It is," said Wilson.

"Yes," said Bassett, "I thought so."

Wilson could hardly bear to ask the next question. It took all his self-control to keep his voice calm, neutral, as if the news didn't signify anything at all to him. "What did he say, Andy?"

"I didn't speak to him myself. Apparently the call came through just after I'd gone into the board. My secretary took the message. I thought I should speak to you before doing anything else. I'm not sure how it works in the States, Mike, but in Britain it's not quite the done thing for the other fellow's investment bankers to start ringing one up. It's not cricket, as we say over here."

"It ain't cricket here, either," muttered Wilson. His mind raced. Obviously, Bassett was more surprised than alarmed by the phone call. There was still time for him to get control of the situation. "Andy, did this guy say what he wanted?"

"No. Said it was urgent, that's all. Apparently said I'd be very interested to speak with him. Wouldn't tell Georgina anything else."

"Okay . . . okay . . ." Wilson was still thinking, still calculating. "Andy, his name wouldn't have been Robert Holding, would it?"

"Yes," said Bassett in surprise. "That's exactly what it says here."

"Listen, Andy. Dyson Whitney has a problem with this guy. He suffered some kind of a personal trauma in the last couple of days and he's gone AWOL. They say he's not a risk to leak anything about the deal, but as you can see he's kind of a loose cannon. They think he's gone off the deep end. Unstable, if you know what I mean. He's just disappeared on them and they'd sure like to know where he is. The thing is, if he calls again, it's probably best if you don't try to speak to him, but if you just get your secretary to get his number or try to—"

"Oh, I have his number."

"You have his number?"

"He left it." Bassett read out a number. "It's a hotel. I'm to ask for room twenty-four. The Bartlett Hotel. Never heard of it myself."

Wilson had grabbed a pen. "Did you say that was room twenty-four, Andy? And how do you spell that, Bartlett? Is that with two Ts?"

Tony Prinzi was appreciative. "Michael, this is very good. If my own employees were so efficient, I would have a lot less problems."

"Can you do something about it?" said Wilson. "He's in London."

"Yes, I believe we can handle that. Just like your business, Mike, my organization is international. I have many associates."

"In London?"

"It's the modern world, Mike." Prinzi chuckled. "Globalization."

"So you'll fix it then? I've got the details. I've even got the room number of the hotel he's staying in."

"Provided the information is correct, we'll fix it."

"And there won't be any more mistakes?"

"Mike," said Prinzi, "there are no guarantees. Personally, though, I do regret the first incident. If we had a picture then, it wouldn't have happened."

"Will your guys in London have a picture?"

"Through the wonder of the Internet," said Prinzi, "I believe they will. Now, give me the information where Mr. Holding is in London."

Wilson gave him the details.

"Very good," said Prinzi. "If this information is accurate, Michael, we should have this little problem taken care of tonight."

"And the girl?" Wilson closed his eyes. "Your guys were going to find his girlfriend. You don't have to worry about her now, right?"

"When the events are in motion, Mike, it is very difficult to stop them."

"But we don't need her. You can call your guys off."

"Best not to act too hasty. Let's first be sure our job is done."

"And then?"

"Then it depends where events got to. If she's not in a position to compermise us, of course, why would we pursue her? I'm not a barbarian, Mike."

"And if she is in a position to compromise you?"

"Michael, best some things not to discuss. Your deal, I leave to you. I trust you to do it as it must be done. My business, you leave to me."

Wilson felt the grip of cold nausea. "Tony, I don't understand. What's the situation? Have your guys found her or not?"

"Let's just say we're waiting for her to come home."

51

The Amtrak service to New York had pulled out of Rochester just a couple of minutes behind schedule at eight-thirty that morning. Rose Bridges settled in for the seven-hour ride. She was a small woman with dark hair cut in a bob, a bright smile, and a pointed chin. Emmy, who was a lot taller than her, had gotten her height from Marty. Rose carried a capacious, multicolored patchwork bag with wooden handles that contained everything she needed for a stay of a few days at Emmy's apartment, including a couple of novels and a sweater she was knitting to keep her occupied on the train. She always enjoyed the ride to New York. She did it at least four times a year to visit her only daughter.

This morning, however, she was too anxious to relax. She tried to read but couldn't concentrate. By the time the train pulled through Syracuse, the first stop out of Rochester, she had tried Emmy's cell phone half a dozen times. She knew it was ridiculous to try so often, but she couldn't stop herself. The man in the seat beside her glanced at her and Rose smiled apologetically. She put her cell phone in her bag. But ten minutes later she couldn't resist the temptation to pull it out again.

"Is everything all right?" said the man.

Rose nodded. "There's just someone I'm trying to contact."

"And they're not answering?"

"No."

"Well, that happens a lot. I'm sure they're okay."

"It's my daughter," said Rose.

"Is there anything I can do?"

Rose smiled. "No. Thank you. I'm sure everything's okay."

"So am I," said the man.

But Rose wasn't. All night, terrible thoughts had kept her awake. Marty, who always thought Rose pushed things out of proportion, wasn't sure what to think himself. It wasn't like Emmy to go off the radar without any explanation, and Rose kept saying she had been terribly upset the last time they spoke. Although Emmy had lived in New York for six years, Marty still thought of her as his little girl alone in the big, uncaring city. When Rose said she was going to New York that morning, he didn't know whether he should try to dissuade her. Maybe it was the right thing to do.

Rose pulled her knitting out of her bag. The needles clacked. The man glanced at her. And again.

"I'm sorry. Is this disturbing you?" she asked.

He shook his head. She could see it was, but she couldn't stop. At least it was something to do with her hands. If she had nothing to do, she'd dial Emmy's number every minute.

The man got up and went to the snack car. When he came back

Rose was still knitting. He found himself a vacant seat elsewhere. She saw him get off the train at Albany. Rose called Marty to see if he'd heard from Emmy. Nothing.

Impatiently, Rose waited for the train to complete the last few miles to New York. Over the course of the trip it had fallen a little further behind schedule, finally pulling into Penn Station at ten to four, fifteen minutes late. Rose rang Marty again as she walked quickly across the concourse. She took the escalator up to the Thirty-fourth Street exit. A minute later, she was in a cab.

"Where to?" asked the driver.

"West Seventy-sixth Street."

The driver headed into the traffic.

Rose called Emmy once more. She left a message to say she'd just arrived and was heading over to her apartment. Then she searched in her bag for the key she had to Emmy's apartment.

52

By now, Steve Engels and George Nabandian were just about certain they knew who had killed Greg Ryan.

The two detectives had spent a day interviewing Greg's colleagues and friends and drew a total blank. That morning there had been more interviews. According to Greg's supervisor at the DA's office, there were no known threats against him, and he was sure Greg would have told him if he had received any. No one else could remember Greg mentioning anyone with a grudge who might want to harm him. As for knowing that he had been staying at Holding's apartment, it was news to them that he had even moved out of his girlfriend's place, as it was to his parents, for that matter. The ex claimed to know only that he had gone, not where he had gone to. She herself had a rock-solid alibi, having been in Boston until Sunday morning, and she gave them the names of ten different people who could verify it. Nabandian and Engels stopped checking after a half dozen.

The picture was utterly consistent. Ryan, it seemed, hadn't told anyone else, not family, not friends, not colleagues, as if he were hoping he might make things up with his girlfriend and move back in before anyone found out what had happened. Which meant that only Holding, who had found the body, and his girlfriend knew where Ryan actually was the night he died.

Holding had the time to do it. His two colleagues at Dyson Whitney put him leaving the office that Saturday night at around ten-thirty. But it could have been ten-fifteen, they agreed when pushed. And the phone records showed him making the call to Ryan's cell phone at eleven-fourteen. Say he had actually left the office at ten-ten. Say he got to his girlfriend's apartment at eleven-twelve, making the call a couple of minutes later. That gave him almost an hour. In an hour you could just about get from Forty-fifth Street, the Dyson Whitney office, to the apartment on West Thirty-ninth, where Greg was killed, and then to the girlfriend's apartment on West Seventy-sixth, with a few minutes to commit the murder. If you got lucky with cabs.

But there was one problem they couldn't get past. There was only one call recorded for Holding's cell phone that Saturday night, and it was the one to Ryan's number at eleven-fourteen. Since the girlfriend stated that she witnessed Holding making a call from his cell phone, that must have been the one she witnessed. The records showed that that call resulted in a conversation lasting three minutes and eight seconds. Holding's call to Ryan on Sunday afternoon—which was also on the record and timed at five forty-three P.M.—diverted to Ryan's voice mail, exactly as you would expect if Ryan were dead. The call on Saturday night hadn't. It had been answered, which meant Ryan was still alive to take it—alive *after* the only time during the period in which the coroner said Ryan had died when Holding had the opportunity to kill him.

They couldn't get around it. They returned to the precinct in the afternoon when they had finished their interviews. A DA was dead, and they were under pressure to come up with a lead. They went through the facts over coffee at their desks. Everything pointed to Holding, and yet the phone records seemed to say that Ryan was alive when Holding should have already killed him. Engels had the phone records in front of him. The records seemed to be mocking him, just as Holding had seemed to be mocking him when he told him to go check the records in the first place. They were missing something, they had to be. Engels wanted to go pick Holding up and bring him back to the station and put a little pressure on him to see if they could find out what it was.

Nabandian shook his head. "We've got nothing."

"He doesn't know that."

"We need something, then we can crack him open."

"Come on, George, we can crack him anyway."

"Not yet," said Nabandian. "It's too early for us to try going in there with nothing. He was a lawyer, remember? We start pressuring him now and he starts yelling harassment, then we can't go near him. We need something first."

"What?"

"I don't know."

Engels threw himself back in his chair in frustration.

A couple of desks away, a cell phone rang. The detective who sat there, Jimmy Bartok, reached into a pocket and pulled out a phone. He cursed and shook his head and pulled out a second phone from another pocket and answered it.

"Yeah?" he said brusquely. He listened. "Yeah . . . yeah . . ."

Engels watched Bartok sitting with a phone in each hand, talking into one, holding the other.

"Yeah . . . Fuck that . . . No . . . Yeah . . . all right." He switched the phone off. He caught Engels looking at him and grinned ruefully. "I got so many fucking phones, I never know which one's ringing. Look, I got another one as well." He began to reach into a pocket.

"Why don't you give them different ring tones, you idiot?" said Gobineau, another detective.

Bartok frowned. "You know, that's not such a bad idea."

Gobineau shook his head in exasperation and turned back to what he was doing. So did Bartok. But Engels kept gazing at him, thinking about it. Two hands . . . two phones . . .

He turned to Nabandian. "I've got it! He had the phone, George. He had the fucking phone!"

Nabandian looked at him skeptically. "What are you talking about?"

"At eleven-fourteen, it's Holding who's got Ryan's phone. He calls it—but he's got it himself! Ryan's dead. Holding's killed him, but he's taken the phone with him. He gets to the girl's place, makes the call. Ryan doesn't answer, of course, but Holding talks anyway. The girl hears him talking to Ryan, or so she thinks. Bingo! He's got his alibi."

Nabandian reached over for the phone record. "Someone answered that call." He held the record up for Engels. "Remember? The Sunday call goes to voice mail. The Saturday one doesn't. Which means someone answered that call."

"Exactly. *Someone.* Holding. He's got the phone, he presses to receive the call. Bingo! The call's answered. Not by Ryan, by him."

"The girl saw him make the call."

"So?"

"Don't you think she would have noticed if he was holding a second phone?"

"It's in his pocket."

"She didn't hear it ring."

"It's on silent."

Nabandian thought about it for a moment. Then he shook his head. "I don't buy it."

"It's on silent, George." Engels savored the moment, sensing that this really was the final piece in the puzzle. "It's in his pocket, it's on vibrate. That's how he does it!" Engels's voice was rising in excitement. "He's at the apartment. He kills Ryan. Takes the phone, puts it on vibrate, leaves it in his pocket, gets to the girl's place, calls the phone, presses it in his pocket, and talks to himself for three minutes and however many seconds. What does she know? She hears him talking, thinks Ryan's talking back. He thinks we'll think Ryan's talking back as well once we see the records, and *that's* why he wants to make sure we check them. That's why he tells us to!"

Other people in the office were glancing impatiently at Engels.

"Solving a crime here, people!" said Engels.

Gobineau applauded sarcastically.

Engels took a bow, then turned back to Nabandian. "Huh, George? Come on, that's how he does it."

"The girl didn't see him press to receive the call."

Engels didn't say a word. Instead, he stood up, took out his cell phone, switched it to Silent, held it up to Nabandian, and turned it front to back, back to front, like it was some kind of exhibit in a magician's trick. "Close your eyes."

Nabandian hesitated.

"Close your eyes, George."

Others were watching now, Bartok, Gobineau, the whole room. Nabandian closed his eyes. Engels put his phone in one of his pants pockets. He put his other hand in the other pocket.

"All right, open them. Now call me. Come on, George. Call me."

Nabandian got out his cell phone. Engels stood in front of him with both hands in his pockets. Reluctantly, Nabandian called Engel's number. The call went through.

"I just pressed to talk, right? Listen to your phone. Right? Now, tell me which pocket I've got the phone in."

Nabandian's eyes moved from one pocket to the other.

"Left," called out Gobineau.

"Right," said someone else.

Engels grinned. He pulled the phone out.

"All right," conceded Nabandian. "It's possible. But how does he get the phone back there?"

"Where?"

"Ryan's phone's in the bedroom when he's found, remember? How does Holding get it back there?"

"Easy," said Engels. "He puts it there."

"When?"

"Don't you remember, George? It was Holding who found him!"

The older cop frowned. He thought about that. Engels was watching him, grinning like a chipmunk.

"We need to check the phone for his prints," said Nabandian.

"Sure, but even if they're not there, what does it prove? He was careful."

"We still need to check."

"We need to get them first."

Nabandian nodded. He looked up at Engels. "I think it's time to have another chat with Mr. Holding."

He wasn't at work, didn't answer his phone, and wasn't at his apartment, where the police tape across the door had been removed. He had said he'd be staying at his girlfriend's. They headed for the Upper West Side.

They rang the doorbell, but no one answered. They got into the brownstone by ringing another doorbell at random and telling the person who answered that they were police and had some questions for them. Then they went straight to apartment 7. Engels listened at the door. He knocked.

Silence.

Engels knocked again. He put his ear to the door.

"You hear anything?" whispered Nabandian.

Engels shook his head. His eyes narrowed. A creak. Maybe from inside.

"What is it?" whispered Nabandian.

Engels put a finger to his lips. He couldn't be sure. Beyond the door, there was silence. But there were small noises as well. But you get small noises in empty apartments. The breeze through an open window, for example.

"She got a pet?" he whispered to Nabandian.

Nabandian shrugged.

"Is there a fire escape out of this building?"

"Probably."

Engels listened again. Now he did hear something. Definite. Footsteps. Some kind of muffled noise as well. He glanced at Nabandian and drew his gun. Nabandian drew a gun as well.

Engels pounded on the door. "Open up!" he yelled. "Police!"

There were more footsteps inside. Engels pounded and yelled again. He jumped back and slammed into the door. Again. The door splintered off its hinges and Engels went stumbling in.

Nabandian ran past him. The living room was empty. He kept

going, gun held out in front of him, swung around a corner, and then he pulled open a door.

One man was disappearing onto the fire escape. A second stood at the window. He turned, coughing.

"Drop it!" yelled Nabandian, glimpsing a gun in his hand.

For an instant the man looked around, at the fire escape, now empty, then back at Nabandian.

"Drop the fucking gun! Police! Drop the—"

Gunshots rang out. Five, six. The man smashed back against the glass and fell over the sill, his head and chest outside, his legs in the room, twitching.

Nabandian looked around.

"How many times were you going to tell him to drop it, George?" said Engels. "Were you going to wait till he killed you?"

Nabandian didn't say a word. He was frozen, trembling.

The man's legs had stopped twitching. Engels approached him cautiously, gun held at the ready. He leaned out the window and felt at his neck for a pulse.

"He's dead."

"There was another one," said Nabandian. "He went down the escape."

Engels looked at the street. A small knot of people had gathered below. He couldn't see anyone running. He looked back at his partner. "You okay?"

Nabandian nodded. He came to the window and looked down at the dead man. He was sandy-haired, with a small, pinched nose and a couple of days of stubble on his chin.

"You recognize him?" said Engels.

Nabandian shook his head.

"Neither do I. What the fuck was he doing here? You think they killed her?"

Nabandian opened the wardrobes in the bedroom, looking for a body. Engels checked under the bed. He looked in the bathroom, pulled back the shower curtain to see if there was anything in the bathtub.

They went into the living room. Against one of the walls stood a long wooden chest.

The detectives glanced at each other. It was big enough for a corpse if the limbs were bent.

Nabandian stepped forward. He lifted the lid.

There was a noise behind them. Both cops spun, guns aimed.

"Drop the bag! Drop the fucking bag!" yelled Engels.

A small woman stood in the opening where the door to the apartment had once been, carrying a big multicolored bag. She stared in shock.

"*Drop the fucking bag!*"

She dropped it.

"Put your hands on your head!"

She raised her hands.

Engels approached her, gun still aimed. He pushed her against a wall and searched her quickly. Then he stepped back. "Who are you?"

"Rose Bridges," she whispered, still facing the wall.

"Who?"

"Rose Bridges."

"What are you doing here?"

"I'm Emmy Bridges's mother."

Nabandian had opened her bag and found her driver's license. "You can turn around, Mrs. Bridges."

Rose turned. Her face was pale.

"We're police," said Nabandian. "I'm Detective Nabandian and this is Detective Engels. I'm sorry if we gave you a fright."

"What's happened?" said Rose. "Where's Emmy?"

"We don't know."

"Is she all right?"

"That's what we're trying to find out."

53

"You should go out," said Emmy. "Go on. It'll be fine."

"He might call."

"Rob, it's ten-thirty. He's not going to call. Anyway, I'll stay. If he calls, I'll answer it."

Rob looked at her doubtfully.

She laughed. "Go!"

He had been cooped up in the hotel room all day, waiting for Bassett's call. Nothing to do but watch cruddy British TV while he waited. Emmy had been out to get food. He said he didn't want much. She had brought him back snacks, muesli bars and corn chips, but now he was hungry and a little stir-crazy. And Bassett wasn't going to call now, Emmy was right. Besides, she could take the call.

"I won't be long," he said.

"Take your time."

"Lock the door behind me."

"Yes, Mr. Paranoid."

Rob looked at her seriously. "Lock it."

"Of course I will."

He went down the stairs. The reception desk was deserted. The night clerk must be doing something, he thought. He wondered if it was the same guy as the night before. He let himself out. The night was cool. He took a deep breath. It felt good to be outside.

He walked away to find somewhere to eat.

The night clerk, Waldemar, slouched in a chair in the room behind the reception desk. The room had a small table and a portable TV. There were dirty mugs and an ashtray full of ashes and cigarette stubs on the table. The TV was on, grainily showing an episode of *CSI Miami*. A suspect was being interrogated. Waldemar watched with a frown of concentration, trying to follow the dialogue.

The night bell rang.

Waldemar watched the interrogation on the TV for a moment longer, then got up to answer the door. Outside was a young man with a thick shock of blond hair.

"This is . . . Boston Hotel?" said the man in heavily accented, halting English.

"No," said Waldemar. "Is Bartlett."

"Boston?"

"Bartlett." Waldemar pointed to the name gilded on the glass of the door. "Bartlett."

"Where is Boston?" asked the man.

"I don't know," said Waldemar. "What you speak? You speak Polish? *Czy mówisz po polsku?* German? *Sprechen sie Deutsch?*"

"Boston. I want Boston."

Waldemar shook his head. "Not Boston. Bartlett. What you speak?"

"Where is station?" asked the man.

"Station? Paddington?"

The man nodded quickly. "Friend . . . I meet . . ."

"You meet friend at station?" said Waldemar. "At Paddington Station?"

"Yes! Yes! Very good. Where is?"

"Go to corner," said Waldemar. "Then left. You see station."

"Left?"

"Left."

"Where is left?"

"Left!" said Waldemar. "Left!"

"You show." The man pulled on Waldemar's elbow. "You show."

"At corner. Left."

"You show. Please. You show." The man was backing down the stairs.

Waldemar sighed. "All right. I show."

He went down the stairs. He pointed toward the corner in the darkness. "There. Left!" he said, and he waved his hand to the left.

The blond-haired man looked up the street, then looked back at him, frowning.

"Left!" said Waldemar. "There!"

The man peered up the street. He took a few more steps, pulling the night clerk with him away from the steps to the hotel.

Waldemar shook his head in exasperation. He pointed, jabbing his hand toward the corner. "There! See? There!"

"There?" said the man.

"There!" yelled Waldemar. He waved his hand toward the left again. "Left!"

Behind Waldemar, a second man came out of the shadows in a doorway. The blond man saw him head up the steps to the open door of the Bartlett and disappear inside.

"Left! See? Left!"

"Left?" said the blond man to Waldemar.

"Left!" yelled Waldemar, still gesticulating.

"Ah? Left?" said the man, his face creasing in a big grin.

"Yes. This is what I say. Left!"

"There?"

"Yes! There! Left!"

The man grabbed Waldemar's hand. "Thank you. Thank you. Station. There. Left."

"Yes," said Waldemar, pulling his hand away from the man.

"Thank you."

"Is all right," said Waldemar.

"Thank you. Thank you."

"Is all right," repeated Wally impatiently. "You go, find friend."

"I find friend!" said the man, still grinning. He headed off down the street.

Waldemar watched until he went around the corner. Then the night clerk went back up the steps and closed the door behind him. He went back to the little room behind the reception desk.

"Ah," he said in disgust, looking at the screen where the credits were rolling. "Is finished!"

Upstairs, Emmy heard a knock on the door.

She got up. There was another knock.

"Rob?" she said.

There was another knock.

"Who is it?" she demanded.

"I'm from downstairs," said a voice on the other side of the door. "I'm looking for Mr. Holding."

"Why?"

There was no reply.

"Did someone call?"

"Yes. Someone called."

Emmy opened the door a fraction. The man outside was wearing an overcoat and gloves. It didn't look as if he were one of the hotel staff. And suddenly she realized he wouldn't have said he was looking for Mr. Holding. That wasn't the name Rob had used when they checked in.

But it was too late. He pushed the door back, sending her stumbling, and then he was inside, jerking her up on her feet and slamming the door shut with a kick.

"Where is he?" he demanded.

"He's not here."

"When's he coming back?"

"He's not!"

The man shook her, hard, his fingers biting into her arm. *"When?"*

"He's gone."

"Is he?" The man flung her onto the bed. He pulled out a gun from under his coat. The pistol had a silencer on the end. Pointing the gun at her, he sat down on the chair behind the door.

"He's not coming back," said Emmy.

"Really? Well, I might just wait and see for meself, eh?"

54

Rob bit into the hamburger. It was his second. He had eaten the first one in about four bites, hardly even tasting it as it turned to pap in his mouth. Later on, he knew, he'd feel sick and regret it, as he always did after he ate at McDonald's. But he had been too hungry to care. All he'd had during the day were snacks. He hadn't realized just how hungry he was until he got out of the hotel. Maybe it was the night air that had done it. The McDonald's was open and it was familiar, and it was the first place combining those two qualities that he had found after leaving the hotel, so he went right in and ordered big. Two Big Macs, two large fries, and a large Coke.

There weren't many people in the restaurant. A large black guy was sprawled in one of the booths. A couple of kids in hooded sweatshirts were huddled together over a mobile phone. An Indian couple came in and Rob watched them go to the counter and order.

Rob took another bite out of the burger. The first one was already starting to sit heavy in his stomach. He took a big handful of fries and stuffed them in his mouth.

He took a slurp on the Coke. He slowed down a little now, took a couple of fries, nibbled them thoughtfully. He wondered what had happened with Bassett. Maybe Bassett had called and they hadn't put him through. Anything could happen in a place like that. Or maybe the secretary hadn't given him the message. He could try again tomorrow. But what if the secretary had given Bassett the message and he hadn't called? Say he'd chosen not to call. Say he wasn't going to call, or refused to meet him? What was plan B?

Rob took a bite out of the burger. He had no plan B.

He finished the burger, then the fries. They were cold now, but he ate them anyway. He looked around at the other people in the restaurant. What could be more depressing than eating in a McDonald's late at night? One of the staff members was mopping the floor in a closed-off section of seating. Looked about sixteen. Rob watched him.

He'd try again tomorrow, he thought. And tomorrow he wouldn't just wait all day. Mr. Bassett might need a little hassling. Maybe even a little doorstopping. That, he decided, was plan B. Emmy could come with him. Two doorstoppers would be better than one.

Maybe not. Bassett still might call. Maybe Emmy should wait by the phone.

He left the restaurant. He didn't go back directly. He walked around the streets for a while, enjoying the cool freshness of the night air. Eventually he started to feel cold and headed back. He rang the bell and waited, peering through the glass panel at the reception desk at the end of the hall.

The night clerk came to the door. He grinned as he opened it.

"Hello," he said.

"Hello," said Rob.

"You are again late today."

"Yeah," said Rob. He went inside.

"And the Mrs. Smith?" said Wally, closing the door and following him up the hall. "She is not here?"

"No, she's upstairs."

"Ah, what you do today? You see London?"

Rob stopped at the foot of the stairs, hand on the banister. He shook his head. "What about you? You study?"

Waldemar nodded.

"How do you study if you're up all night?"

"I not up all night." Waldemar winked.

"You sleep?"

"In chair."

Rob chuckled.

Waldemar shrugged, then laughed as well.

"How long you been in this job?" asked Rob.

"Two months." Waldemar held up two fingers. "The man before, he stay two weeks."

"That good, huh?"

Waldemar laughed again.

Rob turned to the stairs.

"You go tomorrow?" asked Waldemar.

Rob stopped. "I don't know. I'll have to see."

"You say by ten o'clock. If no, they take money, you stay or no stay."

"Thanks, Wally, I know." Rob turned to the stairs again.

"Last night, is good?"

Rob smiled to himself, remembering what Emmy had said. The poor guy, starved of conversation.

"You sleep good?"

"Yeah. It was all right. It's not the Ritz."

Waldemar gazed at him uncomprehendingly.

"It's not like the Ritz Hotel," explained Rob. "You know the Ritz Hotel?"

Waldemar shook his head.

"It's a very good hotel. I'm saying this hotel isn't as good as the Ritz."

"Ah," said Wally. He grinned.

"You understand?"

Wally nodded.

"Okay, Wally. I'm kind of tired. I'm going up now." Rob already had one foot on the stairs. He stopped again. "You know what? Since you ask, the faucet in the bathroom, it keeps dripping. It dripped all night."

Waldemar had that uncomprehending look on his face again.

"The faucet . . ." said Rob. "In the bathroom. Dripping. The water. Drip, drip, drip."

"Ah!" Waldemar nodded his head quickly. "Water?"

"Yes. The water."

"From tap?"

"That's right. The faucet. The tap. They said they'd send someone up to fix it, but they didn't do it."

"I fix."

"You can fix it?"

"I fix water. In Poland."

"You're a plumber? I thought you were an engineer. Roads, bridges . . ."

"I am engineer. I am also . . . fix water . . ."

"A plumber?"

"I am also plumber." Waldemar laughed. "Little bit plumber."

Rob grinned. "Great."

Waldemar held up a finger. "Wait . . . wait . . ."

He disappeared through a doorway under the stairs, and a couple of minutes later came back with a wrench and a hammer. "Come," he said.

He went past Rob and started up the stairs.

"You meant to do this?" asked Rob.

"Ah, I do! No problem!"

"All right," said Rob.

He followed the clerk up the stairs.

They got to the door.

Rob knocked. "Emmy? Honey? It's me."

"*Rob!*"

There was silence.

Rob frowned. He glanced at Waldemar. Then he knocked again. "Honey, I've got the night clerk with me."

Silence.

Rob tried the door. It was locked. He didn't have the key.

Waldemar grinned. He pulled out a master key and held it up proudly.

"Well, she's in there . . ." said Rob.

But Waldemar already had the master key in the lock. He opened the door and walked in.

Rob heard Emmy shout. He saw something appear from behind the door and aim at Wally's head. He threw himself against the door and there was a scream and a muffled pop as a gun flew into the air, putting a bullet in the ceiling. Rob shoved the clerk out of the way and swung around the door and saw a man on the floor between the door and the wall, clutching his wrist and trying to get to his feet. Then he saw Emmy staring at him from the bed.

"Go!" he yelled as he slammed the door against the man again. There was a cry of pain.

Emmy ran. Rob slammed the door once more and ran after her, shoving Waldemar out of the way. He took the stairs two at a time as Emmy turned the corners of each landing ahead of him. At the bottom they raced for the door. Outside, Rob took the steps to the street in two leaps. Emmy hit the pavement beside him.

They ran down the street, swung left around the corner, across the road, down the next street, and into the mouth of the railway station. Rob threw a glance over his shoulder and kept going. They raced across the almost empty concourse. Cabs stood in a line on the other side.

He ran at the first one, pulled at the door, waited for Emmy to jump in, and then dived in after her.

"Where to, guv?" asked the driver over his shoulder, pulling back the glass.

"Piccadilly Circus!" said Rob, blurting out the first thing that came into his head.

55

The cab stopped. The driver half-turned in his seat and glanced back through the glass divider that separated him from the passenger compartment.

"Here we are, guv."

Rob looked up. A wall of bright neon rose in front of him.

"Piccadilly Circus," said the cabdriver. His voice came out hollow, as if from far away, through the microphone system in the cab. He fiddled with his meter. "That'll be twelve pounds eighty."

Rob looked around. Cars went past. Other cabs.

"Twelve eighty, guv."

"Keep going," said Rob.

The driver looked at him doubtfully.

"Keep going!" said Rob, and he pulled a note out of his wallet and thrust it at the driver.

The driver slid open the glass divider and took it. He looked in his mirror, waited a moment, and swung out into the traffic.

"Where to?" he asked.

"Don't know. Just keep going."

The driver shrugged. He drove.

He and Emmy hadn't said much in the time it had taken to get here, instinctively feeling that it wasn't safe to talk, even here. They said just enough for Rob to find out that she was okay. He held her hand grimly.

The cab went around a couple of corners. Rob saw the entrance of a lane coming up on the left.

"Go in there. Turn left."

The driver turned.

"Pull over," said Rob after they had gone about fifty yards down the street.

They pulled over. Nearby was a ramp that led down to the basement at the back of a large building.

Rob turned around and looked out the back window of the cab.

"You getting out?" asked the driver.

"Wait," said Rob.

He watched. The lane was deserted. A minute passed. Then another. He could see the lights of cars going by in the road at the end of the lane. No one turned in. He was fairly sure now that no one had followed them.

"Where does this go?" he said.

"This? Clifford Street. That's the corner up there. Follow it 'round, then into Bruton Street, we'll come out in Berkeley Square."

It meant nothing to Rob. He threw another glance behind him. Still nothing. "Keep going," he said.

"You want to go to Berkeley Square?"

"All right, let's go there."

The driver started moving again.

The cab came into a big square with an area of grass in the middle. "Berkeley Square," said the driver. "Keep going, I suppose?"

"Yeah."

The cab went three-quarters of the way around the square and exited onto another street.

"Maybe you want to go back to Paddington," said the driver, and he chuckled.

Rob ignored him. But they couldn't keep driving around forever.

"We need a hotel," he said.

The cabbie glanced at him in the rearview mirror. "Why didn't you say so at the start? It's like bloody cops and robbers!"

"You know any hotels?"

"How much do you want to spend?"

"I want something quiet. Not showy."

"Plenty of hotels 'round here."

"Out of the center."

"I could take you to Swiss Cottage," said the driver.

"Where's that?"

"A few miles away. North London. My manor. Couple of hotels there. That be all right?"

"Okay," said Rob.

"Suits me," said the driver. He glanced at his watch. "Time to knock off, anyways."

The cab swung left and then right, and came out into a big road with a wide grass divider down the middle. They went through a gap in the divider and started heading in the other direction. There was a huge park on the left. The cab motor growled now, picking up speed.

Rob thought about the moment he saw that gun coming out from behind the door. A black muzzle. He wasn't even sure if he had recognized what it was. Something just made him throw himself against the door. Maybe it was Emmy's shout. He just reacted—reflex, not thought.

He didn't know how that man had come to be there. Once they'd made it out of JFK, he had thought, they were free. And a day later there was someone waiting in their hotel room. How? He couldn't work it out. Had there been someone waiting to follow them at Heathrow? But if there had been, they'd have to have known that he and Emmy were flying there in the first place. And how could they have known that? Someone would have had to have seen which flight they boarded out of JFK. But to do that, someone would have had to have known they were going to JFK. But they didn't know that themselves until just before they left Emmy's apartment. Which meant someone would have had to have followed them from there. But he was fairly certain no one had trailed them. And besides, if someone had, that made no sense at all. If they were able to follow them out of Emmy's apartment, why wouldn't they have gotten to them then, in New York? Why let them get all the way London and then wait an extra day? That was crazy.

And how had they known exactly where he was? Not only the hotel, the exact room. He wasn't even in the ledger under his real name. He was Bill Smith. There was no one who could connect the name Rob Holding with room 24 in the Bartlett Hotel. The only person who could do that was . . .

Rob froze.

Andrew Bassett?

Surely Bassett couldn't be involved in this. He was the one Leopard was trying to buy. He was the one Rob was trying to help. But then . . .

Why not? Maybe Bassett *was* involved. Why was he so quick to do the deal with Leopard? Maybe Bassett was as deep into the murky side of this deal as anyone. Maybe he had his own reasons for wanting it to go ahead, and go ahead quickly. In fact, who was to say it wasn't Bassett, not Wilson, who had instigated Greg's death and the hunt for him that seemed to be following it?

Who else had known where he was staying? No one. Who else could have found him? Again, no one.

So what was he supposed to do now? He felt caged in, blocked at every exit. If both sides were after him, if Andrew Bassett was . . .

No. To be precise, he hadn't talked to Andrew Bassett. He hadn't given him the details of his location. Not directly. In fact, he didn't even know whether Bassett got the message. He had given it to his secretary.

That made sense. Or more sense, anyway. They could have gotten to his secretary, told her to let them know if he turned up. Rob remembered her voice. A cold, efficient English voice. Could they have gotten to her?

He glanced at Emmy. He almost wanted to laugh. This was absurd. He didn't know who he could talk to. He didn't know who was on whose side. It was like a movie. Stuff like this didn't happen in real life.

He thought through everything again. The conclusions were the same. He didn't know who was on whose side. That meant he could trust no one. He would have to work on the assumption that everyone—within the Buffalo as well as the Leopard—was against him. It was insane, but he didn't have a choice.

They had stopped. The cab was outside a hotel in a narrow street of terrace houses. Rob peered at it out of the window.

"Don't like the look of it," he said.

"Can't be too picky this time of night," replied the driver.

"Do you know any others around here?"

"If you like. Won't be no different, though."

The cab moved off. They drove around a couple of corners and came to another, similar-looking hotel in another street.

"Fine," said Rob. "How much more do I owe you?"

He paid and they got out. The driver gave him one last quizzical glance and drove away. The cab went around a corner. The sound of the motor faded into the night.

Rob waited until it was gone.

"Aren't we going in?" said Emmy.

"Not here."

They walked back the way they had come and went to the first hotel they had stopped at.

The room was drab, shabby. The voltage in the light was low. The carpet was an old floral pattern of dark blue and violet and the floor-boards creaked as he walked in. Rob felt safer once they were inside, once he had locked the door behind them, but it was a false sense of security, he knew. They had found them once, they had gotten into their room. What was to stop them finding him again?

At last they could talk. Emmy told him everything that had happened. She thought the man had kept her alive in case Rob didn't come back and he was going to need her to get to him. He had said nothing else in the hour that he had held her captive, even when she tried to get him talking. Just told her to shut the fuck up, told her he'd kill her if she said anything when Rob came back.

"But you shouted."

"I had to. I couldn't let you just walk in."

"What did he do?"

"He put the gun against my head. He only took it away when the door opened." Emmy closed her eyes, remembering. "That was the worst moment of my life, seeing that door open. I was sure I was going to see you die."

Rob squeezed her hand. He tried to imagine what it must have been like for her, waiting there, unable to warn him, unable to do anything but wait for the knock that she wished would never come.

"I should have kept shouting," she said.

"No."

"Of course I should. I should have kept shouting until you went away."

"And he would've shot you. And what would I have done? I would have come straight in to see what happened."

"I didn't want to be a liability." Emmy put her head in her hands. "I should never have come. You were right."

"Emmy, are you insane?" Rob took her face in his hands and forced her to look at him. "You saved my life. If you hadn't been here I would have been in that room by myself when he came. If we'd gone with my plan, right now, you'd be at your folks' in Rochester and I'd be dead on the carpet in that hotel room. You know what? Your plan was better."

Emmy smiled.

"You're the bait, by the way. Didn't I tell you that? You're the bait."

"Don't push it, Rob."

Rob sat back from her, raising his hands. "Hey, you're the plan-meister, Bridges. Just tell me what to do next."

She shook her head. "You think Wally got out of there?"

"He should have. He wasn't hurt. He probably ran like hell, just like us."

"So what now?"

Emmy had worked out for herself, of course, that either Bassett or his secretary must have been the one who provided the information about where to find them. Rob said that he had decided to trust no one, either in the Leopard or the Buffalo. Yet he still had to get to Bassett. He had to put the information to him, challenge him to ignore it.

But how? Phone calls, e-mails, faxes, everything, Rob knew, to the CEO of a company like Buffalo would go through his secretary.

"You need someone like Nicole," said Emmy. "Our receptionist at Lascelle. She'd make sure you got through to him."

"Not every company's lucky enough to have a Nicole."

"True."

"Besides, it may be the secretary who gave us away."

Emmy frowned. "You know what you need? You need to get him at a public event, like a book launch or something. Something where there are people around and you can say what you want and there are witnesses so he can't ignore it."

"I don't know if Andrew Bassett's written any books lately."

"Whatever. You need to get him in public."

Rob thought about it. Emmy was right. If Bassett was involved in all this, then even if he had a meeting with him one on one, Bassett could simply listen and walk away and ignore everything Rob said. But if the allegations were made in public, if he demanded that BritEnergy investigate Grogon and ExPar in front of a roomful of people, with a couple of journalists or photographers in attendance, Bassett would have to do it.

But how would he get to him in public? You'd need to know where he was going to be, and when, and how to get access. In other words, you'd need to know his daily schedule. And that, of course, was with his secretary.

Or you'd need an event so public that everyone knew about it. An open event, one that didn't have invitations, an event where people were expected simply to turn up at the time . . .

Rob broke into a smile. "Emmy, you're a genius."

"Don't tell me he's launching a book."

No, it was better than that. Way better. It was the perfect event. It was already scheduled, Rob knew, to take place in two days' time, right here, in London, in front of a roomful of journalists. And Andrew Bassett was going to be the star performer.

56

The call kicked off at nine-thirty A.M. Thursday Louisiana time. Originally it was meant to have been a brief discussion between Mike Wilson, Andrew Bassett, and Amanda Bellinger to cover off the last details of the announcement. But things never work like that. By now, the day before the announcement, the circle of people who knew about the deal had widened and everyone who could claim a right wanted to have a say. There were people sitting in all over the world. In Baton Rouge Mike Wilson, Doug Earl, Lyall Gelb, and Jackie Rubin were gathered around the speakerphone in Wilson's office. Calling in from separate offices in New York were Amanda Bellinger and Pete Stanzy. In London were Andrew Bassett, Anthony Warne, Oliver Trewin, and Francesca Dillon, BritEnergy's head of public affairs. Caspar Johnson, head of the Morgan Stanley team advising BritEnergy, was on a line from Vienna.

The two in-house public affairs people, Jackie Rubin and Francesca Dillon, were both angry because they had been told about the deal just the day before, only to discover that Amanda Bellinger had been working on a media strategy for a week. They also had the most to lose. Not too far in the future, they realized, they would probably be competing for the same job. Hence they were desperate to have some kind of impact, to change something, anything, to show how important they were. Amanda knew exactly what was going on and played them perfectly, taking a suggestion from each of them over trivialities and navigating skillfully around the important points, on which she had no intention of giving ground. Mike Wilson let Amanda handle it and tuned out as the discussion continued. After forty-five minutes he had had enough.

"Is there anything else we absolutely have to cover?" he demanded in the middle of some excruciating argument between Jackie and Francesca over the order of the contact numbers for the public affairs offices in the online press release.

Jackie and Francesca fell silent.

"All right," said Wilson, "we're done then. Amanda, you work out any outstanding details and let the others know."

In New York, Amanda Bellinger smiled.

"Doug? Anthony?" said Wilson to the legal guys. "Anything critical from the legal side?"

"No, I think we're all right at this end," said Anthony Warne.

Doug Earl, sitting across the table from Wilson, nodded. Wilson glanced at Lyall Gelb. Gelb shook his head. He hadn't said a word throughout the conference.

"Anything else from anyone that absolutely can't be dealt with off-line?"

Silence.

"Okay," said Wilson. "Andy, you want to say anything?"

Andrew Bassett cleared his throat. "I'd just like to thank everyone for all their hard work on this. The presentation looks excellent. Pete, thanks to you and your team at Dyson Whitney. Caspar, well done to your chaps as well. Amanda, what can I say? You've made Jackie and Francesca's work a hundred times easier. Thanks to everyone. Now you just have to watch Mike and me mess it up!"

There were laughs all around.

"Well said, Andy," said Wilson. "I second that. Thanks a lot, guys. Now, let's do it! Andy, Mandy, you want to stay on the line, please? Everyone else, thank you very much."

There were murmurs of good-bye. "Mike," said Stanzy. "I'll call you later."

"Fine," said Wilson. Doug Earl and Lyall Gelb were leaving his office. "I'll need to talk to you later, Lyall," said Wilson. Gelb nodded. Jackie was still hovering at the table, trying to say something about setting up time with him that afternoon to go over things. Wilson looked at her impatiently. Jackie persisted. "Jackie, I've got people on the line," he said pointedly. "Talk to Stella." At last she left. Wilson waited until she had closed the door. "Andy, you still there?"

"Still here, Mike."

"Mandy?"

"Yes."

"Jesus Christ," said Wilson, "I just hate crap like that. Everyone's got to make sure their prints are on the paper."

Amanda and Andrew Bassett laughed.

"Okay. Listen, Andy, I just wanted to check. Everything okay for you? You happy with the presentation?"

"Yes."

"The FAQs?"

"Yes. Very good. Very happy."

"The FAQs are a guide, right? We can ad-lib a little there. But the presentation we do exactly by the script. Agreed?"

"Absolutely, Mike."

"All right," said Wilson. "Mandy? Everything set?"

"Yes. Andrew, you start at three P.M. sharp. Mike, you go at ten, so you're exactly synchronized. By the way, Mike, Bloomberg's covering you live in New York."

"That came through?" said Wilson. "Great. Well done, Mandy."

"Andrew, there'll be no live TV with you, but I believe Sky Business and CNN Business News will be shooting video. Have you done that before?"

"I'm sure I'll manage," said Bassett.

"I'm sure you will," said Amanda. "You'll have a Hill Bellinger person with you. Her name's Sophie Greene. She's coming in today and she'll be with you at the Royal Gloucester. Your secretary has her details. She should be with you in the office at . . . if she's not there already, she should be with you very shortly. If you want to practice anything, do some trial runs, whatever, do them with Sophie. I'd recommend that. She's terrific. Really very good."

"Best one in the agency after you, Mandy, isn't that right?" quipped Wilson.

Amanda laughed. "Mike, you still coming in tomorrow morning?"

"Yeah. Right before the conference."

"You sure you don't want to come in this evening and go through it?"

"No, I'm fine, Mandy."

"You're going to have to get up awfully early."

"The jet's leaving at four-thirty. On the ground by eight-fifteen Eastern."

"Okay. If that's how you want to do it."

"We'll have lunch tomorrow afterward. Keep it free."

"I already have," said Amanda. And she wondered what else they'd have. She fantasized. Back in Wilson's suite after the press conference at the Four Seasons, both of them a little celebratory, a little high, maybe some champagne to mark the occasion . . . Who knew what might happen, with the chemistry between them and the high of the day? She'd let him take her. Urgent, explosive. A little rough maybe. A power fuck. What if it really happened? She felt a tingle thinking about it.

"Okay, Mandy, I've got to have a word with Andy."

It took a second for Amanda to get back to reality. "Gentlemen, you'll do fine."

"Thanks, Mandy," said Wilson. "I'll see you tomorrow."

"Thanks, Mandy," said Bassett.

Amanda went off the line.

Wilson paused for a moment. "Well, Andy. This is it, huh?"

Bassett laughed.

"No cold feet?"

"Funnily enough, no."

"How many times you been married, Andy?"

"Just the once," said Bassett. "I suppose I'm rather a traditional chap."

"Me, twice. Damned if I didn't get cold feet both times." Wilson laughed. "Should've taken the hint, huh?"

"Well, that's—"

"Anyway," said Wilson. "Point is, I've got no cold feet about this one. I'm looking forward to working with you, Andy. Hell, I think we're going to do some great things with the company we're creating."

"Yes," said Bassett. "My feelings exactly."

"Say, Andy. I wanted to ask whether you heard anything else from that guy you mentioned yesterday."

"Which guy do you— Oh, you mean the Dyson Whitney chap?"

"That's the one."

"No," said Bassett. "Not a squeak."

"No more calls today?"

"Not that I've been told about. I'm sure Georgina would have told me. What's the situation with him, anyway?"

"Don't know," said Wilson. "I guess they must have gotten to him. It was kind of a sad situation. You know, he had this personal thing. I hope they've found him, because it sounds like he needs help. I just hope he doesn't . . . you know, do something silly." Wilson had a sudden stroke of inspiration. "To himself, I mean. I just hope he doesn't."

"Do you think he might?" asked Bassett anxiously.

"Who knows? Doesn't sound like he's thinking straight. It's possible he blames himself for whatever it is that's happened. The sooner they get to him, the better."

"Oh. Well, I hope they do."

"Investment bankers, huh?"

"It's a wonder any of them are sane."

"What?" said Wilson. "You know a sane one?"

Bassett laughed. "Touché, Mike!"

"Well, good talking with you, Andy. Good luck tomorrow. We'll talk afterward."

"Good luck to you, Mike. I just regret I won't be able to watch you live on Bloomberg."

"Hell, Andy, you already know what I'm going to say!"

They both laughed. Wilson shut down the line.

He leaned back and gazed out the window. He was there, almost there. The great game of bluff that he was playing was almost his. It was virtually inconceivable that he was going to pull it off, considering how high the stakes were and how little he held in his hand. A reputation, that was all. A name, Louisiana Light. But the higher the stakes, the more likely a bluff to succeed. Against amateurs. And Andrew Bassett, thought Wilson, was nothing if not an amateur.

Everything else was on track. Even Lyall Gelb seemed to have been pretty much okay for the last couple of days. But he hadn't won yet, Wilson knew. You only had to blink once. You only had to lose your nerve for an instant. It was the oldest trap in the book, to think you've won in that last split second before your opponent finally makes his call, to let your mask slip just a moment too early. The closer you get, the harder you have to concentrate.

There was still one potential fly in the ointment. But from what Andy Bassett had said, it sounded as if that had been taken care of.

Mike Wilson just couldn't resist finding out for sure.

57

He waited for the familiar, nasal voice to come on the line.

"It's done, right?" Wilson barely dared to draw a breath. If only the answer would be what he wanted to hear, if only he could hear that it was finished.

"Not exactly."

Wilson's heart sank.

"The information you gave was good, Mike," said Tony Prinzi. "I thank you for that."

Wilson clenched his fist, trying to control himself. He was boiling over. What use was information if Prinzi's goons couldn't get things right? "What happened?" he muttered through clenched teeth.

"There are no guarantees, Michael. I have told you this before."

"So you killed someone else?"

"No."

"Then where is he?"

"That, we don't know."

"Jesus Christ!" Wilson exploded, no longer able to bottle up his frustration. "I give you guys the exact place, all the details, and you can't even fucking go and—"

"There are no guarantees, Michael," said Prinzi slowly. His voice was very soft. Something about it chilled Wilson's blood.

Mike Wilson took a deep breath. "What are you going to do now?"

"Well, this is a problem. We're working on it."

"What are you doing?"

"I said we're working on it. Let me remind, you, Michael, that it is I who is doing you a favor here."

"You said it was a thing of honor! You said you'd—"

"We're working on it," said Prinzi again.

A wave of anxiety swept over Mike Wilson. He was seized with a horrible, visceral dread, so deep it was beyond rationality. He felt as if he were doomed. Wilson remembered that young, smiling face gazing out from the Dyson Whitney website. The smile seemed to be one of mockery. Was there no way to stop him? He seemed to keep bouncing back, no matter how often he was supposed to be knocked down. Like some kind of jinx. A curse.

Suddenly, all the tension that had built up in Mike Wilson from maintaining the masquerade, day after day, week after week, broke out. Prinzi was the one person he wasn't trying to bluff. The fear in his heart took over. He forgot where he was, forgot the thinness of the wall separating him from Stella. "If he does something before this announcement is made . . . if he does something, there's no money for either of us." Wilson's voice rose. "You hear me, Tony? You can kill me, you can chop me up! Doesn't matter! There's nothing, nothing—"

"Michael, calm down. You're panicking."

"The hell I am! There's nothing for anyone, you understand? If this motherfucker gets to Bassett before—"

"Who's Bassett?"

"Who's Bassett? Who the fuck do you think—"

"Michael!" yelled Prinzi. "Calm the fuck down!"

The loudness of Prinzi's voice, so rarely raised, was like a slap in the face.

"Excuse me for cursing. Now, who is this Bassett? Michael, tell me the truth. You know why Holding is in London, don't you?"

"Yes," whispered Wilson.

"Why?"

"He's trying to get to Bassett." Wilson closed his eyes. "Andrew Bassett. He's the head of the other company."

"The one you're buying?"

"Yes. We're making the announcement of the deal together tomorrow."

"How do you know he's trying to get to him?" asked Prinzi.

"He called him."

"What did Bassett do?"

"He didn't talk to him," said Wilson. "He told me where Holding was. That's where I got the details I gave you yesterday."

"So Bassett knows you're trying to—"

"No!" cried Wilson in horror. "No, he has no idea."

"Then why didn't he talk to him?" asked Prinzi.

"Because he's from my investment bank. It's not the way you do things."

Prinzi chuckled. "Not the way you do things. I like this. I must remember it."

Mike Wilson rolled his eyes.

"And if Holding talks to Bassett, you think this might damage your deal?"

"Yes," said Wilson. Not damage it, he thought. Kill it.

For a while, Prinzi said nothing. Wilson listened to his breathing on the line with loathing.

"Mike," said Prinzi at last. "One thing I don't understand. Holding is in London, correct?"

"Yes," said Wilson impatiently.

"Yet you and Bassett are making an announcement together tomorrow."

"Yes," hissed Wilson.

"So he'll be with you in New York."

"No," growled Wilson. "He's making it in London."

"Bassett?"

"Yes!"

There was silence. Wilson's impatience was almost choking him. He could just imagine the Neanderthal thought processes going on in Tony Prinzi's skull.

"We're listed on two exchanges," he said. "We're making the announcements—"

"You should have told me this," said Prinzi softly.

The tone of Prinzi's voice stopped Wilson cold.

"Let me understand, Mike. Tomorrow, this Mr. Bassett stands up at the same time as you and makes the same announcement. Only he is in London and you are here."

"That's right."

"What time?"

"Ten o'clock in New York. Three o'clock in London."

"In front of the press?"

"Of course it's in front of the press!" retorted Wilson. "You can do that when you're in a legitimate business."

Prinzi ignored the jibe. "Mike, I think you better tell me where this announcement is going to be made."

"The hell I am! If any of your guys go in there and fuck this up—"

"Did it ever occur to you, Michael, that this might be Holding's plan? To go there. He wants to talk to Mr. Bassett, but Mr. Bassett won't talk to him, correct? So if Mr. Bassett won't talk to him, maybe he will try to find a place where Mr. Bassett will have to listen. In front of people, I mean."

Wilson was silent. All of a sudden, Tony Prinzi's thought processes didn't seem so Neanderthal.

"Maybe we should have a few people there in case he makes an appearance," said Prinzi. "Do you think this might be a good idea, Michael?"

"Tony, if your guys fuck this announcement up, if they make some kind of a scene, that's it. You understand? That's it!"

"Michael, it'll be very discreet."

"Like killing his best friend? Is that what you call discreet?"

"Michael, I think there are some things it's better you don't keep talking about. I've explained how this happened. Now, tomorrow, this is very delicate, I understand. I think for this my brother will go personally, in a supervisory capacity."

Wilson didn't say anything.

"Michael, I hope you appreciate this thing that I am offering you. This isn't something I would normally do."

Wilson frowned. The idea of Prinzi's goons hanging around Andrew Bassett's press conference didn't exactly fill Mike Wilson with confidence, even if one of them was Nick Prinzi himself. He didn't want to think about what might happen if they screwed things up. But Prinzi was right, Wilson was certain of it now. That must be Holding's plan.

"Michael? Where is the announcement?"

Wilson hesitated a moment longer. "The Royal Gloucester Hotel," he whispered.

"What was that?"

"The Royal Gloucester. The Royal Gloucester Hotel."

"Wait. I have to write this down." There was silence for a moment. "Okay. What's it called again?"

"The Royal Gloucester," said Wilson. He spelled it out.

"Oh, that's a spelling!" said Prinzi in delight. "'Gloster,' you say, and that's how you spell it? That's one for the books."

Jesus Christ, thought Wilson.

"Now, the name of the gentleman you mentioned?"

"You're not going to touch him!"

Prinzi chuckled. "That's funny. What's his name?"

"Bassett."

"Spell it."

Wilson spelled the name.

"What's the name of his company?"

Wilson told him.

"Okay," said Prinzi.

"What does that mean?" demanded Wilson. "'Okay'? What does that mean, Tony?"

"It means okay. If Mr. Holding decides that he'd like to attend Mr. Bassett's announcement, we'll be waiting. In fact, we might just have a couple of people waiting at your announcement also, in case Mr. Holding decides to catch a plane home and come to that one instead. Where is this going to be, Mike?"

Wilson closed his eyes. He didn't want any of Prinzi's thugs within a thousand yards of him.

"Mike?"

"The Four Seasons," said Wilson.

"In New York? Very nice. Let me write it down."

Wilson waited. "I swear," he said suddenly, "we're *this* close. If you and your goons fuck this up for me, I swear I'll . . ."

"What, Mike? Tell me. What will you do?"

Wilson took a deep breath.

"It's okay, Michael. I understand. You're upset. This is very stressful."

"Yes. It's very stressful."

"Of course. We'll forget you said the last thing, Michael. Threats . . . I don't like threats. Threats are disrespectful."

"I'm sorry, Tony. I didn't mean it. I do . . . appreciate the special care you're taking."

"Thank you, Michael. Now let me finish writing."

Wilson grimaced. It was all in the hands of Prinzi and his brother now. One wrong move, and the announcement was gone.

"Please, just tell them to be careful," said Wilson quietly.

"Yes. I understand. Leave this with me, Michael. You must relax now. You have an important announcement tomorrow, isn't that right?"

"That's right."

"Can I see this announcement?"

"On Bloomberg," said Wilson. He almost wanted to laugh in despair.

"At ten o'clock, correct? I'll be watching." Prinzi chuckled. "When you look into the camera, Mike, think of me."

Wilson closed his eyes.

"Tony?" he said. "What about the girl? Holding's girlfriend."

"What about her?"

"You know . . . he's in London . . ."

"Apparently she's there with him. I'm afraid, Mike, that puts her in the line of fire. I don't understand young men today. A man takes his woman into such a situation? A woman should be at home where she's protected. Although we did have an unfortunate incident at her apartment, I have to say."

Wilson barely dared to ask. "What kind of unfortunate incident?"

"Let's just say that Mr. Holding's friend is not the only person to have been killed."

"For God's sake!" For an instant, Wilson couldn't breathe. It just kept getting worse. "I thought you said you didn't kill anyone else!"

"One of my own employees, Michael. A very good man. Very reliable. Shot by the police. You don't think I'm unhappy? Normally, this would cost you. But in this instance I can't say we're without fault."

"So now the police have got one of your guys, and they're going to trace him to you, and—"

"Michael, be calm. He's dead. Dead. What's he gonna tell them? They can trace what they like. You think *I'm* gonna tell them something? Be calm. What am I telling you? Be calm."

Wilson nodded. He took a deep breath. "Okay."

"We'll look after this. Relax. Get a good night's sleep tonight. You ever use pills? To sleep?"

"No."

"Me neither. Sometimes, if something's really on my mind. Get a good night's sleep, Michael. You want to look nice on the camera. Tomorrow, we'll be there. Don't worry, Michael. If Mr. Holding thinks he's gonna come along and make a noise at your party, he's gonna find a welcome committee waiting."

58

They had left the hotel that morning. Rob made a point of stopping by the front desk to ask what the weather was going to be like and how they could get to the nearest subway station, and he mentioned that they'd be back late that evening. He managed to mention it at least five times. He wanted it to stick with the clerk, in case anyone came asking for them. He paid for another day in advance. Then he and Emmy walked out, with no intention of returning.

Outside, it was a bright, blustery day. Cool, but the wind had blown the clouds away. The subway station was at the junction of a couple of big roads and nearby there was a long strip of shops. They kept walking until he found what they wanted. It was a grimy shop, with worn, threadbare carpet, but there were rows of computers inside. Rob paid for an hour's Internet surfing from a guy who sat behind a cash register near the front of the shop and was handed a paper slip with a password. They went to the row of computers at the back of the shop.

After that, it took all of about two minutes. As Emmy watched over his shoulder, he typed "BritEnergy" into Google, got their home page, clicked on the button called Investor Relations, a couple more

clicks, and there it was. Press conference tomorrow, Friday, three
P.M., in the Raleigh Room at the Royal Gloucester Hotel. London
W1. Rob glanced at Emmy and wrote the details down. Easy.

He went to the Royal Gloucester website to find out where the
hotel was. The home page came up with a picture of the facade, a set
of steps leading up to big doors with polished brass handles attended
by a pair of top-hatted doormen. Rob imagined himself walking up
those steps tomorrow. He pulled up a map. Curzon Street. He noticed Berkeley Square near the hotel on the map, an oblong with a
green oval at its center, and remembered swinging around a parklike
area in the cab the night before. But it had been dark, and he hadn't
noticed much else. Then he did a search on other hotels in the area
and checked their locations. He found one a couple of blocks away,
the Norton, that didn't look too obtrusive, but not a dive like the
places they had stayed in for the last couple of nights.

"What do you think?" he said to Emmy.

"Can't we stay somewhere really horrible again?"

Rob smiled. He went on the website and checked room availability. He started to make a reservation, but stopped when the screen
came up for his credit card details. He'd have to put his name down.
His real name. He didn't want to do that. He'd pay cash. He wrote
down the phone number of the Norton instead and took a note of
the nearest subway station. Then he went back to the map. He asked
the guy at the counter if he could print a web page. On the map, he
marked the locations of the Norton and the Royal Gloucester. A
couple of hundred yards from one to the other, he estimated. If that.

He logged off the computer, paid the extra fee for the printing,
and they left.

Outside, he went into a phone box. As Emmy waited, he called
up the Norton and asked if they had a room for a couple of nights.

"What name, sir?" asked the woman on the phone, after she had
confirmed availability and price.

Rob thought. They were Leopard. What was he?

"Poacher," he said.

"Mr. Poacher," said the woman, typing the name in. "Initial?"

"B," said Rob at random.

"Good. Thank you, Mr. Poacher. We'll be expecting you."

Rob left the phone box.

"You need fresh clothes," said Emmy, looking him up and down.

"You think so?"

She nodded. There was an old-fashioned kind of men's store nearby and they went in. What would a journalist wear? Emmy picked out a pair of blue trousers, a pale blue shirt, a black jacket as a pair of old men who ran the store danced attendance. Rob added fresh underwear.

"That's you," she said. They found a women's clothing store and Emmy came out with a black suit, a pale purple blouse, and black shoes.

"What do you think?" she said. "Journalist?"

"Secretary."

"Thanks a lot."

"One more thing," said Rob. He went into a supermarket and bought a whole bagful of snack bars.

Then they headed for the subway.

Half an hour later, Mr. Bernard Poacher paid cash over the counter and checked into the Norton Hotel. They went straight to the room, hung the DO NOT DISTURB sign on the handle, and locked the door behind them.

One more day, thought Rob. Three o'clock tomorrow afternoon. All he had to do was make it to the Royal Gloucester alive.

He sat down at the desk and examined the map he had printed. Emmy lay on the bed, propping herself up on an elbow and watching him. The map showed a crowded area, lots of little streets. Rob traced out the route with a pencil. Left out of the hotel, and he would come to a street called Chesterfield Hill. Right at Chesterfield, then over Hay's Mews, then Charles Street. At Charles Street, it looked like a kind of dogleg into Queen Street, then down Queen a short distance to Curzon. Lots of little streets, but not far. The Royal Gloucester would be right across Curzon from Queen, according to the map, almost diagonally opposite the corner.

Emmy got up and looked at the map. "So that's the route we're going to take?"

Rob glanced up at her. He had known what she was planning ever since she had bought herself the new clothes. Now he hadn't missed the "we," and she knew that he hadn't. It wasn't a question, it was a statement.

She gazed at him steadily.

Rob nodded. "That's it."

Emmy smiled. "Good. Looks easy. How far do you think it is?"

"Couple of hundred yards."

"We should try it."

"Good idea."

That afternoon, they walked the route. In less than five minutes they were standing at the corner of Queen and Curzon, looking across the street at the steps of the Royal Gloucester Hotel and the top-hatted doormen from the picture on the Net.

They went up the steps, past the doormen, and inside to find the Raleigh Room.

59

The four men came up the steps just after nine o'clock on Friday morning. They wore suits. Three of them wore ties, the fourth a gray turtleneck under his jacket. He was a large man, broad-shouldered, with a nose that had been broken one way and then another. The other three hung back as one of the doormen opened the door, making space for him to go through first. Then they followed, a thin man with a rodentlike face, then a man of medium height with a plaster cast on his left wrist, and finally a younger man with a shock of blond hair.

They stopped and looked around the lobby.

First impression, gilt and marble. Reception desk on the left. Bank of elevators directly in front of them. Wide stairway on the right leading up to a mezzanine floor. Farther to the right, down a couple of steps under the overhang of the mezzanine, a big space with low tables and chairs and a bar beyond.

The man in the turtleneck glanced meaningfully at the thin man, who went to the concierge desk. He had a short conversation with the concierge and came back.

"It's up the stairs," he said. "Those ones over there."

"And it's three o'clock this afternoon?"

"Yeah."

The man in the turtleneck turned to the other two. "It's busy here on a Friday?"

They shrugged.

"Okay," he said. "You wanna have a look outside? Right around? See where else you can get in or out."

"If that's what you want," said the one with the cast. "After all, we're here to help."

There was more than a hint of sarcasm in his voice. Together with the blond man, he had picked up the other two off the red-eye from New York earlier that morning, taken them to a hotel, waited around while they freshened up, then brought them here, all so they could do what he believed he and his associate could manage perfectly well themselves.

The man in the turtleneck glanced at him for a moment. "Okay," he said. "We'll meet you back here. Down there." He pointed to the tables near the bar.

The two men walked away.

"Let's go up, Frank," he said.

They went up the stairs. There was a lobby area in front of the elevators, and corridors leading off the space to the left and right. In the lobby were tables stacked with urns and cups and pastries on plates, ready for the morning breaks of the groups that were using the meeting rooms on the mezzanine.

"It's over there," said Frank.

They went into the corridor on the right, past a plaque listing the names of three rooms, the Drake, the Hawkins, and the Raleigh. They passed the first two, each with its name in gold lettering on the door. They came to the Raleigh Room.

The man in the turtleneck tried the door. It was locked.

"Anything else down there?"

Farther along were a ladies' and men's bathroom, and then the corridor ended blind. They went into the men's bathroom and looked around and came out again. The man in the turtleneck glanced meaningfully at Frank. Frank went into the ladies' bathroom to check it out.

They walked back past the Raleigh Room and stopped in the lobby again.

Frank glanced around. "He's gotta come past here, Nick. This is the only way to get there."

Nick's eyes narrowed. "We wanna take him outside."

"So we wait outside?"

"Here and outside. What if he's in one of the hotel rooms right now? What if he comes down the elevator?" Nick looked around a little longer. "Better if we can, we take him outside. Come on. Let's go down. See what those two morons found."

Frank grinned.

They went down the stairs and took a seat at a table near the bar in the lobby. The other two men weren't back yet.

"Go ask at the desk. See if he's booked in. Might have been dumb enough to use his own name."

Frank went to reception and asked. He came back to the table, shaking his head.

Eventually the others returned.

"So?"

"There's a side entrance." It was the man with the cast who replied. "Over there, past the reception desk." He pointed. From this angle, it was possible to see that there was a corridor on the far side of the reception desk. It opened into the space in front of the elevators, directly opposite the stairs that led to the mezzanine. "There's a few shops and then it comes out into the street."

"What's out there?" said Nick. "Some kind of alley?"

"A side street. Then there's a staff entrance and a loading bay around the back."

"Is that two entrances round back?"

"Not really. The staff door is right next to the loading bay."

"Okay."

There was silence.

"I think we should—"

"Shhh," said Nick. "Please. I'm thinking."

"Yeah, but we could just put a man—"

"Mr. Prinzi's thinking," said Frank. "Huh? Let him think. Maybe he can sort this out. If you guys could've done that yourselves, we wouldn't have to be here, would we?"

"Who asked you to come?"

"Well, we wouldn't, if you hadn't fucked up."

"Excuse me, who fucked it up?"

Frank tapped the cast on Kevin's wrist. "That doesn't look like a fuckup?"

"What was your friend doing on our manor?" demanded Eddy. "What kind of a fuckup was that?"

"We had the wrong information. You at least had the right information."

"At least we didn't kill the wrong guy."

"At least I didn't get my arm broken."

"At least—"

"Hey, hey, *hey*!" said Prinzi. "Enough. Shut the hell up, the all of you. Jesus fucking Christ . . . Frank, shut the hell up here!" He paused, looking peremptorily at Frank, then at the others. "All right, listen up. I wanna take him outside if we can. Away from the press conference. We put two guys out the front. Around the back, one guy should be enough."

"You think so, Nick?" said Frank.

"It's an insurance policy. He's not coming through there. He's smart. He knows we're looking for him. He knows we're going to be waiting for him. The whole reason he's coming, if he's coming, is because he wants the protection of being in public. So he's not coming in through some alley at the back. Huh? Think about it. He's coming straight in that front entrance where everyone can see him. We've just gotta get hold of him without anyone noticing. Subtle. Discreet. Move him quickly away and 'round to the car."

The three men turned and looked at the entrance. As they watched, one of the doormen opened a door to let someone out.

"All right, we have two upstairs in case he gets through. Two out the front. One out back. I'm here in the lobby to watch and make sure everything goes smooth. You got communication?"

Kevin nodded.

"You can get more guys?"

Kevin and Eddy glanced at each other.

"I'll talk to Mr. Bailey," said Kevin. "What about the side entrance?"

"Can we put a car out there?" said Prinzi.

"It's not legal. If we have someone sitting in it, it should be all right."

"We gotta have a car. Where else can we put it?"

"That's the only place."

"So that's where we put it. Someone sits in it, watches that entrance as well. If he has to leave it, what happens?"

"The car gets removed. But that's only if the traffic warden finds the car, and then it takes fifteen minutes, maybe. They have to call a truck to come and do it."

"So he can leave it if he has to? If he has to get out and go after Holding. He can leave, we get back, the car's still there."

Kevin nodded.

"You sure?" said Prinzi. "I don't want to get back to a car that's gone. Huh? How would that be, Frank? Look like a bunch of fucking morons then."

Frank shook his head in disgust.

"Maybe we should have two in the car if we can. One to stay if the other one has to get out. All right. So that's . . . seven men, including Frank. You can get five more guys?"

"Four," said Kevin.

"Him," said Prinzi, pointing at Eddy. "He's not there."

Eddy's face creased in anger. "Why not?"

"Your lovely blond hair, that's why not. No offense, but who's gonna forget it?"

"Like putting a fucking sign up saying, 'Notice me,'" muttered Frank.

Nick held up a hand. "Frank, I think he's got the message. You want to cut the hair off, you know, get yourself maybe a cut with the clipper—"

"A marine look," said Frank, smirking at Eddy.

"Yeah, a marine look, whatever. You want to do that, you come back. Fine. Otherwise, good-bye." Nick turned back to Kevin. "Five men. Four at the minimum, but then we have one in the car."

"I'll talk to Mr. Bailey," said Kevin.

"All right. You talk to Mr. Bailey. I appreciate that, Kevin. He understands the importance. Now you, with this arm, normally I would say, go away with your friend here, good-bye, but you're the one who saw the girl, right?"

Kevin nodded.

"You any good with that arm?"

"It's my left arm."

"So you can still jerk off," said Frank.

"Hey, Frank! The man's helping. You can describe the girl?"

Kevin shrugged.

"Okay, you want to wear something that covers this thing a little more? We don't want people remembering it. Maybe a coat with a sleeve." Nick tapped the back of Kevin's hand to show where the cuff should come to in order to cover the cast. "We'll put you upstairs in case the girl's the one who comes. If she comes, she has to pass you. Someone else will be there with you to help, right? We have two upstairs."

Kevin nodded.

"Nick," said Frank, "you think he's going to send her?"

"No. Where did our friend here find her? In the hotel room, right? Sitting by herself. He's protecting her. He figures she's safer with him than by herself in New York so he brings her with him."

"That's not so dumb," said Frank, who knew what had happened at Emmy's apartment.

"Sure. Who said he was dumb? He's going to stash her in some hotel room and then he's going to come down here by himself."

"So why do we need Mr. Broken Arm?" said Frank, as if Kevin weren't at the same table.

"Insurance," said Prinzi. "Now, what do we say? Frank, it starts at three, right?"

Frank nodded.

"So everyone's in place by two o'clock? Not too early, we don't want people to think we're hanging around." He looked at Kevin. "Take me back to the hotel now, you'll get everyone there by twelve, I'll brief everyone. And everyone should know what he looks like, huh? We got pictures of him. Frank, you got the pictures?"

"I got the pictures."

"Good." Prinzi got up. "You," he said to Eddy. "Thank you for your contribution. Maybe I'll see you again without the hair. You wanna get lost right now?"

Eddy glanced at Kevin. Kevin shrugged.

Nick Prinzi watched him pointedly. Eddy got up and left.

"Show me the side entrance," said Prinzi to Kevin.

They walked across the lobby. They went past a series of shops and came out into a narrow street. A couple of delivery vans were waiting, wheels up on the pavement.

Prinzi grunted. "We'll put the car there, huh?"

Kevin nodded.

"Okay." He headed for the corner up ahead. He stopped, looking up and down Curzon Street. Then he crossed to the other side. He gazed at the entrance to the Royal Gloucester, diagonally across the street.

"Frank, you'll go there," he said, pointing to one side of the steps. "The second guy, over there." Prinzi nodded to himself. "What do you think, Frank?"

Frank nodded.

"I'll give Tony a call to let him know it's all set." Prinzi looked at his watch. Ten-thirty in the morning in London, five-thirty in New York. He'd wait a couple of hours.

Nick Prinzi looked up and down Curzon Street again, then gazed at the hotel entrance. "I'm getting sick of this Holding guy. Let's hope he's got the balls to turn up."

60

Friday was set to dawn cool and misty in Baton Rouge. Lyall Gelb was awake long before the sun rose. Silently, as Margaret slept, he got ready.

When he was done, he looked in at each of the children's rooms. He stopped at Becky's doorway. She had an orange night-light beside the bed. She slept peacefully, one cheek to the pillow, one of her hands poking out from under the cover.

Lyall remembered the night he had come home and found her with appendicitis. The look of pain and fear on her face. His heart contracted at the thought.

Lyall knew that a father shouldn't have favorites. He loved each of his children. Perhaps he even tried harder with the others, to make up for the special bond he felt with Becky. He didn't know where this bond came from. Sometimes he thought he might be punished for it one day. Yet the Lord must have forged it, so it must be a holy thing and shouldn't be denied.

He gazed at her. Minute after minute. Just watching her, as if he would never be able to watch her enough. Becky. His Becky.

"Honey?"

He turned with a start. Margaret was standing behind him.

She came closer, scanning his face. "Honey, what are you doing? You all right?"

Lyall nodded. Suddenly he reached for Margaret and hugged her tight.

"Honey . . ." Margaret laughed softly. "Honey, you're squeezing me."

Lyall loosened his embrace. Still, he didn't let her go.

"Lyall?" Margaret's voice was more serious. "Is everything all right?" Margaret pulled back from him. She tried to look into his eyes.

"Lyall?"

Suddenly it was all too much, it had been too much for weeks, and it was all about to come pouring out.

"Margaret, there's something—"

Outside, a car horn honked.

Lyall fell silent. He kept gazing at Margaret, an expression half self-reviling, half imploring on his face.

"Lyall? What is it?"

Lyall glanced quickly toward the door.

"Lyall, what were you going to say? Were you going to tell me something?"

He shook his head.

"Lyall?"

"I've got to go."

"You sure?"

"Yeah. I've . . . Mike's waiting."

Margaret gazed at him. "We'll talk about it tonight, huh?"

Lyall nodded quickly. "Tonight."

Margaret gave him a kiss. He went to the door. She followed him halfway down the hall.

He opened the door, then stopped. "Margaret . . ."

She waited.

Lyall couldn't speak. How could he tell her how much he loved her? And how desperately sorry he was. There weren't words enough even to begin.

There was a knock on the door.

Margaret smiled. "Go on, Lyall. I'll see you tonight."

Outside, Mike Wilson was sitting in one of the company limos. He was on the way to take the jet to New York and wanted a final run-through on the trickier questions that might come up. If they did come up, he knew, they would most likely be about the size of the extra debt Louisiana Light was taking on. Wilson wanted to have the facts and figures word perfect.

Lyall asked him questions. Wilson answered. Gelb added a point here and there.

"You sure you don't think you should come?" Wilson asked.

Lyall Gelb shook his head. "I'm not much good in front of cameras."

"Still, maybe we should have you there."

"You've got to sell this deal, Mike. You don't want to turn to your CFO for backup. Won't look good, you want to go out bold and confident. Anyway, you don't want to get into detail. You have me there, you're inviting it. This way, you can say they have to talk to me and you don't have to deal with it."

That wasn't much of a reason, and normally Wilson wouldn't have accepted it. He was more than capable of being bold and confident with Lyall Gelb on a podium with him. But Lyall had pretty much refused to go, and if he forced him, that might just be the straw to break Lyall's fragile back. The risk was too great. If Lyall was going to fall apart, Wilson didn't want him doing it live on Bloomberg.

"All right," said Wilson. "Let's keep going."

They drilled the questions all the way to the airport. They kept going inside the plane as the pilot did the last few things he had to do before they could take off.

"Okay, Mr. Wilson," said the pilot over the intercom. "We're ready to go."

Wilson looked at Gelb and grinned. "This is it, huh?"

Lyall nodded.

"You sure you don't want to come?"

Lyall shook his head.

"You going to watch?"

"Sure," said Lyall, and he got up.

"Lyall."

Gelb stopped.

"It's going to be okay, you know that."

Lyall stared at Wilson for a moment. Then he got off the plane.

He walked quickly to the limo. As he got in, the plane started taxiing away. The sky was still dark. Lyall watched the lights of the plane heading for the end of the runway.

Lyall Gelb knew he should have been in that plane. He should have been there for backup, in case Wilson needed it, to field the curly ones. But he couldn't bear the thought. He couldn't bear the idea of the cameras filming him as the deal was announced, as the big lies were told. He saw it in his mind like one of those pieces of footage that get dragged out whenever there's a story on corporate fraud, like the footage of Bernie Madoff in his prime. They showed that kind of stuff for years. He didn't want producers to be dragging out footage of Lyall Gelb for years to come.

"You ready, Mr. Gelb?" said the driver.

"Oh. Sure," said Lyall.

"We going to the office?"

"Yes, please."

The limo moved off. It turned out of the airport exit.

Lyall stared silently out the window at the dark scenery of the ride downtown. Mike Wilson was wrong. It wasn't going to be okay. You couldn't pile lie on lie. It got too heavy. Eventually, the whole edifice would topple. Already, he could feel it crushing him. He felt as if he were holding the whole thing up all by himself. The weight was unbearable.

He went over it all, for the hundredth, the thousandth time, starting from the first words that had kicked it all off, from that first Hungarian venture. There was no point, but he couldn't help himself. He traced every step on the primrose path that led to this hell he now seemed to inhabit. He felt a stab of pain in his belly. He was tired of the pain. He was tired of everything. Like a juggler who's been juggling so many balls for so long he just doesn't think he can keep even one of them in the air another second.

The car turned onto North Street. St. Joseph's Cathedral came into view. Lyall watched it as they approached, the pale bulk of it coming closer in the predawn mist. It was disproportionate. He had always thought so. The steeple with its metal spire was too tall for the narrow mock-gothic building it surmounted. Lyall had never been inside the building. For six years, every day, he had passed it and kept going.

It came closer. A faint light filtered out of the windows.

"Stop," said Lyall suddenly.

"Here, Mr. Gelb?"

"Yes."

The car pulled in. Lyall opened the door.

"Should I wait?"

"Yes," said Lyall.

He got out. The driver watched him walk toward the cathedral. The door was open. Lyall took a couple of steps inside.

The interior was bare, severe. The light was coming from the altar. Rows of pews ran in shadow down the nave. A large, pointed arch of stone soared above the altar. On the wall behind it hung a big wooden crucifix.

A priest in his cassock was leading an early Mass. His voice carried as a low, burbling murmur up the nave. A few worshipers sat scattered in the front pews. For a moment, the scene felt foreign to Lyall. Then memories came rushing back at him out of his childhood, and suddenly it was familiar, as if he had never turned away.

He moved in a little farther and sat in a pew at the back.

The indecipherable burble of the priest's words in the stone cavern of the church was lulling, almost mesmeric. Lyall stared at the crucifix above the priest's head. The figure of Christ was plain wood, the same color as the cross. A long, narrow body. Thin, gaunt. Arms stretched, knees flexed, head down.

The Lord on the Cross. Dying in agony for our sins.

Suddenly it was as if Lyall were seeing the cross for the very first time. It was all clear. You made your choice. Heaven or hell. One side or the other. Lyall had made his. He had made his pact with the devil. His deal. A deal that was bigger than anything Mike Wilson could ever dream up.

He stared at the cross. In his mind, Lyall didn't hear the priest in front of him now, but Father Ahern, just as if he were back in the old priest's Sunday-school classroom. The words of the catechism that the father had drummed into him, Sunday after Sunday. The sins. The seven deadly sins. The list. How many times had he heard it, read it, repeated it under Father Ahern's malevolent gaze? Pride, Avarice, Envy, Wrath, Lust, Gluttony, Sloth.

That was his, right at the top of the list. Pride. Lyall knew it now. The things he had done, they weren't out of greed, or envy, or out of a lust for power. He was unmoved by those. They were for pride. The sheer joy of doing things that no one else could understand, the satisfaction of weaving his web around the rules that other people had created. The pleasure of outsmarting people and seeing them fail to discern it. The sheer sinful love of being cleverer than everyone else.

And Wilson had known it. Lyall could see that now. Had recognized it, manipulated it, exploited it. His own overweening, corrupting, self-congratulating, sinful pride.

Lyall stared at the crucifix, stared hard at the downcast face of the Lord. Downcast as if in disappointment at him. In grief. My son, what have you done? Where has your pride led you? Your pride. Your pride, your pride, your pride, your pride . . .

He sat in a reverie of self-recrimination. The Mass had finished. Around him, the congregation shuffled out.

Still Lyall sat.

"Excuse me."

Lyall turned with a start.

It was the priest. "I don't mean to disturb."

"No . . ." murmured Lyall. "It's okay . . ."

"I don't know who you are, my friend. This is a house of God, and you are welcome to pray, whatever your faith. I wonder, though, if you need anything more."

Lyall stared at him, not understanding.

"To talk."

"Oh."

The priest gazed at him expectantly. "Are you a Catholic? Do you need to confess?"

Lyall didn't reply.

The priest waited a moment. The way he looked at Lyall, Lyall wondered whether he knew. "The Lord forgives, my son." He pointed at a door. "I'll be through there if you need me."

Lyall nodded.

The priest walked away. He opened the door and disappeared.

Lyall thought about what the priest had said. But he wasn't a Catholic. He didn't believe in confession. Could a few whispered words expiate what he had done? Years of pride? A whole lifetime of pride?

Lyall looked at the crucifix again.

He got up and went back to the car.

In his office, Lyall turned on the computer. He opened a spreadsheet and buried himself in work. Figures. Numbers. They had always comforted him. The hours passed. Gradually, outside his window, over the river and the factories, the day brightened and the sun broke through the mist. At about eight-thirty he got a call from Doug Earl to tell him the TV was being set up in the boardroom so they could watch Wilson's press conference live on Bloomberg. Lyall put down the phone and his stomach contracted in pain. He had a terrible feeling of dread.

God wouldn't allow it to happen. He wouldn't allow Wilson to get away with it. He wouldn't allow him, Lyall Gelb, to get away with it.

Lyall got out his keys and opened the locked draw under his desk. He reached for the three envelopes he had put there. He had written the letters weeks ago, and they had been in the drawer ever since, in case the time came for them. Lyall lifted them now. The feel of the envelopes gave him a kind of comfort. They were white, crisp, heavy. The edges were sharp and clean. There was a kind of purity in them. He looked at them, one after the other. One was addressed to the Securities and Exchange Commission. One to the police. One to Margaret, his wife.

61

At nine-thirty in New York, Mike Wilson was in a suite at the Four Seasons, going through the presentation with Mandy Bellinger for the last time. A couple of minutes later, just after two-thirty in the afternoon in London, a Bentley pulled up outside the Royal Gloucester Hotel and Andrew Bassett and Oliver Trewin got out. They crossed the lobby, waited at the elevators, then emerged at the mezzanine floor. They didn't notice the two men standing near the steps to the hotel, or the man in a turtleneck sitting in the lobby in a spot from which he had a full view of everyone coming in the door, or the two men having a conversation across from the elevators on the mezzanine level, one of whom wore a long overcoat that appeared slightly too large for him.

In the Raleigh Room, Sophie Greene, the Hill Bellinger associate who had flown in for the announcement, and Francesca Dillon, the BritEnergy head of public affairs, were making sure everything was in order as the camera operators from Sky and CNN set up. The Sky team positioned themselves at the back of the room and the CNN operator selected a spot halfway to the front on the right. Francesca Dillon took Bassett and Trewin to a small waiting area behind the main room.

The camera crews were just about set. A few minutes later, Sophie Greene opened the doors of the Raleigh Room and the journalists started to arrive.

On the mezzanine level, the man in the overcoat put his right hand to an earpiece, keeping his left arm lowered so as to hide the plaster cast at his wrist. "No," he murmured. "No sign." He glanced at the second man, who had his eye on a couple of journalists coming out of the elevator. The other man shook his head.

Downstairs in the lobby, Nick Prinzi listened to the response and kept his eyes on the entrance. He spoke via his mouthpiece to Frank, and the man in the car opposite the side entrance, and the man posted at the back of the hotel. No one was reporting anything.

At four minutes to three, Prinzi stood up. "Anyone see anything?" He heard the negatives come in. "All right, looks like he chickened out. I'm gonna head to the room anyways, make sure he hasn't gotten past us. Keep watching. No one comes in the room without I tell them first. Got it? Whatever happens—*no one* comes in without my word. You do that, I'll deal with you personally. We don't fuck this up."

He went up the stairs and walked past the two men on the mezzanine, exchanging a glance with them as he went into the corridor. In the lobby area near the elevators, coffee and pastries were set up for afternoon breaks for groups in the other meeting rooms.

He stopped outside the Raleigh Room. "Anything? Anyone?" He listened. All negative.

"Nick." It was Frank. "You want we should stay out here?"

"Stay until I give the word," said Prinzi. "I'm gonna go in and make sure there aren't any surprises."

He walked into the Raleigh Room just before Sophie Greene closed the door for the press conference to begin.

Outside, Rob and Emmy were running.

They had left the hotel at ten to three, nervous as hell, but with plenty of time, to judge from their trial run the previous afternoon, to get to the Royal Gloucester, get up to the Raleigh Room, and take a seat as the conference started. He didn't want to get there too early. They turned down into Chesterfield, just as they had done the previous time, went over Hays and over Charles. But there was some kind of blockage on Queen. Some kind of cordon. Police. No one was going through.

They turned around, back up Queen. There'd be another way. Rob still had the map he'd printed. Quickly, he tried to orient himself on it. Right and left again. Or was it left and right? He spun the map. Right and left. "This way," he said to Emmy. They started walking. Right. Left. Then there was a dogleg, wasn't there? They did the dogleg. They reached a cross street. Wait. This wasn't Curzon. Suddenly he was confused. Wasn't this meant to be Curzon?

He pulled out the map again.

"Where do we go?" said Emmy.

"I'm looking!" He could feel time ticking. He was starting to sweat. He looked around for a street sign. Shepherd Street. Where was Shepherd Street? He checked the map. They were way past Curzon! He looked at his watch. Almost three. Did they let you into press conferences if you were late? He focused on the map again, trying to figure out the quickest way. They had to go right, left, then they'd be in a big street, then left again. Right, left, left, he said to himself. "Okay." They started walking quickly. Right left left, right left left. They turned right. Rob checked his watch. Three. He threw a glance at Emmy and started running. The big street. Left. Okay. Should be the next left. He weaved around people, trying to get past them, glancing at Emmy to make sure she was with him. Here was the left. "Come on!" he said and swung into it. There was a sign up ahead of him. Royal Gloucester. Not the entrance he knew from yesterday. Must be another one. Didn't matter. They ran for it.

The two men stationed in the car at the side entrance were watching the corner of Curzon Street up ahead. They hardly glimpsed the two figures running from the other direction before they were past them and turning into the hotel.

They looked at each other in alarm.

"Christ . . . was that?" One of them pulled the lapel of his jacket up to his mouth. "This is Mick. I'm not sure, but—"

There was a tapping on the window. Mick looked around with a start.

"Can't park here, sir," said the traffic warden, shaking his head and wagging a finger like a schoolteacher. "No, no, no."

Rob and Emmy ran into the lobby. "There," said Rob. The stairs to the mezzanine were directly opposite.

They raced past a startled Japanese couple waiting for the elevators. Then onto the stairs. Emmy looked up. A man glanced down from the balcony of the mezzanine.

She knew that face. For an hour, she had sat opposite it at the point of a gun.

"Rob!" she yelled.

He looked up. There were two of them, running across the mezzanine toward the stairs.

The door of the Drake Room opened. For the hundred and fifty people who were inside, it was time for afternoon coffee.

Suddenly the mezzanine flooded with people.

Rob reached for Emmy's hand and grabbed it as they got to the top of the stairs. They charged into the crowd, pushing people out of the way.

Prinzi's men plunged in from the other side. People were falling, shouting. Rob pushed Emmy ahead of him, looked around, and shoved someone back into the path of one of the men. He felt a hand grab for him on the other side and he struck back hard with his elbow. There was a scream of pain. Emmy was through the crowd. "The third door!" he yelled. She ran. He looked around. One of the men was almost at him again. He felt a hand grabbing at his jacket and he chopped at it, tried to accelerate away. He could see Emmy at the door. She was opening it. The hand grabbed again, clutched him at the shoulder for a second, and then came away as the man behind him fell, throwing himself at Rob's feet. He clipped his heel. Rob stumbled, tried to keep going, tumbling. He lunged for the door that Emmy had opened and fell into the room.

A woman standing by the door looked around angrily as Rob got to his feet. Outside, two men had pulled up at the room, panting.

"Are you coming in?" demanded Sophie Greene, the Hill Bellinger associate, in a forced whisper.

They looked at each other helplessly.

"All right," she snapped, and closed the door.

She looked at Rob and Emmy disapprovingly, put her finger sternly to her lips, and turned away. People at the back of the room, who had been staring at them, turned their attention once more to the front. Andrew Bassett was speaking on a podium.

Finally, thought Rob, Bassett would have to listen. He took a couple of steps forward and opened his mouth to speak.

He felt something slam into his chest. It knocked him back against the door, taking the wind right out of him.

"All right, ladies and gentlemen," growled a man in a suit and gray turtleneck. "Don't be alarmed. Security." With his free arm he grabbed Emmy around the neck and pulled her against him.

"Get off her!" cried Rob.

Emmy yelled.

The man slammed his weight into Rob again, pulling Emmy down and muffling her shouts. "No problem, ladies and gentlemen. It's all under control."

Faces turned. Sophie Greene stared at what was happening.

"Andrew Bassett!" Rob tried to shout. "Andrew Bass—"

The man in the gray turtleneck short-jabbed him in the face. *"Shut the fuck up!"* he hissed, teeth clenched.

"Andrew Bass— Ahhh!"

"Shut the fuck up!" Prinzi jabbed him again, then drove his elbow into his windpipe to choke off his voice. Prinzi was a massive

man and he had all his weight leveraged against him, holding onto Emmy with an ever-tighter arm around her neck as she kicked and twisted to get loose. He had Rob against the door, and at the same time he was reaching for the handle, but the door opened inward and he couldn't get it open. "It's all right, folks, I'm security," he said as he struggled to do it.

"Andrew—"

Prinzi drove his elbow in again.

"Excuse me," said one of the journalists, a big, lanky guy with unruly hair, "is that really called for?"

"If you help get this door open I'll remove these people and you can get on with your press conference."

"Bloggers," muttered another journalist. "They're probably bloggers."

"Still, that's fucking rough," said the lanky journalist. "One of them's a woman."

Prinzi hauled them both back from the door. "Now, if you'll just open it for me—"

Rob managed to get an arm up and hit at his face. Prinzi knocked him back, but in the process his grip on Emmy loosened. She twisted free and ran down the room. "Andrew Bassett!" she yelled, hair disheveled, jacket half ripped off her shoulders and her eyes blazing. She stopped and pointed at the back of the room. "That's Robert Holding from Dyson Whitney. You refused to talk to him! *Andrew Bassett!*"

Bassett looked at her in confusion. He had stopped speaking. There was silence. Emmy realized that every eye in the room was on her.

Suddenly Emmy saw that she was standing beside a television camera. She grabbed the end of it and swung it around. "Film him! Film that man!" she yelled at the startled CNN cameraman.

At the back of the room, Nick Prinzi still held Rob with an elbow to his neck. Now he found himself looking straight down the barrel of a television camera. Flashes started to go off from photographers in the room. He took his hands off Rob and backed away.

Rob came forward. The journalists watched him. The only interruption to the silence came from the click of cameras.

"I'm Robert Holding from Dyson Whitney," he said loudly. Then he repeated it. "Andrew Bassett, I'm Robert Holding from Dyson Whitney."

"Dyson Whitney," said one of the journalists. "Isn't that the bank that's acting for the acquirer?"

Rob went farther toward the front. The television camera swung to follow him. At the back of the room, Nick Prinzi cut his losses and slipped quickly out the door.

On the podium, Andrew Bassett wondered what he should do. He could see the journalists glancing through the text of the announcement that he was making, which they had been given at the start of the conference and which was embargoed for another half hour.

"Andrew Bassett," yelled Rob. "I'm here to tell you the truth."

"Get out!" said Bassett. "This is unauthorized! I'm telling all of you here, this press conference goes no further until this man leaves."

"Don't you want to know the truth?" said Rob.

"What is the truth?" demanded one of the journalists. "Let's hear it!"

Rob was at the very front now, standing right below the podium. "Do you want to know the truth or not, Mr. Bassett? I have names. I have proof. Do you want to know the truth or do you want to end up like Enron?"

"Enron?" said a journalist. "Did he say Enron?"

"What names?" demanded another journalist.

Andrew Bassett glanced at Oliver Trewin, who was on the platform with him. Trewin came closer and murmured something to him. Bassett frowned.

"I'm going to give you two names, Mr. Bassett," Rob was saying loudly. "You investigate those two names, and *then* decide whether you want to—"

"That's enough!" said Trewin. He took the microphone out of Bassett's hand. His voice boomed. "Don't say another word! Ladies and gentlemen. We're going to have a slight delay." He tugged on Bassett's arm and virtually dragged him off the platform.

There was silence for a moment as Bassett and Trewin came off the podium. Trewin grabbed one of Rob's arms and began to take him with them. They went past Emmy and headed for the door.

"What about the names?" shouted one of the journalists. Then others shouted it as well, or something similar, all demanding the names that Rob had promised.

"What about you?" one of them shouted at Emmy. "Can you tell us?"

Sophie Greene came forward. "Please stay in your seats, ladies and gentlemen. Stay in your seats!"

That was the last thing they were going to do. The journalists were on their feet, shouting, gesticulating. A couple tried to intercept Bassett as he headed for the door. Oliver Trewin fended them off.

"Please stay . . . please stay . . ." Sophie Greene gave up saying that. Suddenly she saw there was a greater danger. "Turn off your cell phones!" she yelled. "Turn them off!"

"Make us!" growled one of the journalists.

"Turn them *off*!" she shrieked. And then, as Bassett and Trewin left the room with Rob, she ran to the back and locked the door behind them.

"You can't do that!" shouted the lanky journalist. "You're fucking imprisoning us!"

By way of reply, Sophie Greene stretched out her arms and pinned herself against the door. Bassett and Trewin and Robert Holding, whoever he was, were gone, and martyrdom would come to her before any of those hacks got out to follow them.

62

The only place they could think of to go in a hurry was the men's room. There was no one there. Andrew Bassett turned on Rob.

"Now, you tell me what this is about! And let me tell you, if you don't want to be arrested for creating a public nuisance, it had better be good."

"I told you in there," said Rob. "I've got details. I've got names. Louisiana Light is an Enron waiting to happen and if you let them buy you, they'll take you down with them."

"What the fuck are you talking about? You're not stable! They told me about you. You're disturbed."

"Just listen!" said Rob.

Bassett glanced impatiently at Oliver Trewin, who was stationed at the door to keep people out.

"Louisiana Light is in debt up to its neck," began Rob.

"Tell us something we don't know," retorted Bassett.

"*Off* the balance sheet, Mr. Bassett. And another thing, Lousiana Light has been booking revenues ahead as fast as it can."

Bassett scoffed. "How can it do that?"

"That's something you ought to ask Lyall Gelb. There are two main vehicles it uses to do things. I'm going to tell you their names. Grogon and ExPar. Grogon's a subsidiary registered in Hungary. ExPar's a JV in Delaware. If you don't think there's anything wrong with it, just go look at its list of directors. Lyall Gelb's wife is one of them."

"And?" said Bassett.

"Just go look at those companies and you'll see what I'm talking about."

Bassett stared at him incredulously. "You've come here to tell us to *look* somewhere? They were right about you. Get out of my way! We're announcing this deal. We're going back right now and—"

"A man is dead," said Rob.

Bassett stopped.

"One man is dead already over this. I've had thugs chasing me for the past week. My girlfriend was held hostage with a gun at her head. Now you listen to me. If you just do the due diligence about these companies, you'll find out the truth. It's as simple as that. Just do the due diligence."

"We've done the due diligence."

Rob looked knowingly at Trewin. "How much time did they give you, Mr. Trewin? How much information did they supply?"

"Plenty!" said Bassett. "You've never had more information, have you, Oliver? Isn't that what the team said?"

"Exactly," said Rob. "Mr. Trewin? Can you honestly swear that you know, to the best of your ability, that these two companies are aboveboard? Grogon and ExPar, Mr. Trewin. Those are the entities I'm talking about. Tell me you've looked at the financials on those companies and you're satisfied with them, and I'll go back in there and make an apology and walk away. Huh? Can you honestly tell me you're satisfied with them?"

Trewin shook his head slightly. "Never heard of them," he murmured.

"Oliver!" said Bassett. "What do you mean—"

"Come on, Andrew!" retorted Trewin sharply. "Let's stop pretending, shall we? They have two hundred entities, the likes of some of which I've never even seen. You know just as well as I there wasn't time for us to do the due diligence properly. Heavens above, Andrew! You never expected us to. You as much as told me not to."

"I never did!"

"Oh, grow up, Andrew," muttered Trewin.

Someone opened the door of the men's room.

"Out of order!" said Trewin brusquely, and bundled him out.

"Look," said Rob. "It doesn't matter what you have or haven't done. You still have the opportunity to do the due diligence now. Just tell Wilson you need to look at the books on those two companies. See what he says. You know what? Just see what he says. It's as simple as that. My bet is his response will tell you everything you need to know."

Andrew Bassett backed up against a wall between a pair of hand dryers. He crossed his arms. Then he began to shake his head. "I can't do it. It's too late. It'd be an insult. It'd be an insult to Mike. To Louisiana Light. That'd be the end of the whole thing. And how could I go back to the board? What would they think?"

"What would they think?" said Rob incredulously. "What would they *think*? What about your shareholders, Mr. Bassett?"

"The deal's good," said Bassett quietly. He repeated it again, as if it were some kind of mantra that was his only hope of security. "The deal's good."

"The deal is not good!"

"The deal's good."

Rob came closer to Bassett. He was shaking with rage. "You listen to me. My best friend is *dead* because of this deal that you think is so good. You understand that? My best friend's dead and my girlfriend's almost been killed and I've been chased over *two* continents. . . . And if you think you're just going to ignore what I've got to say . . . if you fucking think you're just gonna shake your head—"

"What if I do?" demanded Bassett. Suddenly he regained his belligerency. "What if I do, Mr. Holding? You come here with your ungrounded suspicion, disrupt a press conference, publicly humiliate me and your client, I might add. And you *bet* I'd get a certain response? You bet? I need more than your bets, Mr. Holding. Maybe one day, a long time from now, when you've grown up a bit, you'll understand something about responsibility."

Rob stared at him. "Responsibility?" He shook his head. "Screw you, Andrew Bassett! I came here to give you a chance. But you know what? I'm done with you. You do what you want. I've just said, in front of the cameras of the world's press, that you're doing a deal with the next Enron. And you know what I'm going to do next? I'm going to go right back in there and give them every last detail I know. But yeah, you go ahead. Ignore it. And when it's all shown to be true, you can just tell everyone you never knew. You never had a clue. And you know what? If they all get a case of amnesia, they might even believe you."

Rob turned and headed for the door. Trewin stopped him from leaving.

"Get out of my way! I'm done here."

Trewin continued to block him. "Just wait a minute," he said to Rob. Then he turned his gaze on Bassett.

Bassett snorted. Trewin continued to stare at him. If Oliver Trewin had to make a choice between believing Mike Wilson or the young man who stood in front of him, he'd take this young man every single time. Nothing about Wilson or his deal smelled right. Trewin had known it since the moment Mike Wilson upped the cash without even being asked to. And Andrew Bassett knew it as well.

Reluctantly, Bassett looked Rob in the eye. "What if it's not true?" he said. "What if you're lying?"

"Why would I lie?" said Rob. "Do you think I've got a job after this? What can I possibly have to gain?"

"What if you're misinformed, then?"

"Sue me."

63

In New York, Mike Wilson was on his feet. He had started speaking at precisely ten o'clock.

"Ladies and gentlemen," he began, reading the script. "Thank you for coming this morning. As I speak to you, my friend and soon-to-be-colleague Andrew Bassett is making this same announcement in London. I am here to tell you that our two companies, Louisiana Light and BritEnergy, have agreed to join forces to create what we believe is the first truly global electricity generation and supply company. Although in technical terms this is an acquisition of BritEnergy by Louisiana Light, in all other senses it is a true merger of equals. In the next few minutes, I am going to describe to you what makes this such a compelling deal."

Wilson paused to heighten the sense of expectancy. As Mandy Bellinger had suggested, he avoided the temptation to glance straight at the camera, but maintained his gaze at the center of the audience, showing his strong left half profile to the Bloomberg cameraman.

He continued. "In many ways, this is the culmination of the strategy that both our companies have been following for some time."

On the screen in the boardroom in Baton Rouge, Wilson looked masterful as he spoke. Stan Murdoch, Lyall Gelb, Doug Earl, and Jackie Rubin watched. Jackie was ready to go with an e-mail to all staff the minute Wilson stopped talking.

"In terms of our assets," said Wilson, "the portfolio that we will create is second to none."

The shot on Bloomberg cut back from Wilson's face to include a display behind him showing a map of the world girdled with dots representing the combined assets of the two companies.

Doug Earl glanced at Jackie Rubin and smiled. Stan Murdoch watched the screen stone-faced. Lyall Gelb gripped his stomach, unconsciously grimacing.

Mike Wilson moved smoothly through the first part of the presentation. Even fifteen minutes into the announcement, to the four people watching in the Baton Rouge boardroom, it seemed as if everything was still going to plan. Only a slight frown that had appeared on Wilson's face gave a hint that anything unexpected might be happening. And then the way he was starting to look from side to side, not in the way of someone trying to make sure he includes all his audience, but in the way of someone trying to work out what the hell his audience is doing.

In front of him, all over the room, journalists were pulling out cell phones. Wherever Mike Wilson looked, as he tried to maintain his poise and keep going, he saw journalists gazing at texts or even holding their phones to their ears.

They had to knock to get back into their own press conference. Sophie Greene let them into the room.

Bassett and Trewin went back up to the front. Rob waited below the podium with Emmy.

A number of hotel security men had appeared in the room now. The journalists watched the BritEnergy CEO sullenly. The mood was hostile, to say the least. But for the moment they stayed silent, waiting to hear what Bassett had to say, sensing that the event unfolding in front of them was going to be something special. It had all the hallmarks of a great story—climbdown, scandal, humiliation. Deep down, the journalists in that room were salivating. If there turned out to be a sex angle as well, it would have everything. A huge number of photos of Emmy had been taken while the journalists had waited. She was young, attractive, and disheveled. They hoped like hell she had been sleeping with someone she shouldn't as the lynchpin of the drama.

"The announcement that I was going to make today . . ." began Bassett. "Ah . . . we'll be delaying this for a short time."

Cameras clicked. Bassett made the mistake of pausing, and instantly the shouts came thick and fast.

"How long?"

"Why?"

"What have you just been told?"

"Is Louisiana Light the next Enron?"

"Please!" said Bassett. "Please! I would advise you not to publish anything you can't fully support."

"And I'd advise you not to lecture us after this disgraceful shemozzle!" threw back one of the journalists angrily.

There were shouts again.

"We have further due diligence to carry out," said Oliver Trewin, stepping in. "That's all we can say."

"Why didn't you carry it out before?"

"What's it about?"

"What have you just been told?"

"What's wrong with Louisiana Light?"

Bassett raised his hands for silence, then thought better of saying anything else and left the podium, accompanied by the hotel security men. The journalists crowded after him, shouting questions as he headed for the door.

Then he was gone, and the journalists turned. Suddenly the questions were coming at Rob from every direction.

"I have nothing to say," said Rob, over and over, pinned against the wall along with Emmy. Everywhere he looked, a journalist seemed to be shouting at him or a camera was flashing.

"Come on, let's let them out, shall we?" bellowed Oliver Trewin, and he pushed his way into the middle of the throng, elbows flailing, and extricated them. He took them out of the room.

They strode down the corridor, heading away from the journalists who had come out of the room and were shouting after them. Trewin kept going with them, down the stairs, across the lobby, and out the door.

Trewin stopped at the top of the steps to the hotel and looked around.

"Typical! Andrew's taken the car." He nodded at the doorman, who tipped his hat and walked out into the street to hail a taxi. Trewin looked at Emmy. "I suppose you're the girlfriend."

"I don't know if I like to think of myself as 'the girlfriend.' "

Trewin nodded. "Well said. My apologies for everything that's happened to you. I understand you've been caught up in this frightful mess we seem to have got ourselves into. Your young man says you were held hostage and threatened with a gun. That's appalling."

"Worse things have happened."

"I understand they have. You must be an incredibly brave young lady. What I saw from you today is evidence enough."

Emmy frowned. She didn't know whether the tall, officerlike old man was trying to pay her a compliment in his stiff British way or being extraordinarily condescending. It had been a hell of a few days—she decided to give herself the benefit of the doubt.

"Thank you," she said.

He nodded curtly. "Ah, here we are." A cab pulled up. "Don't suppose I could give you a lift? Anywhere you'd like to go?"

"We can manage," said Rob.

"Nonsense! Least I can do. Well?"

"How about Heathrow?" said Rob.

Trewin looked at him for a moment, then nodded. "Can't say I blame you."

Even in Baton Rouge, now, it was obvious that something was wrong. The screen showed Mike Wilson constantly looking around the room. His frown was deep. He had lost concentration and was stumbling over the text.

"What's going on?" said Jackie Rubin. She glanced at the others. No one replied. Jackie looked back at the screen.

The shot widened back. In the corner behind Wilson, Amanda Bellinger had appeared. She was talking into a phone.

The shot zoomed in on Wilson again. He was in close-up, bemused, uncertain. Noise was coming from the audience. It wasn't possible to hear exactly what was being said or shouted. Wilson was trying to keep going. Suddenly, uncharacteristically, there was something vulnerable about him. It was painful to see. Jackie Rubin glanced anxiously at the others in the boardroom. They were transfixed by what they were watching on the screen. Doug Earl's mouth had dropped open.

Amanda Bellinger appeared beside Wilson. As the shot stayed close in on them, she whispered something into Wilson's ear. In an instant, his face changed. First a look of disbelief, then panic. Utter, naked panic.

Only one person in the boardroom had ever seen a look like that on Mike Wilson's face.

Lyall Gelb had watched the last few minutes unfold in growing dread. He knew it was over. He knew it, as if he had always known the moment was going to come, right here, right now, just like this, in front of his eyes on a plasma screen in the boardroom.

Doug Earl's cell phone rang. Doug listened for a moment. "Say *what*?"

There was pandemonium on the screen now. The shot had cut right back. Journalists were on their feet. Wilson was trying to say something.

A banner started scrolling across the bottom of the screen.

BritEnergy delays announcement of Louisiana Light acquisition.

Lyall Gelb watched. Not in horror now, in resignation. Suddenly, he felt calm. The dread had disappeared. The pain in his belly, which had seemed to be constantly with him these last few days, was gone. It was over. All over.

"Is it true?" demanded a journalist who had somehow gotten hold of a microphone. "Has BritEnergy just delayed announcing this deal?"

"I'm not sure about that," Wilson said. "I'm hearing . . . I'm afraid you're ahead of me on that . . ."

Amanda Bellinger stepped up to the microphone on the podium, virtually shoving Wilson aside. "We're bringing this press conference to a close. Thank you very much for coming and we'll give you further information as . . ."

In Baton Rouge, no one was listening. They were all staring at a second banner scrolling at the bottom of the screen.

Louisiana Light is next Enron, says investment banker. . . .

"Is that true?" demanded Jackie Rubin in disbelief, and she looked around at the others.

"Can't be," said Doug Earl. "It's just . . . it's wrong."

Lyall Gelb and Stan Murdoch didn't say a word. Lyall could feel Stan's eyes on him.

The scene on the screen continued.

Quietly, Lyall got up.

"You okay, Lyall?" said Doug.

Gelb nodded.

Doug turned back to the TV. The screen was showing Amanda Bellinger ushering a shocked-looking Mike Wilson out of the room. After he was gone, the Bloomberg reporter talked into the camera, a roomful of frenetic journalists behind her. The banner at the bottom of the screen kept rolling.

It was like some horrible, macabre thing you just can't take your eyes off for as long as it keeps going. Doug and Jackie watched it, transfixed. Stan couldn't bring himself to move.

"This would have to be one of the most extraordinary press conferences I have ever attended, Dave," the Bloomberg reporter was saying to the anchor, wincing against the noise behind her. "There's utter confusion here. We were given the text of an announcement before the press conference started, but no one seems to know whether—"

Lyall Gelb's office was barely twenty yards away. Close enough for everyone in the room to hear the gunshot.

64

Oliver Trewin came with them in the cab all the way to Heathrow. It was awkward. It felt as if Trewin wanted to say something, but didn't know how to start. He pointed things out on their way through the city, sights here and there, like he was some kind of tour guide. A concert hall. Some kind of museum. Harrods. Just a sentence or two, a snippet of information, and then his voice would peter out. Then they got onto the highway that leads to Heathrow and there wasn't anything else of note. For twenty minutes there was only the rumble of the cab's engine.

At last the turnoff for the airport came into view.

"Which terminal?" said the cabdriver from the front.

Trewin looked questioningly at Rob. Rob shrugged. "We came in on American."

"That'd be terminal three," said the cabbie. "Right you are."

They swung off the highway. Ahead of them, in the distance, were the airport buildings. In another couple of minutes they'd be there.

"I always knew there was something wrong with this deal," said Trewin at last. He shook his head reflectively. "Everything about it was wrong. Should've known, eh? Should've done something about it while I could."

Rob didn't reply. He didn't think that did Oliver Trewin much credit.

"Empty my desk this afternoon, I expect." Trewin smiled ruefully. "Thirty years. What a way to end it." He took a deep breath. "Well, there we are," he murmured.

At the airport terminal, he dropped Rob and Emmy off.

"Good luck," he said after they had gotten out.

Rob shrugged. "Thanks."

"I admire you, Mr. Holding. And you, Ms. Bridges. There was a time when I would have done the same. Youth, perhaps. Eh?"

"Maybe," said Rob.

"Well . . ." Trewin paused a moment longer. "Good-bye."

He pulled the door closed. The cab headed off.

Rob and Emmy went inside.

They got seats on the next flight out and went through passport control. In the waiting lounge, a large-screen TV was showing the BBC news channel. They watched it as they waited for the flight to board. Eventually the business wrap came on.

"In extraordinary scenes today, electricity company BritEnergy first announced and then distanced itself from an acquisition offer by

Baton Rouge–based Louisiana Light. Details remain confused, but in what appears to have been an agreed bid, BritEnergy was to have . . ."

It was surreal. Behind the announcer the screen showed the logos of the two companies. Apparently the BBC didn't have visuals of the press conference yet. There were no further statements from either of the companies involved. The report ran for maybe thirty seconds and the announcer moved on to something else.

The flight home was strange, both too long and too short. Time seemed to move slowly, and yet there didn't seem to be enough time to get anything straight. So much seemed to have happened since Greg died. Rob thought about Greg. The feelings were unfreezing, coming out, everything he had locked away.

He knew that now there would be time to grieve, time to think of him. To speak to his parents. To pay him his due. Or to make a start, anyway.

There were other things. Lots of things. There'd be explaining to do to the police. In New York, in London. And at Dyson Whitney. He thought about that. Pete Stanzy . . . Phil Menendez . . . the Shark . . . Rob shook his head, it was so absurd. The way Phil terrorized them. The way they let themselves be terrorized. Over what? Rob was pretty sure there was no place for him at Dyson Whitney anymore. He wasn't sure he wanted it, or at any firm like it. Did he want to end up another Pete Stanzy in ten years' time? Was that the best he could aim at? He had started to get an idea. Maybe there was something else he could do. Something better.

Emmy glanced at him. She took off her earphones. "What are you thinking about?" she asked.

He shrugged. "Greg, I guess."

"You want to talk about it?"

"No."

"Okay." She rested her head back. Then she put the earphones on. He touched her arm.

She took the earphones off again.

"Actually, there is something I'd like to say."

Rob looked around. The plane was about three-quarters full and there was no one else in the row with them. The lights had been dimmed. The people he could see were dozing or watching movies.

"You know you said to me it was all or nothing? Do you remember?"

Emmy nodded.

"I never really thought about it like that. I never really thought about it the way you said until that morning."

"You want to be careful what a woman says when you wake her up at four o'clock."

"I'm serious, Emmy. It was like I got it, for the first time. You need to know, don't you?"

"Yes, Rob. I need to know. So do you. You need to decide. Not just for my sake, for yours."

"Yeah. I'm not very good at talking about this kind of stuff." He paused. "It's all, Emmy. The whole lot. Forever."

"You sure?"

"I'm sure. I've never been surer of anything in my life."

Emmy smiled. She leaned toward him. Their foreheads touched. "Hell of a place to tell me, Robert Holding."

"You think I shouldn't have?"

"Oh, no. I think you should have. I definitely think you should have." She kissed him, her eyes moist. "Okay," she said, and she settled back in her seat, holding his hand. She closed her eyes. "Okay," she murmured again, a smile on her face.

By the time they landed at JFK, the story had moved on. On a TV screen in a bar off the concourse, Rob saw Lyall Gelb's face. It was the picture from the directors page in the annual report. There were words under the face: BUSINESS SUICIDE.

"What is it?" said Emmy.

Rob nodded toward the screen. He felt sick.

The segment cut to a shot of Mike Wilson being hurried off a podium by a thin, nervous-looking woman. Rob went closer to hear what was being said.

"Rumors of an Enron-style collapse of the company began to circulate as CEO Michael Wilson was announcing a bid for British-based BritEnergy. In London, a simultaneous press conference was disrupted by a man claiming to represent New York–based invest-ment bank Dyson Whitney . . ."

And there he was! Him. The TV showed him shouting at Andrew Bassett from the side of the Raleigh Room. Behind him, as he called out to Bassett, the man in the turtleneck who had assaulted him slipped out the door.

Rob looked around, thinking that everyone would be staring at him. But people were walking past. No one on the concourse was taking any interest in him.

Suddenly it occurred to Rob that the shot he had just seen on the TV, of the guy in the turtleneck slipping out the door, was going to be pretty important. It might help track down whoever it was who had been after them. Might even lead to the guys who had killed Greg.

The anchor was on the screen now. "Dana, what's the latest?"

The picture cut to a woman standing in front of an office build-ing. It was dark, and she was lit by camera lights. A caption on the screen said BATON ROUGE.

"Dave, I'm here in front of the headquarters of Louisiana Light. Employees who were coming out of the building earlier today looked understandably shocked. So far there's no further word on the alle-gations about the company's financial state. However, about an hour ago, Corporate Affairs chief Jacqueline Rubin issued a statement describing CFO Lyall P. Gelb as a wonderful colleague and family man and said his death was a tragedy the company would take some time to come to terms with. Dave."

"Any word from CEO Michael Wilson?"

"Officially, Dave, all we have is the statement from Ms. Rubin. Michael Wilson himself has been unavailable for comment. How-ever, we are hearing rumors that Lyall Gelb, the CFO whose death has just been announced, has left a note to the Securities and Ex-change Commission. Dave."

"Any idea what's in that note?"

"I'm afraid not. And I should stress that the existence of this note is just a rumor at this stage, Dave."

"Well, as we just heard, the latest from BritEnergy is that Louisiana Light's bid remains under consideration. That does sound as if they have their concerns as well. Dana?"

"As I said, Dave, no official word from the company on that yet. But the apparent suicide of the chief financial officer only hours after these allegations surfaced doesn't look good. Dave."

"Where there's smoke there's fire?"

"Time will tell, Dave."

"That was Dana Feldman in Baton Rouge. And we'll keep you up to date with that breaking story. In other business news, pharmaceutical giant Arena today announced the withdrawal of their blood pressure drug Elevestar after persistent concerns . . ."

Rob turned away.

Emmy was watching him. "You're a TV star."

"Doesn't feel like it," he said wearily.

"That suicide? That was because of this?"

Rob nodded. A family man, the reporter had said. A family man. What must that family be going through?

They headed for the exit. Across the concourse, Lyall Gelb's face flashed up on another screen. People went past, ignoring it. Just another face on another TV screen. Here today, thought Rob, gone tomorrow.

65

Rob had never been in the Captain's office before. It wasn't a place analysts went.

It had been ten days since he and Emmy came back from London. They arrived to find her apartment a crime scene and two detectives with a lot of questions. And a mom with even more. But things soon became clearer. Nabandian and Engels hadn't recognized the man they shot dead in Emmy's bedroom, but they recognized the man on the footage shot inside the Raleigh Room in London. So did just about every other detective in New York. They had already discovered that the man they had killed was one of the Prinzis' foot soldiers. Now it was obvious that the Prinzis themselves were involved.

When questioned, Mike Wilson denied all knowledge. He admitted that he had borrowed money from Tony Prinzi. He admitted that he was in debt to him, that he had spoken with him by phone on a number of occasions, that he may even have mentioned Robert Holding's name as the person who was leaking information to the press. But he denied that he knew anything about murder. Perhaps, he offered, when Prinzi discovered that Robert Holding was about to scupper the BritEnergy acquisition, the gangster had concluded that he wouldn't get the money owed him if Holding succeeded and had decided to eliminate the threat. The police were fairly certain that Wilson was lying. But since Tony Prinzi was hardly likely to come forward to refute the story, and since Nick Prinzi was hardly likely to be more forthcoming, they didn't know if they could make a murder charge against Mike Wilson stick. But given time, they knew, Wilson would probably figure out that his best option was to make some kind of charge stick himself. If the Prinzis could find a way to get to him, he was a dead man. There was no way to grant him witness protection unless he provided testimony, which meant he would have to incriminate himself. But witness protection was unlikely to work for a semipublic figure like Mike Wilson, whose face had been all over the media since the announcement fiasco and probably would be for some time to come. One way or another, if he didn't go to jail, the Prinzis would get him. For the foreseeable future, unless he had the money to hire a small army to protect him, the only safe place for Mike Wilson was in a high-security penitentiary.

His lawyer had asked for police protection on his behalf, which the DA had arranged while Wilson figured all this out for himself. In any event, he was almost certain to end up in jail for his financial crimes. At the moment he was denying any knowledge of Lyall Gelb's activities, which were being discovered on a daily basis by a team of external auditors. The collapse in the Louisiana Light share price after the announcement and Gelb's suicide had triggered a cascading call-in of its loans. Rumors about the company's finances started to leak. It had taken all of four days for Louisiana Light to be forced to file for Chapter 11 bankruptcy. But no one who knew the way Louisiana Light operated believed for a moment that Lyall Gelb could have done these things under the radar. Nothing that happened in Louisiana Light happened without the say-so of Mike Wilson. It was only a matter of time until the evidence was unearthed.

Rob followed it in the newspapers, like anyone else. His knowledge of the financial wizardry of Lyall Gelb had been limited to two words, Grogon and ExPar, and those were soon communicated to the police. Lou Caplan, the head of Dyson Whitney legal, had left a message on his cell phone by the time he landed back from London, asking him to call him as soon as he could. He went into Dyson Whitney to meet him. People stared at him. A hush fell wherever he walked. Caplan and another lawyer said they were carrying out an internal investigation and asked him to give an account of Project 40. They asked him specifically if he had ever raised any concerns with his superiors. They took notes. At the end of the session they cautioned him about his contractual responsibility to maintain confidentiality regarding anything related to Dyson Whitney and gave him a copy of his contract, with the relevant clauses highlighted, in case he had needed reminding. Then they said they would be in touch. He wasn't being suspended, there just wasn't any work for him. He would continue to be paid. He wasn't expected to come into the office until he heard from them.

So he stayed away, making his own plans, talking them over with Emmy, making phone calls, going to meet people, and waiting to see what Dyson Whitney would do next.

And then the call came to ask him to come to the Captain's office at eleven o'clock on that Monday morning, ten days after everything blew up. Caplan said he could bring an attorney with him.

It was a corner office overlooking Forty-fifth and Sixth. Lou Caplan and Frank Nardini, head of mergers and acquisitions, were there with Browning. They sat at a meeting table, Caplan, Browning, and Nardini on one side, Rob on the other. He had foregone the attorney. He'd see where this went. If he needed one, he'd get one later.

"Well," said the Captain. "So you're Mr. Holding."

Rob watched him.

"Congratulations. You've shown remarkable determination in . . ."

"Surviving?" said Rob.

Browning smiled. "Actually, I was about to say in knowing what's right and sticking to your guns. A dishonest client's a bad client, for Dyson Whitney, for any bank. The bank needs people like you who are prepared to question a client's honesty and do what needs to be done. We need more people just like you, Rob."

Rob looked at him in surprise.

"Unfortunately," continued Browning, "the bank also needs people who other people want to work with. I don't think you fall into that category."

"Bernard Fischer has been trying to staff you in the last few days," said Nardini, "and to be frank, Rob, you're not high on the list."

"As you know," said Browning, "you only succeed at an investment bank if people want to work with you. At your level, that's how you get your utilization. You don't get your utilization . . ." Browning shrugged. "You're out. It's the same for everyone."

"So you're terminating me?" said Rob. "Is that what you're saying?"

"No," said Caplan hurriedly, "we're not terminating you. Absolutely not. If you want to stay at the firm, that's your decision. It's the same deal as when you joined us three months ago. If you can get your utilization, you succeed."

"We're just saying that's not very likely," said Nardini. "We think it's best to be frank."

"We could terminate you," said Browning. "Your actions constituted an outright breach of your confidentiality commitments both to Dyson Whitney and to your client, and under normal circumstances that would be grounds of instant dismissal, isn't that right, Lou?"

Caplan nodded.

"But we recognize there was a strong public interest argument in favor of what you did. And we accept that you first tried to use the normal internal channels to raise these issues, and in this case the channels were blocked. Our internal investigation has shown that, and as you'll have seen, we've been totally up front and transparent with the press. When there's a problem at Dyson Whitney we're the first to raise our hands. We had two bad apples and we're big enough to admit it."

Rob had seen the results of that so-called transparency. The internal investigation had taken all of about two days, and the reports in the media, while praising Rob by name for his honesty and determination, attributed Dyson Whitney's involvement in the affair to two rogue executives who had wilfully ignored company policy on dealing with concerns.

"As you know, Rob, Peter Stanzy and Philip Menendez have both decided to leave to pursue other opportunities. We want you to be confident that these problems are not systemic at Dyson Whitney. They're not part of the culture. It was the two individuals concerned, a pair of rogue individuals, that were responsible."

"Our investigation showed that very clearly," said Caplan.

Nardini nodded.

There was silence. The three men looked at him.

"We're not terminating you," said Caplan again. "I want to make that clear."

"It's clear," said Rob. Something else was going on here. He waited.

"Like Lou says," said Browning. "We're not terminating you. We think, though, that you might want to leave."

Rob waited.

"We know that leaving under these circumstances isn't easy," said Browning. "And because of that, and because you've done a fine job in helping remind us of why we're all here in banking, of what this profession can be at its finest, we thought we might like to help you in a small way. If you did choose to leave, that is." Browning held out a hand and Caplan passed him a file that had been sitting on the table beside him. The Captain opened the file. He picked up a check and slid it over the table to Rob.

Rob glanced at it.

"Of course, we'll ask you to sign a confidentiality agreement relating to this sum and all details of any agreement between us," said

Caplan. "You may consult an attorney, but you should be aware this offer stands only until five P.M. tomorrow. After that, it's off the table. You are also reminded that all of your other contractual obligations remain in force despite any agreement we may or may not come to over this. These contractual obligations include the obligation to refrain from any action or statement, explicit or implied, that may be construed as putting Dyson Whitney in a negative light both while you are employed at Dyson Whitney and after you have left. You should be forewarned that Dyson Whitney will vigorously pursue its rights in this respect. Furthermore, this is not an admission of liability on the part of Dyson Whitney. If you do choose to accept this offer . . ."

Catch-22, thought Rob, looking at the check as Caplan continued speaking. That's what Cynthia Holloway had said. They only pay you to leave when you don't want to. But not always, he thought. Once in a while, maybe once every ten years, they must sucker themselves into paying someone to leave who wants to leave anyway.

"Double it," he said to Browning, cutting right across the lawyer, who was still citing an endless list of caveats and conditions.

"Mr. Holding!" said Caplan. "Dyson Whitney is offering you two million dollars purely out of concern for your welfare and is under no obligation to offer you any payment whatsoever and you are more than welcome to continue your employment if that is—"

"Lou," said Browning. "Enough."

Caplan fell silent.

"Double it, Mr. Browning," said Rob.

"Don't you think you should look at the confidentiality agreement first?" said Browning.

Rob held out his hand. Browning took a set of three stapled pages out of the file and gave it to him.

Rob glanced over the pages. He looked up and nodded.

"Four million?" said Browning.

Rob nodded again. Four million for walking away from a place he had decided to leave anyway, for keeping quiet when there was nothing more he could really say. Browning was right. Rob knew the internal investigation was a whitewash, but even if he wanted to, he would never be able to prove that what had happened was because of the culture of the bank itself. He had only ever dealt with Stanzy and Menendez, and Browning had made sure they had already taken the fall.

But they wanted him gone, and were prepared to offer him two million to make it happen. If they were prepared to offer him that, Rob figured, they were prepared to offer him more. No one ever started with their bottom line. Not in a bank.

On the other side of the table, Nardini and Caplan glanced at Bob Browning, waiting to see what he would say. Creatures of Wall Street themselves, they all assumed the analyst across the table wanted a career on Wall Street just like them and would fight for it. Well, if Holding had a career, it wasn't going to be at Dyson Whitney. As long as he remained at the bank, he would be a walking indictment of everything they were, a focus of subversion boiling away in the bullpen. The MDs had met. Not one of them was prepared to work with him. They wanted him gone, any way they could get rid of him. But he couldn't be terminated, not yet. Publicly, the bank had just praised him for his honesty and determination. And if they terminated him in three months, or six months, or a year, and if it turned out that he hadn't been staffed on a single project, that he'd been turned into some kind of pariah because of the honesty and determination the bank had praised, they'd be under fire all over again. That was the last thing the Captain wanted. As it was, they were going to struggle to recover from this. Clients were already pulling out of engagements and taking their business elsewhere. This had to go away as quickly as it could, not come back a second time around. Any deal lost because of this—even one lost deal—would cost the bank a lot more than Holding, on the other side of the table, was demanding.

"Done," said Browning. He tore up the first check, pulled out a second, blank check from the back of the file, and filled it out. He signed it and passed it over to Frank Nardini for a countersignature. Then he took back the agreement from Rob, crossed out the sum mentioned on the first page, and wrote in the new sum. He did the same with a second copy of the agreement.

"Sign them," he said.

Rob turned to the back page and signed. He initialed the pages. He repeated the procedure with the second copy of the agreement.

Browning did the same. Then he handed the check and a copy of the agreement to Rob.

"We're done," said Browning.

Nardini grinned cruelly. "You'd better make that last, son. I don't think you'll be getting a job on the Street anytime soon."

"I don't think I'll be looking," said Rob.

"Really?"

"See, I had a friend. He'd be alive today but for the problems at Dyson Whitney, which your internal investigation proved aren't part of the culture. I think I might do what he was going to do."

"And what was that?" said Browning.

"Hunt down corporate crooks. Bring them to court. Put them behind bars. You know what? Turns out the DA's quite keen to have me on his team. Thinks I might know a thing or two. It doesn't pay that well, though." Rob picked up the check and smiled. "I would have walked away without this. But thank you. I appreciate it." He put the check in his pocket. Then he took his copy of the agreement and got up. "I sure hope you're right about the problems here, Mr. Browning. Not being part of the culture, I mean. Every one of your associates has my number. You take care. I'll be watching."